RETURN TO SHIABA

Willie Orr

RETURN TO SHIABA © 2024 William Orr

William Orr asserts the moral right to be identified as the author of this work in accordance with the Copyright, Designs and Patents Act 1988

This is a work of fiction. Names, characters, places and incidents are either the result of the author's imagination or are used fictitiously.

All rights reserved. No part of this publication may be reproduced, stored in or introduced into a retrieval system or transmitted in any form or by any means (electronic, mechanical, photocopying, recording or otherwise) without the prior written permission of the author.

Isbn: 978-1-914399-66-4

This book is sold subject to the condition that it shall not be resold, lent, hired out or otherwise circulated without the express prior consent of the author.

Printed and bound in Great Britain by Clays Ltd, Elcograf S.p.A

Cover Design © 2023 Mercat Design, images courtesy of Dreamstime. All Rights Reserved

By the same Author

Non-Fiction

Deer Forests, Landlords and Crofters (1982)

Discovering Argyll, Mull and Iona (1990)

The Shepherd and the Morning Star (2019)

Fiction

Mick (2019)

Shiaba (Book One) 2023

Introduction

In the winter of 1846, the potato crop in the Highlands and Islands of Scotland, infected with blight, turned to slime. Thousands, dependent on the crop for survival, faced starvation, eviction and death. Those in the remote township of Shiaba on the Isle of Mull were not spared. This is the story of a couple torn apart by hunger and disease.

On the Ross of Mull, when the potato crop fails, the Factor, John Campbell, offers work to the starving tenants, but the wages are so mean that Calum MacGillivray leads a strike. His wife, Catherine, fearing for the lives of her children, takes them to Glasgow, but he remains and the dispute develops into a prolonged contest between him and the Factor. David and Goliath.

Calum is close to collapse when an agent of the Relief Fund intervenes and offers him training as a fisherman. He regains his strength and, through his fishing, helps to feed the people of Shiaba.

In Glasgow, Catherine lives with her cousin, Sine, and Sine's husband, Duncan. She finds work with a widowed teacher, Eoin Lamont, a Chartist and free thinker whom she comes to admire. He teaches her to read and write. Their friendship, however, is broken when a cholera epidemic strikes. As with the potato blight, no-one knows the cause. No-one has a cure.

After a storm, Calum finds a wreck with casks of valuable fulmar oil and feathers. Salvaging the cargo is his salvation. He comes across a starving woman and her sickly children, takes her in to his house and, infatuated, shares a bed with her. Catherine, in the meantime, has found work in a museum, thanks to Lamont.

When Calum sails to Glasgow to bring Catherine back to Shiaba, he finds a woman whose whole life and aspirations are changing, a confident, literate, person, not keen to return to the poverty and hardships of Shiaba. His children too, Mary and Archie, have matured.

Prologue.

There is no road to Shiaba. A grass track serves the isolated settlement. Twelve houses, not quite in a row, their drystone walls a yard thick and no higher than a man, corners rounded to spill the storms, base stones bigger than a bullock, they squat on a remote hillside defiantly facing the sea and the twin peaks of Jura.

The men who built them with their bare hands chose well, settling on a stretch of kind, fertile land. Behind them, the heather slopes of Cruachan Min gave summer grazing for their black cattle, the beasts which were their living and paid the rent. In front, a steep drop down to the rocky shore and, to the east, the wild cliffs of Carsaig. Two small windows, facing the sea, gave some light to the dim interior where the beasts shared space with the people.

No English was heard around the hearthstones or out on the peat banks. There was the sweet scent of peat smoke and butter milk, the groans of hand-mills and thud of churns, the taste of ewe cheese and bere bannocks. They built a school for their children and then a mill for their corn. More than twenty families lived here until the winter of 1846.

Now there are none. Only the stout walls of the houses stand as a monument to the Gaels who built them. Nothing remains of the roofs and grass grows over the hearthstones. An air of melancholy pervades the ruins as if the people, when departing, had left their sorrow in the stones. This is their story.

1

Catherine stopped on the bridge, gazing down the Clyde where she had watched Calum sail away earlier that day, a solitary figure with a hand on the tiller and his eyes on the sail. A flock of gulls was quarrelling over the floating carcass of a dog, one of them balancing unsteadily on its back. A seaman rowing past in a small dinghy stopped to fling a piece of coal at it, which caused the whole flock to rise screeching into the air. The carcass reminded her of Calum and the dangers of the journey back to Mull. His craft looked so small and frail beside the tall sailing ships berthed on the Broomielaw. She imagined it in a storm, swamped in a massive swell and Calum's body floating in the tide, gulls swooping to feast on his eyes. She shook her head to dismiss the vision.

Calum would never leave Shiaba, that collection of stone houses scattered over the remote hillside on the Ross. She knew that now. His father's people, he was forever reminding her, had built his house with their bare hands and cleared the land for grain and potatoes. He was born there. The milk in his mother's breast was nourished with the water off Cruachan Min, the bread that he ate, the fruit of Shiaba's soil. The land was him. Yet many, like her, had left. When the potatoes failed, what else could they do? Listen to their children cry with the pains of hunger and watch them grow thinner by the day? She had made the choice, coming to Glasgow to save her children while Calum, as stubborn as ever, had refused to come and was still clinging to the place.

She compared him with Eoin, who had just found her work in the museum, an educated, cultured man, passionate about education and his profession as a teacher. He had taught her to read and write and given her a gift of Tom Paine's Rights of Man. Most of all, though, she admired his bond with his three boys. Having lost his wife to fever, he had taken sole charge of them without hesitation, caring for them with love and understanding, healing the wound inflicted by the loss of their mother. His love for his young wife transferred to his sons. Calum seemed to care more for Shiaba than his children. They had almost died of hunger and disease. She could not forget that. Now she had a new life in the city.

She searched in her pocket and took out the letter from Eoin, touched by his kindness. He had only begged her to leave when cholera struck her cousin's household in the Gorbals because he cared for the boys.

Dear Catherine,
I hope this finds you well and that none of your relatives or friends have been infected by this dreadful disease. After you left, I was overwhelmed with a sense of guilt, having turned you away in such a peremptory manner. I have since heard that the mill is laying off hundreds and must assume that your relatives will be among those declared redundant. I can't imagine the distress this must inflict on the household and particularly yourself.

I have, therefore, taken steps to compensate for your loss of employment with me and, recalling the wonder and amazement in your eyes when we visited the Museum, have approached the curator, who is a personal friend, to see if you could obtain a position with the Museum. He replied that he would be happy to provide you with work cleaning the premises, menial work I know and not generously remunerative, but it may give you some respite in these terrible times.

If you would be interested, do call at the Museum and take this letter with you.

I hope, when this plague has passed, that you will resume your position here. Both myself and the boys miss your presence in the house. The place is very dull without you.

Yours faithfully, Eoin Lamont.

She folded it carefully, slipped it back in her pocket and set off for the museum. She was nervous entering the building, there being several gentlemen in the anteroom. She wondered if she should sign the visitor's book. She was not really a visitor, being there on business, so she pretended to be interested in the butterflies. Carefully and slowly she read the title of Papilio Menelaus, repeating it to herself until she could say it fluently. When the room cleared, she went over and signed the book, pleased with her new skill. In the saloon she saw a gentleman locking one of the cabinets and, guessing that he might be a member of staff, approached him quickly.

'Mr Lamont asked me to speak to the curator and to hand him this letter.'

'I'm sorry I don't know Mr Lamont and the curator is very busy.'

'Could you give him a message for me? Tell him that a friend of Mr Lamont is here and would like to speak to him. I will wait here.'

'Very well. but you may have a long wait.'

She was astonished by her own impudence. Having Mr Lamont as a friend and being able to sign the book gave her a new confidence. She felt in charge of what was happening, no longer a puppet in the hands of people superior to herself. When the member of staff returned, she was examining the sea fan on the mantlepiece.

'This is from the India Ocean?' she asked, having read the information.

'Yes. ma'am. Amazing, isn't it? Mr Fullerton will see you now. He's in the gallery. Do you know where to go?'

'Yes, thank you. I have been here before.'

She swept through the saloon and up the grand staircase, passing the stuffed birds and animals. She recognised the eider duck, remembering its plaintiff call across the sea at home, the otter and the seal. As she entered the gallery she had to stop, transfixed by the colours on the walls around her—vast landscapes, bright seascapes, portraits of people and animals.

'I see you are admiring our Wouverman—Hunting the Stag.'

'I'm sorry, sir. They have taken my breath away, these pictures.'

'They are a magnificent collection. I believe you are a friend of Eoin Lamont. He comes here often and brings the children. A tragedy about his wife. So young. Still, the boys seem to have taken it in their stride. Now, I believe you have a letter for me.'

She handed it to him, and he read it carefully.

'Well, Catherine. Eoin seems to think very highly of you. As it happens, we could do with an extra cleaner. You do realise that the work would be in the evenings or very early mornings?'

'Yes, sir. I thought that it would not be through the day.'

'I have a couple of women who see to the floors, washing and mopping the tiles and polishing the wooden floors, so your duties would be cleaning and dusting all the cabinets and exhibits—an endless task you will be pleased to hear.'

'I would be happy to work in any way required of me.'

'You're not from the city I can hear.'

'The island of Mull, sir. The Ross of Mull.'

'The Duke's fiefdom. Your English is very clear.'

'The schoolmaster in Shiaba taught me to speak English.'

'He did well. Good. Come here tomorrow night at six and someone will show you what to do. Five shillings a week is the normal rate. Is that acceptable?'

'Indeed it is. Most generous.'

'Good. Till then, I wish you good night.'

'Thank you, sir. Thank you very much.'

On her way back she stopped on the bridge again. She was delighted that she had found work, particularly in such an exciting place, and yet accepting it meant that she could not return to Mr Lamont., except for an occasional visit. She would have to see him anyway to thank him for his reference. That would be the excuse, for she really wanted to spend more time in his company, to listen to him reading to the boys, to watch his eyes fired with passion as he taught, to feel close to him, part of his world.

It was almost dark and the gas lights, one after another, were blinking into life on the river. Behind her, carriages and carts still rattled across the bridge but fewer people hurried past. She wondered where Calum would sleep that night and realised that she hadn't asked him about his journey down. Perhaps he slept on the boat, or did he put ashore and beg a night's sleep in a barn? She wondered if she would ever return to Mull. The new paths opening out before her were exciting, promising, illuminating. She wanted Calum to share the adventures, to be beside her as she travelled. Stubborn, wilful, rash he might be, but he could be kind, imaginative, child-like and loving. Probably he had betrayed her, in his heart if not in his actions. She tried to decide whether she could forgive him, but a final answer eluded her. There were times when she longed to feel him close to her, to hear him laugh, to see him smile, but there were other moments when she imagined him with the other woman and found the thought of his touch repulsive. She wanted to suppress these visions, to cut them out of her memory, obliterate them so that they no longer troubled her mind, but they persisted and surfaced every time she thought about him. Perhaps, she told herself, they would fade with time and her love for him would overwhelm them.

§

'You must be Catherine,' the tall lady in the long black skirt and pristine white blouse greeted her with a smile. She had arrived early and, when she asked the woman mopping the floor in the anteroom for Mr Fullerton, she called for a Miss Armour.

'Mr Fullerton told me to expect you. I supervise the cleaning in the museum. Alison Armour. Come this way and I'll show you where we keep the cleaning materials. Have you come far?'

'The Gorbals, miss. The south side.'

'Ah Yes. I've been to the Necropolis there. A nice walk on a Sunday.'

Catherine noticed the blue brooch with the white figures at her throat and the tortoiseshell hair grip tying her chignon. Trim and elegant and probably fastidious yet friendly and sincere.

'Bella is still mopping the anteroom so perhaps you could start in the saloon. The glass on all the cabinets has to be kept clean. Children, I'm afraid, have a tendency to dribble on them or leave greasy finger-marks on the glass. The loose exhibits can be dusted with a feather duster. When you've finished in the saloon, there's the room on the left. I'll be up in the gallery, if you need anything. I'm sure you'll enjoy it here.'

'I will, I'm sure. Thank you.'

She watched Miss Armour glide away, her small heels clicking on the floor.

With a damp chamois she started to clean the cabinets holding the birds, exotic creatures with brilliant plumage she had never seen before. Delighted to be able to read their names, she set herself the task of learning them. A white spoonbill, a bittern, a parakeet, a paradise tanager, a pheasant, a crested boat bill. There were so many she decided to learn six every night. There was one she knew already, having seen it standing at the water's edge at home, as still as it was in the cabinet, waiting for fish, but she had never seen its name written. She wanted to learn about these strange birds, the countries they lived in, their habits, their diet. Further on, she was so entranced with the two tiny hummingbirds, one on a nest, that she had to stop and study them, but then remembered that Miss Armour might be watching.

In the centre of the saloon was a cabinet of minerals such as jasper and agates of various colours. There were two bell jars, covered in dust, which had clearly not cleaned for some time, containing pottery urns of some kind. She was afraid to touch some of the ornaments—a beautifully clear amber bottle and an amber vase shaped with the figures of boys on its pedestal. There was a sea-urchin like the ones she had seen on Shiaba shore but this one had long, bright purple spines.

'I wouldn't touch that,' Bella said as she passed carrying a pail and a mop. 'They say the spines are still poisonous.'

'These amber things are wonderful, aren't they?'

'You're a Highlander?'

'From the island of Mull.'

'You have Gaelic?' she asked in her language.

'I have.' From then on, they spoke in their native tongue.

'My people are from Barra, God help them. Evicted they were, along with more than six hundred others. The roofs burned off the houses and the doors barred. He shipped them off to Canada, John Gordon of Cluny, the poor people so ill-clad that the wife of the master on the ship took pity on them and sewed up empty bread bags, old sails and blankets to make clothing for them. One man dressed only in a woman's petticoat. And Cluny one of the richest men in the kingdom.'

'They have no heart these people. Were you evicted too?'

'No. My husband saw how things were going and came south to work on the railways. I've heard it's just as bad on Mull.'

'It is a wonder that the clerks in Tobermory get any sleep at all with the number of summonses they have to write. Hundreds. Ulva, Quinish, Ardmeanach and all across the Ross, including ourselves. Soon there will be no-one left but shepherds and flockmasters.'

'Who will fight their wars then, eh? We had better get back to work or we will be joining the hordes on the streets. You go through to the anatomy room while I mop this floor.'

Catherine carried her pail with the cleaning materials through to the other room. She had noticed this area when she visited with Mr Lamont and did not relish the prospect of cleaning it. In the cases, there were hearts, lungs, kidneys, the blood vessels all coloured brightly with scarlets and greens and whites. There was a case with two babies joined together by chest and abdomen, a baby without head and arms and skin covered with down like a pig. The one which she found most revolting was of a woman's thighs with the womb sliced open to expose a foetus ready for birth. She knew that they had been assembled by a doctor but she wondered why the most monstrous and bizarre were the ones chosen for display. Whatever she felt, she had to clean all the glass and exhibits.

She was still cleaning when Bella came to tell her it was time to leave.

'Where do you live, Catherine?'

'Over the river. Gorbals.'

'Pity. I live near Albion Street or I would walk you home. It's not very safe for a woman on her own so late at night. Just be careful.'

'I will. Good night, Bella.'

'Good night.'

It was not far across the river to the Gorbals where she had found shelter when, in desperation, she left Mull. The children were dying of hunger, fading before her eyes to emaciated, sickly creatures, Mary with the flux, while Calum was on strike for wages to buy meal. She remembered the set of his jaw and, although he too was starving, his defiance. A battle between him and the Duke's factor, John Campbell, the Factor Mor, who was in charge of famine relief. A desperate time and she had brought the children to her cousin, Sine, in Glasgow. There were times when she had felt sorry for Calum, left on his own with nothing to eat but shellfish yet he had survived, survived and flourished, now looking the healthiest of the family.

2

When she arrived home her son, Archie, was already asleep. Downstairs Sine and her husband, Duncan, were nursing their daughter, Sarah, deathly sick with cholera. Catherine was dreading the day that her own daughter, Mary, or Archie would show the symptoms. Mary was seated at the table with her cousin's older girl, Marion, in the dim light of a single candle.

'How is Sarah?'

'She has had a drink of tea. She's a little better,' Marion replied.

'That's great news. Is Duncan downstairs?'

'Yes. He's going over to the slaughterhouse tomorrow.'

'Is there work there?'

'He says so.'

Catherine told them about the museum, trying to convey her enthusiasm for the wonders she had seen, but they listened politely and did not show any sign of understanding her passion for dead birds or butterflies.

'You must come one day,' she said, 'and see these things for yourselves.'

'One day perhaps,' Mary said. 'There's some stew in the pot. Will I heat it for you?'

'No thanks. I'm not hungry. Has your mother pen and ink downstairs, Marion?'

'There's a pen but no ink. You look tired, Catherine. You sleep in the bed tonight. I'll go downstairs.'

That night Catherine slept with her children, Archie on one side and Mary on the other. The sensation, a feeling of affection and motherhood, reminded her of their home in Shiaba and the life they had before the potatoes turned to slime. The summer days cutting peats, Calum slicing them from the bank while she and the children laid them out to dry. At harvest time, the rattle and sweet scent of ripe oats as she bound the sheaves. In winter the crack of flails at thrashing time and the nights around the fireside telling stories. She fell asleep remembering.

§

Next day Mary and Marion left the house to search for work while she took Archie to buy ink. When she returned, she called in with Sine to find her cooking over the fire and with some colour in her cheeks. Sarah was sitting up.

'Well, Sarah. You have joined us again. I'm so pleased. You look much better.'

'I thought I was going to die.'

'You're too young for that and too strong, strong inside.'

'I've made porridge,' said Sine. 'There's enough for us all, Catherine. Sit in and I'll fill a bowl for you and Archie.'

When they had eaten, Catherine left Archie with them and went upstairs to write a letter.

Dear Mr. Lamont,
I wish to thank you for your help in finding me work at the museum. I would never have got it without your letter. It is fassinating work and I intend to learn the name of all the birds and butterflies.

I hope your boys have not had the kolera and that I will be able to visit you when the sickness has passed. I miss the lessons with the boys and your stories of the Roman times.

If the girls here and Duncan can find work, I will try to send Archie to school. I know that you would approve of that.

I hope we will meet again soon
Yours faithfully, Catherine MacGillivray.

She was very pleased with her effort and sent Archie round to push it under Lamont's door. It was true. She did long to see him again, to listen to his voice and to watch him reading to his boys. She had so much more to learn from him.

On her way downstairs again, she met Duncan returning from the slaughterhouse, his expression of despondency indicating that he had not been hired.

'The place is full of Irish who will work for wages that would not feed a mouse.'

'Is there nowhere else? Surely someone is hiring men.'

Catherine could see her plan of paying for Archie's schooling fading.

'I don't know. We should leave this country. All of us. There's nothing here but starvation and disease and hardship and heartache. There's work for everyone in Canada. Those who have the courage to leave have found a good life over there. You don't have to go round begging for work, pleading on your knees for a few pence. You don't have to crawl like a whipped dog whining for offal. You can be a man with some dignity and pride.'

She could see the hurt and anger in his quivering lips as he raged against the injustice of his circumstances, a strong, able man willing to work for his family.

'The people from the Ross did not fare so well in Canada. Half of them died in the snow before they reached Owen Sound.'

'I know. I know, but I hear of others who have done well. And there is gold in Australia. You can claim a plot in Ballarat and find a fortune overnight.'

'And dig for years and find nothing.'

She found herself opposing emigration, having argued with Calum so vehemently in favour of it. Meeting Mr Lamont and her new employment had changed her view, inspiring a feeling of optimism, of hope for the future.

'We will manage, Duncan. The girls have gone to look for work and I have the museum. Sarah will recover and Sine will be free to work.'

'It's always like that. Just scraping by, counting pennies to see if you can afford a pair of shoes. I'm tired of it.'

'I think you should go in and try to cheer up Sine. She has had a hard time and doesn't need to hear your sorrows.'

'You're right. Yes, you're right. I shouldn't be so miserable. I have my health and a loving family after all. I will go look and look for work this afternoon.'

She turned and returned to her room, leaving the couple together.

When Archie came back he was breathless with enthusiasm.

'I've been given work!'

'What? What kind of work?'

'Cleaning chimneys. A man stopped me in the street and said he would pay me handsomely—that's the word he used—handsomely.'

'No, Archie. Definitely not. You've no idea of the dangers. Boys have to climb up inside chimneys in the pitch dark, mouths, noses, eyes full of soot. Sometimes they get stuck up there and other boys have to climb up after them and haul them down, dead sometimes. No, no, no. Anyway, I'm going to send you to school so we must practise your English and your reading and writing. It was good of you to think about earning money for us.'

He was so dejected she took him in her arms and hugged him.

'I miss Father,' he mumbled into her belly.

'I do too, Archie. I do too.'

Shortly afterwards, Sine came up the stairs.

'I want to thank you, Catherine, for everything you've done.'

'I have done very little.'

'You have been a rock in the storm, someone strong and steady. Without you I could not have carried on. Believe me. And, without Calum's money, we would be starving. He's a good man.'

'They all have their moments.'

'Anyway, thank you. I wanted to say that. When Sarah is better, I'll speak to the foreman at McBride's. I know they're laying people off, but he seems to have a soft spot for me, always brushing against me as he passes and smiling across the machines. Worth a try.'

'Of course. I think I'll try Mrs McBride. Her maid may not have heard about Sarah's cholera. You never know and I won't say a word about it. Worth a try.'

'You're already working at night. Is that not enough?'
'We need the money, especially with Duncan off work.'
'The girls may find a place.'
'And they may not. There are so many—men, women and children.'

§

Report in The Scotsman December 1850 on people evicted from Gordon of Cluny's estate on Barra. Edinburgh Town Council debate.

Mr Ross from Glasgow said, *"In the month of September the Highland Destitution Board suspended relief and Colonel Gordon immediately ordered a large number of his poor tenants to be removed which was accomplished by demolishing their cottages and then, after they were cast out desolate on the fields, getting them shipped off the island. About 132 families were sent in this way to Tobermory. Of these, 37 families had made their way across to Ardrishaig and from that to Glasgow. The authorities there could do little for them and some of them accordingly came to Edinburgh, and more are on their way, with the idea of seeing Colonel Gordon ..."*

Dr Begg said, *"I never saw objects more fitted to call forth compassion ... the course which occurs to my own mind is as the best that could be adopted is an application to the Secretary of State ... I and the other members of the deputation come here as men, as citizens and as Scotchmen who have had their feelings outraged by this occurrence ... the poor people cannot speak a word of English."*

At the same time The Witness reported that Rev. Dr MacLeod said that in Glasgow, *"the doors are besieged by poor people from the Highlands in a state of destitution, inquiring what they should do. The steam boats are frequently arriving crowded with them. They are now forming a Protection Society in Glasgow to guard against these inundations and to give all the assistance they can to the poor people. Last year 70% of the smallpox cases were from the Highlands and there was also cases of fever ..."*

Letter from the Home Office to MacLeod of MacLeod concerning destitution:

"Sir George Grey is not aware of the existence of any sufficient grounds to justify expectation, which you say prevails extensively, of assistance from the Government, an expectation which can only lead to disappointment and to neglect of ordinary means of relief ... it is not in Sir George Grey's power to hold out any hope that the population, which for the last several years has been largely assisted by charitable subscriptions, can now be maintained by public money, the consequence of such aid apparently not to effect any permanent improvement in the condition of the people but rather to generate and perpetuate a feeling of dependence on extraneous and precarious subsistence ..."

3

She was horrified. As she was heading back to the museum, Catherine met an elderly man whose clothes barely covered his nakedness. Through the shreds of his trousers she could see his emaciated thighs and, through the threadbare sark, the skeleton of his shoulders. What was left of his shoes flapped on the wet pavement.

'Would you have the price of a loaf for my family, mistress?' he begged in Gaelic.

She could see that such pleading did not come easily to him. The dark eyes, sunk so deep in his skull they were barely visible, pleaded with such expectation of failure, that she reached out and touched his arm.

'You're from Barra?' she asked in the same tongue.

'I am, God help me.'

'A long way from home.'

'A home I fear I will not see again. Cluny drove us out like lepers. Set fire to the house and the barn. There is nothing there now but a black ruin. He shipped us to Oban and we have walked from there without bread or shelter, sleeping in barns where there was kindness, under the trees where there was none. We have nothing. We are driven to begging. We knock on doors here and they can't understand what we say. Some drive us away, their voices raised in anger, some shut the door in our faces. I don't know why. We have done nothing to harm them.'

'There must be some in the city who are not so harsh.'

'I can count them on the fingers of one hand. A few kind souls.'

As he spoke, his wife, her clothes as worn as his, joined us with two young children, their bare feet smeared with filth. The older one was dividing a half loaf between them. Catherine took them to be grandchildren. She searched for her purse and gave him all that she had.

'God bless you, mistress.'

'The woman who works beside me is from Barra. Bella MacLeod. Do you know her?'

'I have seen her and her man at mass a few years ago. She was not one for the priests as I remember, and he was not of the faith. Good people, though.'

'She's been kind to me. She has only one room or I would send you there. I live on the south side. I can give you shelter and food.'

'Thank you, mistress, but the young ones are ahead of us. We must follow on the way to Edinburgh.'

'You're going to walk?'

'Walk. Walk and not faint. The Lord giveth power to the faint. We will walk to Edinburgh. Cluny, we are told, lives there.'

'God go with you, then, seanair. I will tell Bella we met. What name will I say?'

'MacIvor. Iain MacIvor. God bless you, mistress.'

The small group walked on, the children wanting to stop for a rest.

When she walked into the museum, Bella was mopping the floor at the door. It had been raining in the afternoon and visitors' shoes had carried in a layer of filth from the street. Catherine saw that Bella's eyes were red and crusted with tears.

'I wish these gentry folk would wipe their shoes before they come in,' Bella said.

'Have you been upset?'

Bella plunged her mop into the bucket and thumped on the floor.

'Upset? I'm furious, raging and ashamed. Have you seen the state of my people from Barra? Trying to beg round the doors and them with no English.'

'I met a family of them just now. MacIvor. Iain MacIvor, they're in a fearful state. Walking to Edinburgh to see Cluny.'

'No better than Cluny's slaves in Tobago.'

'He has slaves?'

'Hundreds. Africans torn from their people, branded like beasts and sold like cattle and his people in Barra treated no better. I met one of ours, a man who had been a neighbour. I didn't know him at first. I spoke but he said nothing. Too proud to beg, he pleaded with his eyes and I had nothing to give. How do you think that feels?'

'Terrible. Can no-one help?'

'Oh they could, they could, but, like Pontius Pilates, the city fathers want to wash their hands, they want Cluny to pay. They're getting tired of being asked for money, the rich folk in the town.'

'What's he going to do, your neighbour?'

'Walk. Walk like the others. Walk and beg.'

'I wish I could help, Bella.'

'I know but it's not up to the likes of us. I just feel so helpless. Anyway, you've heard enough of my woes. You have troubles of your own, I'm sure. You'd better go and polish your companions in the bird room.'

Catherine went through to collect her materials and decided to clean the room to the left of the saloon, which she had not cleaned the previous night. There were six large glass cases almost as tall as the ceiling in the centre of the room, and several other cabinets. She was intrigued by the colourful cloaks from the Pacific and stopped to examine how they were made. Reading the description, she found that they were made of pine tree bark, beaten into a kind of flax. She wanted to absorb all this information, store it in her memory so that she could tell the children. There was a bracelet made of boar tusk, a knife carved in wood with shark's teeth, fishhooks fashioned in mother-of-pearl. In another case there were extraordinary insects that would fascinate Archie—a Great Mantis, a Tarantula, a scorpion. She read the descriptions hungrily as she cleaned the glass.

She thought of the Barra people and Colonel Gordon, wondering why some rich landowners could be so cruel and have slaves in the distant parts of the Earth. Remembering Jacob, the black servant who had saved Mary's life on the ship, she wondered if he was branded as Bella said. She could not see him as a slave labouring in a cane field. He had given her herbal medicine to stem the flux. And Baillie, his master from Glenelg. He was a kind man and other landowners like MacLeod in Skye and Campbell in Islay cared for their people. She wondered why some could be generous and others so callous, and tried to decide into which category she would place the Duke of Argyll. Calum detested him and all Argylls. She did not know the man. Perhaps, unlike Gordon, he was doing his best by helping the people of the Ross to leave. If he had said to her, 'Catherine MacGillivray, I will pay for your passage to Canada, if you want to go,' she would have thanked him and left. Perhaps it was not the Duke who wielded the whip in the Ross but John Campbell of Ardmore. He was a cruel creature. She had threatened her children with him as a bogey man—'Go to bed or the Factor Mor will get you!'

She was ruminating when Miss Armour startled her by appearing behind her.

'Ah, Catherine, I see you're admiring the sea-horse.'

'Yes, miss. What a strange creature.'

'Hippocampus—sea monster. The males produce the young, you know.'

'Really? What a good idea!'

'Indeed. Mr Lamont was here today with his boys. He tries so hard to keep them in the Roman section but they are desperate to be with the elephants and the gory medical cases. He asked me to give you a message. He will be here tomorrow afternoon and is hoping that you could join him. I explained that you worked at night and might have other work in the afternoon but he said to tell you anyway.'

'Thank you. I will try to be here.'

'We have just acquired a new painting in the gallery. Sadly, the packing has left quite a mess and Mr Fullerton needs some assistance to clear up. Could you go up and help? Take a sack from the store.'

'Of course.'

Catherine left her cloths and cleaning materials in the pail and hurried up the stairs.

'Well, Catherine,' Mr Fullerton greeted her enthusiastically. 'Come and see Lady Maynard.'

He beckoned her over where she could see the painting.

'Isn't wonderful. What does it say to you, Catherine?'

'I don't know what you mean.'

'When Sir Joshua painted this portrait, he didn't just try to reproduce an image, he also tried to convey something of the character of his subject, tried to tell you about her, what kind of person she is. So what do you learn about her?'

'That she is rich.'

'Yes indeed. I think that's an ermine mantle around her and I'm sure her delicate hands have never scrubbed a floor. Anything else?'

'She's beautiful.'

'Beautiful and rich—what a combination. Have a look at her left hand, the first finger extended towards her cheek, almost coy, demure certainly. A necklace too, tight around her neck like a shackle—imprisoned in her wealth or convention. Is she happy? Now there's a question. Not a Mona Lisa smile anyway. See how the paintings speak to you?'

'I do. I'll look at them differently now. Shall I clean up the wood shavings?'

§

As she walked home that night, she thought about the way he spoke about the portrait and the things he could see in it and she made up her mind to study the other paintings in the same way. She tried to recall the painting of the stag hunt but could only remember her feeling of sorrow for the stag as it was hunted down by the hounds and the men on horseback. The stag was a small delicate creature compared to the ones which she had seen on Shiaba, sturdy, swift, majestic beasts, whose roar at rutting time echoed around the shore. How could men slaughter them?

Trudging through the filth in the streets, she could not help thinking kindly of Shiaba, its clean, fresh air with stars at night, the scent of peat fires, the moon rising in the east and casting a long, rippling beam across the sea and the silence broken only by the lapping of the swell on the rocks. Silence, stars and clear air. Suddenly she realised she had been happy there, happy there with Calum before the hunger. She had never really thought about happiness or what it meant but now she knew and it was something precious, something which had to be held close and nurtured. The happiness which came from their love for each other was greater than his time with the other woman. She could forgive him.

When she reached home the girls had returned from the city and were sitting at the table in the candlelight.

Mary jumped up to throw her arms around her.

'I have a job, Mother!'

'What?'

'Both in the same house. Housemaids in the same house, Mother. Me and Marion.'

'Well done. Where is the house?'

'St Vincent Street. Not too far. Anyway she wants us to live in.'

'Live in? I don't want that, Mary.'

'Marion will look after me, Mother, and we are allowed a day off to see our families.'

Catherine could feel her daughter slipping away from her, not only growing up but choosing her own paths.

'There'll be more money in this house,' Marion pointed out. 'We will not need to be fed here and we can give you and Ma our wages. Ma is very pleased.'

'Who are these people?'

'Respectable people, Mother. He's a merchant and she is a rich lady and really kind. The other maids say she is very generous and easy to work for.'

'If Marion will look after you, I suppose I'll let you go but you must promise to come home on your day off.'

Mary hugged her again, clearly delighted.

§

The next afternoon, Catherine walked briskly across to the museum, excited by the prospect of meeting Mr Lamont again.

Waiting for him in the anteroom, she spent the time studying the butterflies and the cases of strange insects like the enormous Hercules beetle with its long horn and velvet belly and the bronze-backed scarab beetle sacred to the Egyptians.

When he arrived, Hector, his oldest, ran across and threw his arms around her waist.

'Hector! Do behave,' Lamont said. 'You don't embrace a lady without invitation. I'm sorry, Catherine. His manners leave much to be desired.'

'It's perfectly alright. It's good to see him. Thank you for the welcome, Hector.'

'Let's go down to the elephant room. The boys can amuse themselves down there and allow us time together. I do miss adult conversation. I don't see much of the other staff in school. How are you enjoying the work here?' he asked as they descended the stairs. 'Mr Fullerton speaks very highly of you.'

'It could not be better. It's a fascinating place.'

The boys hurried ahead, leaving them to talk in his favourite area, the room with the Roman artefacts.

'I wanted to come and see you,' she said, 'but Sine's daughter had cholera and I didn't think you would welcome a visit.'

'That was most considerate. The woman next door died of it, I'm sad to say. I was worried that you might be ill so I was delighted to hear that you had spoken to Mr Fullerton.'

'Yes. I have to thank you for the letter. I would not have been given the position without it.'

'I'm sure you would, Catherine. You underestimate your capabilities. It would give me great pleasure if you could come and visit. The boys, particularly Hector, really enjoyed your company.'

'I would love to come. I'm free most afternoons.'

'Splendid. You know our routine. Now tell me about your work here.'

4

'That must have been a difficult journey, John,' Sir Charles said.

Sir John McNeill, just returned to London from his brother's funeral, was sitting across from his friend in Charles Trevelyan's office.

'Yes, we took the steamer Briton from Stranraer up to West Loch Tarbet and then a boat to the island of Gigha.'

'Why Gigha? I thought you were from Colonsay.'

'Our McNeills are buried in Gigha.'

'I see. Your brother was there?'

'Yes, and Alexander's sons. The whole affair has been dreadful. Three weeks before Alexander's body surfaced. All at different times too. Anne and the two girls. The waiting was the worst part. Always hoping that they might be found alive.'

'I can imagine how painful that would be.'

'Some of the survivors saw him in the water, clinging to a floating spar. They say that he was trying to encourage those struggling in the water around him until his strength failed him. His last words, they say, were "For God's sake save yourselves. I have done all I can."'

'A warrior indeed.'

'Yes. In that ancient graveyard in Gigha, there are stones so old and worn by the weather that the carvings are almost obliterated, but they can still be seen—warriors with helmets and swords. McNeills perhaps from the years when the birlinns of the Lords of the Isles sailed through the islands. An ancient family.'

'Remarkable.'

'However, Charles, I'm sure that you didn't invite me over to hear about my troubles.'

'I was keen to see how you were faring under the circumstances but, true, I did want to hear your views on the Emigration Society, the finer details that is. I am anxious to see that we have everything covered, that we leave nothing to chance. It must succeed.'

'It will. I'm sure of it and it will leave the Highlands much more independent and able to survive future crises. It is the right course to pursue.'

'Well, let's settle on the character of emigrant we wish to send to Australia. I think we must give priority to families—they are less likely to abscond to the gold fields.'

'Indeed. Single men would certainly be tempted, but single women might be useful as domestic servants.'

'True. Let us say that we will only take single women if they travel with their parents or a close relative. Certainly no women with illegitimate children.'

'That would preclude half of our aristocracy! And we don't want any with pox. I think they should all be vaccinated.'

'Or have had smallpox. George had a letter from a clergyman, pleading the case for a woman from Mull with children whose husband was a convict. I am unsure about that. One could argue that the husband would be less likely to cause trouble and more likely to settle successfully. I have not replied.'

'She might be a criminal herself and cause havoc on the ship.'

'Yes. I had thought of that. What are we to do about clothing? Many of these miserable Highlanders have only rags. We can't have them disembarking in such a state. I think we may have to advance them money to buy clothes, provided, of course, that they dispose of any goods of their own first.'

'What clothing do you think they should have on boarding? Could be four months on board.'

'For men let's say six pair of socks, two pair of shoes, two full sets of exterior clothing. What do you think?'

'That sounds perfect. And the women?'

'Heavens, John, how am I to know what working class women wear under their skirts?'

'I should think many of the Members in the House would be able to help.'

'John! To be serious, let's say, as they are going to pass through extremes of temperature, two gowns, two pair of shoes, six pair of stockings, six shifts, two flannel petticoats and I think towels, sheets and soap.'

'I'm most impressed, Charles. I take it that there's to be a surgeon on board.'

'Yes, yes and an assistant.'

'What about their spiritual needs?'

'Ah yes. Most of the emigrants will be Free Church so I will ask the church authorities to select a minister, a qualified catechist and a teacher. I will write to Dr MacLeod in Glasgow to see if he can provide Gaelic psalm books, catechisms and bibles.'

'Splendid. And the ship?'

'I've been considering the Hercules which was to be based as a floating barracks in Hong Kong but would be better employed in this capacity, and I had hope to employ Commander Baynton, whom you know already, as captain.'

'I think I know the ship too. Isn't she berthed here in London?'

'Yes. We must walk down one day and inspect it for ourselves.'

'Good idea, Charles. Now, I'm meeting with the Reverend Cumming in Covent Garden shortly so I'll have to leave.'

'Of course, John. He's a very popular preacher, I believe. A trifle too extreme with his fulminations against Rome for my taste, though.'

'Believes that the famine is a warning from the Lord, Charles. That should appeal to you.'

He laughed as he lifted his hat and left.

The mention of Covent Garden reminded Trevelyan of his encounter with the poor family from Tiree in Covent Garden and his promise of financial to the father. He wondered if George had looked into the matter.

5

Calum sat on the pier, gazing down at his new boat. All the others were at sea so he had peace to admire it. It was much longer than he expected and he had to look up to see the top of the mast. Climbing down, he sat in the stern with his hand on the tiller, absorbing the details—the elegantly curved oak knees, the shining blocks, the scent of shellac, the lapping of the tide against the new planks. He ran his hand along the gunwale, admiring the long sweep from the stern to the bow. His boat. There was plenty of room for creels and lines. He stood and moved forward to hoist the sail, finding the new halyard rough in his hands. It took most of his strength to haul up the sail and fasten the halyard around the pins. He was going to need crew.

Climbing back to the pier, he walked back towards Bunessan to speak to Catherine's brother, hoping that he had not been carousing the night before.

'It's yourself, Calum MacGillivray,' her mother said as soon as his shadow crossed the threshold. 'We thought perhaps you had abandoned us in favour of the delights of the city.'

She was sitting by a flameless fire, picking whelks out of their shells with a pin.

'Is John not here?'

'You can see for yourself that he's not.'

'Has he been drinking again?'

'Whisky has not passed his lips since you were here last and anyway his habits are no concern of yours.'

'They will be, if I take him on as crew.'

She looked up, her sightless eyes searching for him.

'Crew is it? Getting too lazy to lift creels on your own?'

'Where is he, Mima?'

'In the barn at the back, looking for bits of peat.'

Calum was glad to turn his back on her and walk across to the barn. He found John on his knees, picking out small pieces of peat.

'Well, John. On your knees at last. I'm sure the Good Lord will welcome your penitence.'

John did not rise but turned and glared at him silently.

'You have no peats, then?' asked Calum.

'I would not be scraping through the chaff with my bare hands if I had. I was up on the bank above Saorphin searching but the Tiree women have it cleaned.'

'There's some by the empty houses with us. I'll bring you some. I came to ask if you would crew for me.'

'For payment?'

'Of course. Two shillings a day. A pound of meal if we're stormbound.'

'I have never been in a boat and I have never been to the fishing.'

'You can learn. I had to learn. Will you join me or not?'

'I will, Calum, and thank you, a charaid.'

'Be on the pier at first light tomorrow. Have you meal for tonight?'

'We have'

'Good. I will see you tomorrow.'

He walked round to see MacQuarrie.

'Well?' the merchant said. 'What do you think of her?'

'A fine boat. Bigger than I expected; plenty of room for creels.'

'They say these Loch Carron boats handle well and are steady in a gale. I'm very pleased with her myself.'

'I have asked Catherine's brother to sail with me. I don't know the people in the village well enough to choose one of them. You must know them well. Who do you think would be suitable?'

'There's young Hugh Cameron, the carpenter who mends boats. He would be a good man to have and there's men in Kintra who have given up the fishing.'

'I'll try Hugh first. Can I borrow your horse and cart to take Peggy's creels to the pier.'

'Yes, that'll be fine. I have heard nothing of Peggy. I hope she reached Australia safely. And what news of Catherine ?'

'She's well and working in a museum till I can save enough to bring them all back.'

'A museum? That must be interesting work indeed. She's a remarkable woman.'

'She is. Can I get the horse?'

'In the stable.'

Calum walked away quickly. MacQuarrie always had to insert Catherine's name into the conversation, like a flick of a nettle-leaf. It was very annoying.

He harnessed the mare, backed her into the cart and led her round to the creels.

§

That afternoon, as he returned to Shiaba, he met Hector MacKinnon hurrying towards the village. Calum was surprised by his urgency and a hint of shame in the way he could not look him in the face.

'You're in a hurry, Hector.'

'I am.'

'It will not be to dance a reel at the inn, then.'

'I'm going to see the Factor.'

'He has asked you to dine with him?'

'Chance would be a fine thing. No, he offered me a house in the village and I turned it down. I will try to persuade him to let me take it after all.'

'You will leave Shiaba, then?'

'I'm sorry. After all you have done to help us, I feel I'm betraying you. There is typhus fever in the end house—the widow MacLean—her son came back with it. I have to think of my children. We have nothing—no seed, no corn, no food, no candles. Nothing.'

'It is no betrayal, my friend. You must see to your family. I hope the Factor will help. He's not noted for his generosity towards those of us who defy his notices of eviction. Go. You have my blessing.'

As he passed Assapol, he thought of the widow who had come from the far side of the island and remembered that she had five children. He had met the oldest girl when he delivered meal to their door and was shocked by the lifeless eyes in the gaunt face. She had thanked him in a tone which spoke of her despair, her submission, her lethargy and he compared it with the vitality he had seen in

Mary and Marion. Perhaps Catherine had been right to leave. He had returned home, infected with the girl's gloom.

Reaching Shiaba, he walked down to the last house and knocked on the door. The same girl answered.

'I heard there was fever in your house.'

Her cheeks were smeared with grime where she had been rubbing away tears.

'My mother is sick and my brother.'

'There are others, though.'

'Four brothers, one a baby.'

'I will take the older two, the ones not sick, and look after them. Less of a burden for you. It is too heavy for you alone.'

'The fever could be passed to you.'

'I will take that risk. See if your mother agrees.'

'She is too sick to say.'

'Send the oldest two to my house. I know them by sight. Have you meal for tonight?'

'Enough for tonight only.'

'I will see you have more tomorrow and I'll ask the Bunessan surgeon to see if he can help.'

'That is kind of you, Mr MacGillivray. Very kind. Thank you. God bless you.'

As he left, he sensed a pleasing spark of vitality return to the girl. Yet he was barely half way to his house when the full implications of his impulsive gesture made him stop. The children would surely carry the fever and, if he were to be infected, he would be of no value to them or to the others in Shiaba. If he died of it, Catherine would be left a widow and his children fatherless. He cursed himself for his folly, his vanity, his need to be seen as a hero. Thoughtless. Yet he could not withdraw the offer now. He would have to see it through, in spite of the risks.

He turned aside into John Campbell's house and carried through some blankets that had been left and two candles. The boys were not far behind him.

The taller of the two, his pallor emphasised by his thin red hair, gripped his brother by the shirt to prevent him entering the house.

'It's fine,' Calum said 'Come in. I've forgotten your names. Which of you is Connor?'

'I'm Connor,' said the tall one. 'He's Niall after Niall of the Nine Hostages.'

'Irish names, then.'

'Our father was Irish. He's dead.'

'Yes. I'm sorry. What age are you, Connor?'

'Nine. Niall is seven. He says he's eight but he's seven.'

'Two strong boys. I need help to carry a bed through from the house next door. Are you fit for that?'

'I am but I don't know if Niall is strong enough.'

'Of course he is. Come.'

They followed him through and helped him carry Lachlan's bed into his house. He noticed how different Niall was to his brother—black hair that hung over his eyes like the dossan of a cow. He had a habit of lowering his head to hide his face.

'Niall, will you take the pail there and fetch some water and we'll make some porridge.'

The boy did not move until Connor gave the command.

After he left, Calum blew the fire to flame.

'Have you ever been in a boat, Connor?'

'My father was a fisherman.'

'So am I. I have a boat in Bunessan. Tomorrow you can come with me—you and Niall—and help me to catch mackerel for bait. And we need to find mussels for the lines.'

'I used to go out with my father. He had nets for herring.'

'Good. You'll be able to help me.'

As the light began to fade, Calum made porridge and fed the boys.

They had just finished when their sister appeared at the door, greatly distressed.

'Mother has just fallen. She was trying to rise from the bed—God knows why—and fell. I can't lift her on my own.'

'Connor you stay there with Niall,' Calum said 'Are there candles in your house?'

The girl shook her head so Calum lifted the candle, resolving to buy some paraffin for his lantern, and followed her back to the house. He was relieved to find the wind had dropped and it was a still night, though moonless and dark.

'What's your name?' he asked on the way.

'Bridget. I think she's going to die.'

'We'll see. Is there fire on the hearth?'

'No. We have nothing to burn.'

The candle flickered as he entered the house. The stench of flux and filth was overpowering. The woman was lying on her back on the floor beside the bed, her mouth open and her eyes shut. For a moment Calum thought that she was dead but saw her move and clutch at the earth by her side. Laying the candle on the table, he slid his arms under her and lifted her on to the bed. It was like lifting a bag of sticks. There was no weight in her frail body and he could feel every bone. She was colder than the floor. She opened her eyes but, as if they were blind, they stared past him. He covered her with the blanket but guessed that she would never be warm again. Her breathing was shallow and quick.

He moved across the place where the beasts had lain, broke the last rails of the pens and lit a fire. In the light of the flames he saw the brother lying against the wall.

'How is he?' he asked Bridget.

'Dead, I think.'

He was shocked by the casual way she announced it, as if she was speaking of a passing cloud. He went across and knew by the pallor that it was true. Still, he touched the surface of the staring eye to test for a response and, finding none, closed them both.

'Where's the little one?'

'In the house next door. They are looking after him.'

He broke as much wood as would keep the fire burning until daybreak.

'I'll come again in the morning, Bridget, but, if your mother is worse in the night, call me. You keep warm.'

He left and was relieved to be out in the fresh air.

6

John Campbell sat on his horse, watching the men building the dyke around his field. In spite of their weakness from hunger, they were manhandling massive round granite stones carted from the shore. He stayed well back from the work, knowing that he would have to listen to their complaints if he came too close. He was pleased that he had been able to use most of the Government Drainage money to improve his own farm and the Duke didn't seem to object. He was keen to see the dyke built to a height that would not only keep his beasts in but would also provide shelter from the cold winter winds.

He noticed a man approaching from the west and, judging by his hurry and the way he swung his arms aggressively, he was in a temper. Campbell was tempted to swing his horse away and head for home, fearing he would have to hear yet another tiresome complaint or pleading. However, he decided to wait and endure it. As he came nearer, he recognised him as one of the tenants from Creich near Fionnphort.

'Can I have a word with you, Mr Campbell?' he gasped, taking off his bonnet. Campbell saw his fingers shaking with fury. One of the MacDonalds.

'A word, I hope, will suffice.'

'Your keeper's rabid dogs have killed half of my sheep.'

'He is not my keeper. He is employed by the Duke. And what makes you think the dogs are his?'

'They are his alright. He has passed my croft often enough.'

'You say they are rabid. What makes you think that?'

'They were foaming at the mouth.'

'Dogs foam at the mouth for many reasons other than rabies. Excitement, exertion, heat.'

'They were rabid. I have lived long enough to know. I will need compensation for this.'

'Did you see them killing your sheep?'

'I did. I was scraping for seed in the rigs and ran. The dogs had them in a corner. By the time I was near enough to fling stones at the dogs, they had killed half of them, the throats torn out and blood all over their fleeces. It was like a battleground. Great gaping wounds in their sides and legs stripped to the bone.'

'I will send the ground officer to ascertain the truth of your allegation and to count your sheep stock. In the meantime you should write to the Duke in Inveraray. The keeper is employed by him.'

He turned his horse and rode away, leaving the crofter standing.

Had the sheep been of any quality, he might have sympathised but he knew them to be poor specimens, barely worth keeping. Pleased with his suggestion that MacDonald should complain to the Duke, he smiled, knowing that such a letter would annoy His Grace and perhaps provoke him into chastising the crofter. Still, he would have to have a quiet word with the keeper.

§

That night he wrote to the Duke without mentioning the matter:

The state of the poor in this island at present I need not say is truly appalling. I cannot move but I am beset with applications for relief. I sent for meal about ten days ago in case any thing might happen and, on the arrival of the vessel at Bunessan, it was like a market day, they congregating there beseeching for meal, saying that some of them had not tasted food but shellfish for days together—this I know to be a fact.

§

The next morning he left the house early to see how his new bull was settling, a bull he had purchased from south Argyll to improve his stock. He had admired it the moment it sauntered through the gate, its bulk, its straight back and broad haunches, even the way it had glanced at him as it passed. The sun had just risen and his boots left a trail in the dew. The sheep in the turnip field raised their heads above the last stumps of what had been a record crop.

When he reached the cattle, the bull was not with the cows but standing alone in a corner with his head down. He hurried down to find that a beard of white froth hung from its mouth. He was stunned.

'Good God Almighty!' he said, turned and rushed back to the steadings to find help.

Dugald Campbell was the first of his workers he encountered.

'Find Angus and Malcolm and go up to the bull field. I want the new bull moved to Iona immediately.'

'Iona?'

'Yes. Immediately. He has foot and mouth and I don't want the disease to spread to the rest of the herd. Say nothing to the people you meet. Nothing. I expect some will see for themselves but I don't want his sickness broadcast throughout the parish. Do you understand?'

'Yes, sir.'

'And take some cloths with you to wipe away the froth round his mouth so that the people won't see.'

The Factor returned to the house, threw his hat on the hallstand, stormed into the study, slammed the door shut and sank into his chair.

'God damn them!' he said and then put his hand over his mouth, regretting the blasphemy, 'They knew! The scoundrels knew! I will have them in court for this.'

He rose and poured himself a whisky, the glass rattling in his shaking hand.

'Blackguards!'

The door opened and his wife looked in.

'What's happened, John? I heard the door slam so I knew something was amiss.'

'The new bull has foot and mouth.'

'Oh, John, that's dreadful. It's not fatal, is it?'

'No. Not always, but if it spreads to the herd, it could set us back years, particularly the dairy cows.'

'Can anything be done?'

'I'm sending him to Iona immediately. Try to protect the herd.'

'He'll infect the beasts there surely.'

'They are poor specimens anyway, Flora. We must look after our own.'

'I suppose you're right. You should not be drinking whisky at this time of day. I'll fetch some cordial.'

'No, Flora. I'm going out anyway. I want to check on the men building the dyke by the road.'

'If you must, but don't be too upset. Your face is quite flushed. You should rest for a while.'

'Later perhaps.'

§

As the light began to fade that night, Dugald called to see him.

'Did you see the bull settled, then?'

'We left him near the abbey ruins. There's shelter there. He's not well, though.'

'I know. I know. It's a worry. I must take some hay across. The land is so bare.'

'If you go over yourself, you should check the hoggs—the ones you sent there for wintering. We saw the Iona men drive them off the grass with their dogs on to the rough ground.'

'Did they indeed? I've had enough these people. Go down to Ross the keeper and tell him he is to take his gun to Iona in the morning and shoot the dogs—every dog he sees on the island.'

'Shoot the dogs?'

'Yes, every blasted one of them.'

§

A fortnight later John Campbell received a letter from the Duke. Worried that His Grace might have received a complaint from Iona, he opened it with some apprehension. It contained only a few trivial instructions but one which pleased him.

I have received a most insolent letter from John MacDonald demanding compensation for sheep killed by the keeper's dogs. See that he is removed from his croft and that his stock is disposed of to pay for any outstanding rent.

It was the reaction he had expected.
He replied.
I will instruct the Sheriff's office to issue a summons immediately and will see
that it is enforced rigorously.

The fishing is doing well in Bunessan with a score of boats prosecuting the trade. Calum MacGillivray from Shiaba has formed a partnership with MacQuarrie in a new boat of thirty feet and is fishing lobsters.

The destitution here is greater than ever and I have employed 194 females in knitting whose labour produced £50 and 36 women spinning. The cost to the estate has been £350 including the cost of yarn, freight etc. The expenditure, however, will have prevented many deaths by hunger.

§

Some months later, at the cattle sale outside Bunessan, the Factor noticed MacDonald had brought his stock to be sold. It was a surprisingly brisk sale, the dealer McClymont being in a generous mood. The Factor walked round to the auctioneer and spoke to him quietly.

'You are not to call MacDonald's stock—the poor creatures over by the dyke—I will purchase them myself.'

'That's rather irregular, Mr Campbell.'

'On the instructions of the Duke.'

'Oh, I see. Well, we had better not offend His Grace. I've no wish to test the hospitality of Inveraray gaol. I'll not call them then.'

At the end of the sale, MacDonald came across to the auctioneer.

'You never called my beasts.'

'I was instructed not to call them. I understand the Factor is to take them for the Duke.'

'But the Factor is not here. He left an hour ago.'

'I'm sorry, Mr MacDonald. There's nothing I can do.'

7

'I'm afraid to say, Charles, that everyone was open-mouthed down at the club—at Brook's—the other day about your plans for the Civil Service, particularly the entrance examination.'

MacAulay, sitting across from Trevelyan in the drawing room, seemed genuinely concerned for his bother-in-law.

'I'm not surprised. For far too long the service has been seen as a refuge for the indolent, ineffectual and corruptible sons of influential people in the corridors of power. It has to be reformed. We both know that.'

'Indeed. But it could be that the time is not right. Be patient. The pear is not ripe, Charles. We have more opposition here than in India.'

Trevelyan lifted his glass of port and admired its crimson hue against the flickering candelabra. He remembered India and the powerful people ranged against them when he and Tom had tried to persuade the Governor General to drop Persian as the official language of British India and to adopt English. They had shared a firm belief in the cultural superiority of England and, together, they had won their case but they had made enemies, the corrupt Sir Edward Colebrooke among them. Lady Colebrooke in India had publicly accused Charles of being a villain and a liar. He was not afraid of making enemies when he knew he was right.

'I feel that I have done what I can in Ireland and the Highland emigration is proceeding satisfactorily—this year we sent out thirteen ships with 2,500 emigrants.'

'I believe there was a mutiny on one of them.'

'Greed, Tom. Greed. The lure of gold. The Georgiana. No sooner anchored at Geelong but the crew demanded to be put ashore, overpowered the master, left him for dead and abandoned the ship and the bewildered Highlanders. I'm pleased to say the passengers did not assist the mutineers.'

'They could have assisted the captain surely.'

'I expect their main interest was disembarkation and finding a place of employment ashore which, I believe, most of them managed to secure.'

'And the mutineers?'

'The last I heard, seven of the eighteen had been apprehended. No doubt the others will have been taken by now. We anticipated that some of them would be tempted by the goldfields. That's why we limited the applications mainly to families. I think the scheme has been an overwhelming success. The letters of gratitude received from the emigrants speak of their satisfaction, if not delight, with their new home. And, of course, their departure must ease the congestion and poverty in the Highlands.'

'There have been some misfortunes, though, Charles. You must admit.'

'Sadly, yes. Disease on the ships. I'm convinced that it has been carried on board by the emigrants and thrives in the airless spaces below deck. Yes, had a report today of the Ticonderoga having to bury seventy in a bay and, it is thought, many more buried at sea. Unavoidable, I'm afraid, but still a minority.'

'What happened to that family we met in Covent Garden market?'

'Died of fever, I'm afraid. Not sure about the children.'

'A shame. Seemed a stalwart sort. Salt of the earth as they say.'

'Yes. We did what we could for him. Tom, I need to find a new channel for my energy. A new challenge. There is still much to be done. Now that Gladstone is Chancellor, we have an opportunity to deal with the Civil Service. Gladstone will support us.'

'Yes, I believe you're right. You know that you are thought to be the object of satire in Trollope's Three Clerks? His Gregory Hardlines, the Civil Servant, is said to be Sir Charles Trevelyan. Have you read it?'

'I don't read novels.'

'You should. It's very amusing. Trivial but entertaining. I believe that Gladstone is considering Stafford Northcote to help us draft a proposal for reform.'

'Really? Good man. Moving force in the Great Exhibition. Could be a great asset.'

'What manner of subject had you in mind for the Service examination?'

'Well, we could start with the basics of classics and mathematics and then history—with your books as compulsory reading of course—jurisprudence and political economy.'

'And modern languages, political and physical geography.'

Trevelyan could feel his enthusiasm, which had been waning under the stresses of the famine, beginning to revive.

'Indeed. I think we should also have regular supervision, don't you? Our novices must feel that their promotion and future prospects depend entirely on their industry and ability.'

'Good heavens! A Civil Service based on merit! Can't have that, Charles. The members in Brook's would have heart failure at the thought.'

'That would do no harm. I become very weary of such resistance. What I would really like to do is return to India, see Simla again.'

'And deprive me of my dear sister and Margaret as well? You would not be so cruel.'

'Just a dream, Tom. Well, perhaps more than a dream. An aspiration.'

'Your aspirations have a tendency to blossom into reality. However, I suspect that your organisational talents will be called upon before your dream—which would be a nightmare for me—can be thrust upon us. I fear the imperial ambitions of Russia in the Balkans will lead to war, an event which, when I reflect upon it, might help to solve the problems in the Highlands. Nothing like a war, the King's shilling and skirl of the pipes to entice young Celtic warriors away from the glens and island retreats.'

8

Calum stood outside the house, leaning against the wall as the boys finished their porridge. A mantle of early morning mist covered the sea below, stretching to the horizon as if the ocean had flooded in the night, swelling to engulf the lower islands. Only the peaks of Jura protruded from the flat, grey surface. A bronze sun was rising in the east and he knew it would soon burn off the mist. He thought of Catherine in the smoke and stink of the city and wished she could be there to share the peace and beauty of the scene beneath him. He was afraid that she might never return, that the attractions of the city would lure her into remaining there. If she made that choice, he wondered if he would be able to leave Shiaba, abandon the fishing and join her. Looking along the row of houses, so many of them empty now, and remembering his father scything hay, he was not sure.

Behind him, he could hear the boys talking about their mother and he thought about Archie, wishing that it was him who would sail with him that morning. He imagined him crawling under the machinery with his face white with cotton dust. A terrible life. Every hour of the long day governed by the flying belts and clattering mules. Better here in the sunlight. As he watched, the Skerryvore lighthouse rose out of the mist, the lens glinting in the sun.

The boys emerged from the house, blinking in the light. He was about to ask if they had shoes but then decided not to draw attention to their bare feet. He noticed their thin ankles and legs below their trousers, brittle and transparent like the legs of a hen.

'Right, boys. Bunessan it is and it's a fine day for fishing. The sun will burn off the mist.'

They set off for the village.

'Which is your boat?' Connor asked when they reached the pier.

'The new one.'

'There's a lot of boats.'

'Too many now and all after the same thing. There'll be no fish left in the sea shortly.'

He looked across to Ardtun to see if there was any sign of John. There was no-one on the road and he could see that the door was still shut. That was annoying. He had hoped that John would prove to be reliable, that the family connection would count for something. He would have to sail without him.

They scrambled over several boats to reach his and he was shocked to find John asleep in the stern, wrapped in the spare jib.

'God Almighty, John! What are doing here?'

'I was afraid I might sleep too long at home so I spent the night here.'

Calum shook his head in disbelief but was relieved. John swung his legs off the thwart, frowning at the boys.

'I've brought two deckhands to help. Connor is nine and Niall is seven, though he'll tell you he's eight.'

'Strong-looking men, right enough.'

'First we'll carry some of the creels down to the boat. We can't take them all as well as the boys.'

Once they had loaded them, Calum cast off and hoisted the sail, heading out of the bay. He had the twin task of teaching John about the boat and showing the boys how to use the short lines with the feathered hooks.

'Here, John. You take the tiller. Get the feel of it on a good day. Keep her heading for Dun I on Iona. To turn left, push the tiller to the right. To go right, pull it left. Have you got that?'

'Yes, I'm fine. You see to the boys.'

He showed them how to pay out the line and take a turn around their fingers when it had reached its depth, how to jig it up and down.

'We'll heave to off the point. When you feel a fish on the line, don't pull it in. Keep it out. Others will come. You might have six or seven on a line.'

When they reached the point, Calum took the tiller, turned the boat into the wind and let go the mainsheet, leaving the sail slack. They drifted along, the boat rocking gently in the current. The sun was warm and a cormorant, watching them from a rock, had spread its wings to dry.

'Have you heard from Catherine?' John asked.

'No.' His curt answer meant to deter any further discussion.

The two men sat in silence in the stern.

'They say she has a new friend, an educated man. A teacher,' John persisted.

'We are all entitled to have friends.'

'She was going to his house.'

'A domestic servant, I'm told, normally goes to the house where they are employed.'

'A widower. A man on his own.'

Calum hauled the tiller round, the boat swung into the wind and the boom smacked John's head. He was beginning to regret taking him on. As the boat steadied, he glared at him to make sure that he had received the message; his silence indicated that he had.

Connor started to haul in his line, several mackerel flapping on the hooks. Calum always took pleasure in the flashing silver, blue and green of mackerel, their sleek shape made for speed and their slim tails. They fought against the hooks, against their fate. Saithe, though, were sluggish fish, submissive, compliant. He disliked them as a species but cooked them when they were caught.

'Can you unhook them yourself, Connor?'

'Ay. Father showed me.'

'How many do you need?' John asked.

'As many as we can. We need plenty for bait and there'll likely be some saithe for the pot.'

'Have you spoken to the Kintra men?'

'No. Not yet.'

'There's much talk of Australia.'

'In Kintra?'

'Some of them worked in the quarry but it is not so busy now that Ardnamurchan light is finished. They fear another winter like last will finish them altogether. Leave or starve.'

'I will speak with them, but I only need one.'

'The Factor is riding around the townlands persuading the poor to leave, telling them it will cost nothing. He is desperate to clear them off the land. They say two sheep men by the name of Elliott have offered £250 for Scoor and Shiaba.'

'They may get the grazing—and I'm sure Campbell will see that they do—but they will not drive us out of our homes.'

'Surely half of Shiaba has gone already.'

'But not me. Connor, can you help Niall? He has too many fish on the line.'

'It's all in a fankle.'

'Right, I'll see to it.'

He moved over to Niall, relieved to find a diversion from John's conversation.

'I can't get the hooks out,' Niall said.

'I'll show you. Look. You work them backwards away from the barb. See?'

'Ay.'

'You've done well. Four in the basket and two in the sea yet.'

'How do you kill them?'

'Hit them on their heads. I'll do it.'

By noon the baskets were full, a mixture of saithe and mackerel, the gleaming bellies stained with threads of blood. Calum showed John and the boys how to bait the creels, opening the cage and sliding the mackerel into place in the twine, then set sail for the back of Erraid, forgetting that there would be traces of the wreck still on the rocks—the wreck from which he had stolen the cargo to buy his first boat.

'Look!' said John. 'There's the wreck, what's left of it. MacLeod's it was. Oil and feathers from St Kilda. His rent. Plundered. He's had the Sheriff's men and constables from Oban asking about the cargo. All over Fidden and Fionnphort they were, asking and searching, poking their noses into every corner. They're sure it was the Fidden cottars.'

'Even if it was them, what would they do with feathers? They're not likely to sleep on a feather bed. The oil they could use maybe.'

He tried to sound casual, but the news of MacLeod alarmed him. He had been so sure that no-one would search for the cargo that he had plundered and sold, the cargo that had transformed his life.

'Feathers make a good price in the city,' John continued. 'MacLeod is desperate to retrieve them. Raging they say. His men were asking in Oban and the Sheriff sent men to Glasgow.'

'I'm sure MacLeod would not miss a few feathers.'

'We should have a look. There might be other things.'

'I'm not taking the new boat in to the rocks. Let's get these creels set.'

He turned the boat into the wind and dropped a creel over the side, feeding out its line with the cork floats. One after the other, he set seven creels before he turned for home.

When they tied up with the other boats at the pier, he gave John a couple of saithe and, passing a string through the gills, made a string of them for Shiaba.

'We will eat well tonight, boys, thanks to you, and we'll take some through to Bridget. You can tell her that you caught them. First, though, we must get candles.'

§

That evening, when he reached home, he found a letter on the table. He did not read it immediately, preferring to wait until the boys were in bed. Instead, he walked round to ask after their mother.

'I don't know,' Bridget answered. 'She's sleeping. She must have the pox. She is covered in rash.'

'See that she is kept warm. I'll find more wood later.'

'Thank you for your help.'

He walked away, leaving her standing in the doorway. There was something about her that reminded him of Catherine, a resilience, a quiet determination to survive.

§

When the boys were settled he read the letter by candlelight. It was from Peggy.

Dear Calum,

I am writing to thank you for your kindness to me and my girls. If you had not taken us into your house and given us food, I am sure that we would have died.

As you can see we reached Australia safely, though many on our ship did not. Ourselves and a family from Tyree were sent to join the ship in Campbeltown. The minister in London Rev Cumming was kind enough to see that our lodgings and our fares were paid. When we got to Campbeltown the ship was already crowded with emigrants from Skye, Uist and Harris, more than eight hundred I was told. We left on Boxing Day but we had to shelter in Rothesay because of a storm and did not set sail till the 14th of January. We were not long at sea when typhus fever and smallpox broke out and we had to go into Cork in Ireland. More than fifty people, including the couple from Tyree, died and all the orphaned children had to be sent home, many to orphanages. We did not leave Cork till the 14th of April and arrived in Adelaide on the 26th of July.

Although I was very ill with sea-sickness on the voyage, the girls did not suffer. I have found work on a dairy farm and live in a small wooden hut. The girls will soon be going to school. I have found where my husband is being held and, although I am not allowed to visit him, I can see him at a distance working with the gang of convicts and can write to him and he can write back. We are both longing for the day he is released.

I hope you and your wife have been reunited and that you are all back in your beloved Shiaba. With many thanks and best wishes for the future.

Yours sincerely, Margaret MacNicol

He was glad that Peggy had reached Australia. He had heard that many emigrants perished on the journey. He remembered the seductive dark eyes, the dexterous fingers as they made the creels and the sensation of Lucia's head on his chest. He wondered what it would be like to live under the burning sun, watching your partner in chains and unable to speak or touch. In chains. He recalled what John had said on the boat about MacLeod and the constables. He could end up in chains himself, if they found any traces of his sales in Oban or Glasgow.

He did not sleep well, waking at one point to find a louse in his shirt but, having crushed it, scratched all night.

9

Catherine gazed at the butterfly in the case, entranced by the brilliant iridescent blue wings with jet black tips. She remembered the name—Papilio Menelaus—and that it came from Brazil, a country which she had found on the globe upstairs. She learnt the names and details of all the ones that she liked. She found it sad, though, to see them pinned out in the cases when they should be fluttering in the sun, flitting from flower to flower. Imprisoned, crucified, preserved for the public, they would never fly again.

On the evenings when she visited Mr Lamont, she drew each one, colouring them with his water colour paints and writing their details in the margins. It was frustrating to find that she could never reproduce the brilliance of the colours yet he seemed truly amazed by her skill and her memory.

'These are wonderful, Catherine,' he had said that afternoon. 'I love the way you portray them in flight or resting on a flower. You bring them to life. You take dead specimens and breathe life into them. Astonishing. Don't you think so Hector?'

'Yes. I wish I could draw like that.'

Lamont had lifted one of the drawings and held it in front of the oil lamp.

'See how the colours come alive. You must paint one for me, Catherine.'

'I want to keep them all here with you, if I may. Safe.'

'Of course. I would be delighted. I will find a special folder for them. How is Archie doing in school?'

'Very well. The teacher says he has an aptitude for arithmetic and has caught up with the others of his own age in reading and spelling. He can recite the Shorter Catechism and parts of the New Testament.'

'Splendid. I knew he would do well.'

It was good to be back with Mr Lamont again now that the cholera had passed. She felt at home there with him and his boys and cooked for them before she left for the museum.

'Have you ever thought about training as a teacher yourself?'

'Never. I'm not clever like you.'

'You are more intelligent than half the teachers I encounter at meetings and you have a remarkable capacity to learn quickly. Don't dismiss the idea. I could coach you for the entry examination to the Free Church College in Cowcaddens—very popular with Methodists—good people the Methodists—and you might even get a scholarship to cover your fees. Now, don't laugh. You could do that. You have a great way with children.'

'I'm very happy in the museum and I'm learning all kinds of fascinating things.'

'Of course you are, but do you not want to return to Mull one day? If you returned as a teacher, you would not have to endure the kind of starvation and poverty you have had to face in the past.'

'Of course I want to go back, but only when the famine has passed and God knows when that will be. Things are as bad as ever. Neither seed nor crop. No. Not yet.'

'Think about what I've said, Catherine. If a tenth of my pupils had your talents, my daily task would be a pleasure. I would help you.'

In his enthusiasm he had placed his hand on hers, quite unconscious of the gesture, but she felt the smooth, gentle fingers and enjoyed the sensation. As she looked down, he realised what he had done and quickly withdrew his hand. She would have preferred him to keep it there.

'I will think about it,' she said quickly, 'I promise.'

'The subject on which they concentrate at these auditions is knowledge of the Bible and Catechisms. Naturally, I object to that strongly but that's how it is. How well are you versed in such things?'

'My father used to read from Gospels when I was small and Mary learnt them at school but I know very little really.'

'We will have to work on that, I'm afraid, but you have a great memory so it should be no trouble to you. Then you can forget all about it and return to Tom Paine!'

§

As she gazed on the butterflies she thought about his proposal. Being far more interested in the exhibits in the museum and all their fascinating details, she was reluctant to abandon her studies of them in favour of tedious texts of the Gospel and the Catechisms. Yet the prospect of returning to Mull as a teacher had its attractions, not least the salary and security but also as proof of her worth, particularly to Calum. She wondered how he would react to her transformation from housewife to professional, from chrysalis to butterfly. He might resent her being seen as a respectable lady, perhaps even jealous of her status. He had little time for figures of authority and made his contempt quite obvious. Mary, though, would be delighted and, were she to consult her, would be enthusiastic in her support for the training. Archie would be pleased whatever she did as long as she was happy. She decided to ask Sine what she thought.

§

When she arrived home, she called on Sine to find Duncan sitting at the table with a blood-stained bandage around his head.

'In God's name, Duncan, what happened to you?'

'The bloody Irish,' Sine shouted before he could answer.

'I went to see if there was work on the railway and I was lucky. They were taking on a few men and I joined a gang from Skye.'

'He should never have gone, Catherine,' Sine interrupted. 'I said there'd be trouble.'

'An argument broke out between our boys and the Irish—I don't what it was about—something stupid anyway—and one of our young bucks clouted an Irishman with a shovel.

The whole gang of them took off to the nearest town for reinforcements so we sent word up the line for assistance.'

'You knew there was to be trouble. You should have come home.'

Duncan ignored her intervention and continued.

'We gathered about two hundred Highlanders but the Irish appeared in the late afternoon—I'm sure there was a thousand of them, armed with pokers, rails, stobs—a fearsome sight I can tell you. A few of us had dirks but against that wild army we would have been massacred so we fled. They flung a few stones after us and one caught my head.'

'Well, you're not going back and that's final.'

'No. We've had a talk, Catherine,' Duncan said,' and we've decided to leave, to emigrate. Australia can't be any worse than here and some folk have done well there. I just can't take any more scraping for every penny and fighting over scraps like dogs at a table and dodging disease round every corner.'

'All of you? The girls too?'

'We haven't spoken to them but I'm sure they'll come. You should come too, you and Calum and the children.'

'Calum will never leave Shiaba. You know that. And he seems to be doing well at the fishing. This is a shock. I don't know what to say. I can't bear the thought of you leaving and it's so far away. I may never see you again.'

'People do come back,' Sine said, 'but it will be hard for us too, leaving everybody and everything, leaving the place where we were born and where our people are buried. I know it will be hard but thousands of others are leaving, a lot of them not driven out like the people of Barra and Ulva and Shiaba but leaving by choice.'

'I know. I will miss you so much. I feel part of the family here.'

'You'll still have the children and Calum. You have a future here.'

'I suppose so. Actually I do have plans myself.'

'You're going to move in with the teacher!' laughed Duncan.

'No. I'm not. I'm thinking of training to be a teacher.'

'What?' said Sine, her tone of disbelief verging on insult.

'Mr Lamont thinks I could pass the entrance examination with his help.'

Duncan clapped his hands.

'Well done, girl! You do that. I think that's a great idea. A clever woman like you would be a gift to any school.'

Sine, realising her mistake, took Catherine's hands in hers.

'Of course you should do it, Catherine. You took me by surprise there.'

'I know. I'm surprised myself. It was Mr Lamont's suggestion but what am I going to do without you here at my back? I just can't bear the thought of it. Yet I do understand, Sine, and you're probably right. A new start, a new country.'

'And if we can't find work,' said Duncan, 'we can go to the gold diggings.'

'You'll do nothing of the kind,' said Sine firmly. 'We will find work. Don't you worry.'

'Where are the girls?' Catherine asked.

'Upstairs. Marion is still at work. Sarah is with Mary.'

'I'm going up. Will I send Sarah down?'

'Yes. I suppose we'll have to tell her sooner or later.'

Catherine embraced Sine with tears in her eyes and left the room.

She found Sarah and Mary sitting at the table, their faces pale in the candlelight, and Archie asleep in the bed.

'I thought you would be in bed,' she said.

'I was telling Sarah about our room in the attic where I work and the luxury in the rooms below.'

'They're not unkind to you, though.'

'That's true. The lady is really thoughtful, always asking after you, Sarah. In fact, she was saying that she could use you in the bedchamber.'

'I don't know if Sarah is strong enough yet,' Catherine said quickly. 'By the way, your mother wants you downstairs.'

'What for? I was talking to Mary.'

'I don't know but she seemed keen to speak to you.'

'Oh well. If Mother calls, I'd better obey.'

She rose, hugged both of them and left.

'What's the matter, Mother? You look upset.'

Catherine joined Mary at the table.

'I didn't want to say anything in front of Sarah but they are going to go to Australia.'

'What? Sine and Duncan?'

'All of them.'

'That's terrible. Why?'

'You know why. I think the trouble on the railway was the last straw. They can get work but they never know from one day to the next whether it will last. Never safe. One day you have work, the next you're out on the street. One day there's bread on the table, the next day there's none. You can't live like that. They're sure it will be better in Australia.'

'Why Australia? All the Ross people went to Canada.'

'Cheap fares I suppose and the men have gold at the back of their minds. The promise of a fortune. The dream of finding a nugget that will keep them in luxury for the rest of their lives.'

'And how many find nothing? Greed. That's what drives them. Does Marion know?'

'I don't think so.'

'Maybe she won't go. Maybe she'll stay with us.'

'I doubt it. She'll want to go with her father.'

'Would you go?'

'No. Never. I want to go back to Shiaba.'

'When will we be going back?'

'I don't know. I want to train as a teacher first.'

'What?'

'Mr Lamont suggested it. He thinks I could pass the entrance test.'

For a moment Catherine thought that she was going to object, place all kinds of impediments and arguments in the path of her plan, but her eyes shone in the candlelight and she rose and threw her arms around her.

'Wonderful! Absolutely brilliant idea! You can do it, Mother, I know you can and I will do everything I can to help. How much will it cost?'

'There are scholarships, he says.'

'Does Father know?'

'No. Not yet. He will not be pleased, I fear.'

'Never mind. He can wait. Do it! You will be a wonderful teacher.'

10

Calum sat on the edge of the bed, a film of sweat cooling on his face. A crippling nausea pinned him to the bed and every limb ached. His heart fluttered like moth's wings. The boys were still in bed behind him.

'Connor. Go and fetch Bridget.'

He lay back on the bed, flinging his left arm across his brow. He knew what had happened. The fever which had killed their brother had passed to him. He lay, staring at a patch of damp in the thatch high above him and planning to see to it later. He did not hear Connor return with his sister until she stood over him.

'You have the fever,' she announced, her voice seeming to come from the shore.

He looked up to see a frown above her worried eyes.

'You will have to see to the boys, Bridget.'

'Yes. I'll fetch you some water.'

He closed his eyes and heard her speaking quietly to the boys. Then there was silence.

He saw himself up on the roof with an armful of straw, a gale from the sea whipping the bundle so violently that he could barely hold it, a hot relentless wind which brought no relief. Every time he tried to slip the new straw into the thatch, it blew him back, his eyes streaming so that he could not see. The rope beside him, holding down the thatch, snapped and he heard the great boulders on either end crash to the ground. Then another rope parted and one after another until there were none and the gale lifted the entire roof, wrapping it around him, smothering him in a hot shroud so that he could not breathe. Catherine was calling him. He tried to answer but his voice came in a croak like a hooded crow. She called again but it was not her voice.

'Calum! Take a drink.'

Bridget was standing over him with a cup of water.

'Take a drink,' she repeated.

He tried to haul himself upright but fell back.

She slipped her arm under his head and helped him to drink. The water was cool and comforting. He took a few sips and shook his head.

'Thank you, Bridget.'

He sank back and closed his eyes.

He found himself at sea in his new boat. Catherine was there with the children, hauling in long lines laden with fish, so many fish that the boat sank low in the water. He told them to stop, to leave the lines but they continued to lift more and more fish aboard. A steamboat was heading towards them with the Factor at the helm. He tried to alter course but the boat would not move. The steam ship kept coming. He could see the Factor's stern, expressionless face with glazed eyes staring straight ahead. He stood and shouted and waved his arms but the ship did not swerve. Black smoke poured from its funnel and twin plumes of white flew from its bow. He called out to Catherine and the children but, not hearing him, they were laughing as they hauled in the fish. The steamship hit his boat midships, cut it in two and steamed on, oblivious. Catherine and the children sank and he was left standing in the stern, roaring her name.

'It's alright, Calum. It's only a dream.'

He opened his eyes to find Bridget bent over him, bathing his forehead with a cold cloth. Soothed by her calm presence and gentle touch, he slid back into sleep.

§

Bridget returned to her house to cook some meal but found four women with her brother's body wrapped in a blanket on the floor. She glanced at her mother but she was sleeping soundly.

'We were afraid to wash him,' the oldest said, 'him having the fever but we have laid him out as best we can and the men will come with a door and carry him to Kilvickeon.'

'I could have washed him myself and laid him out.'

'He does not need to be washed to go to the place appointed. The Lord will welcome him as he is. Anyway, you have enough to do. It is good of you to look after Calum.as well.'

'He has been kind to us.'

'We have brought you a few peats for the fire. It's all we have.'

The women left, the oldest calling back,

'The men will be here shortly.'

Bridget went over to her brother and rolled back the blanket so that she could see his face. He looked quite peaceful, though his lips were blue. She bent down and kissed his eyes and his mouth, wondering if he knew, if he was still there or if he had left with his last breath. She imagined him walking into heaven, a garden where warm sunlight fell on banks of flowers, a place where there was no hunger or pain or sickness, a place among fields of barley heavy with grain and lochs alive with herring. She imagined the Christ that she had seen in pictures taking his hand and leading him in.

Yet, when the men arrived, placed him on the door and carried him out, the comforting visons melted and she broke down and wept. He was leaving, leaving in the hands of other people, and she would never see him again. Why was he chosen? Did it mean that her mother would join him? She looked at her in the bed and was comforted by the way she was sleeping so peacefully.

The old woman came to the door and spoke kindly to her.

'Are you going to Kilvickeon, child?'

'No. I will stay here with the others and look after Calum.'

'Very wise and it's kind of you to see to Calum. You're a credit to your mother.'

The woman left and Bridget sat on the bed beside her mother She had decided not to follow her brother to the graveyard. She could not bear to watch him being lowered into the cold ground.

She wondered if she should walk to Bunessan and fetch the surgeon for Calum. He would probably have enough money to pay the fee. Yet she was loth to leave her mother and the children.

She went outside and leaned against the wall, weak with fatigue and poor nutrition. On the horizon a ship seemed to be becalmed, its slack sails motionless in the still air. She wondered where it might be going and longed to be on the deck, sailing away to a new land, free from the life in which she was trapped. She envied the boys, free to sail with Calum , but immediately felt guilty. She should be happy to stay with her mother and help in the house.

She pushed herself off the wall and went to see Calum. He was still the same, thrashing around and speaking to people in his dreams. She dipped a cup in the water and held it to his lips but his head rolled from side to side, ignoring the drink. Looking at his face, she tried to decide if he was a handsome man, studying the long nose, the beard so sparse that the chin shone through the hair, the jaw heavy and thrust forward, the lips cracked with the wind. He was not handsome but she remembered him out in the sun, thinking that his kind eyes and slightly mischievous grin made him most attractive. Yet, poor man, he lay there, sick and tormented, a husk of the man outside.

She was about to leave when the doctor arrived and stepped into the house, a young man vibrant with energy and enthusiasm. She had expected an older man with grey whiskers and spectacles but she knew it was the doctor by his leather bag and the faint scent of disinfectant.

'Good afternoon, young lady. I'm Doctor Beveridge. Is it your mother who is ill?'

'Yes.'

'But she's not here.'

'She is next door, sir.'

'Is this your father?'

'No, sir. My father is dead. This is Calum MacGillivray.'

'I see. It was he who sent for me to examine a woman with fever.'

'Yes. He said that he would send for you to cure my mother but now he is sick himself.'

'I can see that and you have been looking after both?'

'Yes.'

'You're a remarkable young lady. Now, let me have a look at Mr MacGillivray.'

He moved across to the bed.

'Has he been vomiting?'

'He has but there is little inside him to come out. He has been having terrible dreams and screamed that he had a broken head.'

'Yes, a severe headache is one of the symptoms. He has typhus. Now, this may seem strange but we must move him outside. Fresh, cold air is the only answer. Can we get help?'

'The men are all away at the funeral, burying my brother.'

'Your brother had the fever too?'

'He died of it.'

'It's curious that you have not been affected. Are there others in the house?'

'My two younger brothers and my mother.'

'The boys are not ill?'

She shook her head.

'Are any of the women left at home? The young ones that is.'

'I can go and see.'

'Yes. We need help. We must move him as quickly as possible.'

'Is he going to die?'

'I don't know. He is very ill. Go and find the women.'

When she returned with two younger women she found that the doctor had stripped the blanket off Calum and laid it on the floor.

'Right ladies, help me to lift him on to the floor.'

'Should he not be kept warm?' one of them asked.

'No. Let me explain. This treatment was discovered during Napoleon's campaign in Russia. Fresh, cold air. I've seen it work many times. Now, come on. You take his feet.'

They hoisted him off the bed on to the blanket, lifted the bed outside and carried him out. Calum was too ill to object, allowing them to haul him about without complaint.

'Now wrap his hands and feet in cloth to keep them warm. If it rains, cover him with a tarpaulin. Do you have such a thing?'

'There's a bit in the mill I think,' said the woman.

'Take me to your mother,' he said to Bridget. 'What's your name?'

'Bridget, sir.'

She led him along the row of houses to her own where they found the boys huddled around the last glowing embers of the fire.

'Well, boys,' he said, 'you must be Bridget's brothers. Is that the last of your firewood?'

'There's a few pieces in the empty house next door,' Bridget answered.

He walked over to the bed where her mother lay, tugging the blanket modestly up to her chin and her eyes dark with suspicion.

'I'm Doctor Beveridge. Calum MacGillivray asked me to come and examine you but I see you're over the worst. There's nothing more I can do. You will recover very quickly. In two days' time you will wonder how you could have been so ill. An unpleasant memory. As it happens, I am Inspector of the Poor and I'm going to arrange for a load of peat to be sent to your door, some clean blankets and a bag of meal. Your daughter here is doing a sterling job of looking after you all. A remarkable girl. Now I must return to the village. I will call tomorrow to see Calum.'

'Is he to be outside through the night?' Bridget asked.

'Yes. In the cold night air. It does not look like rain fortunately.'

'Is he going to die? I don't want him to die.'

'As I said, I don't know.'

He hurried out of the house, relieved to escape from the foul air inside.

11

John, Catherine's brother, walked into his house on the shore.

'What are doing back so early?' his mother asked from her bed.

'Calum has not turned up.'

'Not like him to lie in bed, unlike yourself.'

'I'll swing the kettle on.'

'You'll do nothing of the kind. You will start walking out to Shiaba and find out what has happened. There is something wrong. Go now. Now!'

John considered ignoring her instruction and returning to the boat to lie in the sun but he knew that she would find out. She had an uncanny way of discovering his misdemeanours. He set off for Shiaba, quite sure that he would meet Calum and the boys on the track. Still, it was a fine morning with the larks spiralling into the sky above the glebe. Ahead of him he saw a stranger on a pony, a young man, he reckoned, sitting upright in the saddle with a bag slung over his shoulder. Clearly in a hurry, he disappeared over the hill. John tried to work out who it was but could think of no-one like that.

However, meeting the cattleman from Scoor, he asked him.

'Who was the man on the pony, Donald?'

'The surgeon. Beveridge.'

'Is he going to Scoor?'

'No. He turned off for Shiaba.'

'Must be for the widow, eh?'

'I expect it is. They say Calum MacGillivray is very sick. I must be on my way. There's a heifer calving.'

'Of course. I hope she's alright. Good weather for it anyway.'

Donald walked away, leaving John considering whether to walk to Shiaba or have a seat in the sun and wait for the surgeon returning. A seat on a heather bank in the sun was very appealing but he decided that he had better be able to give a full account of events to his mother.

When he reached Calum's house he was shocked to find the bed out in the sun with Calum asleep under some blankets, Connor at his side. The surgeon's pony was tethered at another house.

'Well, Connor,' he said quietly, 'I wondered why you did not appear at the boat.'

'He has the typhus.'

'What did the surgeon say?'

Just then Calum woke and, turning to face him, was about to speak but winced with pain. Calum's pallor and face creased in agony frightened him.

'Don't trouble yourself, Calum. Just lie still and rest.'

'My head,' was all he could say.

'Why is he outside, Connor?'

'The doctor said.'

'The doctor said to put the bed outside? Nonsense.'

'He's in with my mother. Go and ask him.'

John hesitated then reckoned that it must be true.

'No. I'll get back to the boat. Make sure it's safe.'

He hurried away, leaving Connor standing by the bed.

When he reached home he told his mother what he had rehearsed while walking back.

'He's gravely ill.'

'Gravely is it? That's a big word for you, John.'

'Like a living corpse, screaming in pain.'

'A corpse does not scream.'

'They have his bed outside and him in it out in the cold.'

'Why would they do that? There must be a reason.'

'Connor says the doctor ordered it.'

'If the doctor ordered it, it must be right. I'm sure he will not be as sick as you say. You always exaggerate. Still, we had better tell Catherine. Go to the store and fetch paper and ink.'

'He's not as bad as that, surely.'

'A living corpse you said. Make up your mind. Is he gravely ill or not?'

John's enthusiasm for the drama he had created withered.

'I don't know. He has typhus the boy said.'

'People do recover from typhus. Get me the paper nonetheless.'

When he returned she was searching at the end of the bed for her coat. He helped her to find it and sat at the table as she tugged it over her shoulders.

'Now I will tell you what to write.'

John, however, knew that he could choose the words himself and that she would never know.

§

When Catherine read the letter she carried it immediately down to Sine.

'I will have to go to Mull. It says here that Calum is gravely ill with typhus.'

'Oh, Catherine. That's dreadful. Of course you must go.'

'Will you look after the children for me?'

'You know I will. Mary will be at work anyway and Archie is no trouble. You go the shipping office this morning and I'll get word to the museum and Mr Lamont. Don't worry. I'll see to everything here.'

'That's wonderful. You're so good to me.'

'I've not forgotten your help with Sarah, with all of us. Go now. Have you the price of the fare?'

'Yes. I have some wages saved.'

§

Early the following morning, Catherine caught the steamer from the Broomielaw. It was a strange experience, gliding steadily through the water against the wind, speeding past fields and woodlands, overtaking sailing ships. Yet it was far from peaceful as the engines roared and shook the deck beneath her feet and the paddles thrashed the calm water into a foaming wake. She watched the stokers frantically shovelling coal into the boilers as they gathered speed in the estuary and saw a thick mass of black smoke vomit from the funnel. A scene from hell over there.

Having called at Lochranza, it was dark when they reached Campbeltown and, unable to afford a cabin, she found a seat sheltered from the wind and tried to sleep but the night chill kept her awake. At four o'clock in the morning, when the steamer reached the open sea round the Mull of Kintyre, it began to sway and dip alarmingly, the windward paddle barely biting the water at times. She began to feel sick, the nausea not helped by the cold. The turbulence did not last long, however, and subsided as they turned north towards Gigha.

As dawn broke over the Kintyre hills, the rising sun staining the hills of Jura blood red, she walked forward to see if the hills of Mull were visible above Islay. She had forgotten how beautiful the west could be on a clear day and thought of Sine and Duncan choosing to leave for Australia. They might never see this land again. Although they were exiled in the smoke and filth of the city, they could always return to the islands, they were never far away. Australia was on the other side of the world, the home of Papilio Ulysses, that brilliant turquoise butterfly, she remembered. She could not leave like them nor could she settle in the city, in spite of the museum and her affection for Mr Lamont—Eoin as he insisted.

As the steamer passed Scarba she could see the cliffs above Carsaig and the hills above Shiaba. She thought of Calum and wished that she could be there beside him. People did die of typhus, she knew that, and she didn't want to lose him. He was strong now, recovered from starvation, so surely he would be able to fight the sickness. She imagined what it would be like to arrive in Shiaba to find him cold and laid out for burial. The thought brought tears to her eyes. To think of him passing away when she was not there was unbearable and she rubbed her eyes vigorously to wipe away the image. She wanted to be with him again, to hear his voice and feel his arms around her.

As the ship sailed through the Firth of Lorn and into the Sound of Mull she watched the hills above Shiaba until they disappeared. In the late afternoon they reached Tobermory, where she was forced to spend a night in the inn. Exhausted through lack of sleep and chill, she slept well and awoke refreshed. By good fortune the mail coach was heading for Bunessan and Fionnphort the next morning so she did not have to wait.

Arriving in Bunessan, she stepped down from the coach and was turning back towards her mother's house when she met Calum with two boys. She was speechless. They stood facing one another, paralysed by shock and uncertainty. Neither moved, unsure, hesitating to embrace or speak. It was Catherine who broke the spell.

'I thought you were dying,' she said.

'I thought I was.'

'You can't have been as sick as they said.'

She felt hot fury erupting in her breast.

'I have come all the way from Glasgow for nothing. They said you were gravely ill. I thought you must be dying. You are perfectly well, able to walk from Shiaba, able to go fishing by the look of the lines in your hand.'

'I was ill and I recovered quickly, almost a miracle. Sick one day, better the next.'

'I don't believe you. Just go fishing. Go to hell if you want.'

She stormed off, heading for her mother's house.

She was still furious when she reached it. Her mother was sitting in a chair by a weak, flameless fire.

'What is this nonsense about Calum's sickness? There is nothing wrong with him.'

'It's yourself, Catriona. It was the custom at one time to greet one's mother respectfully.'

'You have lied to me. How can I respect you?'

'I never tell lies. You should know that.'

'You said that he was gravely ill, a living corpse. That's what you said.'

'I did not but I can see what has happened. These are your brother's words. I told him what to write and he has twisted every word. He has betrayed me as always.'

Catherine, seeing the source of the exaggeration, began to calm down.

'I have come all the way from Glasgow for nothing.'

'You might as well stay now that you're here.'

'I have no intention of staying. The children are in Glasgow.'

'I'm sure Sine will see them onto a steamer for you.'

'Sine is leaving for Australia soon. In any case, I have to prepare for an examination for training college. I am going to train as a teacher.'

'You always had ambitions above your station.'

'You should be proud of me.'

'Proud of a woman who leaves her husband, who takes the children to the city and leaves her old blind mother to starve?'

'I don't see you starving.'

'Thanks to the husband that you left. He looks after me. That should be your duty.'

'As a teacher I will have a salary, enough to see you don't starve.'

'Your place is here with your husband, not flaunting your charms before other sinners in a college.'

'I am going back to Glasgow whatever you say.'

'Honour thy father and mother, it says. It's vanity that drives you, Catherine. You will come to a bad end.'

'Goodbye, Mother, and don't write to me again or, if you do, find a reliable scribe.'

Wondering why her mother was so spiteful towards her, she walked back to the village with tears in her eyes. Realising that she had nowhere to stay as she had no intention of returning to Shiaba, she headed for the inn. Calum, however, was still standing by the roadside, the boys no longer with him.

'It's not my fault,' he said. 'The doctor tells me that, if you don't die of typhus, you get better very quickly.'

'My brother told me you were gravely ill. A living corpse. You can see why I came so quickly.'

'It was good of you, Catherine. I hope you'll stay now that you're here.'

'Not yet, Calum. I want to train as a teacher.'

'A teacher? '

'Why are you so surprised? Am I not clever enough?'

'Of course you are and you must do it. I want you to do it, Catherine. When I saw you on the road, I thought my prayers had been answered as I've prayed for you to come back every night and day. I really want you to come back but you must do the training first, if that's what you want. Who knows? Maybe there will be a post here for you one day.'

He stepped forward and took her hands.

'Come back to Shiaba. Even if it is just for one night.'

'No, Calum. If I go to Shiaba tonight, I will never leave. I'm afraid of that. Please, please, understand.'

'I don't, but I won't lean on you. I know that you will do what you think is right. I trust you. Just promise me you will come back when you have finished.'

'I promise.'

He took her in his arms and they stood together, holding each other as if they would never meet again.

12

'Mr Fullerton wants to see you,' Bella announced as Catherine returned to work.

'Did he say why, Bella?'

'No. He didn't seem cross, though, so that's a good thing. How's your husband?'

'Completely recovered. He can't have been as ill as they said. A wasted journey.'

'Better to be sure, though.'

'True. I'd best go and see the lord and master.'

She left Bella mopping the floor and climbed the stair to the gallery where the door was open.

'Ah, Catherine. You've returned safely. I'm so glad. How is your husband?'

'Recovering slowly, sir.'

'Good to hear that. Very worrying for you. Dreadful disease, though I understand that victims who survive recover remarkably quickly.'

'I hope Calum is one of them.'

It crossed her mind that she might have misjudged him.

'Indeed. Now I wanted to speak to you about another matter.'

Catherine's fingers tightened into fists, expecting criticism.

'We are being overwhelmed with offers of artefacts at the moment, so much so that we need help with compilation of catalogues. Most of them are labelled on arrival and we have to transfer the description to a ledger. I know you have a great interest in our exhibits and I wondered if you would consider assisting us. I'm afraid it would entail a change in your working hours, but also an increase in remuneration. Would that appeal to you?'

She hesitated, trying to decide whether to confess that reading and writing were new to her, an admission which might prejudice the offer, or whether to be silent and hope that she could cope with the work. She saw the warmth in his pale blue eyes and the kindness in his smile and could only choose the truth.

'I have only just learnt to read and write, sir.'

'I know, Catherine, but I'm assured that you have learnt with such extraordinary speed and accuracy that you will be perfectly capable of mastering the work I'm proposing.'

'Mr Lamont told you?'

'The source is irrelevant. It is reliable and that is all that concerns me. Now, what do you think? Does my offer appeal to you?'

'Of course, sir. I'm sorry if I appeared to be ungrateful. I will do my very best.'

'Splendid! I'm very pleased. Come in on Monday morning then.'

'Thank you, sir. Thank you.'

She almost reached out to take his hand but contained herself and left the gallery, hurrying down the stairs to tell Bella.

'Bella! Bella! Mr Fullerton has offered me a new job here.'

Bella leaned her mop against the wall and wiped her hands on her apron.

'A new job?'

'A day job, helping with the catalogues.'

'That's great, Catherine. Wonderful. You'll be on the staff. No more cleaning. No more nights. One drawback, though.'

'What's that?'

'I'll miss your company. It was good to have another Gael in here.'

'No, no, Bella. I'll see you every night. I'll wait till you start. I will. I promise.'

'You don't need to do that.'

'I will. You've been a good friend.'

She gripped her arm and held it, looking into her eyes.

'I will. Now, I had better go and find my cleaning things in case I am dismissed before I've started.'

§

That night she arrived home to find Mary and Sarah in tears in each other's arms and Archie seated at the table, staring sorrowfully at the candle.

'What's happened?' she asked.

'They're leaving tomorrow,' Archie answered.

'So soon?'

'Duncan has the tickets. Steamer to Liverpool first.'

She turned and hurried down the stair.

Sine, Duncan and Sarah were sitting around the table, their faces shadowed in the candlelight. Sine looked up, forcing a faint smile of greeting, rose and threw her arms around her, saying nothing. The two women remained locked in that embrace for some time, Catherine finally breaking the silence.

'So you have the tickets?'

'Duncan collected them today. Now that I see them, I'm crippled with doubt.'

'You were very sure two days ago, even trying persuade me to come.'

'It's the right thing,' Duncan said. 'Right for us. Right for the girls. This is no life. There's opportunity out there. Work for us all, Sine, you and the girls. You were keen enough yesterday.'

'Yesterday it was still just a dream, a game, like a play on a stage. Tonight it is real.'

'I'm sure it is the right choice,' Catherine said. 'In Bunessan I passed a crowd waiting for the meal store to open. At first I thought they were strangers and then I realised I knew them, people I had known all my life, their faces so wasted with hunger that I could not tell who they were. Walking skeletons, shambling along with eyes as blank as cod fish, pleading for meal, many of them, unable to pay rent, evicted from their homes. Our people should never be reduced to that. Go when you can, Sine. Hundreds have gone before you so you'll find fellow countrymen out there.'

'She's right, by God,' said Duncan.

She wanted to tell them about her new employment but held back, deciding that it was not the time to display enthusiasm and prospect of a better life.

'You'll have much to discuss, so I'll go back upstairs and comfort Mary, who is upset. I'll come with you to the Broomielaw tomorrow.'

She returned to her own quarters to find the girls holding hands across the table.

'Can I sleep here tonight?' Marion asked.

'If your mother is happy with that, yes.'

§

Late that night, Catherine sat at the table to write to Calum. Behind her, the two girls slept in each other's arms in the bed beside Archie. She gazed into the flickering flame of the candle, composing the letter, imagining Calum holding the paper in his hands and sitting by the fire in Shiaba. She tried to recall the scent of peat smoke and the sweet smell of the beasts beyond the bed, the feeling of her brow against a warm flank and the hiss of milk in the pail, the purring of hens in the rafters and the wind in the thatch. Outside a full moon would be casting dark shadows behind the houses and lighting the snow on Beinn Cruachan. Above the house the stars of the Great Bear would hang from the one that never moved. Calum's home. Calum's land. She longed to feel his arms around her, his fingers gentle on her cheek, hear his laughter and the small noises he made in his sleep. She dipped the pen, surprised to find her vision blurred with tears.

My Dearest Calum,
I am writing to tell you that I have been given a new position in the museum. I will no longer be a cleaner but will be helping to write out catalogues of things given to the museum. I will be a member of staff and will not have to work at night. I will have more pay but I do not know how much. I will be able to study at night for the college.

Tomorrow Duncan, Sine and the girls leave for Australia. I will walk with them to the Broomielaw where they will board the steamship for Liverpool. It will be very, very sad to see them go but I will pray *for God to be with them on the dangerous journey. I am sure that it is best for them to be leaving and that, with God's help, they will prosper in the new country.*

Mary is very happy with her work and the lady of the house is very kind to her maids. I know that she will miss Marion and will be very sad for a long time but she is good at making friends and maybe she will find another to take her place. Archie is doing very well at school and talks of finding a place in an engineering works.

I long for the day I can return to the Ross and to your arms.
Your loving wife, Catherine.

She slept fitfully with her head in her arms on the table, waking with a stiff neck and still tired. Stoking the fire, she made porridge and woke Marion, amazed as always by the mane of red hair on the pillow. As Marion swung out of bed, she filled four bowls and placed the last of the milk on the table.

Mary suddenly leapt out of the bed.

'What time is it?' she asked.

'Six o'clock. You have plenty of time.'

'I have not, Mother. I meant to wake at five to be on time.'

Sliding to the edge of the bed beside Marion, she hauled on her shoes but, in her haste, her trembling fingers could not tie the laces. Catherine knelt in front of her.

'I'll see to it. Calm yourself. There is plenty of time.'

Marion put her arm around Mary's shoulders.

'Her ladyship will understand, Mary.'

Still flustered, she stood and rushed across for her coat.

'At least have your breakfast,' Catherine said.

'No, no. I'm late.' She ran back to Marion and, flinging her arms around her, buried her face in her hair and wept.

'Please don't go. I can't bear it. Please stay. I'll never see you again. Never. I can't let you go. I can't.'

Marion stood and, holding her at arm's length, looked straight into her eyes.

'I'm going to make you a promise, Mary. I will come back. Only illness or death will stop me. I will find work there and save and one day I'll be back. Now go before your clothes are soaked. Go!'

When she had left, Marion wept too.

Archie struggled out of the bed and the three of them ate in silence.

§

As the steamer pulled away from the quay, Sine stood with one hand on the rail and the other lifted in farewell to the two figures slowly fading into the crowd, Catherine holding Archie's hand and waving a handkerchief. As the tumbling wake spread across the river below, a claw clutched her heart, tore it from its roots and hauled it back towards the city. She gasped with the pain of its leaving. Her eyes did not see the black ribbons of smoke, the debris in the river, the filth in the streets or the skeletal mothers in the vennels. She saw only the place where her girls were born, the bridge where she had met Duncan, the room where they had lain together for the first time. She did not see with her eyes but in the empty space which held her heart.

She remembered the island where she was born, the shell sand blinding white in the sun, the crescents traced on its surface by murram grass tossed by the wind, the crystal-clear sea and the machair blazing with wild flowers, the summer breeze rolling in waves over the meadow grass. She saw the muscles of her father's arm rippling as he swung the scythe, his joy as he cut the last stand of corn, her mother behind him smiling as she bound it into a sheaf. She would never see them again, never watch her mother's hands shaping bannocks, never hear her sing the songs in the tongue of her people. All that she held dear would be left behind.

Duncan came beside her and seeing her sorrow, placed his arm over her shoulder and held her tight against him.

'I know,' he said, 'I know, but we will be together Sine. We will share the grief and the good things and we will have the girls. A better life, Sine. It has to be.'

13

Calum rose early while there was still a sheen of frost on the land, though this would soon melt as the sun rose behind Beinn Cruachan, its summit still white with winter snow. Lifting his spade, he walked round to the rigs, which had lain empty for six years, and started to turn over the soil. His hair, now flecked with grey, glistened in the dawn and his hands, more familiar with wet ropes and fish, seemed paler than the ones which had lifted rotten tubers from the soil. As he worked, he could feel the muscles in his back object to the new task but he was determined to turn over as much ground as he could before the boys appeared.

He had ordered seed corn and, having spoken to Duncan MacIntyre, the farmer in Knockvoligan, he had obtained seed potatoes from England, hoping that they would be free of disease. Promising himself that he would bring the Shiaba land back into cultivation, he imagined rows of healthy potato shaws, green and blossoming, and the corn ripening in the sun. The soil was heavy, though, still sodden from the February rains, and sharp pains in his back hindered his progress, as he straightened now and then to rest. He had turned only a few yards when Connor called for him.

Heading back to the house with his boots weighted with soil, he saw Bridget approaching his door. It pleased him to see her restored to health and striding along purposefully. Kicking the mud off his boots, he stooped into the house.

'How's your mother?'

'She is better and is eating again. She saw you out in the rigs and told me to come and help.'

'Tell her I can manage but thank her for the offer.'

'I could carry seaweed from the shore.'

'You could. I had not thought of that. You and the boys. I will make some porridge and then the three of you can go to the shore. There's creels in the barn.'

After they had eaten, he pointed out the best parts of the shore for seaweed.

'There should be banks of it there after that last storm. When you carry it up, tip it out beside the rigs I was digging this morning. I must go and see to the creels. There's bread and cheese inside, if you're hungry. I'll be back in the afternoon.'

He hurried away towards Bunessan.

Arriving at the pier, he found most of the boats had already left, and John sitting in the stern enjoying the sun.

'You could have gone for bait,' Calum growled.

'The tide was not right.'

'Always an excuse, John.'

Calum climbed down into the boat.

'I've been thinking I would join the army again,' John said, still lounging in the stern.

'Oh? If a recruiting sergeant saw you just now, he would laugh in your face. No respectable regiment would have you. Why would you want to go anyway? Do I not pay you well enough?'

'It is not that. I want some adventure, to see new places. They are recruiting troops to fight the Russians.'

'And what of your mother? Who will see to her?'

'I thought Catherine could come back.'

'Just so that you can waltz away in a kilt as a soldier? I think not. You're a dreamer, John, with a head full of nonsense.'

'I'll find a way.'

'I dare say, but not with Catherine as a substitute. Now, cast off that stern rope and I'll hoist the sail. At least look as though you are working for your wages. We have to call at Kintra for Dugald MacArthur. He's agreed to join us.'

'There you are. You have a replacement already.'

Calum ignored him, hauled on the halyard and wound it round the pin. The mainsail filled and they headed out to sea.

'I'm quite serious,' John said as Calum took over the tiller.

'You can't leave your mother.'

'I'll find somebody.'

'It won't be Catherine. She is training to be a teacher and she will not sacrifice that just so that you can go and get killed by the Russians.'

'I will write to her. She can make up her own mind.'

'No-one can stop you.'

He tried to appear unconcerned but he was worried that she might succumb to such persuasion. Still, it would bring her back, but, if she came, he knew she would always regret abandoning her course and might never settle happily on the island.

'It's her turn anyway,' John continued.

'Who was there last time when you were away soldiering? Who looked after the whole house for all your young life, John, eh? '

'It was her place. She should be there yet.'

'I think it is well that you leave to join the army.'

The two men fell silent, a silence broken only by the slapping of the bow in the sea and the cry of a tern as it swept past.

Calum took the boat into Kintra where Dugald MacArthur was waiting.

'A grand day, Calum. Well, John, how is your mother?'

'Fine, thank you.'

He stepped into the boat and sat near the mast. Calum hauled in the main sheet and they headed through the Bull Hole for Erraid.

'Tell me, Dugald,' said Calum, 'Is there anyone else in Kintra who would crew for me?'

'My brother Archie might, and one of the MacPhee's, but they are all thinking of Australia.'

'Emigrating?'

'Oh yes. The MacPhees and ourselves and Colin Campbell, Sandy MacLean from Ardfenaig, Angus MacDonald from Bunessan, the MacFarlanes and the Campbells from Iona.'

'Good God! There'll be no-one left.'

'Isn't that what the Factor wants? He can give the whole Ross over to his friends from Islay and the sheep men from the south.'

'And you are going too?'

'When the time comes.'

'See,' said John. 'It is not so easy to get crew.'

They sailed round to Erraid to haul the creels. Dugald was the first into the bow to catch the cork floats as Calum let the sail go slack. Clearly he was experienced as he lifted the first of the fleet of creels into the boat, opened the cage and pulled out a large lobster, its shell mottled blue and studded with barnacles. Holding it out towards John, its claws waving angrily, he waited for him to tie them shut with twine.

'Hurry up, for heaven's sake,' he said as John dithered with the twine, 'or we will be here till dark.'

When the claws were secure he dropped it into a pail.

'You bait the creel while I haul up the next one.'

Calum was impressed by the way he took command. It was a relief to have found a replacement. He moved forward to help John fix a mackerel into the cage.

They had a good haul that day, with enough lobsters to fill the crate that Calum had anchored in Bunessan. On the way back he sailed into Kintra to let Dugald off near his home.

'You will not need to come here tomorrow,' Dugald said, stepping ashore. 'I've a cousin in Ardtun. I'll stay with him to be near the boat.'

'That would be a help indeed. We need bait for the lines.'

'I'll meet you at the pier then.'

Calum swung the boat around and headed home.

'You'll need to watch him,' John said, 'The way he orders you about, he'll take over the boat.'

'He's an able man and not afraid of work. When you swagger off to conquer the Tsar single-handed, I'll be pleased to have him as crew.'

They sailed into the bay at Bunessan and John lifted the crate, already containing a few lobsters, and placed the new ones in beside them.

'They'll need to go off tomorrow,' Calum said. 'I'll speak to Shaw. You will be here tomorrow, will you?'

'Yes. I have not made up my mind yet and I've to write to Catherine.'

'I'll see you tomorrow then.'

§

When he reached home that evening, he found a great pile of seaweed by the rigs. He was so impressed that he hurried in to thank the children, but the house was empty. The fire was still smouldering on the hearth but there was no-one there. He turned and walked down to the widow's house. As he approached, he could hear laughter and he stopped to listen. It was a wonderful sound, a sound that he had not heard in Shiaba since that terrible winter and he stayed still just to enjoy it, a music sweeter than song, reminding him of his own children laughing as they tossed chaff in the air by the thrashing floor. He remembered the chaff blowing over them like golden snow as the wind caught it in the doorway and their sheer joy as it covered their hair. The memory swelled painfully inside him, bringing tears to his eyes.

He wiped them away and went to the door. The boys were blowing at a hen's feather, trying to keep it in the air and contain their laughter at the same time. They stopped as soon as his shadow fell on the floor. The widow rose from the fire and came to him.

'How are you, mistress?'

'I'm well, thanks to you, Calum. I will never forget your kindness.'

Looking at her, with her gaunt face and shrunken limbs, he knew her claim to be well was far from true.

'I came to thank the children for carrying up the seaweed.'

'It's the least they could do. They are not as strong as they were, but they were keen to help. The boys can stay here with me now.'

'They are not a trouble to me.'

'Maybe not but there's no need for you to be looking after them. I'm well enough now and I have Bridget to help. You are planting potatoes?'

'Yes, and some corn.'

'Will they not rot?'

'God knows, mistress. The seed is from the south. Time will tell.'

'We will pray for a good harvest.'

'Indeed. Have you meal in the house?'

'No. The last of the meal you brought is finished.'

'I will bring you some tomorrow and some fish.'

'God bless you, Calum. My name is Tina, by the way. Baptised Christina but never known as that.'

'I will see you tomorrow, Tina. Good night to you.'

He returned to his own house and sat at the table. The bread and cheese were untouched so he broke off a piece and cut a slice of cheese with his knife. In the silence and solitude he thought again of his children and Catherine, remembering her sitting by the fire grinding corn before the famine, her eyes glistening in the candlelight, her lips fastened tight with the effort. He wondered if she would ever return. She had promised but she was changing as a person, tasting a life which was foreign to him, rich with fascinating new experiences and opportunities. And there was that teacher who had offered to prepare her for examination. Clearly there was a bond there and that worried him. Perhaps John might persuade her to come back. Perhaps his letter to her might succeed. The thought prompted a smile but it was a brief movement. He knew that she would resent a return under such circumstances. He composed a letter to her in his head:

My Dearest Catherine,

Your brother John, who as you know is working as my crew, is threatening to go back to the army. He cannot leave your mother on her own so he is writing to you to ask you to come back. Please do not be persuaded. I want you to pass the examination and to finish your training. I long for you to return and to see you sitting at our table and to hear your voice again but you must seize this chance of a better life for yourself, even if it makes you a different person. I will still love you as I always have and always will. Maybe you will find life here tedious and mundane after the city but I will do everything I can to make up for that.

I have taken on Dugald MacArthur from Kintra as extra crew and he promises to be a good hand and he says that there are others. We are doing well at the fishing and the lobsters are selling well. I should be able to pay off the boat soon. There are only four fires in Shiaba now counting mine. All the others have gone, scattered to the ends of the earth.

Do write to me, my dearest,
Your loving husband, Calum.

14

Catherine and Lamont sat by the coal fire in the evening, Lamont smiling as he read out the questions.

'Now this is question 60 regarding the fourth commandment: How is the Sabbath to be sanctified?'

She closed her eyes and chanted,

'The Sabbath is to be sanctified by a holy resting all that day, even from such worldly employments and recreations as are lawful on other days; and spending the whole time in the public and private exercises of God's worship, except so much as is to be taken up in the works of necessity and mercy.'

'Well done! Well done! Word perfect.'

She sat back, pleased by his praise.

'It's in that last phrase,' he continued, 'those words "works of necessity". They provide the employers with their justification for working their hands seven days a week. I suppose they would define tending power looms as "works of mercy". However, don't repeat what I'm saying at the interview.'

'Am I expected to know every word of the catechism?'

'Being a new Free Kirk college, they would be impressed if you did. They will try to catch you off guard by asking for the longer answers such as this one or ones with difficult words. Let's finish with 61. What is forbidden in the fourth commandment?'

She closed her eyes again and squeezed her hands together.

'The fourth commandment forbiddeth the omission, or careless performance, of the duties required, and the profaning the day by idleness, or doing that which is in itself sinful, or by …'

She struggled to recall the words.

'Unnecessary,' he prompted.

'...unnecessary thoughts, words, or works, about our worldly employments or recreations.'

'Well done. That's enough for tonight. I disapprove of this emphasis on the formalities of Christianity instead of its substance but it is almost universal. Children having to learn lists of the prophets and kings of Israel. But we have to prepare you for interview and hopefully scholarship. Tomorrow we will look at some geography.'

'Good. I prefer that to the Catechism. I never did learn it properly.'

'Dull, isn't it?'

'Very. I'll call Archie through. We must get back or I will never rise in the morning.'

'You could stay here, you know. There's plenty of room.'

Catherine looked at him, trying to see if the invitation was a step towards intimacy, but she saw only innocence and concern.

'Thank you, Eoin, but I quite enjoy having time to myself late at night.'

'Of course. It was just a suggestion to save walking through the streets in the dark.'

'I know. Thank you.'

She called Archie and they set off east towards their flat. Frost had frozen the wet streets and made walking on the cobbles treacherous. Twice she slipped and had to catch Archie's arm. Passing McBride's works, the roar of the machinery echoed in the street.

'Poor souls,' she said, shaking her head.

'It was fun when Marion was there.'

'Not fun for her, though. Morning till night at that machine.'

The nearer they came to the old village, the darker the street. Outside the spirit merchants, a crowd had gathered to watch two men fighting, jostling for a view and bawling encouragement. As she hurried past, she caught a glimpse of blood streaming from broken teeth. She had to grip Archie by the collar to haul him away.

She had taken over the lease of Sine's flat and had scrubbed the floor, washed the walls and fitted a new pane in the window.

She had bought an American clock and an oil lamp with a mantle which gave better light. There was a new horse-hair mattress on the bed and clean blankets. She had made the place into a home. What was missing was Calum and she worried about him, living on his own. He had succumbed to temptation before and she wondered whether he could resist it, if some unfortunate woman came to his door, craving help and comfort.

Archie removed his boots and went to bed. She opened The Rights of Man and started to read. She knew that she should be reading the Catechism but could not face the tedious passages. Paine was much more interesting.

The natural, civil and political rights of man are liberty, equality, security,

property, social guarantees, and resistance to oppression.

Some of it she did not understand and would ask Eoin to explain but she thought of the Duke in the luxury of Inveraray castle and her mother in the squalor of her home in Ardtun when she saw the word "equality". "Resistance to oppression" landed men in prison or on a ship to Van Diemen's Land.

Every man is free to publish his thoughts and opinions.

The Chartists in Edinburgh didn't find that to be the case.

Education is the right of everyone and society owes it to all its members equally.

Except for those who can't pay, she thought. Eoin had said that it should be free and available to everyone. She agreed with that.

To aid the needy is a sacred debt of society ...

That was a Christian teaching too. She thought of Bella and the people from Barra. Who had seen to their needs?

The more she read, the more she understood and the more injustice she saw in the country. Yet the enlightenment did not inspire her to violence. She could never approve of that. She had heard of the guillotine and the bloodshed of the first revolution in France and the stories filled her with horror. There the echoes of "Liberty, Equality Fraternity" had been heard in the streets again recently and stories of the violence appalled her. She was not a violent person. She could be angry, certainly, and instances of injustice made her grip her fists in fury, but she would never strike another person and had never physically chastised her children. Reading Paine made her angry and inspired her to take action, however small, however insignificant in the great scheme of things, but she resolved to do what little she could to leave the world a better place.

§

In the museum many of the artefacts which were donated came from countries the location of which she had no knowledge. Studiously she found them in an atlas and learnt everything she could about them—their climate, their main flora and fauna, their place on the globe, their people and their capital cities. Many of the exhibits came from Polynesia and she became entranced reading about the islands and their exotic cultures in Captain Cook's journals and about New Zealand in Richard Cruise's descriptions. She learnt how the marriage of Ranji and Papa, the Sky and the Sea, created the world and all that was in it. She read about Tahiti and the Marquesas and, on her way out at night, looked again at artefacts from Polynesia in the room beside the saloon.

At lunchtime she continued to draw, copying not only the butterflies but insects and sea creatures like the sea horse and the angler fish, taking them back to show Eoin and the boys. They asked her to draw the tarantula and the bird spider, the mantis and centipedes. Eoin requested copies of the Roman exhibits and the Egyptian mummy. They all seemed to look forward to her visits and all too often there was little preparation undertaken for her examination.

Archie joined her at Lamont's house where she cooked a meal for everyone. She was pleased with his progress in the Sessional school which, although it housed over two hundred pupils, had a good reputation. She helped him with his grammar and spelling while Eoin assisted with arithmetic, the table littered with books after the meal—Rae's English Grammar, Gray's Geography, Cromley's Arithmetic. Hector struggled manfully with Tacitus, Moore's Greek Grammar and the Odyssey.

At the end of the year in June she went to Archie's prize-giving, delighted to find that he won the arithmetic prize. Eoin insisted that he and the boys would join her so the announcement of Archie's success received raucous applause, much to his embarrassment. Without that moment of triumph, the boys' patience might have been sorely tried as proceedings were slow and tedious with hymns, marching songs and long recitations. Catherine was relieved that Archie had not been chosen for a solo performance.

On those evenings when Mary was free, she and Archie came home and she cooked for them. She liked to spend time with Mary, listening to her accounts of the dinner parties held by her employers with guests from exotic places like Jamaica, Guyana and Virginia. At times Mary's enthusiasm for these distant lands worried her, thinking that, if she were to be offered an opportunity to work there, she would leave Scotland. She didn't mention this concern, however, and didn't try to balance the attractions of these places with descriptions of the hazards of living there. There would be time enough for that, if Mary was tempted to go.

'Have you heard from Father?' Mary asked one evening.

'Yes. He is doing well at the fishing. Your Uncle John is working for him but he is thinking of joining the army again.'

'He can't. Who would look after grandmother?'

'He will expect me to go back.'

'No. You mustn't do that, Mother. You must sit the examination and, when you pass, finish the course. You must not go back just because he wants to swan off again. You can't turn down this chance.'

She looked across the table at her daughter, who had reached out and taken her hand, and marvelled at her maturity and confidence. She felt proud of her, her sincerity and concern. She had grown and was becoming a young woman, beautiful too in spite of the pallor and shadows of fatigue under her eyes.

'We will see. John has not asked me yet. Maybe he will change his mind at the last minute.'

'And so he should. It's selfish of him to think about leaving Grandma. I'm sure Father pays him well. He doesn't need to go.'

'No. He doesn't need to go. He was always a restless creature. Now, it is time you were in bed. You have an early start.'

§

Mary arranged to come home the evening before her mother's examination, bringing with her a new dress and shawl given by her employer.

'When I explained to Lady Caroline why I wanted this evening off, she immediately went to her wardrobe and handed these to me. "I hope your mother will not be offended but I would like her to have these," she said. "They would be ideal for interview. Tell her I wish her every success."'

'That's very kind. I must find some way of repaying her.'

'She won't want payment. She has a huge wardrobe of dresses and she has asked me to be her lady's maid so I will be in charge of them.'

'Mary! That's wonderful. She must think very highly of you. A trusted position. Well done!'

'You'll have more money,' said Archie.

'Trust you to think of that.'

Mary laid the dress out on the table to examine it. The sheen on the fabric glistened in the lamplight as she and Catherine felt it with their fingers.

'Good heavens, it's silk,' said Catherine. 'That's far too grand for me.'

'Nonsense, Mother. It's very plain compared with the fashion today. But what a beautiful colour—emerald green. It will suit you perfectly and I'm sure it will fit. Archie, go upstairs till Mother tries this for size.'

'It's dark up there and cold too.'

'Take a candle then and a blanket in case you perish.'

Archie grudgingly shambled out of the room.

The dress fitted perfectly.

'It shines in the light,' Mary said, 'and there's a petticoat to go with it.'

'No. No petticoat. I don't want to look like a knitted tea-cosy. Anyway, to appear before Free Church worthies dressed like a duchess would be the height of folly. I will be nervous enough without worrying about them criticising my clothes.'

'Are you really worried?'

'Of course. Terrified. Imagine appearing before a group of men for inspection like a mare at a horse fair with them staring at you.'

'Maybe they'll like what they see.'

'I don't think so. Anyway, can you unhook the back of my dress so that I can escape from it?'

15

Catherine took a cab to the new college in Cowcaddens and was shown up to the examination hall. She could feel the nervous sweat seeping down the bodice of the dress. Lamont had assured her that she would pass the written papers with ease, but she was convinced that he was just being kind. His detailed description of the procedure, however, was reassuring for, just as he had said, there would be pen and ink on the desk beside the paper.

She took her place in a row with the other candidates, several of whom were women, most of them younger than her. She caught the eye of one of them who smiled nervously in return. The invigilator stood behind his raised desk at the front of the hall below the clock, the hands of which were just approaching ten o'clock.

'Ladies and gentlemen when I say the word, you may turn over the examination paper on your desk and begin to answer the questions. Remember to write your name at the top of the page and the number of the question you are attempting to answer in the left-hand margin. You may start now.'

Catherine flipped over the paper entitled Bible Studies and was relieved to find that the questions all concerned stories with which she was familiar. The second paper on geography she found even easier but, when it came to the fractions in mathematics, she knew that she was making mistakes and began to panic. Remembering that Lamont had told her to put down her pen and breathe deeply if that happened, she followed his instructions and sat back, trying to regain her composure. It seemed to help and, when the English paper appeared, she was relaxed and able to deal with the parsing and grammar successfully.

When the written test was finished, the candidates made their way out into the street and she found herself beside the girl who had smiled at her.

'How did you find it?' she asked Catherine. 'I was completely lost in the geography.'

'I'm sure I will have failed mathematics. I should have taken my young son in with me. He would have done better.'

'You're not from Glasgow, are you?'

'The island of Mull.'

'Good God! You've come a long way.'

'I'm staying in Glasgow.'

'Are you? We must meet. Where do you live?'

'In the Gorbals.'

'Really? Not the most salubrious quarter. There was cholera there, was there not?'

'Yes. My cousin had it.'

'Really?'

Catherine saw the girl step back as though she might be infectious.

'Which church do you attend?'

'None.'

'Oh. You had better not admit to that in the interview. Leave me your card and we'll arrange a meeting.'

'I don't have a card.'

'Oh. Well perhaps we'll meet on the course. If you'll excuse me, I have just seen a friend. Good luck in the interview.'

She swept away, leaving Catherine standing in the street and wondering if the others would treat her with such disdain. She didn't relish the prospect of sharing a classroom with younger students who might regard her as inferior. She re-entered the building, admiring the long corridors, bright with light from the profusion of windows, the wide twin staircases, the white tiles of the tall narrow quadrangle at the back. There seemed to be light and air everywhere; it was like walking in the sky. It was beautiful. It gave her a sense of freedom. She compared it with the dark, cramped rooms in the Gorbals and knew that, to do better, she had to succeed in the college. She walked into one of the classrooms and tried to imagine the desks full of children, all working studiously under her direction. The vision was alarming. She had no idea how to manage a group of children. Surely the college would teach her how to control them … if she was admitted.

In the afternoon she was interviewed by four men, including the rector. Her shoes echoed in the empty room as she walked across the floor towards their desk. Lamont had told her not to curtsy or bow but to smile and wait to be asked to sit. She followed his instructions, worried that her forced smile might be more of a grimace than an expression of friendliness.

'Please sit, Mrs MacGillivray,' said the rector. 'I see you are from the isle of Mull.'

She was surprised to find that he was not an ogre, not a fierce inquisitor, but a kindly gentleman who put her at her ease. He didn't seem interested in her knowledge of scripture or the Shorter Catechism but asked for her thoughts about children and about her life on Mull, impressed by her honesty about her illiteracy and by her years of caring for her mother. His last question was more difficult to answer.

'You have a remarkable understanding of children. Can you tell me why you would like to become a teacher?'

She was unprepared for that. Lamont had told her not to be rushed into answers but to take time to assemble her thoughts. There was an awkward silence but eventually she replied.

'I know what it is like to be unable to read and write. I know how it hurts when you can't help your children with their lessons, when the words are only a blur on the page, and I know the feeling of relief and joy when you find out what the words mean, when a new world opens in front of you and you can picture each word in your mind. Every child should be able to read and write, whether they are rich or poor, and to get that feeling of success when words come to life. If I can help them in that way, I will have done something worthwhile.'

Surprised by her own fluency and vehemence, she blushed.

'Thank you, Mrs MacGillivray. Most eloquent.'

The others did ask questions about the scriptures and education which she answered with ease. The Rector thanked her again and told her that she would be informed of her results within a fortnight.

Leaving the building, she had no idea whether she had impressed the panel or whether she had passed the written papers. She did not relish the long wait for the result.

§

Returning to work, she passed through the visitors and climbed the stairs to the gallery where she found Mr Fullerton.

'Well, Catherine. How was it?'

'It is difficult to say, sir. I was able to answer most of the questions.'

'Splendid! I'm sure you'll have done well. I am, however, in two minds about your application. On the one hand. I would be delighted were you to succeed. On the other hand, I can't help hoping that you fail so that I can keep you here. You have become a great asset to the museum.'

'Thank you, sir.'

She was annoyed to find herself blushing again. Twice in a day.

'In fact, I chastised Mr Lamont for writing such a complimentary reference.'

'I didn't know that he had.'

'I suggested it. Being a pedagogue himself, I thought it would carry more weight than mine.'

'He has been very kind to me.'

'I'm sure you deserve a little kindness. I'm afraid another batch of anatomical exhibits—heart and lungs I think—has just arrived from the infirmary. Not your favourite items, I know, but perhaps you could catalogue them for me.'

'Of course, sir.'

She left him admiring a small oil painting of the Virgin and Child.

§

She did not wait for Bella that evening but hurried round to see Lamont. By then it was raining, and a dismal mist hung over the streets. The hem of her dress was soon sodden and heavy, catching her ankles as she walked, and the drops from her bonnet soaked her shawl. She was shivering by the time she reached his door.

'Good God, Catherine, you're soaked. You should have taken a cab. Come in to the fire and get warm. I will make some hot chocolate.'

She could hear Archie and the boys in their room as Eoin pulled a chair over to the fire for her.

'Take off your bonnet and shawl and I'll hang them to dry.'

He fetched a rug from the drawing room and draped it over her shoulders.

'I don't want to hear all the details of the interview or the written papers—we can leave that for another night—but I would like to know how you are feeling about the experience. First, though, some chocolate.'

The boys came tumbling through, laughing and taunting each other.

'Boys! Boys! Have some respect.'

The silence was immediate.

Archie left the group and came over to his mother.

'Hello, Ma. Did you pass?'

Surprised by the new form of address, she raised her eyebrows as she looked at him, but then realised that he was copying other children.

'I don't know yet, Archie. I wish you had been there for the mathematics. I'm sure you would have answered all the questions correctly.'

'When will you know?'

'A fortnight they said.'

Lamont handed her a cup of chocolate. She held it in both hands to warm her fingers.

'I have made some lamb stew so that you didn't have to cook,' Lamont said.

'That's really kind of you.'

'Well, you usually make a meal for us. It's the least I could do.'

'When I am older,' Archie announced, 'I'm going to be an engineer.'

'Splendid idea!' Lamont said.

Catherine was about to describe all the difficulties of realising the ambition but thought it wiser to follow Lamont in encouraging it. He would discover the hurdles for himself.

'Perhaps you could find part-time work in an engineering works.'

'Yes,' said Lamont, 'there are plenty of those around here. I will make a list, but you must not neglect your studies, Archie, particularly your mathematics.'

§

Later that evening, when she and Archie had returned home and he was in bed, Catherine sat by the fire, thinking about him and his sister. They seemed to be slipping away from her—Mary happy in her new position, Archie with his strange ambitions. There would be little call for an engineer in Bunessan and the duties of lady's maid on Mull would lack the excitement of working in fashionable city houses. Neither of the children might return to Shiaba. Perhaps she should have stayed and let them grow up in their own culture, speaking their own language, entertaining more limited ambitions. There would have been more chance of them becoming good, honest, caring people, being isolated from the all the temptations and hazards of the city. Yet she remembered Eoin, who knew little of the countryside. If they grew into people like him, she would be delighted. Calum, in spite of his stubborn and impulsive nature, was a good man too, a model for his children. Perhaps it was not the place that mattered but the nature of the people around you. She would keep her children as close to her for as long as she could.

§

When Mary appeared on her next night off, she bounced in the door, ebullient, vivacious.

'Mother, I've been offered a wonderful chance! Those close friends of the Grants have asked me to accompany them to Jamaica as nursemaid to their children.'

'Jamaica! Who are these people?'

'Buchanans. They have a plantation in Jamaica and are very rich.'

'That doesn't make them good people, Mary.'

'Mr Buchanan is a real gentleman and she is the kindest person in the world and the children have such good manners and speak like English folk and they have an African maid. They would pay all my fare and let me come home if I was unhappy. Please, please, can I go?'

Mary knelt beside her and took her hands in hers.

Catherine looked down at her bright eyes and her worried brow and remembered the reservations which had surfaced the previous week.

'I will have to think about it and meet these people before I agree, and I'll have to ask your father. In fact, you can write to him and ask his permission.'

'Oh, thank you, Mother, thank you. I thought you would say no.'

'I have not said yes.'

She remembered the African who had helped Mary with his exotic medication. He said that he had been a slave and she wondered if these Buchanans had slaves in Jamaica. She had read Uncle Tom's Cabin and had been appalled by its portrayal of slavery. She would have to ask Eoin about this family and seek his advice. In the meantime she would have to prepare herself for the possibility of losing her daughter, as she would not deny her a chance of stretching her horizons, if the enquiries were favourable.

16

Glasgow Herald 26th March 1855:
Highland Destitution

The Sheriffs, in the respective districts, Ministers of every religious denomination and the poor sufferers themselves, having certified, in every manner that cannot be doubted, that severe and almost unprecedented distress prevails in the West Highlands and Islands of Scotland and that, but for the large supplies of food already sent to the rescue, there would have been ere now many deaths by starvation. A benevolent public is earnestly solicited to contribute towards the relief of those who are suffering from hunger. Every day is added to the number of the destitute. The causes of this extraordinary destitution are the complete failure of the potato crop and the great failure in the corn crop last year. This, coupled with a total failure if the herring fishing, the famine and war prices of food and the bad state of trade has brought very large numbers of the inhabitants of the West Highlands to the brink of starvation ...

Calum returned from the fishing in the late afternoon to find the people of Shiaba gathered round the widow's house. With them, the Factor on his horse, the sheriff's officer and his men, nailing boards across the door and windows. One of the women had her arm around the widow, who was sobbing on her shoulder. Bridget was struggling in the grip of a constable, biting his arm and kicking his shins. Calum reckoned that she had been "obstructing the officers in their duties." The boys stood on either side of their mother. The small crowd was silent, apart from Bridget's cursing.

Calum approached the Factor and stood in front of him.

'What's happening here?'

'This is the Duke's business and none of yours, MacGillivray.'

'This woman has been ill with fever.'

'She has no lease. She is not one of the Duke's tenants. She has no right to be in this house.'

'And, if you turn her out, where is she to go?'

'That is no concern of mine. She is not from this parish. We cannot have every vagrant in Argyll sneaking on to the Duke's estate.'

'Where is your Christian compassion now, Mr Campbell? A widow with four children and no means of support.'

'My duty is to my employer. She should seek support in her own parish. If she or anyone here breaks into the house after I leave, they will be charged.'

'She can live in my house then.'

'If you take her in, I will have you removed, the roof pulled down and burned.'

'I have a lease and I am not in arrears. I'm not afraid of your threats nor your summonses of removal.'

'The Duke will see to it.'

'I'm sure the Duke knows very little of what his factor does here or how his factor improves his own farm without expense.'

'Be very careful what you say, MacGillivray.'

'I'm always careful, Mr Campbell. When I sup with the devil, I use a long spoon.'

'Time to go!' Campbell shouted at the men. 'Leave that, Mr Lawrie.'

He swung his horse round and rode off, followed by the sheriff's men. The constable flung Bridget towards her mother and marched off.

Calum walked across to her.

'Are you hurt, Bridget?'

'No. My arms are sore where he held me and my foot is hurt where I kicked him.'

'When they are out of sight, we will break down the boards and open the house,' he said to her mother. The crowd murmured its agreement, but Tina was worried.

'No, no. Calum. They'll have me in prison. I will be blamed. I don't want to cause trouble. We will leave.'

'Nonsense, Tina. You've nowhere to go. There are five empty houses. You can move into John Campbell's. Are your belongings all outside?'

'They threw everything out and doused the fire. We don't have much anyway.'

'We will help somehow. We could fetch more seaweed,' Bridget said to Calum. 'Me and the boys'

'There's no need.'

'We have to help and we'll help you with the harvest when the time comes.'

He admired the girl's resilience and strength, reminding him of Catherine, the same firm jaw and eyes that hid nothing.

§

That evening, as the sun dipped towards the sea behind the Torran Rocks, Calum carried a sack of seed potatoes out to the rigs and started to plant them, examining each tuber for signs of rot or disease. Bending over, he placed them carefully in the drills, handling each one as gently as he would hold an egg. When he had completed three rows, he looked back with satisfaction at the neat lines, then covered them with seaweed and soil, sure that, in a month or two, these rigs would be bright with new green stalks, healthy and heading for flowering.

He stood for a while in the dusk, admiring the results of his labours. This was a statement of his faith in the future, a display of his attachment to the land and determination to defy any attempt to drive him off it, a message to the Factor. He imagined Mary, a grown woman, binding sheaves behind him and Archie lifting creels with him behind Erraid. He saw the old school re-opened and Catherine walking down to him, her arms laden with books. Smiling, he left the rigs and walked back to the house.

§

Early the following morning he left for the village. At the top of the hill above Shiaba the wind snatched at his jacket and trousers and forced him to lean forward. The surface of Loch Assapol was whipped into surf. There would be no fishing until the gale eased but he carried on, feeling that he should check the boat.

At the pier he found Dugald already lashing the mainsail securely to the boom.

'Where's John?' he asked him.

'Gone to be a soldier.'

'What?'

'He said to tell you.'

'He's out of his mind. Did he say anything about his mother?'

'No. Said he was weary of Bunessan and fishing was for fools.'

'I'll need to go back and see to his mother. We won't go out today. See if you can talk a couple of the Kintra men into crewing for me.'

'I will surely.'

Calum turned and hurried back towards Ardtun.

'Well, Mima. What's this about John?'

'He's gone to fight the Russians. A brave man, unlike those who choose to stay at home.'

'And who is to take his place?'

'Catherine.'

'She has agreed?'

'He says that she has.'

'Nonsense! He's lying.'

'He wrote to her.'

'And he read her reply to you?'

'No.'

'Catherine will not be coming back, Mima. She is training to be a teacher.'

'Her duty is to her mother. Honour thy father and mother.'

'She sacrificed her schooling to honour her mother. She will not be coming back. I will find someone to help here.'

'It's the least you could do.'

He left the old woman sitting over the fire, staring blindly at the wall, and walked into the village to see if there was mail for him. The post-master handed him a letter from Catherine which he opened and sat on the sea wall to read.

My Dearest Calum,
I have just heard that I have not only passed the examination but have been awarded a scholarship to help with my fees. I was so surprised and delighted that I walked all the way up to Mary to tell her the news. We danced round the kitchen when I told her.

She has been given the chance to go to Jamaica with a respectable family, but I have told her she must seek your agreement first. I am in two minds about it. On the one hand, it would be a great adventure *and she would learn so much about another world. On the other, there would be all kinds of dangers, not least the journey across and back. I am sure she will write to you herself but tell me what you think.*

I'm sure John will see sense and not leave mother. He has always suffered from these silly notions and did not enjoy his last adventure in soldiering no matter how much he bragged about it in the village.

Archie is doing very well at school and making great progress. He tells me he wants to be an engineer but I pointed out that that there was not much demand for engineers in Shiaba!

I hope you are looking after yourself, my dearest. I worry about you being all on your own. I would far sooner be with you than living in this dismal place. Will you talk to Mr MacQuarrie and find out if there is likely to be a place for a teacher in the Ross?

With all my love, Catherine.

He folded the letter and, still holding it in his fingers, sat down on the parapet of the bridge, his feelings in turmoil—delighted for Catherine but disappointed by the prospect of a delay in her return, shocked by the thought of Mary going to Jamaica. He had heard of Jamaica and its sugar plantations, its fevers and hordes of Africans, the licentious overseers and dissipated proprietors. A dangerous place for Mary. Yet, as Catherine said, it would be an adventure for her, an opportunity to experience a different way of life and learn about another culture. Reluctant to let her go, he still wanted to hold her close, to protect her from all the dangers she might meet, shelter her from the harsh realities of life. His little girl. Yet she had survived the fever and was earning a living in the city and one day she would meet a young man and fall in love. He squirmed at the thought of her in the arms of a stranger but it was going to happen. In many ways, she was already lost to him. He had to release her, allow her to lead her own life. She might resent any attempt to stop her.

Deciding to allow her to go, he rose from the bridge and set off for Shiaba. Reaching the top of the hill above the houses, he was forced forward by the storm. Bundles of white grass, gathered by the wind, tumbled past him. When he reached the shelter of the houses, he called on the widow in John Campbell's.

'I have an idea, Tina. John, who crews for me, lives with his old mother, who is blind. He has taken it into his head to join the army so she is left alone and needs help. I wondered if Bridget could move in with her. She's an able girl and I would pay her, but I was worried that you might not manage without her.'

'She's old enough to answer for herself, Calum. I am stronger now, thanks to you and the food you bring us, and could easily manage on my own. She has gone to the empty house next door. Go and ask her.'

'She would not be far away in Ardtun, Tina, and you could see her at any time. I will still take the boys on the boat, if that would help.'

'I might need them here.'

'Whatever is best for you. I'll go and see Bridget.'

He found Bridget gathering scraps of dried dung from the old cow stall.

'You're busy, Bridget.'

'This burns well. Saves peat.'

'I need your help. You know John who crews with me?'

'He was here when you were sick. He didn't wait long. I think he was frightened of catching the fever.'

'I didn't know he was here. Anyway, he lives with his blind mother in Ardtun but he has decided to swagger off to be a soldier, leaving her on her own. She needs help. Could you move in with her and look after her? I would pay you for it.'

'Have you asked my mother about it?'

'Yes. She thinks she would manage.'

'I don't need paid as long as there is food in the house and the blind lady isn't crabbit.'

'With you, she'll be as sweet as honey. She has little time for me because I stole her daughter. I'll take you to meet her tomorrow.'

17

Trevelyan sat in his carriage as it crossed the Thames heading south for Clapham, the newspaper in his hands trembling, his face pale with fury as he read

> ... *the same reckless waste of money, the same outrageous audacity which marked the administration of funds appropriated to the relief of Irish distress, and the same wretched confusion, had prevailed in the two cases and the consequence had been the destruction in Ireland of two million of the population and, in the East, the destruction of our army. There was not a soldier who would not congratulate himself on his escape from that baleful influence..... the failure of the Commissariat under Sir Charle Trevelyan.*

'Arrant nonsense!' he spat out, shutting the paper.

Arriving home, he slammed the door of the carriage behind him and strode into the house, tossing his hat on to the hatstand and turning into the drawing room where he found Tom MacAulay relaxing in an armchair by the fire.

'Good heavens, Charles, you look quite apoplectic! Come and sit down.'

Trevelyan lifted a decanter, poured a glass of cognac and sat opposite MacAulay.

'It's that man Colonel Dunne again in the House. Keen to blame me for every failure of the army in Crimea.'

'Yes. I've read his speech. Intemperate nonsense. Bilious. Too much port. Ignore it, Charles.'

'Of course there have been failures in Crimea—in care of the wounded, in transport of food and ammunition, in uniforms, the list is endless—but these were not my responsibility, Tom. The conduct of the Commissariat has been irreproachable. If anyone is to blame, it is the Quarter Master General—mismanagement of transport, the chaos in the harbour of Balaklava and worse in Constantinople.

That Rear Admiral—what's his name—oh yes, Boxer—completely incompetent. No, not my responsibility.'

'No indeed. The furore over the conditions there has been whipped up by the press—Russell of the Times and all these letters from the front line published in the newspapers.'

'Yes. Perhaps, when editors recognise the damage inflicted on public morale, they will desist from publicity of that kind. It sells newspapers, I suppose. We should have followed the French and censored everything.'

'We should have followed them in every way—better officers, better equipment, better medical care. What a brilliant idea—panniers on the mules to carry two wounded men off the field.'

'Ingenuity is not a common complaint in the army, Tom. I have consistently voiced my admiration of their intendance militaire—so much more professional than our Commissariat. I'm glad it's being transferred to the War Department. I'm sure Dunne will see it as a personal rebuke of my administration but it is a relief. I'm tired of trying to defend the weaknesses which I inherited. I would really like to return to India.'

'And steal my beloved sister from me?'

'I was remembering a journey from Hyderabad through the valley of the Musi—the river often a great swollen torrent, brown with monsoon rain—and leaving the parched land of the plateau to descend through cotton scrub beneath coconut and toddy palms. I remember, in the early morning, the wonderful scent of champa flowers, the blanket of brilliant blue lotus flowers on the lakes, a mantle of mist clinging to the road ahead under the palms. Magical really.'

'You're really an incurable romantic at heart, Charles, under that stern exterior.'

'I felt at home in India, particularly in the north, as you know. I'm tired, Tom. I've devoted the past ten years to rescuing Ireland from its sloth, superstition and rebellious priests, the Highlands and islands of Scotland from their indolence and primitive tradition. the mills of Yorkshire from a famine of Australian wool. I have borne the weight of famine relief in Ireland, the Highland Destitution fund, the Poor Law and now the Emigration Society. Once I see the reform of the Civil Service completed, I will return to India.'

'The last ambition may be the most arduous and controversial.'

'Nevertheless, I want to press ahead, and we have Gladstone on our side and, in spite of its veiled criticism of my methods, the Reform Association with Dickens and Thackeray is a useful ally.'

'Scribblers should remain behind their desks—apart from myself, of course.'

'The Commission should be in place this year—not exactly the Board of Examiners which we had in mind—but progress, Tom. Civil Servants selected on merit and the principle to be applied to army officers. Modest success, I think.'

'Indeed.'

18

Catherine and Mary took a cab up to the Buchanans' house in the north of the city, Catherine wearing her green dress and new shoes. The house was in a crescent, in the middle of which was a fenced garden with trees and shrubs. At the top of the steps, they hesitated, facing each other and checking their clothes. Mary adjusted the clasp in her mother's hair before she raised the brass knocker and tapped on the door.

It was opened by a tall young lady with coal-black hair and eyes as blue as butterfly wings. Catherine had never seen a creature so beautiful. Even among the portraits in the gallery, none had features as perfectly formed as hers, from the almond-shaped eyes like those of a pharaoh to the long, elegant jawline. Her appearance did not fit with her uniform.

'Good morning, madam. Can I help you?'

'We have an appointment with Mrs Buchanan.'

'Mrs MacGillivray is it?'

'Yes, and my daughter, Mary.'

'I know Mary. Please come this way,'

They were shown into the morning room, where Mrs Buchanan rose to meet them. Expecting a large middle-aged matron, Catherine was surprised to encounter a young, vibrant and friendly lady, who seemed to float across the room. Her fair hair and rose-petal complexion contrasted with her servant's swarthy skin.

'Mrs MacGillivray. Please sit down, and Mary of course. Please.'

Issuing them to the chairs opposite her, she lowered herself into hers. The room bore all the signs of wealth but, unlike McBride's with its heavy ornate furniture, everything was light and delicate. The windows, tall and wide to allow the morning sun to glint on the crystal vases, were framed with curtains so light that they swung gently as people moved past. There were no dark corners, no gloomy landscape paintings, but roses on every table except the one in front of them.

'Could you bring us some tea, Martha, please? '

'Certainly, madam,' answered the tall servant.

'I know you'll be anxious about Mary leaving Scotland, Mrs MacGillivray …'

'Please call me Catherine, madam,' she interrupted.

'Thank you, Catherine. Christian names are so much easier. Mine is Ruth. I was saying that you must be apprehensive about Mary coming with us to Jamaica and I do understand, having children myself, but let me assure you that she will be safer on our estate than in the streets of Glasgow. We are well away from Kingston on the north-west side of the island and have never had any trouble. Being in the hills, we have a breeze to keep us cool and a splendid view over the valley. Mary will have no heavy duties—there are plenty of servants to see to that—and will have plenty of free time. I have every confidence in her, Catherine, she is a credit to you. I can think of no-one better to look after my children and help with their education.'

'Yes, she is a clever girl, Mrs Buchanan. Jamaica seems so far away and strange, though. Is it truly a safe place?'

'Very safe, I can assure you. Twenty years ago—long before my time—there was a slave rebellion with much destruction of property, but it was quickly suppressed by the militia and order was restored.

Since then we have lived in peace and complete safety. Mary will be perfectly safe.'

Martha carried in a tray with a silver teapot and sugar bowl and three fine porcelain cups and saucers.

'Thank you, Martha. I will see to it myself.'

Martha left the room and Mrs Buchanan poured the tea and handed them a cup.

'Is there a minister of the Free Church on the island?' Catherine asked, holding the saucer very carefully.

'I'm not sure but I can make enquiries for you. I know we have a Church of Scotland Minister and there are many Baptists—indeed I believe the leader of that rebellion was a Baptist. Would you need to know before making a decision?'

'No. Not at all. It would be a comfort, that's all. Something familiar.'

'Of course. If I can find a Free Church minister, I will make sure that he visits, even if I have to pay him to come from the far side of the island.'

'Thank you. I would appreciate that.'

'I will do everything I can to make Mary happy. She would be far too valuable to neglect her welfare. You would be losing a daughter, but I would be gaining a member of my family. She has a rare and remarkable way with children.'

'They are lovely children, ma'am,' said Mary, 'clever and great fun.'

'Too clever at times but certainly great fun. They would be delighted, Catherine, if Mary could come.'

'I fear I have little choice. Mary is desperate for my agreement and would not forgive if me if I denied her the opportunity.'

'That's very good news, Catherine. I promise I will look after her.'

Mary spilt some of the tea in the saucer as she put it on the table and rose to embrace her mother.

'Thank you so much, Mother. I'm sorry, Mrs Buchanan, I was so pleased I had to hug my mother.'

'No need to apologise. I would do the same thing in your position.'

They discussed the journey and suitable clothing as they finished taking tea. After Martha showed them to the door, Catherine found herself sorry to leave the lady's company. She seemed to be honest, open and kind, quite unused to dissembling or affectation. She liked her and trusted her with Mary.

'I will write every day, Mother,' Mary said, as they waited for a cab.

'No you won't,' Catherine laughed.

'I will. I will.'

'Write when you can. Don't make promises you can't keep.'

Catherine thought of her sitting in the shade of palm trees with butterflies fluttering around exotic flowers—the lime swallowtail, nemoleus, with its chequered wings and the bright orange dryas iulia. She saw pink frangipani, oleander, purple garlic vines and Mary, tanned and healthy, frowning as she tried to think of things to write. Gleaming white sand and an azure sea. A kind of paradise except for the slaves. She had read abolitionist pamphlets about slaves being whipped until there was no skin on their backs, staked out in the burning sun to die of thirst, their heel tendons sliced if they fled. She had thought of handing a pamphlet to Mary but felt that she would suspect her of trying to turn her against the Buchanans, to interfere with her plans, so she decided to let her find out for herself.

§

As Catherine crossed the bridge on her first morning in college, she stopped for a moment to calm herself and to watch a small steamboat pass beneath her as it sailed up the river against the current. A cloud of smoke enveloped her and made her cough. She was worried that she might not cope with the work and that she might appear to be stupid in the eyes of the other students. She had not forgotten the dismissive manner of the other woman on the day of the examination. In spite of all Lamont's reassurances, she was so nervous that she felt slightly sick. The best way to deal with it, she decided, was to walk briskly up the road and not stop until she was in her seat in the college.

One of the teachers, a formidable woman in a tweed skirt and jacket, whom she later found to be Miss Caughie, was stationed inside the main door to direct the new students.

'Your name, please?'

'Catherine MacGillivray.'

'Ah yes. A scholarship student. Welcome to the college,' she said kindly. 'Your room is upstairs, turn right, along the corridor and third door. You're in good time. Some of the others are there.'

Catherine thanked her and climbed the stairs. In the room she found a strange collection of students, the men standing by the window, the women along the back wall. The ages of the men seemed to vary as much as their attire. Two middle-aged men, one rook-like in a black coat might have been a minister, the other corpulent with frock coat, yellow waistcoat and watch-chain a shopkeeper. Among the other younger men, one looked as though he was dressed for cycling in tweed knee-breeches, another as though he had descended from a steam yacht with a reefer jacket. They were all pretending to ignore the women.

As she approached the women, she was examined courteously but thoroughly with glances at her shoes, her dress, her bodice, her hair—a quick assessment of her class, her age, her profession. Most of them smiled politely and carried on with their conversation but one middle-aged woman broke with the others to greet her.

'I'm so pleased to find someone of my own age,' she said. 'The others are so young.'

'Yes. Young and full of confidence.'

'I'm Phoebe. You're from the North, I think.'

'The island of Mull. Catherine MacGillivray.'

'That girl with the red hair is from Lewis and speaks Gaelic. You must meet her. Come, I'll introduce you.'

'No. No thanks. Later perhaps.'

'Of course.'

At that point the Rector swept into the room, his gown flowing behind him.

'Good morning, ladies and gentlemen. My name is Mr Hyslop, the Rector. On behalf of all our staff, I would like to welcome you to the college. Please be seated.'

The men sat in the desks on one side of the room, the women on the other. No-one directed them to follow this procedure—it seemed to occur naturally.

The Rector explained the rules of the college and outlined the curriculum—three periods a week of Scripture, six of Maths and Arithmetic, five of History and Geography, four of reading, composition and grammar and four of Teaching Practice and School Management. The women, however, would miss out on some Maths, Latin and Political Economy to study Sewing and Domestic Economy.

'Disgraceful,' whispered Phoebe. 'Why can't the men learn to cook and sew?'

'Might poison the pupils or sew their breeches to their bottoms.'

'God forbid.'

The Rector finished his introduction by asking them to write a short composition about themselves—their schooling, their background and ambitions—and left the room, saying that he expected full concentration and no conversation.

That was Catherine's introduction to her new life.

§

Phoebe became her friend, the pair indulging in what the tutor referred to horse-play in the cooking class. Catherine discovered that Phoebe's fees were being paid by the War Office as she was training to be a regimental schoolmistress.

'Good heavens. I didn't know there were teachers in the army,' Catherine said.

'There are battalions of illiterate soldiers. My father is an officer in Crimea.'

'What a dreadful place to be. I hope he is somewhere safe.'

'Dreadful indeed. Soldiers betrayed. Let me tell you. Exhausted men on the front line with no water, a single piece of salt pork or beef to eat with sugar rice, frozen clothes crawling with lice, a tot of rum to keep them happy. That's what it's like. Not enough ambulances to carry away the wounded, cholera and dysentery sweeping through the ranks, horses pulling the supply wagons dying of starvation, soldiers having to walk back for supplies and ammunition. Hell on earth. London's fault. Father blames Trevelyan, Sir Charles Trevelyan. I'm sorry for the rant. It makes me so angry. Father is safe for the moment behind the lines.'

Her vivid description of the conditions shook Catherine, reminding her of John.

'I know of Trevelyan. It was him who stopped the famine relief in the islands when people were starving, so I'm told. A cruel man.'

'Cruel and incompetent, a dangerous mixture.'

'My brother is in the army, just re-joined.'

'Really? What regiment?'

'I have no idea. I have heard nothing. I don't know where he is. I hope it's not Crimea.'

'That's upsetting for you. Let me know which regiment when you hear. I may be able to help.'

'That's kind of you. I will. I suppose we had better go into sewing and learn how to make bloomers for elephants.'

They laughed and walked arm-in-arm to the classroom.

§

At the end of the day, Catherine was leaving when one of the young men approached her on the steps, a handsome youth with thin, straw-coloured side whiskers and long hair.

'You are from the island of Mull, I hear.'

'Gossip travels like heather fire in the college it seems.'

'I have been deer hunting there with Johnnie Campbell—the 'Dragoon' they call him—on Torosay. Do you know him? '

'No. I'm from the far side of the island next to Iona. Is he Campbell of Possil?'

'Yes. A splendid fellow. We had a marvellous time there with violins and dancing and singing in the evenings and hunting through the day on Ben Vearnach. Magnificent scenery. You're very lucky to live there. Where are you staying in the city?'

'On the south side.'

'Let me take you home. I'm hiring a cab anyway.'

'No, thank you for the offer. I enjoy walking.'

'On a fine day perhaps but that east wind is piercing and you look perished. Do allow me to rescue you—it's always been my ambition to rescue a lady—as a knight on a white charger.'

He was a handsome young man with an air of innocence and recklessness which she found attractive and she was flattered by his attention.

'We have not been introduced, Sir Knight. You might be a highwayman.'

'My apologies, madam. I'm Charles MacLaine.'

'Of Lochbuie?'

'Nothing so grand, I fear. Perhaps distantly. Are you a MacLaine?'

'MacGillivray. Catherine MacGillivray.'

'So to which part of the city can I take you, Catherine?'

Feeling ashamed of the Gorbals address, she chose to visit Lamont.

'Oxford Street, if you please, Sir Knight.'

On the way she told him of the famine on Mull, sparing no detail, and how hunger had forced her to leave the island for the sake of the children. She told him about the queues for meal, the starvation wages, the fever, the Factor and the evictions. He listened quietly, frowning and shaking his head, until she had finished.

'I had no idea. How can I not have known? I met Johnnie here once and all he talked of was the Free Church and meetings in a gravel pit. You have had a dreadful time. I'm sorry.'

'It is not your fault. The Minister—the Duke's man—said it was the hand of God laid on a wicked and wayward generation.'

'What nonsense!'

When they reached Oxford Street, he stepped out of the cab, opened her door and handed her down politely.

'Thank you, Sir Knight.'

'My pleasure. My real pleasure. I have learnt more about my country in the past ten minutes than in years at school. Enlightening and humbling. I hope you will allow me to take you home again, Catherine.'

'Perhaps.'

'I will see you tomorrow in Scripture class.'

He spoke to the driver and the cab clattered away into the night.

19

'You allowed him to take you home?' said Phoebe, 'That was very brave.'

'I think he's harmless, certainly not a Lothario. Quite child-like really, which I find attractive.'

'You would have him as a lover? To introduce him to the "sins of the flesh"?'

'Certainly not, Phoebe. He's young enough to be my son.'

'Virgin soil, awaiting the seed.'

'Phoebe!'

They were standing in the college corridor after lunch, waiting for the Geography tutor.

'I'm not looking forward to teaching a class, facing the ranks of pupils staring at me,' said Phoebe. 'I'm rather frightened of children, the way they study every stitch of clothing, every line on one's face, searching for the cracks in one's armour. Predatory, ready to pounce. Have you children?'

'A girl and a boy, Mary and Archie. Mary is leaving for Jamaica soon as a governess with a respectable family. I'm not entirely happy about it but it is an unusual opportunity. Archie is still at school. He announced the other night that he wants to be an engineer.'

'Really? That was my brother's ambition. He succeeded too. He works for a firm in Tradeston now—McOnie and Mirrlees. Loves every minute. I'm sure he would find Archie a place there when he's finished school.'

'Really? That would be wonderful, Phoebe.'

'His firm builds steam engines, sugar mills, boilers and sends them to the West Indies—probably to Jamaica. That family to which Mary is attached, are they involved in sugar? '

'I don't know. I didn't enquire.'

'Do find out. It would be extraordinary if Phillip was sending out engines to them.'

Catherine saw the men trooping along the corridor, led by two who, by their ecclesiastical attire, were preachers or licentiates of the Church. Charles, more flamboyantly dressed in a checked jacket, was in the middle of the throng, nodding politely in her direction and smiling as he passed into the classroom.

'Good heavens,' said Phoebe, 'I believe he was blushing. I wish I had that effect on men.'

'He's just a boy really.'

'A most attractive one, though.'

The rest of the women appeared and they followed the men into the art room. This was Catherine's favourite subject and the only class in which the students were allowed to move around and see each other's work. She never took advantage of the freedom, only looking at other drawings if invited. Asked to draw a still-life of a bowl of fruit, she was so involved in her work that she didn't see the tutor standing behind her.

'Excellent work, Mrs MacGillivray. Now think about how to teach this skill to children.'

'I will, Miss.'

The tutor moved on to Phoebe but was not so complimentary about her drawing, taking her pencil and showing her how it could be improved.

Towards the end of the class, Charles wandered across.

'That's brilliant, Catherine! Perfect. I can almost taste the fruit. Don't you think so, Miss Carter?'

Phoebe came over to join him.

'Extraordinary. I'm so jealous. You have real talent, Catherine.'

'I just draw what I see.'

'I try to do that, but my hand has a life of its own and doesn't follow what's in in my eye.'

At the end of the class, Charles joined her as they left the room.

'Where did you learn to draw, Catherine?'

'I didn't. No-one taught me.'

'Extraordinary. Do you draw at home?'

'When I can get paper. All the time, if I could.'

'May I see them—the work you do at home?'

She thought for a moment he was inviting himself to her home and hesitated, but he realised immediately what she was thinking and, blushing, clarified his request.

'I mean could you bring them in? I would love to see them.'

'They are not worth carrying in. Not meant for other people. They were done for my pleasure.'

'Even so. Would you mind? I would not show them to other people.'

'Very well. If you promise not to show them to anyone else, I will.'

'Splendid. I'm so pleased.'

§

She did not escape his attention at the end of the day. As she and Phoebe walked down the steps, he followed them and, undeterred by Phoebe's presence, asked if he could take her home again.

'No thank you, Charles. I'm determined to walk. It's a fine day and I need some fresh air—well, as fresh as the city can offer.'

'May I walk with you, then?' he persisted.

'I can't prevent you, can I? What would I do? Call the constables?'

Phoebe, grinning, excused herself and walked away.

They stopped on the bridge over the Clyde to watch a barque in full sail pull away from the quay. With the east wind behind it, it slid quickly out of sight behind the ships still moored above the Broomielaw. Behind it, white gulls wheeled above the brown water. Its departure reminded her of Mary's leaving for Jamaica.

'It always makes me feel sad, a ship leaving,' she said. 'Reminds me of all the people who have left, sailing to Canada or Australia, people that I will never see again. That's what worries me about my daughter leaving for Jamaica, that I might not see her again.'

'There are ships sailing to and from the West Indies every day,' Charles said. 'Of course you'll see her again.'

'Who knows?'

She imagined Mary waving goodbye from the stern of a ship as she stood on the quay and could feel already the sensation of sorrow and loss.

'I really want to see your drawings,' he said. 'I always wanted to be an artist but my father insisted I should become a man of the cloth. I can't think why. There's no tradition of it in the family. Perhaps so that he can obtain absolution for his sins, which are legion, an easy path into heaven.'

'You wanted to be an artist?'

'Yes. All my young life.'

'You should do it. We only have one life and it's yours not his.'

'He would cut my allowance immediately.'

'There's always a way, if you put your mind to it. When you take the first step, things fall into place. It happens, believe me. Now, I must press on. I have dinner to cook.'

They left the bridge and headed for Oxford Street where, raising her hand to his lips, he left her.

§

'Who was that handsome young man?' Lamont asked.

Catherine, sensing a hint of jealousy, smiled and walked past him into the kitchen.

'A fellow student.'

'Doesn't look old enough to be a teacher.'

'Oh? Perhaps he's older than he looks.'

'Perhaps. What were your subjects today?'

'Scripture followed by Mathematics, Penmanship and Art. In the afternoon school management and preparation for teaching practice.'

'Sounds rather dull. It's a disgrace that they deny women Latin. It forms the basis of English.'

'Latin can be dull too with nominative, vocative, accusative and so on.'

'Without the basics of grammar one can't aspire to the wonders of the Iliad.'

'I can read it in translation.'

'Never the same. This young man—he will learn Latin?'

'I expect so. He really wants to be an artist.'

'An artist? So what is he doing at college? Clearly he is not committed to teaching. He will never make a good teacher. He's wasting the time and effort of the tutors.'

'I expect he or his father is paying for their services.'

'You seem very keen to defend him.'

'As you are to attack him without knowing anything of his character.'

'Perhaps you have a romantic attachment to the youth.'

'Eoin! You should know me better than that. I think I should leave before I get really angry.'

She called Archie and left, hurrying home, furious with Lamont. Clearly he was jealous and that annoyed her, for jealousy implied some sense of ownership. He had no right to imagine that he owned her in some way. She had been attracted to him, that was true, but she was sure that she had never regarded him as anything more intimate than a good friend and he had never made advances to her. Charles was little more than an acquaintance and she tried to convince herself that the attraction was superficial, a passing fancy. She did like him but nothing more than that.

'You look very cross, Mother,' Archie complained as they passed McBride's mill.

'Sorry, Archie, I was thinking of Mary and Jamaica.'

'I wish I could go too.'

'You have to finish school. By the way, one of my new friends has a brother who is an engineer. He works for a firm in Tradeston and might help you to get work with his firm.'

Archie stopped in the roadway, his face transformed with delight.

'As an engineer?'

'Yes. That's what you want, isn't it?'

'Yes, yes. Maybe I could go on weekends—Saturday afternoons and Sundays.'

'I don't know. I'll ask. Be patient, Archie. It may not happen immediately.'

As they walked on, she wondered what Calum would think of the plan. Archie, as an engineer, would never return to Shiaba. Calum would be losing his son. She would be losing her son. She began to doubt her decision to mention the opportunity.

The room was cold and dark when they reached home. She had to feel her way up the stair, through the door and across to the table where she had left the candle and matches. Lighting the candle, she could see in the gloom that the fire was out. Having walked out of Lamont's without cooking, she realised that she would have to make a meal.

'Archie, take the candle and go upstairs. See if there's some kindling up there.'

Lighting the lamp, she passed him the candle. Shivering, she began to regret her impetuous departure from Lamont's and realised that she had left her college book there.

'Damn and blast!' she whispered, shovelling cold cinders and ash into a bucket and searching for some paper to start the fire. Some ash spilt out over her clean dress.

Once the fire was in flame she made some porridge and they sat down to eat it with some bread and cheese. She imagined that Charles would be sitting in his spacious dining room with a glass of wine and a meal of venison and gravy. Perhaps. Then she realised that she knew nothing about him. Maybe he lived in a garret and his meal would be as simple as hers. She looked around the room, the bare board floor, the unclad rafters next to the sarking, the soot-covered chimney breast and the cracked and crumbling plaster around the door. She could not see him being comfortable in such surroundings. Calum, on the other hand, would feel at home here.

She thought of him in Shiaba, remembering their evenings round the fire before the children were born, how he would tell her stories of his childhood, recalling how his grandmother would squirt milk at him when she was milking the cow, how his grandfather, intoxicated with whisky, would whirl around the house at Yule with a burning branch of juniper. She remembered the way he laughed, abandoning himself to the mirth, tears brimming in his eyes, how he would suddenly stop in the middle of harvest, fling down his sickle, and take her in his arms, holding her against him as if they were parting for the last time. Remembering it, she longed to feel it again. She wanted to go back, leave the college, leave Lamont, leave Charles and go back to Calum, where her heart still lay.

20

In the early morning, with the dew still glistening on the grass, Calum stood by the potato rigs, admiring the green shaws. They were healthy and strong, promising a good crop. On the land beside them, the young corn was thriving as well. He wished that Catherine could be there to see the crops. She would surely be proud of his efforts. On the face of the hill above him, the shepherd was herding the sheep down from the high ground onto the hill face. Calum was worried that, when he was away at the fishing, the shepherd might shift the sheep down to his crops, though, so far, he had not ventured in that direction, perhaps suspecting that he still had a gun.

He turned and walked back to the house, remembering that he had to smoor the fire before he left for Bunessan. As he passed Tina, who was outside her door, she asked him to call in with Bridget to make sure she was managing with Mima. He had not intended to visit Mima, but was happy to help. The boys, clearly, were keen to go with him, but she kept them at home.

Mima's house was a bit out of his way, but he crossed the bridge and hurried down to Ardtun, telling the boys to wait at the pier.

'I'm glad you called, Calum,' Bridget said, meeting him at the door. 'I think Mima may have the fever. There's a smell of the flux but she won't admit anything is wrong.'

'I'll come in. When did it start?'

'Last night, I think.'

He went in to find Mima sitting by the fire, not in her usual upright posture, but bent over, holding her belly.

'Well, Calum MacGillivray, what brings you here?'

'I came to see if you needed anything?'

'A new house with a door that you have to knock before you come in.'

'Bridget thinks you are not well.'

'Now there's a grand girl. If I had her for a daughter, I would want for nothing. There's nothing wrong with me that a little Christian kindness can't cure.'

'They say laudanum is good for the cramps.'

'Chinese poison.'

'Have you heard from John?'

'He will be far too busy to write. A brave boy, gone to fight for his country, unlike the cowards who wait behind.'

He was about to retaliate with alternative descriptions like 'rogue' or 'blackguard' but managed to control the impulse. She was, after all, Catherine's mother and a sick old woman.

'Seeing you're so clever, MacGillivray, maybe you could find out where he is.'

It was the first time she had asked him directly to do anything for her.

'I will do what I can.'

He left the house, telling Bridget that he would ask the doctor to call.

When he reached the pier, having called at the doctor's house, he found that Dugald had managed to recruit his brother, Archie, as another crewman. The lines were all baited and carefully coiled and the boat made ready for sailing. He was impressed.

'I think I can persuade one of the MacFees to join us,' said Dugald, 'but they are all weak with hunger, the whole family. I don't know how they will be fit enough to emigrate. They will never make the ship.'

'Do they not get meal from the Board?'

'Donald is too proud to beg for it.'

'He would rather they starved?'

As he said it, he remembered with some shame his own stubborn resistance and the effect on his family. He climbed down into the boat and they set sail.

They had good fishing that day, with plenty of cod and ling and more lobsters than they could fit in the barrel, two of them being left to flick their tails on the deck.

Calum took the boat into Kintra and walked up the hill with a string of fish for the MacFees. When he entered the house, he was shocked by the state of the family. Donald, the head of the household, staggered as he rose to greet his guest, his legs as thin as his wrists, his sunken eyes black with worry. His wife did not even look up but stared at the dead ashes on the hearthstone. The three girls were sitting together in the gloom of the far corner, one of them combing lice out of her sister's lank hair. The boys sat around a bowl of raw whelks, breaking the shells with stones and eating the flesh.

'I have brought you some fish. Have you no peat to cook them?'

'Our peats were finished a month ago,' Donald answered.

'Surely someone in the townland has some? The quarrymen?'

'He won't ask,' said the oldest boy, 'and he won't let us ask either.'

'We have never begged for charity before, never been on the parish lists. We are not paupers.'

Calum looked around the room, thinking that if these weren't paupers, real paupers must look like the living dead.

'I came to see if one of your boys would crew for me.'

Two of the boys stood up immediately, saying together, 'I will.'

'Would they be paid?' asked their father.

'I would not ask them to work for nothing.'

'We will be leaving for Australia soon so it would not be for long.'

Calum knew there was little chance of them leaving unless they regained their strength.

'No matter, but I can take only one.'

'Take Neil then.'

'Good. I'll call tomorrow. I will leave the fish and I'll find you some fuel to cook them.'

'God bless you, sir,' the wife said, suddenly looking up at him.

'I'm not "sir", mistress. Calum is enough. Tomorrow then, Neil.'

He left the house and walked down to the boat.

'No fire, no food, no light at night. What kind of life is that?' he said to Dugald.

'The life of half of the Ross, Calum.'

They set sail for Bunessan to unload their catch and store the lobsters. When they had finished, Calum called on MacQuarrie in Bunessan.

'Well, Calum. A good day's fishing?'

'Fair. I've a good crew now. Dugald MacFee from Kintra. His family are starving. Can you get some meal to them? I will pay for it.'

'Strange. They have never asked for meal.'

'Too proud, I think.'

'A fault I have seen before somewhere. Very well, I will send meal to them.'

'And do you know any house with plenty of peat in the stack?'

'A few. People who left for Canada.'

'Could I hire your horse and cart to take some peat to Kintra?'

'No need for payment. You can take the cart. Is Mima unwell? I saw Beveridge call on her.'

'Bridget thinks she has fever, but the old witch is denying it.'

'She'll be missing John.'

'Not that he was ever much help to her.'

'He was there for her. I saw the Factor this morning, riding through. In a hurry.'

'Spreading misery, no doubt. I'll call in the morning for the cart.'

He set off for Shiaba, carrying a string of fish for the widow and her family.

§

As he came over the hill, he saw a heavy billow of smoke rising from his house. Running down the slope, he found the burning roof had collapsed into the building and a bonfire of all his belongings outside the door. All the other houses were untouched. Shocked, he stood still, watching the flames in the broken window. He could not believe that the Factor would burn him out of his home, that he would dare to do such a thing. He had made threats in the past but had never carried them out. Why would he choose to attack him now? The fury ignited inside him, bursting into flame like his house, stirring one vision of revenge after another—setting fire to the factor's house, hauling him from his horse and slicing open his throat, poisoning his precious cattle, raising the people of the Ross in an army against him. As the wind blew smoke in his face, tears rolled down his cheeks.

'I'll kill him,' he swore.

Suddenly remembering his crops, he ran round the back. Every potato plant pulled out and all his corn trampled.

One of the old men from the small group of people came over.

'He has threatened us with the same. I'm sorry, Calum. We thought he respected you.'

'He respects no-one but himself. I swear I will get revenge. Somehow, somewhere, he will pay for this. Is Tina safe and the children?'

'She left just after the Factor and his men.'

'She left? Where would she go?'

'I don't know. Too frightened to stay, she said. She thought it was all her fault.'

'God damn him! Hell is too good for the likes of him. I could kill him.'

'Do nothing rash, Calum. You're a clever man. Every bit as clever as Campbell. The way to punish him is to stay. You always said you would. Rebuild the roof—we will help you and there is wood and thatch in the other houses. Replant the crops. That is how to punish him. Show that you are more of a man than he is.'

21

'These are absolutely beautiful!' Charles said, looking through her drawings, 'Every minute detail and the colours. Brilliant. Aren't they, Phoebe?'

'You should be studying art, Catherine,' said Phoebe, 'Not the dry, old stuff in here.'

The three were in their classroom at lunch time, with her illustrations laid out on one of the desks.

'You must show these to the art teacher,' Charles said.

'No. Definitely not. No-one else is to see them.'

'You can't hide them away, Catherine. Things of beauty should be shared.'

'No. I brought them in only because you asked and I thought Phoebe would like to see them.'

'I'm really jealous,' said Phoebe. 'Where did you learn to draw like that? And to copy the colours so precisely?'

'I never learnt. I mean no-one taught me.'

'Astonishing,' said Charles.

She folded the drawings into the newspaper in which she had carried them to college.

'I am taking my first class today,' said Phoebe. 'I'm dreading it. Daniel in the lions' den.'

'So am I,' said Catherine. 'I think all of us are facing that ordeal. Are you not, Charles?'

'Yes. I'm not as worried as you. I've faced a congregation which were more interested in hurrying back for lunch than listening to my prattle. Pupils can't be any worse. I'll roar at them, if they misbehave, and threaten them with the Shorter Catechism.'

'I must go and prepare for humiliation,' said Phoebe.

'Me too.'

The trio split up, Charles asking if he could meet Catherine after class.

§

Catherine stood outside the classroom, clutching her notes against her bosom to stop her hands shaking. Inside, she could hear the tutor calling the roll and then explaining that one of the students would be taking the class that afternoon. She heard him walk across the floor and open the door for her.

'Mrs MacGillivray. Come in.'

He showed her to the teacher's desk and then walked to the back of the class where he stood with his arms folded, waiting for her to start. She looked around the mass of small faces, some grinning as they waited for her to stumble, some smiling sympathetically, some frowning with hostility. She had decided to teach them about Jamaica as a geography lesson.

'Hold up your hand if you have tasted sugar this week.'

Most of the class, aged, she thought, between eight and ten, responded.

'Who can tell me where sugar comes from?'

There were many guesses but only three knew of the West Indies. She showed them on the world map hanging on the wall, where Jamaica was to be found and told them how sugar was made. She described the flora and fauna, including the manatee, the crocodile and the hummingbird. Finally, she lifted the chalk and wrote "Jamaica" on the black board and "The Capital is Kingston. The principle exports are sugar and rum" and asked them to copy the words into their exercise books.

After the lesson, the tutor, who had been observing her performance, spoke to her privately.

'I notice that you did not mention slavery, Mrs MacGillivray. Was there a reason for that?'

'I considered that some of the parents might object to me raising the subject and that a geography lesson was not the place to deal with the morality of slavery.'

'Very wise. It might be mentioned with the senior pupils, pointing out that the workforce is mainly of African origin. I thought your lesson was well planned and well executed. You could, perhaps, provide some relief from your monologue by giving them practical work half way through. Otherwise, a very competent start.'

Delighted with the critique, she hurried away to meet Charles and Phoebe. She found them in the foyer, along with other groups of students who were chattering noisily.

'How was it?' asked Charles. 'Mobbing and rioting? Or did you beat them all into submission?'

'They were very well behaved.'

'Good heavens. Hypnotised by your charm. Was the tutor pleased?'

'I think so, except suggesting that the pupils needed "relief from my monologue". That was rather insulting.'

'Mine was a nightmare. I was telling them of Moses and his magic rod—how the rod turned into a snake and Moses caught it by the tail and it became a snake again. They thought this was hilariously funny, particularly when the rubber pipe I was using to illustrate the tale flew out of my hand. "Rather too ambitious" the tutor said. How was yours, Phoebe?'

'It went well until one little boy soiled his trousers and the perfume drifted all round the room, the other pupils reacting with the usual display of exaggerated disgust. I ended by describing conditions in the military hospital in Scutari and what the nurses there had to cope with. I was told that I shouldn't frighten the children. God forbid that they should know what our soldiers have to suffer.'

They left the building, Phoebe leaving Catherine and Charles to walk towards the river, stopping again on the bridge to watch the debris of the city floating towards the sea.

'You should apply to the School of Design, Catherine, in Ingram Street. There's a great future there for a person with your skills, your attention to detail and sense of colour. They need artists in so many fields now—in pottery, in silks and cottons, wallpapers—and they do value women students.'

'My only reason for remaining here is to qualify as a teacher, so that I can return to Mull and to Calum. It's kind of you to think of my future—I really appreciate that—but it doesn't lie in the city. Yours might. Indeed, yours might lie in the school of design. You told me that you wanted to be an artist. You should apply.'

'Compared to yours, my talent is like that of a child.'

'Perhaps you're a poor judge. Let me see your work. Bring it in. I was brave enough to show you mine.'

'When I see the paintings in the museum—Rembrant, Titian, Reynolds—I despair.'

'You've been in the museum?'

'Yes. Often. They had to chase me out at night sometimes.'

'How extraordinary! I worked in the museum before I came to college. Perhaps we passed each other.'

'No, Catherine. Had we passed each other, I would remember. Believe me. In fact, had we met in the corridor, I could not have passed without finding an excuse to engage you in conversation.'

'That would be most impolite, Sir Knight, without an introduction.'

'To hell with manners! Passion is what matters, the baring of the soul, honesty.'

'That can lead to rejection, hurt, resentment—even anger.'

'Is that a warning?'

'No. I was thinking aloud. Come, Sir Knight, we must head for home.'

At the end of the bridge, she decided not to call on Lamont, but turned towards home.

'I'm going to see my son in the Gorbals,' she explained. 'I'll see you tomorrow.'

She walked away, his words about honesty echoing in her head uncomfortably. She liked him, his carefree immaturity, his gentleness and consideration, but his obvious affection for her was worrying because, in the end, she would have to reject it and how to reject it without hurting him posed a problem she would have to face.

§

When she arrived home, Mary was waiting, having stoked the fire and swung the kettle over the heat.

'What a nice surprise, Mary. I didn't expect you home tonight.'

'I had to come. We are leaving tomorrow.'

'What? So soon?'

'The ship is sailing sooner than they thought.'

'You've no suitable clothes, nor anything else you might need in such a climate.'

'I have. Mrs Buchanan has seen to everything. I wish Father could have been here. I wanted to see him before I left.'

'I've not heard from him recently. I hope he's alright. He would want to see you too.'

'I can't stay long. I have to help with the children and their belongings.'

'At least wait till Archie comes back. He should be here. He must have gone to Mr Lamont's to see Hector. They have become great friends.'

'Yes. I'll wait, as long as he's not too long.'

'Are you still sure about this—Jamaica, I mean?'

'Yes, Mother. Very sure.'

'You heard Mrs Buchanan say that there had been a slave rebellion there. Mr Lamont says that there are so many Africans there that they can be controlled only by the utmost brutality. Their anger and resentment will be simmering below the surface, ready to boil over at any time. A dangerous situation, Mary.'

'Stop worrying, Mother. They're not slaves any more. Mrs Buchanan swears that all is peaceful and that the Africans on their estate are happy and paid for their work.'

'I suppose I have to take her word for that. Here is Archie now. I can hear him on the stair.'

'Mary! What are you doing here?' he said as he burst open the door in his usual fashion.

'Come to say farewell. We're sailing tomorrow.'

'Wonderful! I mean wonderful that you have the chance, but sad that you're leaving. I wish I was coming with you.'

'You must stay and look after Mother.'

'Full time work, that is. Is there any tea?'

'I'll see to it,' Catherine said. 'You two sit and I'll hang on the stew as well.'

As she attended to the food with her back to them, she did not really listen to their conversation, but imagined Mary among a crowd of angry Africans, her fair skin and poise a contrast to theirs. She saw her smile and, with reassurance, confidence and friendliness, calm the crowd and persuade it to disperse. That would be her daughter. Perhaps, she thought, she would do well in Jamaica and return with her craving for adventure satisfied.

When they had eaten a meal together, Mary rose to leave.

'I will see you on the quay tomorrow,' Catherine said.

'No, Mother. Please. Please. I couldn't bear that. To watch you standing on the quay as I sailed away would break my heart. No. Say farewell here and now. Please.'

Catherine didn't reply but flung her arms around her daughter and held her close. Archie left the table and joined them. The three stood, locked together in sorrow, their single shadow on the wall hovering over them like a guardian. When Mary broke away and hurried out, mother and son were left with their arms around each other. No word was said, no final blessing, only silence. Their pain was inexpressible.

22

The men came from Lee, Scoor, Saorphin, Uisken, Ardtun—all the neighbouring townships—saying nothing about the task on hand but nodding silently to Calum and joining the others at Shiaba. They might mutter to each other about the dismal spring or the price of meal, but they had no need to talk about the work. Word of the burning had swept around the townlands and of Calum's determination to rebuild. They had come to help, to be with him in his defiance of the Factor. They came because he was one of them. Few of them were in good health, most of them weak with hunger, many emaciated, some could only stand, but they were there for him.

His neighbour had suggested that he could move into one of the empty houses, but Calum had refused.

'This was my father's house and mine when he passed away. I am not going to leave it. The Islay man will not drive me out of my home. I'll take the couples and thatch from the empty house and rebuild.'

Ropes holding the boulders, which weighed down the neighbouring roof, were untied and the thatch stripped then laid in rows on the grass. By noon, only the skeleton of the roof stood above the walls. Then the purlins were untied and finally the couples brought down and carried across to Calum's house. The couples, salvaged yard-arms from a shipwreck, were precious in that exposed part of the Ross where few trees were stout enough to survive the storms. After the couples were hoisted above the charred walls of Calum's house, the purlins were tied and the thatch re-laid. Finally, the ropes were flung across the roof and granite stones hung on the ends. The task was completed before dusk.

Calum thanked them all, apologising for having no whisky, though no-one expected it, any barley grown being for meal. He watched them all walking away, touched by their generosity and their moral support.

'I would offer you our table tonight but there is little enough on it,' said old Duncan.

'Thank you, seannair. I will manage. Does no-one know where Tina was going?'

'She came from Torosay parish. Perhaps she has gone home.'

Calum had not had time to call on Mima and Bridget, but he resolved to do so the next morning.

From the charred remnants of the old roof he scraped together enough kindling to make a fire, discovering in the corner what was left of the old gun. The metal was twisted by the fierce heat, the wood consumed, but still recognisable, however useless. He would have to hide it. He lit a fire and went outside to look for meal. Although the kist had been burnt, there was enough untouched meal in the remains to make porridge. He sat by the hearth, enveloped in the stench of Campbell's fire. The men had cleared most of the debris from the house and carried through a bed from another house. Apart from that, the room was empty. The bare walls blackened, the earth floor baked, the hearthstone cracked. It was hard to imagine the place as it was when Catherine and the children were there. The fire had consumed every trace of them, every living thing, leaving only memories which seemed to float unattached in the air. The place was dead. He would have to breathe life into it, start at the beginning again. He was not sure that he had the energy to face that task but then he remembered what old Duncan had said: "the way to punish him is to stay".

§

Bridget met him at Mima's door as she went for water.

'You're awake early, Bridget. Did your mother come this way?'

'She is in with Mima, laughing and teasing each other. They are the best of friends as if they had been neighbours since childhood.'

'So Mima has made a miraculous recovery?'

'It seems so.'

'And the boys?'

'They'll be in the barn at the back.'

'You are all living here?'

'My mother and the children sleep in the barn. I stay with Mima.'

'What about food? How can you feed so many?'

'MacQuarrie gave me some meal and the boys picked whelks from the shore.'

'That's not enough. I'll bring you fish tonight.'

He turned to leave but Bridget called him back.

'Are you not going to see my mother?'

'No. I'll leave her with Mima. Tell her I'll call tonight.'

He went round to the pier where Dugald and Archie were waiting.

'We're going to head north today,' he said. 'Treshnish. Try the lines there and see if there are any birds' eggs left.'

'It's a bit late, a charaid, but worth a try.'

The soft south-west wind was behind them so they made good time. Calum decided to put in to Lunga, knowing that, on the steep banks of the small island, there were warrens of puffin nests. As they approached the shore, the sky wheeled with birds, screeching and complaining about the intrusion, guillemots, razorbills and swooping terns. Calum thought it proper to call on the only family living there before he searched for eggs, so they climbed up the path and walked to the house. He thought it was strange that no-one opened the door when the birds must have warned the people of their landing.

The house was smaller and lower than the ones at Shiaba, squatting beneath the one hill on the island as if it had emerged from the landscape. When he knocked on the door, it was some time before anyone answered. Eventually, a man opened it slowly.

'Thank God!' he said. 'Thank God. You're an answer to my prayers. My wife is sick and the two children and my boat was smashed in the storm. I would take them to a doctor, if I could.'

'They have the fever?'

'I don't know. They're very sick. My cousin has a farm near Oskamull. Could you take us to Kilninian? I can't pay you, fisherman, but I pray the Lord will reward you in His own way.'

'Yes, I'll take you. Can your family walk to the shore?'

'No. They will have to be carried. I'll take the door off its hinges.'

The Kintra men, who were standing behind Calum, came forward.

'We'll see to the door.'

The man, Hugh Campbell, stepped back into the house, followed by Calum. The woman was lying on the bed, her waxen face slimy with sweat. She did not open her eyes as they approached. The children lay behind her, awake but clearly very sick. The Kintra men laid the door beside the bed, covered it with a blanket and gently lifted her down.

'It was tourists who brought the fever,' said Hugh. 'Folk from the south. They came off a steamer anchored by the shore and walked all over the island, admiring the puffins. A sickly-looking woman came here for water. A few days later Flora took ill.'

The four men carried her down to the shore, laid her in the boat and returned for the children.

'Should we smoor the fire?' Dugald asked.

'No. Let it die. We will not come back. Never. I have had enough. We have no meal, no potatoes and few fish since the boat was wrecked. Eggs and puffins and shellfish. Had to sell the beasts to pay the rent.'

'Is there anything you need to take, Hugh?' asked Calum.

'The family Bible is all. And my father's musket under the bed. The rest can stay and, if any poor soul is shipwrecked here, he is welcome to it.'

'Your father's musket?'

'Yes. There's powder and ball too. I kept it to protect us. We are alone on the island. You may have it for your trouble. I'll have no more use for it. Take it.'

He retrieved the gun and horn concealed under the bed and handed them to Calum.

'I don't need payment.'

'You have saved their lives, God willing. Take it.'

They wrapped the children in blankets and carried them down to the boat. When all were aboard, Calum hoisted sail and they headed north for Kilninian.

Landing at the beach, Hugh jumped into the water and hurried up to the village, returning with a gang of men. Wading up to their thighs, they lifted Hugh's wife and carried her ashore. Calum and Dugald carried the children and laid them on the sand.

'May God bless you, fisherman. I don't even know your name.'

'Calum MacGillivray from Shiaba.'

'God bless you, Calum, and your crew. Thank you for your help. I will never forget.'

They set sail again, heading south against the wind. It was a slow journey and it was dark when they reached Bunessan.

Calum wrapped the gun in a sack and carried it back to Shiaba. Having rescued his oil lamp from the pile outside, he laid the gun on his knee to examine it, admiring the sheen on the stock and its elegant shape. The flintlock and trigger were well oiled and the ramrod slid easily in its tube. It had been thoroughly maintained. He raised it to his shoulder, pointing it to the wall and imagined the Factor in the firing line, sitting on his horse with the supercilious expression that he reserved for people whom he despised. Calum wondered if he could fire at him, actually pull the trigger and send a ball into his heart. It would not be like killing a stag, a beast that could not speak or glare at you as it died. You would surely feel it yourself—the blow of the ball and that second of terror when death was certain. There were times when he might have killed Campbell, but those eruptions of fury did not lead to bloodshed. He did not have a gun at the time. Had he been armed, perhaps the outcome would have been different. He could not be sure. If Campbell, in future, came to his door, he now possessed the means of protecting his home. He would keep the gun loaded.

He rose and laid it on the wall head under the thatch, remembering that he had intended to write to Catherine, but he had neither pen nor ink nor paper. The letter would have to wait.

23

My Dearest Catherine,
I have bad news. The Factor came while I was in Bunessan and burnt down the roof of our house and set fire to many of our belongings outside the door. But there is also good news. All the people in the district came over and we rebuilt the roof. I am back in the house.

The widow from Torosay who lived in the Campbells's house left Shiaba because she was so frightened of the Factor and is now living with your mother in Ardtun. She will be a help to your mother. I do not know if MacQuarrie will continue to give the widow and her family meal as they are not of this parish.

I am doing well at the fishing and the lobsters are selling at a high price.

I do not know what I will do if the Factor comes back but I will not leave this house.

I hope your training is going well and that Archie is working hard at school. Please tell me if you hear from Mary or any news of the family she works for.

Your loving husband who misses you every day, Calum.

Catherine folded the letter and slipped it into her pocket.
'That's appalling,' said Charles, 'The Duke's factor actually burnt the roof of your house. I take it there was no-one inside.'

'No-one inside, but it would not have mattered to him.'

She was standing with Charles and Phoebe in the corridor at college.

'Who is this man? What's his name?' asked Charles.

'Campbell. John Campbell from Islay. Portrays himself as a godly man, a staunch member of the church but he's as heartless as any heathen.'

'I can see that.'

'Where is Calum living now?' asked Phoebe. 'Has he nowhere to go?'

'He's back in the house. He and all his neighbours rebuilt the roof.'

'Good for them. That must be a relief.'

'What if the Factor comes back?' asked Charles. 'He must have issued a notice of eviction surely before setting fire to the house.'

'He sends out summonses like other men sow seed corn. Some people burn them, others are too fearful and leave. Calum ignores them. God knows what he will do if Campbell returns.'

'Calum's business seems to be flourishing, flourishing in the midst of famine. That should be encouraged. You would expect the Factor to be delighted.'

'He has a grudge against Calum. He can't tolerate defiance.'

'That's no excuse. He's there to represent the Duke's interests and I would have thought that Duke would be pleased to see one of his tenants thriving. Leave this with me, Catherine. My friend, Johnnie, knows the Duke. I will speak to him. Johnnie can't abide injustice.'

'It could make things worse. They might resent any interference.'

'Could they be any worse? He would be very discreet, I assure you. Now, if you'll excuse me, ladies, I must go to face questions on Caesar's Gallic wars, about which I have prepared absolutely nothing, but I could talk all afternoon about Titian or my hero Caravaggio.'

'He's kind,' said Phoebe after he left. 'He may be able to help. Are we going to sewing class or will we take a walk to the Green? It's far too pleasant to be shut in a classroom.'

'Yes, let's miss sewing.'

'Splendid! What fun!'

They hurried down the stairs, giggling like a pair of naughty schoolgirls, and walked arm-in-arm down towards the river. The streets were dry and the warmth of the sun filtered down through the mantle of smoke that hung constantly over the city. The open acres of the Green gave a sense of space, a feeling of well-being, as they strolled across the park. A flock of sheep, their heads bent to the grass, moved towards the trees. As they neared the river, scores of women were hanging out washing to dry in the breeze and, further along, ribbons of linen had been laid out to bleach in the sun.

'I live over there,' Catherine confessed, nodding in the direction of a column of black smoke from Dixon's ironworks.

'I thought you lived further west,' said Phoebe.

'No. Main street, Gorbals. I was too ashamed of the filth in the street to direct the cab to my house when Charles took me home. I sent it instead to a house where I worked as a servant, a teacher's house.'

'I don't believe Charles would think less of you because of the place you live. Such things are of little consequence to him.'

'I know. I did him a disservice. I regret that now but, having started the deceit, it is difficult to withdraw. I'm ashamed of it now.'

'Confess the sin,' Phoebe laughed. 'It's trivial. He's so smitten, he would forgive you anything.'

'Yes. That worries me. There's no future in it for him. I have a husband, but I would not wish to hurt Charles by a direct refusal.'

'If you are not sure what to do, do nothing. That's what my father says. I have heard from him, by the way, and he tells me that he can't help unless he knows in which regiment your brother enlisted.'

'We don't know.'

'Yes, that is a problem. He could be with the 74th in India or the Black Watch in Crimea. Depends where he enlisted. I could make enquiries for you, if you like.'

'That would be wonderful. I really want to know where he is. He's such a headstrong and foolhardy young man and yet, with all his faults, I adore him. I hope he's not in Crimea. Might you be sent there when you are finished here?'

'God knows, Catherine. Crimea, India, China—wherever the army is stationed.'

'I will worry about you. Such a dangerous profession. You will write to me, won't you? We must keep in touch. I've never had a friend like you, someone who I can trust.'

'I promise.' Phoebe squeezed her arm to emphasise what she said.

It was true. Catherine had felt an immediate affinity with her. They were of the same age and more mature than the other women in the class. She confided in her, telling her of Calum's infidelity and her own affection for Lamont, an emotion which had shaken her and still led to confusion and irritation.

'Eoin accused me of having a romantic attachment to Charles.'

'So you flounced out.'

'Yes.'

'A prickly subject, evidently. Could there have been just a tiny fleck of truth in the accusation? Could that account for the indignation?'

'No! Well, I am fond of him, but not in an amorous sense, more in a maternal manner. I like his boyish enthusiasm and sensitivity. He's gentle too and kind—qualities I admire—but it ends there. No romance.'

'And what of Eoin Lamont? How does he compare?'

'That's a different matter. So many mixed feelings, a cauldron swirling with incompatible emotions. I was entranced by his intelligence, his wisdom and knowledge. I had never met anyone like that. I felt sorry for him, having lost his wife and left with three little boys, although he has a remarkable bond with them and manages them with ease. I enjoy every minute of his company but I can't imagine sharing a bed with him. I do regret—deeply regret—leaving him that way, though.'

'You must repair the damage, then. Swallow the pride and call on him. He obviously means a great deal to you, in spite of your aversion to his bedroom furniture. The longer you leave it, the more difficult it will be. Do it.'

'You're right, Phoebe. I will.'

Looking across the river, Phoebe said, 'You shouldn't be ashamed of the Gorbals, Catherine. I have seen much more loathsome places than that. We were in Ireland during the worst years of the famine. I regret to say my father's regiment was employed to guard the wagons of grain heading for the English ships. His men had to fight off mobs of starving Irish. I wonder how your brother would feel, if he was ordered to do that.'

'It would test his loyalty certainly, but he would obey orders.'

'I saw some fearful sights there. Much worse than what you might see in the Gorbals. I was in a cabin once—you couldn't actually call it a cabin—more like a sodden hole in the ground—and the whole family lay dead. The place smelt of excrement and rotten flesh and rats scuttled away as I stepped in. Skulls with empty eye sockets staring at the roof, fleshless bones with skin stretched over them, feet gnawed clean by rats. All dead of hunger and my father's men guarding the precious grain. It stretched my loyalty to its limit. It stretched his too, though—obeying orders, government policy, Trevelyan's policy.'

'Yes, I've heard the stories from Ireland. Terrifying really.'

'But we should not be talking of such morbid events on such a beautiful day. Let's go back to the town and find a tearoom.'

She did not return to college that afternoon and, in the evening, she sat at the table after Archie was in bed, thinking about Lamont and how she might apologise for her impulsive exit from the house. She would have to explain her indignation and she was sure that he would suspect that it arose because there was some truth in the allegation. Perhaps there was. Perhaps her vehement denial of her feeling for Charles was not entirely truthful. She did find him attractive. Yet he belonged to a different world, one in which people did not have to starve or to suffer oppression and injustice. The gap was too great to have any future.

Her feelings for Eoin were more difficult to define. She was sure that, if she offered to become his wife, he would be delighted, that he would welcome her into the household with open arms, not only as a companion but as a mother for his children. When they sat together by the fire in the evening, she always felt at home. Yet, although she admired his intelligence, she felt distinctly uncomfortable when she imagined a passionate embrace. She was sure he would be awkward and inhibited, sexless even. She loved his mind, his devotion to his boys, his respect for her, but she could not see him as a lover.

Besides, there was Calum—impulsive, stubborn, unfaithful, selfish Calum. For all his faults, she had no doubt about her feelings for him. She loved him. They might lie together and conceive children, but that intimacy was not what mattered most. There was something that bound them together, something indefinable, a force beyond their understanding, as if they were destined to be together. She might have left him alone in Shiaba to protect their children, but, even as she sailed away, she knew that she would return one day. She wanted to be with him, to grow old with him, even it was in penury and deprivation.

24

Charles hurried over to her as she waited to go into the classroom.

'I've brought you something, Catherine,' he said, handing her a leather briefcase. 'It's for your drawings. To protect them. And it can carry your college work.'

She was so shocked she took it without thinking.

'I can't accept this, Charles. It's too expensive.'

'Of course you can. It's a gift. You have to look after your drawings. I insist.'

'It's very kind of you, very generous. Thank you. Thank you very much.'

'It's a pleasure.'

He disappeared into the classroom to join the men.

She examined it, running her fingers over the shining leather and the bright metal clasp, which had a lock, and the carefully sewn handle and seams. It was beautiful.

'What's this?' asked Phoebe. 'An executive badge of honour, an essential part of a teacher's uniform?'

'A gift from Charles.'

'Good heavens! True love indeed.'

'Nonsense. He's just being very kind.'

'A bit different from a bunch of red roses.'

'It's for my drawings.'

'Of course. By the way, I've written to the Ministry of War, using Daddy's name, to enquire about John. It may lead to nothing, but it's worth a try.'

'Thank you, Phoebe. My mother will not rest till she knows where he is.'

'I think we had better go in. If I never hear about Ananias and Sapphira again, I will not mourn. Can you really believe that a couple could be struck dead by the Holy Spirit because they kept a part of the proceeds of sale to themselves? Good God, Catherine, half of the capitalists of Europe would be in the catacombs, if that were the case.'

'True. I must point that out to the tutor.'

'Better not. You might be struck down too or turned into a pillar of salt.'

They strolled into the classroom and took their places with the other women.

§

Charles attached himself to them at lunch time as they walked out into the street.

'I have news for you, ladies. I'm afraid I will be leaving the college.'

The women stopped and stared at him, speechless.

'It seems that Papa has relented and has entered my name for the Design college.'

'That's wonderful, Charles. What you wanted,' said Phoebe.

Catherine, still shocked by the announcement and wondering how to react, said nothing.

'Papa discovered that I would not, after all, be spending my time drawing naked ladies but would be training for industry and so he changed his mind.'

'You must be delighted,' Catherine said finally.

'You should come with me. You are far more talented than I am.'

'I can teach others. I want to finish here and go back to Mull.'

'It doesn't mean that we can't meet. It's only in Ingram Street. I can walk up here and see you at the end of your day—if you don't object, that is.'

'Of course you can,' said Phoebe with her usual enthusiasm.

'I'm sorry you're leaving,' Catherine said, 'but I'm pleased for you. We will miss you in the college.'

'That's kind of you. I hope you will still allow me to walk you home occasionally.'

'I look forward to it.'

§

That evening after college she called on Lamont, standing for some time outside the door before knocking.

As soon as he answered, indeed before the door was properly open, she blurted out an apology.

'I must apologise for my behaviour the other night. It was rude and rash.'

'Catherine, Catherine. There's absolutely no need to apologise. The fault was entirely mine. I should never have enquired into your private affairs. I had no right to intrude. Do come in. The boys have missed you.'

The grace with which he accepted the apology stirred her affection for him.

'I want to hear all about college,' he continued. 'Perhaps, on the other hand, you would sooner forget all about it, having spent an arduous day wrestling with its dry curriculum. Do sit down.'

'Some of it is very tiresome. I enjoy the English composition but not the grammar, the domestic economy and not the arithmetic. I taught my first class the other day, which was a terrifying experience.'

'I'm sure it was much more of a success than you judged it to be.'

'He said that I did not break up the lesson with enough practical work—I did not give them enough "respite from my monologue".'

Postscript.

'In 1846 and the few following years, the aspect of the population, and of the numerous wretched hovels created by squatting cottars along the roadsides, was most painful. It resembled nothing so much as the descriptions of the poorest parts of the West of Ireland …. I have been most unwilling to hasten the process by dispossessing any crofter who would pay his way at all.

The combined effect of all those operations has been a great and visible improvement in the whole aspect of the people as well as the country …. well drained fields, substantially enclosed by some of the finest "Galloway dikes" in Scotland, have replaced spongy mosses and neglected pastures. Wire fencing on an extensive scale has been erected and substantial steadings have been built …"

Duke of Argyll. Letter to Napier Commission, 1883

'They have to say something. They are handsomely paid to be discouraging.'

'Actually, I think it went quite well.'

'Good. That's what matters.'

'My friend, Phoebe, seems to have had something of a riot with her class.'

'Oh dear. Poor girl. First time, though. It should get better.'

'She tells me that she may be able to arrange part-time work for Archie in her brother's engineering firm.'

'That would be ideal—as long as it did not detract from his studies.'

'I'm sure it wouldn't and it's what he wants to do.'

'I'm quite happy to continue helping with his schoolwork, Catherine. He can call round at any time and there would be no charge. Hector enjoys having him here.'

'That would be very kind. I'll tell him.'

She was about to tell him that Charles was leaving the college, but then decided that it might be too sensitive a subject.

'The same applies to yourself. I would be delighted to see you at any time. I miss the company.'

'Thank you. I will, though it may not be as often, as I find I have to study in the evenings.'

'Of course. I understand. I would not dream of keeping you from your studies. They must come first.'

Just then, a young woman came through who must have been with the boys, a striking girl with long, auburn hair and wide, emerald eyes. She seemed to float into the room with ease and familiarity.

'Catherine,' said Lamont without a hint of embarrassment, 'this is Kathleen, my new helper. Kathleen, this is my dear friend, Catherine.'

Catherine could see the rapport between them and, for a moment, felt a stab of jealousy.

'I have heard a great deal about you, Catherine,' she said, holding out her hand. 'I'm delighted to meet you.'

There was such genuine warmth there that the jealousy subsided.

'Kathleen, as you can probably hear, is originally from Ireland, but she has come to teach the infants in my school. The house in which she had a room was destroyed by fire so I offered the spare room here. It has proved to be an admirable arrangement.'

'He's been very kind,' Kathleen said and moved beside him to place her hand on his shoulder.

'I'm so glad you have found someone to help, Eoin.'

Hector ran in and flung his arms around Kathleen, not noticing that Catherine was there. Her jealousy returned, but again was swept away when the boy saw her and immediately ran to her.

'I've missed you so much,' he said. 'I thought we would never see you again. Is Archie not with you?'

'Not tonight, but he will be coming sometimes so that you can help him with him with his mathematics.'

'He doesn't need my help. He's clever, but he must come. He's good fun.'

'I will tell him. Now, I must leave you. Archie will be waiting impatiently for his tea. He would rather starve than make it himself. It's been a pleasure to meet you, Kathleen.'

She rose, lifting her brief case and passing her fingers through Hector's hair.

'You must come again,' Lamont said. 'As often as you can and do send Archie. The boys miss him.'

'I will surely. Goodbye, everybody.'

As she walked along the road, she tried to arrange her swirling feelings into some kind of order. Kathleen's appearance had been a shock and the stab of jealousy annoyed her. The bond between Eoin and the girl was obvious, the kind of intimacy which she had never shared with him. There was a time, she had to admit, when she craved such a relationship, when she was smitten by his superior intellect, but the cascade of circumstances—the Museum, the admission to college, her new friends—had diluted the enthusiasm. Kathleen's appearance, indeed, provided a sense of relief. She had believed that Eoin would be hurt when she declared her intention to leave Glasgow. Perhaps that was arrogant. She had no reason to believe that he would be upset. She was keen to keep the friendship, to listen to his thoughts on national affairs, to learn from him about education, religion, democracy, but she feared that Kathleen's presence would prevent that. It was over really. Another page of her life turned over.

25

As Calum walked down toward the pier in the early morning, he found a body lying on the grass beside the bridge leading to Ardtun. Assuming at first that someone had died of starvation, he went over to see who it was. As he approached, however, the sour smell of vomit and whisky told him that hunger was not the cause of death. Bending over the carcass, he realised the man was not dead at all, but almost unconscious with drink and rank with incontinence. Examining him closer, he was shocked to find that it was John, his brother-in-law. Unshaven, gaunt, his clothes covered in filth, his hair matted, he was almost unrecognisable.

Calum didn't know what to do. He couldn't carry him to his mother's house. Although she was blind, she would know from the smell what had become of him and that would upset her. He couldn't leave him by the roadside in sight of the whole village. He would have to take him on the boat. Throwing his coat over him, he hurried to the pier to fetch Dugald and Archie.

'Can you help me to carry John to the boat, boys? He's lying by the roadside in the village. It looks as though he has been drinking for weeks and is in a dreadful state. I don't think he went to the army at all.'

They returned to the village and, between them, managed to carry John to the pier. On the way, he began to recover enough to swear at them and protest that he didn't need help.

'Where are you taking me?' he drawled, his tongue rolling the words to make the speech barely comprehensible. 'Not going on your bloody boat, bastards that you are.'

They handled him carefully into the boat and climbed in themselves. He could not sit up safely so they laid him on the bottom boards and worked around him as they set sail. They were well out at sea before John sat up.

'I need to get back to the village,' he said and started to climb over the side.

Calum had to let go the tiller and catch him.

'For God's sake, John! Archie, will you keep a hold of him. He's mad with the drink.'

'Leave me alone, you bastards!' he shouted. 'Turn the boat round. I need to get back.'

'You need to sit down and behave yourself.'

'Aye, Calum. The big man. You going to make me? Come on! Make me then!'

Calum ignored him, watching the mainsail and feeling the tiller. John calmed down for a while and then tried a new approach, smiling and wheedling.

'Lend me a few shillings, Calum. I'll pay you back. I know you're a generous man, a good man. Just a few shillings.'

Again Calum chose to ignore him, knowing that the loan was for whisky, and John's mood swung back immediately to belligerence, trying to fight off Archie's hold and kicking at his legs.

'You bastard, Calum! No good bastard. Adulterer! Betrayed Catherine so you did.'

Calum asked Dugald to take the tiller. He knelt beside John and spoke very quietly and firmly.

'If you don't keep quiet and behave in a civilised manner, John, I will break your jaw so that you can neither speak nor drink. Do you hear me?'

It was the quiet sincerity and vehemence with which the words were delivered that had the desired effect. John sank into a silent sulk and eventually fell asleep. On the way back, Calum told Archie to take the tiller.

'I think we'll have some fun,' he said to Dugald. 'We'll have his trousers off. Give me a hand.'

'What if he wakes, Calum?'

'He'll never wake, maha. Come.'

They slid his trousers off and, though he groaned, he never opened his eyes.

'When we reach the pier, maha, you run up and get a skirt from old Mrs Cameron.'

When John woke, the boat was passing Kintra on its way home with a barrel full of lobsters and a creel of crabs.

'Christ Jesus! Where are my trousers?'

'You never had them on, boy.'

'What?'

'You were trouserless when we found you.'

'Good God. Where was I?'

'In the village street. We helped you to the boat.'

'I was naked in the village? With all the women there?'

'They were too famished to notice.'

'What am I to do now?'

'We'll hide your nakedness, never fear. Dugald will find you trousers.'

John was searching the horizon for solace.

'You never went to the army, then?' Calum asked.

'No. I decided it was too late, that the war was nearly over.'

'Where have you been all this time?'

'Oban mainly. I have friends there.'

'Drinking friends, no doubt. What are you going to do now?'

'I'll go home.'

'Your mother is well cared for now. She has a widow woman and her daughter to look after her. She doesn't need you as a burden.'

'She's my mother. I'll look after her.'

'No. You're coming to stay with me till you prove you can live without drink.'

'Are you going to stop me going home?'

'Yes, John, by whatever means necessary. I have more respect for your mother than you have and I will see that you don't trouble her. She thinks you are away fighting in the Crimea. She can continue to think that for a while yet.'

When they reached the pier, John sat in the boat while Calum and Archie unloaded the catch, clambering over the other boats to reach the quay. Dugald hurried up to the village. Fastening down the mainsail and lifting the rudder, Calum made sure the boat was secure.

When Dugald returned, he threw John a skirt.

'I can't wear that! A skirt, for God's sake.'

'It's all I could get,' said Dugald.

'The folk will have seen your precious possessions already, maha. Better than nothing, eh?'

'Are you able to walk now?' Calum asked John.

'Why would I not be?'

He staggered across, falling twice on the way and barking his naked shins. On dry land, he was still unsteady, as they walked towards the village. As they approached the spirit store, John became anxious and ready to run. Calum took some line from his pocket and tied John's wrist to his, knowing that he was too weak to resist.

'I need a drink,' John pleaded.

'Yes, you probably do, but you're not having one.'

The four of them walked past the stores until the Kintra men left the group to head for Ardtun.

'You'd do well on the dance floor, John,' said Dugald, grinning at Calum. 'Every man in the place would be after you for Strip the Willow'

'Go to hell.'

Calum and John carried on up the hill on the way to Shiaba.

'Can I not have one drink?' asked John,

'I will make tea for you at Shiaba or you can have cool, clear water from the burn.'

'Poisonous stuff, water. It gives you a headache.'

When they reached the top of the hill above Shiaba, John noticed the state of the houses.

'Some of the houses have lost their roofs. What's happened?'

'The Factor. He set fire to mine and burnt it down so I took the roof of the other house and rebuilt mine. Two of the others were pulled down by the sheriff's men.'

'Are you not afraid he will come back?'

'He may come back but I'm not afraid of him.'

They descended and Calum brewed some tea, John consuming most of it to quench his thirst. Calum cooked a couple of saithe and offered one to John.

'I can't,' he said. 'If I eat, I will vomit. I've not eaten for weeks. If I eat, my gut will throw it back and I can't bear the retching that goes with it. I'm afraid of it.'

'You have to eat, John.'

Calum began to feel sorry for him as he sat shivering and fidgeting by the fire, his fingers trembling and his eyes black with fear.

'Did you not eat in Oban?'

'Very little. I had no money. I stole bread and cheese out of stores.'

'How did you pay for drink then?'

'Queued for meal and then sold it. Stole things. Begged for money. Anything.'

Calum eventually persuaded him to eat, but, no sooner had he swallowed some fish than his stomach threw it up again. Calum made some porridge and told him to try again. It had the same effect. At the third attempt, he managed to keep it down and Calum fetched a pail of water to wash his face and clean his clothes. By that time, the light was fading.

'You take the bed, John. You'll sleep now. I'll sleep by the door.'

'To make sure I don't run away.'

'Yes. That's right.'

'A prisoner, then.'

'For your own good.'

He did fall asleep for a short time while Calum lay on a blanket across the door but, within half an hour, he was up, pacing around the house. Calum watched as he struck out at imagined demons with his fists, muttering and swearing at them. Eventually, he lay down again, but only for a short time and this pattern of behaviour continued until dawn. Calum rose, exhausted, shook out the blanket, stoked the fire and hung the pot for more porridge.

'You had a bad night,' Calum said.

'I dreamt I was in Crimea, but I wasn't fighting Russians. It was giant bears with claws like sabres coming at me out of the dark and I couldn't run. Terrifying.'

'It's the whisky. You'll be better tonight.'

They ate breakfast of porridge with bread and cheese.

'You should go and wash in the burn. You stink like a dead beast.'

'Thank you for the compliment.'

He rose and headed for the door. Calum followed him.

'You don't need to come with me.'

'In case you're tempted to go begging. There's no whisky in Shiaba anyway. Every grain of barley's eaten.'

He watched John strip off his shirt, noticing how thin and weak he looked. He heard him gasp as the ice-cold water splashed over his head and pale skin. He was tempted to force him take to off all his clothes and wash the filth off them, but one of the women might appear and he reckoned that John had had enough humiliation for the moment.

After he had washed, they set of for the village, Calum noticing that John struggled to climb the hill.

'I must call on my mother. Let her know I'm back.'

'You'll do nothing of the kind—not until you're well. You're only going to beg off her. You don't care whether she lives or dies. You're coming with me to get bait for the lines. It's spring tides and there'll be plenty of mussels.'

John walked beside him, dejected and silent, as they passed Assapol.

§

For three days Calum looked after his brother-in-law, taking him fishing through the day, cooking for him in the evening and sleeping at the door. On the fourth night, he had to write to Catherine.

My Dearest Catherine,
Your bother has come back to the Ross. He never joined the army. Indeed, he never went further than Oban where he took to drinking

and thieving for drink. He was in a terrible state when he came back. I found him lying by the roadside, drunk and filthy. I made sure that he did not trouble your mother. It would have been a shock to her to see him in that condition. I took him to Shiaba, fed him, made him wash and watched over him till the drink was out of his system.

Every night I slept by the door to keep him in, but I am sorry to say that this morning I woke up to find him gone. I must have slept too soundly. He is not at your mother's house and no-one in the village has seen him. I'm afraid the craving for drink has taken over and he will probably go back to Oban or somewhere else where he can steal.

My greatest worry is that he has taken a musket which was given to me by a man on Lunga whose family were sick and I helped them to Kilninian shore. He did not find the powder and ball but he could easily obtain those elsewhere. I hope that he will sell the gun for drink rather than use it.

I am sorry to be the bearer of such bad news, Catherine, but I thought that you should know.

Your mother is well looked after and thriving. She and the widow and her children are getting meal from MacQuarrie, but I give them fish and peat and candles.

I hope that your college work is going well and that you are looking after yourself and Archie. Have you had a letter from Mary yet? I worry about her in that country where the slaves have been known to rise up against the owners. Although they are right to do so, I fear for Mary in the household of slave owners.

I am doing well at the fishing and the Factor has not been near Shiaba since. I am longing for you to come back. The house is like a tomb without you.

Your loving husband always, Calum

26

'I'm truly sorry, Phoebe, to have put you to so much trouble,' Catherine said, when they met in the morning outside the classroom.

'No trouble at all. I have only written a couple of letters, that's all. It's nothing. I'm glad he has turned up and he's alive. Had he gone to Crimea, he might have been killed.'

'I can't help feeling embarrassed, though. Having returned to Bunessan, he has now disappeared again. I'm afraid he is in the claws of the demon drink.'

'A dreadful affliction, Catherine. I'm sorry. Some people do seem to escape from it. Perhaps he'll be among the fortunate ones.'

'I hope so. My worry is that he steals to pay for drink—so Calum says—and that, if he is caught stealing, he is sent to gaol or, worse, Australia.'

'There's nothing you can do. His fate is in his own hands. Come, we must go in and join the gentlemen. Oh, I almost forgot. I have a letter for Archie to take to my brother in Tradeston. I've spoken to Torquil and he's expecting Archie, but he will need to take the letter to the office. It's addressed to Mr Strachan.'

'Thank you, Phoebe. You're very kind.'

'Nonsense. Anything to help. Let's make an entrance. Sweep in talking loudly about the gorgeous Italian tenor in the opera. I know we weren't there but that'll impress them.'

§

After the class, Charles hurried over to them.

'Ladies, ladies. I have a proposal.'

'To us both?' asked Phoebe.

'Not that kind of proposal. How would you like to come to the opera with me? I can get tickets and I would be delighted to take you.'

Both women stared at each other, their mouths open but stunned into silence.

'I have never been to an opera,' Phoebe said eventually, 'I thought it was all about fat ladies screeching and ageing gentlemen pretending to be young lovers—so my brother tells me.'

'No, no. My mother went on the first night and she says that the costumes are magnificent, the set is amazing and the singing moved her to tears. You must come. You would enjoy it.'

'I've seen the ladies arriving at the theatre, descending from their carriages as their footmen hand them down, all dressed in the latest French fashion with colossal crinolines and lofty hats. I would sooner be on a horse at a fox hunt.'

'They are not all like that. Mama certainly isn't. Those will be the ones in private boxes—the elite.'

'Still, I think I would feel out of place.'

'Nonsense, Phoebe. You looked absolutely ravishing at the entrance exam.'

He blushed, realising what he had just said.

'You two go,' said Catherine. 'You would enjoy it, Phoebe.'

'Certainly not. Both of us or neither.'

'Please come,' said Charles. 'It is a fascinating story, apart from the music, all about the Romans and a Druid rebellion.'

Catherine, hearing mention of the Romans, thought of Eoin. He would approve of her learning more about his favourite people, even if it was in the company of Charles. He might even envy her attendance at such an event.

'What do you think, Catherine?' asked Phoebe. 'Should we condescend to be seen with this disreputable youth?'

She was tempted. It was a unique opportunity to experience something that she would never see again, something that she would always remember.

'Yes, let's. Thank you, Charles.'

Beaming, he took their hands.

'I'm so pleased. You will never regret it.'

§

That night she put on her green dress and took a cab to the Theatre Royal in Dunlop Street. Charles and Phoebe were waiting on the steps, Charles very smart in a grey frock coat, waistcoat and smartly tailored trousers and Phoebe, refusing to follow fashion, in a simple silk skirt and bodice with wide sleeves. Catherine wondered if Phoebe had deliberately chosen her modest costume to avoid shaming her.

Charles took them to seats in the gallery where he insisted on sitting between them.

Catherine was astonished by the auditorium, the dress boxes decorated with scenes from Shakespeare and Scott and magnificent chandeliers suspended from the ceiling. She had never seen such luxury. Charles told her that the opera was called 'Norma' and that it would be sung in Italian and described the plot.

She was startled when the orchestra started to play. The sound seemed to surround her, touching her face, vibrating in her head. It was alive, exciting. She gasped as the curtains opened to reveal the woodland grove, with druids and priestesses circling around the stage, and when Norma sang her first aria, reaching notes which Catherine had never heard from a human voice, its beauty flooded her whole being and swelled until she felt she would burst with ecstasy, a rapture which she didn't believe could exist. It was like floating in a sea of sound. The chief druid possessed a bass which seemed to shake the whole theatre, powerful like thunder in the hills. The experience was so overwhelming that she was relieved when the intervals came.

The final scene, when Norma leaves her children with her father and commits herself to the funeral pyre with her lover, was almost too much for Catherine as she sat with tears streaming down her cheeks. When the house lights were turned on and Charles turned to speak to her, she was embarrassed by her snivelling and tried to hide it with her handkerchief. Her discomfort was eased somewhat when she saw that he had been weeping.

'Wonderful, wasn't it?' he asked. 'Are you glad you came?'

'I'll remember it for the rest of my life. I will write it down when I reach home in case my memory fails me.. Who are the singers? Are they Italian?'

'Yes. Italian. The chief druid was Augostino Susini and his daughter Norma was Giulia Grisi. I'm not sure of the others. The Roman Consul, I think, was Giovanni Mario. All difficult names to remember. I will find a copy of the cast for you.'

When they emerged into the street with the crowd, it was dark but with a dim light cast by the gas streetlights. At the end of the street a row of carriages waited for the fashionable ladies.

'Thank you, Charles,' said Phoebe. 'That was my first opera. From now on I will attend every one staged here. It was wonderful. I'm sure Papa would regard it as frivolous and pretentious but I will take Mama next time. I'm sure she would love it.'

Charles paid for a cab to take them home and joined a group of his friends.

§

Catherine called on Lamont a few weeks later, and was startled when Kathleen opened the door, having prepared herself to meet Lamont.

'Catherine, please come in.'

Her welcome was so warm and genuine that Catherine relaxed and followed her into the living room, where Lamont and the boys were grouped around the table. Hector smiled but, this time, did not rush to greet her. Lamont rose immediately, clearly delighted to see her.

'What a surprise! It's so good to see you again. Please sit down,' he said, showing her to the armchair by the fire, 'Would you care for some tea?'

'No, thank you all the same. I was passing and I thought I should call.'

'Of course. You're always welcome here.'

As she sat, Kathleen took her place beside Hector and Lamont turned his chair to speak to her.

'How are the studies?'

'Doing well, even Mathematics.'

'Splendid. I hope you're giving yourself some leisure time. It is most important to balance your studying with some healthy diversions.'

'I went to the opera. I don't know if that's a healthy diversion.'

'The opera? Really? Which opera?'

'Norma in the Theatre Royal.'

'Ah yes. Norma. The druids against the Romans. A fanciful story. The real drama is far more impressive. The rebellion of princess Boudicca and the Iceni against Suetonius. It's all there in Tacitus and Cassius Dio. There's a wonderful description of the warrior princess in Dio of a tall woman with long, tawny hair hanging down to her waist, a deep, harsh voice and piercing glare—not a woman I would care to meet on a dark night. Sorry. My apologies. I do get carried away at times.'

'Don't apologise. That's a wonderful description. I must read about her.'

'How is Archie? I have not seen him.'

'He's doing well at school now and is going to work at weekends with McOnie and Mirrlees in Tradeston.'

'A great opportunity. I hope he doesn't find it too taxing—along with his schoolwork.'

'I will watch for that. He is very determined to become an engineer.'

'Good to be planning his future. And what of yours? I know you were keen to return to the Ross of Mull. Are there vacancies there?'

'I have asked Calum to watch for one, but, so far, he has not found a position.'

'Remember, if you need a reference, Catherine, I would be delighted to provide you with one.'

'Thank you, Eoin. You're very kind. I may ask you for that at some point. Now, I have taken up enough of your time and I must go home to Archie.'

He rose as she did and accompanied her to the door.

'Please tell Archie to call,' he said on the doorstep. 'Hector does miss him.'

'I will, of course. I'm glad you have found someone to help, Eoin. Kathleen seems a warm, gentle and loving person. I'm sure she will look after you and the boys.'

'Yes. I hope she'll be happy here. I don't want to lose contact with you, Catherine. You will continue to call, won't you.?'

'I will and I will send Archie to see you too.'

As she walked away, she realised that she was relieved. Lamont's obsession with the Classics might have come between them. Although she still admired his intellect and independence of mind, his unwitting display of his knowledge might become tedious. The more she learnt for herself, the less she was in awe of his erudition.

§

When she reached home, Archie was sitting at the table, writing in an exercise book.

'I was worried about you, Mother. Where have you been?'

'I called at Mr Lamont's. He has a new servant living with him—a girl Kathleen.'

'Is she going to be his wife?'

'I don't know. The boys seem to like her. Mr Lamont was asking after you, worried that working at McOnie's might interfere with your schoolwork. He's keen for you to call, partly to see Hector and partly to help you with your Mathematics.'

'I don't need help. Mr Stark would like you to call.'

'Why? Have you done something wrong at work?'

'No. I don't know what he wants. Maybe he's going to offer you work in the office.'

'I doubt it. Besides, I've too much college work to see to.'

'You're always working in the evening. Never just sit and blether.'

'I'm sorry, Archie. There's just so much to do.'

'There's a letter here. I think it's from Mary. Maybe you'll have time to read that.'

Dear Mother,
I have arrived safely in Jamaica after a long voyage across the Atlantic. We were becalmed shortly after we passed Bermuda and were very jealous of a steamship which cruised past us. While we were there a whale and her calf passed close under the bow and we rushed forward to watch them. How can whalers kill these magnificent creatures? We often saw dolphins as they followed the ship. They are so playful and kept the children amused.

When we reached Jamaica, Kingston was full of ships of all kinds—steamships, tall sailing ships, small tenders, barges—it was quite a sight with the palm trees and white sand on the edge of the sea. Many negro women work on the wharves, carrying coal, driving donkeys, carting stone for the roads. In the town, the colours were almost blinding. There were soldiers in red coats, hundreds of negroes in white cotton, women in light printed dresses with wide hats and parasols. There are some fine buildings near the quay, but the houses are mainly made of wood and are only two storeys high with shingle roof and are painted white. There is even a railway here, though it only runs to Spanish Town, fourteen miles away.

As we drove out of Kingston we saw the huts of the negroes, which are made of wattle and thatched. We passed many of the negroes carrying bananas on their heads and saw some working on their small patches of land. They were barefoot and wearing straw hats. I do not know yet if their living is as hard as ours.

The gateway to our plantation is like those of our grandest estates in Scotland with wrought iron and lamps. The house, though made of clapboard, is so big I am likely to get lost in it. It has a veranda along the front which looks over the valley below to the distant hills. From my bedroom I can see the sugar fields and a windmill. There are lots of negro servants in the house—men and women—who are very kind and helpful. The nearest town is Port Antonio which I have not visited yet. I'm told that there is no Free Church there but there is Baptist one and a Wesleyan church.

The children—two boys and a girl—are very well behaved and easy to manage. They seem to like me which is a great help. We have not settled into a routine yet but I'm sure that will come with time. This is only my second night. I am trying to get used to the heat and finding it very difficult to sleep.

I hope Archie is attending to his studies and also helping you with cooking. I will write to father later and again to you with a full description of the island and my duties here.

Have you heard from Sine and Duncan? I would like to write to them but have no address.

I hope you are managing with your studies. I think you are very brave and I really admire you for taking on the training. I miss you so much.

Your loving daughter, Mary.

27

'There is little chance of Catherine being offered a teaching position here as long as John Campbell is the Factor. You should know that, Calum,' MacQuarrie said.

'But he is not on the Board.'

'He doesn't need to be. He has as much influence on the others as if he were there. His word is law.'

'It's not right.'

'No, but that's how it is.'

'What can I do?'

'Nothing probably. You've defied him so often I doubt if he would listen to reason. If you were to leave Shiaba, it might help.'

'Never.'

'There you are then. Stubborn to the end. Even if it means denying Catherine a position.'

'I could talk to him.'

'That would not be wise, I think. He might set the dogs on you or take a whip across your face. I'm not sure he has the capacity to forgive. He'll have heard about the roof.'

'How do you know about that?'

'It's all round the Ross. Calum MacGillivray's act of defiance. He'll know.'

'I will go and see him.'

'Be very careful, then. Your temper has betrayed you in the past and he can be an intemperate man. An unlikely combination for compromise.'

Calum left him yoking his horse for the cart and walked down to the pier. Dugald and Archie had just finished baiting the lines and were carrying them to the boat.

'I hear you have defied the Factor,' Dugald said with a smile.

'Good God! Does everyone know?'

'Good news travels fastest. I'm glad someone stands up to the tyrant. They're all too frightened.'

'If we all stood together, all of us, all the crofters, cottars, we might shake him.'

'That'll never happen. They would sooner leave and sail to Canada than challenge him. They believe he can destroy them, that he's got the power of the Duke and the police behind him. He's like God Almighty.'

'He's only a man and he'll go the same way as the rest of us.'

'Amen. Before we sail, I have to tell you that we'll be leaving soon.'

'What?'

'I told you it might happen. We are leaving within the month.'

'For Australia?'

'Yes. On the other side of the world. God knows what will become of us there, but it can't be any worse.'

'Do I not pay you enough?'

'It's not that. Campbell took all our stock to pay our arrears. We have paid no rent since the potatoes failed. We have nothing, no seed, no stock, no peats. Nothing. You saved us from starvation, but it is no life. Our father is set on going.'

'I'll have to find someone else then.'

'You shouldn't have much difficulty. There are scores of starving men on the Ross.'

They boarded the boat and hoisted sail.

'We'll try west of Iona,' Calum said, 'The Reidh Eilean rocks. There's deep water on the far side.'

It proved to be a profitable move, for they filled the barrels with cod and haddock. Besides, it was a pleasant day's fishing with a soft west wind from Tiree rippling the sea and the sun warming their backs.

At the end of the day, each of the Kintra men carried away a string of fish.

'I'll be sorry to lose you,' Calum said to Dugald. 'A good hand like you will be hard to replace.'

'You'll manage, a charaid. You will.'

§

When Calum reached home that night, he was shocked to find two constables from Tobermory waiting for him. At first, he was tempted to turn around and head back to sea, fearing that he was to be arrested, but then decided that he might as well face the men.

'You are Calum MacGillivray?' the tall one with a thick black beard asked.

'I am.'

'We have bad news for you, I'm afraid. John MacPhail has been found dead. I'm told he's your wife's brother. We didn't want to upset his blind mother—at least until his body has been identified—so we were advised to ask you.'

'Did he take his own life?'

Calum imagined John lying with the top of his head blown off by shot from the gun.

'No. He died of fever along with the family at Arinasliseig, the solitary house across from the marketplace at Torness. You'll have seen it, all on its own with no neighbours. It seems that he found the whole family sick and tended to their needs, carrying water and making gruel, but then caught the fever himself. One of them was still alive when we reached the place and was able to speak but she passed away too. We think it is MacPhail because there was a letter addressed to his mother in his pocket. We would like you to come with us to be sure it is him. Someone will need to take the remains back to this parish anyway.'

'I have a fishing boat, creels to lift and crew to pay.'

'We don't want to deliver the remains to his mother for identification.'

'I don't have much choice then.'

'We have a trap to take us to Torness, if you could meet us at the inn here first thing in the morning.'

'I'll be there.'

Calum, wondering whether John had sold the gun, watched them walk away. Surely they would have mentioned it, had it been in the house. He would have to retrieve it, if it was there.

§

The following morning, he met the constables at the inn, having sent Dugald to lift the creels at Erraid, and rode on the back of the trap as they headed east towards Pennyghael. Fortunately, it was a fine day and, as he had his back to them, he could travel in peace without having to talk. He sat wondering about John—whether it was possible for him to have looked after the family at Arinasliseig. It was out of character for him to be so selfless and yet, in the end, perhaps he had redeemed himself. It was possible and it would be a comfort to Catherine and his mother to know that his better nature had overcome his craving. Maybe he should tell them the better story, even if it were false. That would be kinder.

As they approached the inn at Kinloch, Calum remembered the place where he had first seen Peggy. As they passed it, he saw that there were still several crude shelters like hers on the land, with a plume of smoke rising from one of them. Evicted families no doubt. When they reached the inn, there was a group standing by the roadside, people in such a wretched condition that he felt ashamed of his health. When the constables stopped to go into the inn, the women crowded round them, begging and plucking at their sleeves. The constables had to push them away roughly in order to proceed. Calum, moved close to tears by their condition, walked over to the oldest of the men and quietly handed him the few shillings he had in his pocket. These were proud people, driven by starvation to beg from strangers, their dignity cast aside, their clothes tattered and soiled, their hope for the future bleak.

'God bless you,' the old man said.

'You're living in the tents?'

'Driven off our land and living like frogs, half-in and half-out of the water in the bogland there. We had good homes till MacArthur turned us out. He wanted sheep not people on Ardmeanach. We have nothing now, nothing.'

'It is the same with us. The Duke wants to clear us out, sweep us away, to make room for a sheep farmer. What are you going to do? You can't live over there forever.'

'God alone knows. We have not the means to go anywhere. The misery eats away at our faith. We pray for deliverance like the children of Israel but our prayers are not answered. Still, we try to keep hold of our faith. It's all we have.'

The constables emerged from the inn, wiping their lips on their sleeves, and Calum resumed his place on the trap. As they climbed into Glen More, with the steep sides of Cruach Choireadail on the north side and the black volcanic slabs of Ben Buie on the south, dark clouds passed over the sun and a chill breeze followed their shadow. At the top of the glen, however, it cleared again to reveal the three lochs far below the road, glittering in the bright light.

'We'll go down to Ishriff, down to the loch,' the bearded one said. 'It will be easier to cross the river there.'

They drove down; the constable unhitched the trap and, taking the pony for a drink in the burn, tied it to a rail and left it with a nose-bag of oats. It was a long walk to the remote cottage and the sun was high in the sky by the time they reached it.

'All the other remains should have been taken away by now,' the small man said. 'Only one—the one we think is your brother-in-law—is left. I must warn you that it is in an advanced state of decomposition.'

He seemed to take pleasure in this announcement.

He pushed the door open, beckoning Calum to go in. It was almost dark inside, the small windows having been covered with sacking, and the place smelt of rotting flesh. Calum instinctively covered his nose and mouth. Light from the door fell on John, his body propped against the bare stone wall. The flesh on his face had melted away, leaving only the dry skin clinging like parchment to his skull. The hand lying by his thigh on the floor had been chewed by rats and maggots crawled round his teeth. Still, someone had taken the trouble to close his eyes.

'It's John right enough,' Calum said, looking around the walls for the gun. 'Did he not have a gun, a musket?'

'It was his, was it? It was taken to Tobermory.'

'It was mine. He stole it from me.'

'Can you prove it was yours?'

'The man who lived on Lunga gave it to me. I helped to move him and his family to Kilninian.'

'Get him to write an affidavit declaring it is yours and you can collect it at the police house.'

'You'll keep it for me?'

'If it hasn't been claimed already, we will.'

'Please do. Can you help me move the body to the road end at Ishriff? I will hire a cart to collect it.'

'It's a long way to carry a corpse.'

'On the door. I'll wrench the door off its hinges and I'll lift him myself. There'll be little weight in him anyway.'

'Fair enough, as long as you lay him on the door and we don't have to touch him.'

Lifting the rotting carcass onto the door was a revolting task, but Calum was determined to give John a decent burial in Kilvickeon.

They carried him back to Ishriff and laid him in the barn as the sun dipped below the hills of Glen More.

'We can't take you back to Bunessan, I'm afraid,' said the bearded one.

'I'll walk. There might be a trap or a carriage on the road. Remember to keep my gun.'

'We will. It seems very precious to you. What is it for? I hope it's not for poaching.'

'To kill rabbits. The place is over-run with them.'

The constable smiled at him.

'Fair enough, my friend. See that you confine it to rabbits.'

They hitched up the pony and rattled away up the road. He watched it disappear over the hill as he set off walking towards Bunessan, not relishing the prospect of the long trail through the glen. By good fortune, he was given a lift on a trap to Pennyghael with a servant from Carsaig returning home, having delivered his MacLaine master to the ferry at Grasspoint. Yet it was well after midnight by the time he reached Shiaba.

§

When Calum went to tell Mima of John's death, he was relieved to see Tina there. The old lady remained silent for some time after she heard the news. Tina put her arms around her, but she didn't weep or show any signs of grief or shock.

'How did he die?' she asked eventually.

'Caring for others,' Calum answered. 'The house across from Torness in the glen. The family had fever and he looked after them till he got the fever too. It was the fever that killed him.'

'A good boy. He was always a good boy. He'll be in a better place now. You will see to the funeral for me, Calum?'

'I will.'

'And tell Catherine.'

'I'll go to Glasgow and tell her.'

'Thank you.'

It was the first time she had been civil to him since he married Catherine.

§

It was a small funeral indeed—Calum, the Minister, Dugald and Archie. As the four of them stood around the grave, Calum remembered the last time he had been there with Peggy and the censure in the eyes of the Shiaba people as he walked home with her. He regretted that now, his blind infatuation with her. When the minister had finished his blessing, he and the Kintra men shovelled the loose earth back into the grave, Calum remembering that he had to tell them that he was leaving for Glasgow the following day.

28

Calum took the steamship to Glasgow, arriving in the late afternoon. He was planning to walk up to the college to meet Catherine there, but then realised that he had no idea where it was, so had to head for the flat in the Gorbals. He was glad to leave the ship, the constant drone and vibration of the engines annoying him after the silence of his own boat. As he walked up the Broomielaw and over the bridge, he rehearsed what he was going to say to Catherine, trying to choose words that would soften the blow.

The flat was empty when he arrived. He stopped at the door, astonished by the transformation. The walls had been whitewashed, the roof timbers creosoted, the floors scrubbed and there were bright printed curtains on the window. The ashes had been emptied and the fire set for lighting in the grate. Everything was clean and in good order. Finding the matches on the table, he set light to the fire. There was clean water in the pot so he hung it over the coals and sat down to wait.

There were several books on the table, and he picked up the one which appeared to be the most frequently used and was surprised to find that it was written in Gaelic. Opening it, he saw a dedication to "To Catherine, hoping that this proves to be an inspiration, With warmest regards, Eoin." The words stirred the jealousy he had felt on his first visit and he slammed it shut, imagining, for a moment, her in the arms of the other man. The sensation subsided, though, as he recalled his own failings and the purpose of his visit. There was a folder beside the books which he opened and was amazed by what he found. Unfinished drawings of butterflies with hand-written descriptions of their names and origins. He leafed through them, each one seemingly more striking than the one before it. They must be hers and yet he could not believe that she possessed such a talent or that, if she had, she had never revealed it to him. He found a sense of resentment clouding his first admiration. Why had she never shared this with him? Had she shown it to Lamont or her fellow students?

He had one in his hand when she opened the door. She was so shocked, she dropped her case and lifted her hands to her cheeks. Calum noticed that she was neatly dressed in a new black skirt and tight bodice with a printed patterned shawl.

'What are you doing here?' she gasped,

'That's not a very friendly welcome.'

Running over to him, she threw her arms around him.

'I'm sorry. You took me by surprise.'

He held her against him and looked into her eyes, seeing only true pleasure.

'There was no time to write and I wanted to tell you myself.'

'Tell me what? Mother is sick, is she?'

'No. It's not your mother. I'm afraid it's John.'

'He's been drinking again.'

'No. I'm afraid he's dead, Catherine.'

She stepped away from him, an expression of disbelief on her face.

'How can he be dead? He's not been sick, has he?'

'He was in a house in the glen where the family had fever. He cared for them but they all died and he caught the fever too.'

She sat at the table with tears in her eyes.

'He died of the fever? How did you hear? Are you sure it's him?'

'The constables came for me and took me to the house. I brought him home to be buried.'

'There was a funeral?'

'Yes. He's buried in Kilvickeon.'

'Why didn't you tell me? I should have been there.'

He sat beside her, taking her hands in his.

'There was no time. They were all dead for days in the house before they were found. I had to bury him quickly.'

'Why?'

'Because of the state he was in,'

'Oh God. That's awful. How is Mother? I should go to her.'

'The widow MacLean is with her. She's bearing it well. I think she was half expecting it, with him going to the army. There's no need for you to go. Truly. She's fine.'

'Who was with him? Was he alone?'

'No. He was with the others.'

'Thank God for that. Poor Johnnie.'

'He was looking after the others.'

'He would. He was so kind. Kind to everyone but himself.'

'He'll be at peace now.'

They heard someone running up the stairs and Archie burst in, breathless and grinning until he sensed the atmosphere in the room.

'What's wrong? Why are you here, Father?'

'Your Uncle John has passed away.'

'Was he shot? Shot by the Russians?'

'No. He never went to the army. He died of the fever on Mull.'

'That's horrible. Poor Uncle John. Sarah downstairs nearly died too. I've got the prize for mathematics.'

Calum smiled. Archie had brought them back to the present, hauled them out of the irreversible past.

'Well done, alaochain! Well done.'

Calum placed his hands on Archie's shoulders.

'Yes. Congratulations,' Catherine said, trying to muster some enthusiasm. 'Come and give me a hug.'

Archie came beside her.

'I must go and tell Mr Lamont. He'll be pleased,' he said.

Calum frowned and turned away.

'Not tonight, Archie,' Catherine said. 'Mr Lamont has been helping him with his schoolwork, Calum, and obviously it has proved to be worthwhile.'

'I'm sure it has. Is there food in the house?'

'There's a little butcher meat by the window and meal in the bin.'

'Archie,' said Calum, handing him some shillings. 'Go to the big butcher by the river and get a steak pie. I saw them in the window.'

'A steak pie!'

'Yes. Hurry up before he closes.'

Archie left and a silence moved into the space. Calum regretted his sharp comment on Lamont, knowing that he should have complete faith in Catherine's fidelity. That spark of jealousy was unnecessary, but he still resented Lamont's interference with his son.

'There is nothing between Mr Lamont and myself,' Catherine said. 'Nothing but friendship. I saw your face when Archie mentioned the name.'

'I know. I know. You are the one person in all the world that I trust. It is stupid.'

He took her face in his hands and kissed her brow tenderly.

'He has been good to Archie, Calum. The Mathematics prize is probably due to him. I was worried that the job at McOnie's might be bad for his schoolwork, but obviously it hasn't been affected. Oh. I almost forgot. I'm supposed to call at the foundry. Stark, Phoebe's brother, has asked to see me. Archie swears that he has done nothing wrong so I don't know why he would want to see me.'

'I'll go, if you like.'

'Would you? That would be a relief.'

'Yes, I'll go. Stark, did you say? What does he do there?'

'Torquil Stark, one of the engineers. It was through him that Archie was given the work.'

'Is it far?'

'No. Along to Scotland Street. The office is on the corner of West Street.'

'I'll go in the morning. I have to go back the next day, though.'

'So soon. Can you not stay a while? It's so long since I've seen you.'

'Believe me, I would give anything to stay, but the Kintra men, my crew, are leaving for Australia. I can't leave the boat lying at the pier. There are men there that I don't trust. Campbell would welcome a chance to see my boat meet with an accident. Campbell, by the way, will oppose your appointment as a teacher in the Ross.'

'Good God! Is he so mean?'

'Don't worry. I'll find a way of dealing with him.'

'Nothing stupid, I hope.'

'No. Nothing stupid.'

They heard Archie running up the stairs and Calum squeezed her hand and sat back as Archie presented them with an enormous steak pie, still hot from the oven.

§

The following morning; after Catherine left for college and Archie for school, Calum walked over to the engineering works and asked at the office for Mr Stark.

'He's over in the pattern shop at the moment. If you don't mind waiting, I'll send a boy for him. Who shall I say is calling?' The woman was neatly dressed, a cairngorm brooch on the neck of her white blouse.

'Calum MacGillivray, Archie's father.'

'Ah yes. Young Archie. Clever boy.'

Calum smiled and sat on the bench outside the office. He didn't have to wait long. Stark swung open the door and hurried across with his hand extended.

'Mr MacGillivray. I'm Torquil Stark. I'm so glad you could come. Let's go into the back office—quieter there.'

They passed through the main office where several women were working on orders.

'Please sit down, I wanted to talk to you about Archie. A clever boy, Mr MacGillivray, and a keen worker. The problem is that he is only here at weekends. I would really like to take him on full time. Now, I know that his mother is training to be a teacher and naturally would oppose such an arrangement, but my contention is that he will learn far more on the shop floor than in school. My best engineer left school at twelve '

'His mother would not be happy.'

'I know. I know. Bur his maths are already good enough and he's desperate to learn. Listen, why don't I take you round the works so that you can see what we do?'

'Yes. That would be very helpful.'

Stark, a sturdy young man with sleeves rolled up to expose his muscular arms, led the way across the coal yard where men were loading a roaring furnace from their barrows.

'Much of our trade,' he shouted, 'is with the West Indies. This year we sent off our largest order—four steam engines, five sugar mills, twelve steam boilers and nine steam clarifiers with all the mountings—and we have another order pending.'

'To slave plantations?'

'Yes. The more efficient we can make their production, the less need for the labour of their former slaves.'

As they approached the huge foundry, the noise became deafening, rapid explosions as if a row of cannon was firing one after another.

'It's a steam hammer,' Stark shouted again, 'punching holes in plate.'

The crack of the hammer echoed around the iron roof of the vast shed, adding to the roar of the plate furnaces and steam engines. The place smelt of molten iron, coal and steam and its gloom was lit by the glare of furnaces and ovens. He could taste the smoke and dust in the back of his throat and feel the heat of white-hot metal on his face and wondered why anyone would want to work there.

'We'll go through to the workshop. Quieter there.'

Calum followed Stark through to an extension where there were several lathes and a small forge. If it was quieter there, he barely noticed it.

'This is where Archie works. He's learning to use a lathe and stocks and dies.'

They crossed to one of the lathes and watched one of the men turning a piece of iron. Calum was fascinated by the way the hard metal peeled off like apple-skin, leaving the iron shining and smooth. He imagined Archie standing over the lathe, his brow creased in concentration. A different life altogether. Perhaps, in spite of the noise and dirt, it would be better, more secure and with a sounder future, than anything the Ross could offer.

'This way now.'

He led Calum upstairs to the holding loft and through to the drawing office, where he could be heard.

'This is where Archie would spend much of his time later on. Given his ability with figures, he could be one of our best designers.

As I said, I would like to see him here all the time. He has great potential as an engineer. What do you think?'

'It's not up to me really. I can see the advantage of working here but one day he might regret leaving school, not finishing his education. I can't answer for him. I'll speak to his mother. It's in her hands really.'

'It's a great opportunity. This industry is growing year by year. As an engineer, he could travel anywhere in the world—Russia, America, the West Indies.'

'I can see that. I'll ask his mother and let you know.'

'Good. I'll show you the way out.'

As he walked back to the flat, Calum thought about the proposal. He had hoped that his son would join him on the boat and that one day he would own several boats. It was a trade that he had come to enjoy—out on the sea in clean air with the sun on your back. In charge of your own day. No overseer to tell you what to do. True, there were storms, freezing east winds, sodden clothes as the rain ran down your neck, hands so cold you couldn't feel them, days when creels came up empty and lines with few fish, but there were others when the sea glittered in the sunlight and their catch filled the barrels. Maybe it was not for Archie, though. He wanted to be an engineer. That's what he said. Maybe he should be allowed to try it. That conclusion, however, would lead to an argument with Catherine, a possibility which he wanted to avoid. He wasn't sure what to do.

29

'Your brother must have been very persuasive, Phoebe,' Catherine said as they waited in the corridor outside the classroom.

'In what way?'

'He convinced Calum that Archie should leave school and work full time.'

'I can imagine. He couldn't wait to leave the academy himself. Hated school.'

'Calum tried to be fair, to look at both sides of the argument—for my sake, I think—but I could tell that he had been persuaded.'

'Are you happy about it?'

'No. Not really, but it may prove to be the best choice. I don't want Archie to be standing in the queues for meal in Bunessan, starving because the crops have failed and waiting for the Factor to pull the roof down on his head.'

'Engineers can be paid off too.'

'Not according to your brother. The world's your oyster as an engineer—as he sees it. Russia, America, the West Indies he mentioned.'

'I think that's what he would like to do. Have you seen Charles?'

'No. I think of him every time I pick up my briefcase.'

'Strange. I haven't seen him since the opera. I hope nothing has happened to him.'

'I expect, in the tradition of all aspiring artists, he has fallen in love with his art.'

'That would be in character. Oh God. Here come the gentlemen. Let's go in before they reach us.'

§

That afternoon, they had just stepped out into the sunlight when Charles hurried across the road to meet them, dressed in a white shirt with ballet sleeves which filled like sails as he walked.

'Ladies, ladies! I've timed it perfectly—just as you finished class. I'm going to take you for tea in the Tontine Coffee rooms. Best in town. No excuses. Come.'

He squeezed into the middle between them, taking each of them by an arm, led them down the Trongate.

'How are you, Charles? Are you well?' Phoebe asked as they sat down.

'Never better. I'm enjoying every minute of it.'

Catherine had passed the hotel several times, never thinking of entering the grand arcade along the front, deterred by the elaborately decorated carriages parked outside and the ladies dressed like Christmas trees in outsized bustles—wives of the city's merchants.

Charles led them through one of the ten arches into the carpeted precincts and on into the renowned coffee rooms.

Catherine felt slightly out of place, as most of the ladies were wearing hats, some waving feathers of exotic birds which she had seen in the museum. A waitress came across, her white apron and cap as perfectly ironed as the tablecloths, and her black dress spotless. Charles ordered tea and cakes. Catherine watched as the waitress glided away under an arch which reminded her of paintings of the Alhambra in Spain. Her mind wandered off to think of Mary, remembering how near death she had been, her life flooding away in the flux and the sweat of fever. Looking around the room, with its opulence and comfort, she remembered the agony of hunger and reminded herself that there were people in the Ross still suffering from starvation and deprivation.

'What are you thinking of, Catherine?' asked Charles. 'You look very gloomy.'

'Sorry. I was thinking of the poor people at home, the wretched of the parish.'

'You still want to go back? Return to all that.'

'Yes. I want to go back. I want to do what I can to make life better for the children at home. If I can help a child to read and write and, through that, gain confidence, learn to think for themselves and to care for others, then I will be happy. If I can give them hope instead of despair, maybe they will find a way out of poverty and oppression.'

'Well spoken, Catherine MacGillivray! Worthy sentiments.'

'It seems, though, that I will not be allowed to put them into practice in the Ross.'

'What? Who can stop you?'

'The Duke's Factor. Because Calum has defied him, he will oppose any application I might make for positions in his demesne.'

'Surely not. He is but one man. There must be others.'

'All in his pocket or afraid of him.'

The waitress arrived with a tray full of delicate cups and saucers, a silver teapot, a sugar bowl, side plates, milk jug, three iced cakes and serviettes.

'See,' said Charles. 'I told you they had the finest cakes in the city.'

The waitress laid out the cups and saucers and poured the tea.

'The best Indian tea too,' he added, smiling seductively at the waitress, who blushed and pretended to ignore him.

'Can't you do anything about this dreadful man, Charles?' Phoebe asked. 'I know you have friends in the aristocracy.'

Charles didn't answer immediately, savouring his cake with his eyes closed and his head back.

'This is so good,' he said eventually, 'I'm tempted to ask for another. Do help yourselves, ladies. I will speak to Johnnie again, explain your predicament, Catherine. Nothing will happen immediately, though. It will depend on Johnnie meeting the Duke. Even then, nothing is guaranteed but I'll do everything I can. I promise. How is your baking going, Phoebe? I'm sure the lady of the house here could reveal her secrets, if you asked.'

'And I'm sure she would do nothing of the kind.'

Charles emptied three spoonfuls of sugar into his tea.

'Think of the poor slaves needed to produce that,' Phoebe said.

'I try not to. They're emancipated anyway.'

'But still slaves in all but name.'

'Let's not spoil the afternoon with something serious.'

'You're right. Let's invent some scandal about the tutors. Send a rumour circulating that the ancient Latin tutor is having an affair with young sewing teacher—highly unlikely, I know, given that harridan of a wife of his, but it could be fun.'

'Unimaginable, I would have thought,' said Charles. 'He's a bit of an ascetic, like John the Baptist or that Syrian chap—what's his name?—Simeon.'

'Tell us about your college, Charles,' said Catherine. 'I know you have lady students. Surely some of them are attractive. You must have found a paramour by now.'

'Catherine! I only have eyes for you,' he replied with an exaggerated flourish of his hand over his brow.

'And what about me?' Phoebe asked.

'Ah, Phoebe. The Goddess, the Titan, the daughter of the sun. The Untouchable. Far beyond my reach. Grandmother of Hecate, the witch.'

'Am I so terrifying?'

'You would lure me into the Underworld like Orpheus, never to be seen again.'

'I asked you about college, Charles,' Catherine broke in.

'Ah yes. College. Dull, Catherine. Design. Design for curtains, carpets, wallpaper and so on. Mundane. No naked ladies, no landscapes. Dull.'

'You tried to persuade me to go.'

'Yes. I know. You would have been stifled. Still, I'm learning about design and actually I must admit it is quite interesting. Now, I'm afraid I must leave you. I'm taking a most inspiring lady to the theatre.'

'A fellow student?'

'Mama. My wonderful Mama. I will see to the tea. Do feel free to stay, ladies.'

He dabbed his lips with his serviette and rose to leave.

'No, no We'll come with you, won't we, Phoebe?'

Phoebe, taken by surprise, agreed.

As they reached the foyer, Catherine stopped suddenly to stare at a black gentleman coming down the wide staircase.

'What is it, Catherine?' asked Phoebe. 'Is something wrong?'

'I know that man.'

'What man?'

'The gentleman on the stair.'

'But he's a negro. How can you know him?'

'I do. Excuse me. I must speak with him.'

She left her friends standing in the foyer and crossed to intercept the African as he descended. He was not, as before, dressed as a servant but as a gentleman in a frock coat and trousers.

'Jacob,' she said, 'do you remember me?'

He halted and, for a moment, Catherine thought he had forgotten, but then a broad smile of recognition lit his face.

'Of course, ma'am. The lady with the sick daughter. I remember. Mary. How is she?'

'Thanks to you, she recovered and is now a handsome young woman.'

'I'm so pleased. She was very sick. I thought she might not live.'

'Come, Jacob, you must meet my friends.'

She led him back across the foyer.

'Phoebe, this is my friend, Jacob. Jacob, this is Miss Stark.'

He bowed gracefully and she returned the gesture.

'Charles, this is Jacob. Jacob, Mr MacLaine.'

Charles held out his hand enthusiastically.

'I've never had the pleasure of meeting a negro.'

'I hope I do not disappoint you, sir,' replied Jacob with a smile.

'Of course not. Any friend of Catherine's will be a friend of mine.'

'Jacob saved Mary's life,' Catherine said. 'With a medicament which healed her almost immediately. It was remarkable. I'm very sorry she's not here to thank you herself, Jacob. She is in Jamaica.'

'Jamaica?' Jacob said. 'We are bound for Jamaica tomorrow.'

'How extraordinary! You must meet with her. Please. She is with Mr and Mrs Buchanan on Benmore estate.'

'I know it well. It is on the other side of the island from Mr Baillie—Portland, I think—but I will make every effort to visit and to tell her how we met here.'

'Please do. I would give you a letter or a small minding to carry to her, but there is no time. The personal contact, though, would warm her heart, I'm sure, and mine too. Wait. Will you give her this? A small stone from Iona. They say it saves you from drowning.'

She searched in her purse and handed it to him, touching his arm in her eagerness to use the link with her daughter.

'I will. You have my word. Now, if you'll excuse me, I'm on an errand for Mr Baillie and he does not like to be kept waiting.'

'Of course. My apologies, Jacob. I should not have detained you, but I was so pleased to see you again.'

'The pleasure is mine, I assure you. Good evening to you. Miss Stark. Mr MacLaine.'

He hurried away towards the entrance.

'Where did you meet him, Catherine?' Charles asked.

'On the ship which brought us to Glasgow. Mary was near death with hunger and fever. He noticed and gave me medication and his master gave us the use of his cabin so that Mary could rest, then drove us in his carriage from the quay to my cousin's house. Remarkable display of kindness, an example to us all.'

'Indeed. A good Samaritan. Is Jacob a free man now? I assume he was a slave.'

'He was a slave. I don't know if he has been freed. Perhaps he's a house servant. I don't know. He's a remarkable man whatever.'

The trio walked across the carpeted hall to the door.

30

When Calum came ashore in Tobermory, he went straight to the police house to ask about the gun. The door was opened by the tall constable who had helped to carry John to Ishriff.

'Yes, it's still here,' he replied when Calum enquired. 'Did you find a way of getting your brother-in-law's remains back to Bunessan?'

'We did and he's buried in Kilvickeon. Can I have the gun?'

'It's a fine weapon. Well oiled and polished. Have you need of it in Shiaba?'

'I have. The place is polluted with rabbits.'

'They say a snare's a good way of catching rabbits.'

'Not when there's a plague of them. Can I have the gun?'

'You're sure it belongs to you?'

Calum could feel his temper beginning to boil.

'It does. If I have to prove it, I will go round to Kilninian and find the man who gave it to me and haul him back here by the ear so that you can hear the truth from the man himself.'

'There's no need. I was called to business over there last week and spoke to him. I did not ask him about it, but he happened to mention your kindness to him and the gun he had given to you in return. Wait there and I'll fetch it.'

He turned back into the house and returned with the gun, clearly pleased with his success at annoying Calum.

'Be sure it's only rabbits you kill. If there's one murder in the Ross involving a gun, I will know who to blame.'

'Thank you. I'm not a murderer.'

'That's what they all say. Any man can become a killer in the right circumstances. We all have that evil within us. Go carefully, MacGillivray. I would not like to find the Factor dead in a ditch.'

Calum's jaw tightened, wondering if the man had the second sight, if he had probed his mind and read his thoughts.

'Hundreds in the Ross would celebrate his departure.'

'Particularly yourself. I know all about the hostility between you and him, so, if any misadventure befalls him, yours will be the first door I come to.'

'As I say, I'm not a murderer. Good day to you.'

He did not wait for a reply but hurried into the town to catch the mail coach.

§

He decided to confront the Factor. Choosing a Sabbath, he left Shiaba in the late morning to arrive at Ardfenaig in the afternoon, thinking that Campbell was sure to be at home. Passing the mill at the road end, he walked down the long drive to the house at three o'clock.

At first, he thought of going round to the servant's entrance and then decided to face the man at his front door. When he knocked, the door was opened by one of the maids.

'Is Mr Campbell in?'

'Who shall I say is calling?'

'Calum MacGillivray.'

'Just a minute, please.'

She shut the door and he stood, looking around the garden. It was possible that Campbell would refuse to see him, giving his devotion to the Sabbath as an excuse. He waited for some time before the maid returned.

'Mr Campbell is not available. He suggests you make an appointment.'

'Go back and tell him I will wait on this doorstep till he has the courtesy to see me.'

The door was closed again. When it opened again, it was to reveal the tall figure of the Factor himself, clearly displeased.

'You have a nerve, MacGillivray. I'll grant you that.'

'I'm not calling on my behalf, but on behalf of my wife.'

'Who has left you.'

'She left the Ross so that our children did not starve to death under your management, but she will be back and she will be hoping for a teaching post here. She is attending training college in Glasgow and, when she is finished, she'll come home. I came to ask you not to oppose any application she might make for a school in the parish.'

'As I say, you have a nerve. You have defied me at every turn, poaching, stealing sheep, ignoring my summonses, rebuilding your roof. Why should I assist you in any way?'

'Because you claim to be a good Christian and sit in the pews every Sabbath and must want to see the children of the parish receive the best schooling possible. It is not me you would be helping but my wife and the children of the Ross.'

Campbell's brows drooped down over his eyes.

'I have no say in the appointment of teachers.'

'We both know that is not true. The board will seek your opinion. Your influence extends into every corner of the parish.'

'I don't think I've come across anyone quite as impudent as you are, MacGillivray. I would be a great deal more inclined to listen to you, if you were to vacate the Duke's property at Shiaba, which is let as a sheep farm, and leave the place.'

'That sounds to me a little like blackmail.'

'It is a statement of fact. Now get off my doorstep before I set the dogs on you.'

Calum walked back up the drive, pleased with himself. He had found the strength to face the Factor. He detested the man, his unassailable arrogance and ruthless avarice. but did recognise that he had the power to make his life a misery. If Campbell was sufficiently provoked, he could manufacture a crime and have him in prison without too much effort. He had the sheriff, judges and jury in his pocket. Yet, to ask the necessary favours, Campbell would be in their debt and Calum suspected that he would try to avoid that. He had taken a risk in confronting him, the consequences of which might follow at any time. In an odd way, possession of the gun had given him courage—not that he would use it. He could not imagine himself killing another man.

He was not sure that Catherine would approve of his action. No doubt she would see it as impulsive and reckless, confirmation of her view of him as irresponsible. Yet he had to do it. He had to take action against Campbell's injustice on her behalf, even if it proved have the opposite effect to what he intended and that thought worried him. Perhaps he had made a mistake. Perhaps the consequences would be ruinous. He picked up a stone and threw it far into the hazel scrub in an attempt to dismiss the thoughts.

As he passed the mill again, he remembered that he might not have a crew for the boat. MacQuarrie had mentioned someone, but he could not recall who it was. The lapse of memory annoyed him as he prided himself on possessing a good memory for people. He sat on a bank beneath Campbell's new stone dyke, an impressive piece of work built of single granite boulders and taller than any beast. It seemed to reflect the heat of the sun onto his back, causing him to feel quite drowsy after the stress of the afternoon. Within minutes he was asleep.

He woke with a start to find the Kintra men standing over him.
'We thought you were dead,' said Dougal.
'Not yet, a charaid.'
'I came to tell you that we are leaving tomorrow.'
'So soon, but I haven't paid you yet.'
'We have to go. We have no choice.'

'I'll ask MacQuarrie to send it to you tonight. I'll see that you're paid.'

'We were speaking to him earlier and he said to tell you that Hugh Cameron, the carpenter, is offering to sail with you. He would be good man, Calum.'

'I'll call on him. I'll be very sorry to lose you both. I hope you find a good life in Australia.'

'It can't be any worse.'

He shook hands with them both.

'God be with you.'

He watched them walk away, knowing that he would never see them again—good men, an asset to any township. So many good people had left, draining the Ross of its best. He was sad to see Dugald go. He had come to be a friend, someone he could trust.

He walked down into the village to find Hugh sawing wood for a coffin.

'Well, Hugh, you're busy.'

'Not a task I enjoy. I've made too many of them recently and too often for folk that I know. Mind you, a lot of folk are buried without one, a winding sheet's all they manage. It was good of you to pay for John's. I'm sure Mima would be grateful.'

'If Mima's ever grateful for anything. Dugald Kintra said you might be willing to crew for me.'

'I would be happy to work for you, Calum, but not for the kind of wages you paid to Dugald. I would want a share of the catch.'

'Would you now? And what kind of share had you in mind?'

'On the big boats they say it is a third for the boat, a third for the skipper and a third for the crew.'

'I've heard that, right enough. That's on the big boats, though. The fishing here is up and down. Some weeks plentiful, some poor. And you know what the weather's like—one day a fair wind and a calm sea, the next a hurricane. Some weeks you would have nothing.'

'I'll risk that.'

'A third is too much, Hugh. I'll give you a quarter, if you'll mend the creels.'

'You're as tight as the Factor, Calum MacGillivray, but I'll agree to that.'

'Good. I'll call for you tomorrow then.'

The two shook hands over the bargain.

Calum walked away, grieved that he had been forced into an agreement which was too generous, yet relieved that he had a crew. Besides, he liked Hugh, a young man with a ready smile and unruly fair hair. A good carpenter too, which could be an asset. He wondered if Hugh would be able to build him a boat. Maybe they could start a boat-building business.

§

That evening, as he sat by the fire and looked around the house, the earth floor, the dried dung where the beasts lay, the space above the roof beams open to the thatch, the bare stone walls and the central hearthstone, he decided that it was not good enough for Catherine. If she was going to be a teacher, he would build her a better house, a square house with a chimney and a fireplace, a kitchen and a bedroom, an iron roof and maybe a ceiling. A house for her. He would build it as his father had built his, though his father had every man in the township to help, but they had gone, nearly every man from Shiaba, away to Canada or the city or Kilvickeon graveyard. He would have to do it himself. For her. To show her how much he cared for her.

31

That evening Catherine decided to call at the Museum as she had missed Bella when she had visited Mr Fullerton to enquire about working there for the month of July.

It was a beautiful June evening, with an amber sun setting through the masts of the ships on the river and gulls gliding over the bridge. She always imagined that the air was cleaner there, along the river. The open space of the Green, its green grass and trees, helped to support that illusion. She could have walked straight to the Museum, but wanted some time to herself on the Green. She thought about Shiaba and remembered that, at that time of year, the women used to stay out with the cattle on the high ground, telling stories and singing around the fire with the sparks drifting up into the cooling air. Good days, days which would never be repeated now that the people had gone. There would be no gathering to watch the shooting stars or the dancing lights in the north, no celebration as the last sheaf was cut at harvest time, no cattle in the house to warm the place in winter. All gone. A feeling of melancholy followed her as she headed for the High Street.

She found Bella cleaning the glass cases of the medical exhibits.

'Well, Catherine, it is good to see you and you looking so smart too.'

'How are you, Bella? I've been meaning to call, but Archie's always ravenous at night.'

'I'm well enough and I know you're busy. How are you finding the college work? Is it very hard?'

'I'm coping, thanks, Bella. Standing in front of a class of children is the hardest part. What of the Barra folk? Have you news of them?'

'Not of the ones who passed through, but my aunt from Uist was brought down to me because she was left alone. She lives with me now. She needs a lot of looking after. I might have to give up my work here to care for her.'

'Will you manage without the wages?'

'No. I don't know what I'm going to do. I won't see her in the poor house, though.'

'Is there no-one else to help?'

'Not a soul. And she doesn't take to everyone.'

'Maybe I could help. I could come over at night when you're at work.'

Bella stopped polishing and turned to look at her.

'You have enough to do, with Archie and all your college work. No. I'll manage somehow.'

'I can do it through July. There's no college work then. Really.'

'It would be a great help. Just for July, though. You're very kind, Catherine.'

'I can't start this week. Next week, starting Monday. Will that do?'

'Of course, but she's not easy to handle. I help her to rise and dress in the morning and make her porridge. She sits in her chair through the day but I've to help with her toilet. When she came, she was near death with hunger, weak and so thin it was like lifting a pillow. She's a bit stronger now but there's nothing of her and she's a bit wandered—remembers what year the bull was drowned but not what she had for tea yesterday. At night I help with her toilet, change her and help her to bed. Could you do that for me?'

'Don't worry, Bella. I looked after my blind mother all my young days. I'll manage fine.'

'You're a godsend. Thank you.'

'I'll call on Monday, then.'

As she walked out into the cool evening, she was concerned that she had been a bit rash in making the offer. There would be college work to attend to over the vacation. Still, Bella needed her help and she might yet manage to find someone to look after the old lady.

As she passed over the bridge, swallows were swooping in the still air over the river. All the way from Egypt, the place of the Pharaohs, the source of the mummies in the museum. She thought of the pyramids and the acres of sand, the blue sky and the sun that the Egyptians worshipped, the sun that she saw only through a haze. Why would the swallows leave such a place?

When she arrived home Archie grinned at her, clearly very pleased with himself.

'I've made you a present,' he announced, lifting a poker off the table and handing it to her.

It was not just a straight rod of iron, but had been twisted and turned with a head shaped like a thistle—an impressive piece of work.

'Archie, that's amazing. How did you twist it?'

'When it was white hot.'

'Thank you. Thank you. What a wonderful present.'

'And I've made a stew, so you don't have to cook.'

'Well done! You're spoiling me. I might come to like it.'

'I'm starting in the lathe shop next weekend.'

'That's dangerous surely. You'll have to be specially careful.'

'I will. Don't worry.'

'I'll have to leave you on your own at nights shortly. Bella at the museum needs help with her old aunt and I've told her I'll come over.'

'I'll be fine. I can go and see Hector.'

'Of course. That'll be good.'

'Would you like some stew?'

'Please. That would be just perfect. I'm really hungry.'

Bella lived in a dark vennel near the police house north of the river. The gutters, slimy with waste, spilled out onto the cobbles, making them treacherous for pedestrians, particularly at night. Catherine found the doorway and climbed the stair and was pleasantly surprised to find that Bella kept the room spotless in contrast to the stair which smelt of urine and was covered in ashes.

'This is so kind of you, Catherine. I've hung Nan's night things over the fire to warm and there's a chamber pot under the bed. There's tea in the caddy on the mantleshelf. Come and meet my aunt Nan.'

The old lady was asleep in an armchair in front of the fire and Bella shook her shoulder gently.

'Nan, this is Catherine. She's come to sit with you while I'm out. Remember?'

'Yes, of course I remember. Catherine MacGillivray.'

'I'll be off, then, or I'll be late. I'll be back before eleven.'

As Bella threw a shawl over her shoulder and hurried away, Catherine sat in a cane chair opposite Nan.

'You remembered my name,' she said.

'My memory is better than Bella thinks.'

Catherine glanced at the old lady. The skin on her face, pale yellow parchment, hung from her skull in folds. Her mouth, soft and hirsute, like that of a horse, trembled as she spoke and yet her eyes glittered with vitality and intelligence, studying Catherine with an intensity which she found unsettling.

'You'll be from Mull, then, or Argyll anyway,' Nan said. 'With the name MacGillivray.'

'Bunessan on the Ross.'

'The hunger was bad there, I believe.'

'Worse than '37 anyway. We had the potatoes then.'

'A catastrophe. Like the plagues of Egypt. Our prayers did little to help us. Were there removals there too?'

'Hundreds and hundreds have left for Canada.'

'Our men had no choice, you know. Driven onto the emigrant ships like cattle. Constables came and forced us out of the houses and set fire to the thatch. I saw them chase Donald Smith down the road to Askernish to load him onto the ship in Lochboisdale and poor Lachlan MacDonald hiding in the trench of lazy beds on a wee island and them searching for him with dogs as though he was a convict. They caught him and bundled him into the boat.'

Her eyes grew dim as they gazed inwards at the memories.

'And Angus Johnston, the poor soul, tied up with ropes and given a kick to land him in the boat and him falling onto the boards. The priest, God bless him, interfered. "What are you doing to this man?" he says. "Let him alone. It is against the law." But they threw him into the boat anyway. His four children dead in the house with starvation. Cruel. Cruel.'

'How many, Nan. How many removed?'

'Twenty-seven families from Kildonan and twenty-four from Bornish.'

'Good God. You were put out too?'

'My man and the children died of the famine fever. I was too weak to walk. The neighbours put me in a cart and took me on a ship to Glasgow or I would have died. Bella has been good to me. Will you swing over the kettle there? There's water in it.'

Catherine rose to do as she was asked.

'And I'll need the chanty too. You'll need to help me.'

Catherine fetched the chamber pot from beneath the bed and helped Nan use it. Although she seemed to be so slight, Catherine strained to lift her back into the chair.

'I'll have my broth now,' Nan said.

'Bella said you had eaten.'

'I've had nothing to eat all day.'

'I'll make some tea.'

'John will be here soon. He's late again. Out on the moss, looking for the heifer.'

Catherine guessed that John was her late husband or son and said nothing.

'Would you like some sugar in your tea, Nan?'

'Can't afford sugar, Maggie.'

'There's some here, if you would like it.'

'You're not Maggie.'

'Catherine. I'm Catherine.'

A look of recognition changed the blank expression in Nan's eyes.

'Catherine. Yes. Catherine,' she said, smiling. 'What were you asking?'

'If you would like sugar in your tea.'

'Yes, dear. Sugar. Bella got some specially.'

Catherine handed her a mug of tea.

'We had three cows and followers, good milk cows. John—that was my husband—milked them when he was home but he was away a lot at sea so I did them myself. We had plenty of butter and cheese from them. Never needed sugar. Milk was sweet enough, specially in the summer. A good life then, dear. Before the potato rot. Thrashed more barley than we could use—even made whisky. John got drunk one day and fell in the midden. The stink of him drove the children from the house. They would not go near him till he went in the sea to wash. Do you have children yourself?'

'Only two—a boy and a girl. The girl is in Jamaica, the boy an apprentice in an engineering works.'

'Good for them. The islands are finished. No place for them. The old lairds have gone and the new men have no heart.'

Catherine found that Nan's memory for the life she had was as clear as spring water, but there were moments when her mind seemed to leave her and slip into a whirlpool of unconnected images and thoughts.

That night she helped her to change into nightclothes and into bed. Nan seemed to accept the help like a child, unaware or untroubled by any loss of dignity. When Bella returned, she was peacefully asleep, breathing loudly through her open mouth.

'Was she any trouble, Catherine?'

'None at all. She's a great lady.'

'She has her moments. I can't thank you enough. I didn't know what to do.'

'I've not emptied the chamber pot. Where does it go?'

'Never mind. I'll do it. It goes out in the gutter.'

'Well, then. I'll see you tomorrow night.'

§

For the next few weeks Catherine helped Nan, changing her clothes when they were soiled or wet, lifting her when she needed moved, calming her when she became confused, listening to the memories of her life in Uist. The vacation passed quickly and it was not until the last week that she began to worry about Mary, having had only one letter from her.

32

Dear Father,
I have arrived safely in Jamaica and am living on a plantation near Port Antonio in the parish of Portland. I expected to see fields covered in sugar cane and tobacco, but in these parts much of the land is used for grazing and I have seen some of the finest and healthiest cattle and horses you could find anywhere. You would love it here. The land is fertile and the weather is kind.

The negroes are free, but they seem to work as if they were still slaves. They have little plots of land on which they grow vegetables and there are many fruits that grow wild. The staff here are all negroes and are very kind to me. The oldest house lady has become a special friend and has told me about her young life on the island.

I am getting used to the heat here and all the different plants. I had a very nasty rash after I picked an orange flower they call a cow-itch and it really does itch. My skin came up in blisters and I couldn't sleep.

The children are very well behaved and easy to manage. My work is really very easy because the negroes in the house do all the heavy work. I attend the Baptist church on the Sabbath when I can, in spite of the displeasure this brings to my mistress. The planters still blame Baptist preachers for the rebellion but they seem to me to be sincere, peaceful and compassionate men.

I wish you could come out here. There are many Scots in Kingston—planters, overseers, lawyers, merchants—and all seem to have a good life on the island. It would be much better than scraping a living in Shiaba. Mother could come and teach, Archie could find work as an engineer and you could rent land which is green and fertile. That would be an answer to my prayers.

Your loving daughter, Mary.

Calum folded the letter, rose from the table, and left the house. Outside, a thick mist enveloped the township. He could barely see the other houses and moisture settled on his beard. He stood in the doorway and listened for any sound of a swell on the rocks below, but all was silent. No sign of a breeze. There would be no fishing that day. He walked over to the site he had chosen for the new house, which he had marked out a week beforehand, and gazed at the furrows.

Out of the mist from the direction of the village there loomed a figure, a shawl over her head. He could not see her face, so he assumed it to be one of the women from Shiaba. Yet it was very early for her to be returning from Bunessan. As she approached, he gasped, and, at first, could not believe it was her.

'Catherine! What are you doing here?'

She stopped on the far side of his marks for the house and smiled, slipping the shawl from her head.

'That's not a very friendly greeting, Mr MacGillivray.'

He rushed across to her and took her hands, his sight of her blurred with tears.

'Catherine, Catherine, mo chroidhe, my girl. How I've longed for this day.'

Lifting her hands to his lips, he kissed her fingers. He felt it rising inside him like a whale from the deep, monstrous, unstoppable, emotion rising until he could contain it no longer and it burst from him in a sob that shook his whole body. He could not speak, he could not see, but he felt her fingers on his cheeks and her lips on his. He put his arms around her and held her against him as he wept.

'You've come back,' he said.

He felt her hair on his face, the familiar shape of her body against his. Nothing else mattered. This was all that he wanted.

'I've come back. There's no need for tears.'

She wiped his cheeks with her fingers and, pulling down his head, kissed his eyelids. He looked into her eyes, their enchantment as powerful as ever.

'I couldn't tell it was you, coming out of the mist like a wraith.'

'Maybe you hoped it was a beautiful maiden.'

'You are as beautiful as any maiden could be.'

'Always the flatterer.'

'No. I mean it. No-one else will do. Only you. It's you I love. Truly. Look. The furrow there. I'm building you a new house, a square house with chimneys and gables. For you.'

'For you too, I hope. You can tell me about it later.'

He saw how the moisture in the air had settled in shining stars in her hair.

'Come into the house out of the mist,' he said. 'I'll make some tea.'

They walked hand in hand towards the old house.

He laid fresh peats on the fire and hung the kettle in the smoke.

'It's good to smell peat again after the stink of coal,' she said, sitting on the single chair.

'How did you get here so early in the morning?'

'I confess I stayed in the inn last night. I could not face Mother. I came by steamship and the mail coach.'

'There would not be room anyway with the widow and her daughter there.'

'I have only a few days before the term starts, but I wanted to see you.'

'I'll be glad when you're finished, even if you don't get a position here.'

'I'm still hopeful of that.'

He was about to tell her that he had spoken to the Factor, but reckoned that she would not approve so delayed the confession.

'If there is no position, will you still come back?'

'I suppose so, but it would be a waste of my time at the college, if I did not teach.'

'It would. I had a letter from Mary in Jamaica. It's on the table there.'

'Is she alright?'

'Yes. She's fine.'

'I'll read it later. Tell me about the fishing. Is it doing well?'

'Very well. I have only one man as crew, though. Young Hugh Cameron, the carpenter. We would be out today were it not for the mist. I'm glad it came down and that I was here when you walked in.'

'It may clear yet.'

'Even if it clears, I'm not going. A day with you is worth a whole month's fishing.'

'A month only?' She smiled.

As he handed her a mug of tea, one of the women came to the door.

'Come in, Margaret,' said Calum.

'Catherine! It's good to see you. You're looking well. The city must agree with you.'

'I would not stay there a moment longer than I have to.'

'We may end up there ourselves. God knows where we will go. I came to tell you that we're leaving, Calum. Hector is worried that the Factor will pull down the roof over our heads and that the children will suffer. Another summons arrived. We can't defy Campbell the way you do.'

'I'm sorry, Margaret,' said Calum. 'The place will not be the same without you. You have been the best of neighbours to us. Where will you go?'

'They say there's an empty house in the village. Maybe the Factor will leave us alone, if we go there.'

'The children will be nearer school there,' said Catherine.

'I'm not thinking about school just now or anything like that. I'm thinking how we are going to live.'

'I could use another man to crew for me.'

'Could you, Calum? That would be an answer to our prayers. You have been so kind to us anyway. We will never forget that. I must go and tell Hector. Thank you.'

She hurried away, leaving a silence behind her, as Calum and Catherine gazed after her, each clearly troubled by their own thoughts of the future and the fate of Shiaba in the years ahead.

'Soon there will be no-one here but us,' Calum dared to say, testing her reaction.

'Who knows? Let's not talk about it. It was good of you to offer Hector a job.'

'He has never been to sea in his life and he's a nervous creature anyway so he may not take the offer.'

'Well, you made it anyway. That's what matters.'

Later in the morning Hector called to thank Calum and to say that he would join him on the boat. Throughout the day, neighbours called to welcome Catherine back to Shiaba. At the turn of the tide, the sky cleared and the sun burned away the dew left by the mist. The twin peaks of Jura seemed to move nearer in the clear air and the sea below glittered in the sunlight. Calum and Catherine stood together outside the door, holding hands and leaning on the wall.

'It is beautiful here,' Catherine said.

'More beautiful because you're here.'

She leaned against him and squeezed his hand.

'I wish the children could be here,' he said.

'They are fine where they are. Let's enjoy the time together.'

He made a meal that night of lithe and bread and cheese, which they ate by candlelight. As it neared time for bed, Calum's usual calm assurance was upset by apprehension. He felt like a youth meeting his lover for the first time. He did not know what to do, whether to suggest that they lie down together or whether he should offer to sleep on the floor. He found his fingers trembling and his mouth like sand. It was Catherine who rescued him from the dilemma.

'Come,' she said, 'let's pretend we are young again.'

They stood at the same time and he looked into her eyes, touching her cheek tenderly with his quivering fingers. Her face was older, but her eyes still shone with the same sincerity, the same affection and candour.

'We don't need to be shy,' she said and, moving over to the bed, started to remove her clothes.

When they lay together, her skin warm and soft against his, the longing for her, which had sunk beneath the struggle to survive, suddenly surfaced and overwhelmed him in its intensity. All he wanted was to hold her, to protect her, to envelope her with tenderness. Driven not by passion or lust for fulfilment, he felt only gentleness and love for her. He kissed her forehead and her eyelids and, when he kissed her lips, he felt them touch his with the same tenderness. It was as if they needed no more than this, to touch, to breathe together, to relish those precious moments and hold on to them forever. As the candle on the table guttered and died, they joined together with the same gentleness and restraint, though he could taste the passion on her breath and feel the yielding in her flesh, absorbing him, loving him. He could not believe that such ecstasy existed.

'I love you,' he whispered.

§

The next day, they avoided discussion of Shiaba, either his attachment to it or her aversion to it, and Calum still didn't tell Catherine of his confrontation with the Factor. She sailed with him on the boat, taking over the tiller as he worked with Hugh on the creels. Hector did not turn up, so Calum assumed that he was too fearful of the sea to join them. Catherine stayed with him for several days and he was just becoming accustomed to having her home when she had to leave.

That was the hardest time for him. Standing by the mail coach in Bunessan, he held her in his arms and kissed her, feeling as if he would not see her again, the dread of something, some accident or tragedy, which would keep them apart. As he watched the coach depart, he felt as if a part of him had left with her, torn from him, leaving a gaping wound where his heart might be. Parting after the days of pleasure was painful.

33

Calum hired MacQuarrie's horse and cart to carry heavy stones from the shore for the foundation of the new house. The Oban contractor who had built the new church in Bunessan had taken most of the good stone from Kilvickeon chapel, but there were still some cornerstones left and he carted these to Shiaba. It was heavy work and his hands, unused to heaving stones, blistered badly. He decided to use mortar instead of dry stone, which meant ferrying lime from Lismore and sand from the shore below Scoor. The building proceeded slowly as he couldn't neglect the fishing, working on the house only when gales or mist prevented him going to sea. Hugh proved to be invaluable, offering to help with the building and woodwork.

Every day Calum watched the path leading in to Shiaba for the Factor, expecting him to ride in with constables to stop him building or to evict the four remaining families. As summer passed into harvest time and a skin of frost settled on the grass, he began to wonder if Campbell had chosen to leave him in peace. Nevertheless, he kept his musket oiled and powder dry.

As he drove down to the shore below Scoor, he could see the workers in the big field cutting down the oats, the men slicing a pathway with their scythes and the women behind them binding the sheaves. Youngsters were gathering the sheaves into stooks of six to dry. He could hear the rasp of whetstones on iron as the men stopped to sharpen their blades. Sitting on the rim of the cart with his feet on the trams and the reins in his hands, he remembered the harvest days at Shiaba, with Catherine behind him, the children helping and the hens scratching in the stubble. They seemed so long ago, those days when they did not worry about hunger, days when a dozen potatoes came out of the ground where he had planted one. All in the past. He had to face that. The Catherine he knew then was not the Catherine who came back in the summer and he wondered if she would ever be content to live in the house when he finished it. Perhaps he was working for nothing. Still. It was his gift to her, a symbol of his devotion. For that reason alone, he would finish it.

It was a long sail to the island of Lismore, north of Oban, but the kilns at An Sailean provided the best slaked lime in the district. He was not keen to have the bottom boards burnt on the boat so he paid for the delivery by smack to the shore at Scoor. It was an unpleasant substance to work with, stinging any crack in the hands and burning the skin, but he learnt to wash it off quickly and keep it from his clothes. Hugh showed him how to make mortar and, by Martinmas, the walls were almost high enough for the door and window lintels and still the Factor had not appeared.

By then, the days were short and it was the best season for lobsters so progress was delayed. In the long evenings he found time to write to Mary.

Dearest Daughter,
I have at last found some peace and time to write to you. I am building a new house so that your mother has a decent place to live when she comes back. I don't suppose it will be as grand as the house you live in, but it will have a chimney and separate rooms. I don't think we will have negro servants either to do all the work.

There have been some bad gales here. On Coll one of those iron steam ships was blown ashore and badly damaged and had to be towed to Glasgow. Our boat, being tied up in Bunessan, was untouched. It is now very cold and it is hard to keep warm at night. When I'm shivering, I think of you complaining of the heat. Maybe we could change places for a night or two.

It is strange to think of a negro Baptist preacher, but I suppose he could be as spiritual as any man and just as sincere. Slaves are said to be free now so maybe things will get better for them.

You will need to be careful about displeasing your mistress. It would be a terrible fate to be cast adrift in an island so far from home. Still, it is good that you attend the church on the Sabbath. That will please your mother. As you know, I have little faith in any of them, although I respect the Baptists here.

I am looking forward to the day she comes back but I worry that there will be no work for her here as a teacher. The Factor Mor is against her because I have defied him and his shadow is cast over every appointment. We will not starve, though, because the fishing is doing well.

I do not think we will ever leave the Ross, unless we are driven out. I hope that you will come back, though. By then, no doubt, you will be a young lady, familiar with the ways of the world and too sophisticated for any of the beardless youths here.

Your loving father.

By the time the first leaves appeared on the trees at Assapol and the skeins of wild geese had flown north, the walls of the house had reached their full height, although scaffolding had yet to be built for the gables. Two more families left Shiaba, leaving the township almost deserted, and still the Factor had not appeared. Calum began to worry. Perhaps Campbell was waiting until he had finished the house and would arrive to claim it for the Duke or for his sheep-farming tenant. Campbell had a way of knowing everything that was happening in the Ross. Still, he was determined not be deterred. Catherine's house would be built.

They were hauling creels behind Erraid when Hugh told him of the ploughing match.

'The Factor is organising it. They say he has more than a dozen ploughs entered. All the worthies of the Ross will be there, I'm sure, dressed in their best. We should go, just for the craic.'

'Why would I go to watch a ploughing match? I have enough to do.'

'A holiday. A day away from work. There'll be a crowd going, I wager.'

'It sounds as though you would like to go.'

'I would. It might be a grand affair.'

'You're welcome to it. When there are still folk starving in the district, it is shameful to arrange an amusement for people who have nothing better to do.'

Hugh dropped the topic of conversation, but announced the evening before the match that he would be going. Calum, remembering that Hugh was just a young man who might like to meet with some of his peers, decided to encourage him.

In the morning, Calum's curiosity overcame his objections and he walked over to the farm. The Factor was there, strutting around the field in his polished leather boots and talking to the more prosperous tenants. As Hugh had predicted, there were fourteen ploughmen, struggling to keep the furrows straight as the nodding horses strained ahead of them. Calum watched the ploughs slicing into the grass and turning the soil over into neat furrows. Far quicker and easier than the hand plough he had used. He realised he was witnessing the future.

The three judges strolled around the field, studying and discussing the efforts of each contestant, while quite a large crowd watched from the higher ground. One of the judges was Elliott, the flockmaster and tenant of Scoor and Shiaba, and Calum noticed that the Factor spent much of his time in his company. Later in the morning, the two men came very close to where he was standing and Calum waited to see if Campbell would acknowledge him.

He not only acknowledged him but brought Elliott across in his direction.

'I didn't think you had any interest in modern agriculture, MacGillivray,' he said in English.

'I don't. I came to find my crewman, who is enjoying his holiday.'

'Mr Elliott, this is Calum MacGillivray from Shiaba.'

'From Shiaba?' Elliott said. 'I thought the township was cleared.'

'It will be, I assure you. MacGillivray's wife, it seems, has some very powerful friends.'

'Indeed? I hope they will have the wisdom to exercise their power according to the law.'

'Whose law would that be, sir?' asked Calum.

'The law which states that I am the sole tenant of Shiaba and that no-one else has the right to be on my land.'

Calum realised that he would have to tread carefully and did not reply, wondering whether either of the men knew of his new house.

'His Grace the Duke,' Campbell said, 'granted Mr Elliott the lease on the understanding that there would be no small tenants or cottars on the land.'

'His Grace was ill advised then. His tenants in Shiaba had never failed to pay their rent. There was no reason to evict them.'

'Except when the potato failed and the arrears mounted. In any case, the rent was pitiful compared with Mr Elliott's offer and the farm is now in his hands and the land has to be clear of people. That is how it stands. All of you are offered accommodation in other parts of the estate, in your case nearer the sea and nearer the schools.'

'I will keep that in mind.'

'Do that, MacGillivray.'

As they walked away, he heard Elliott mutter, 'What an insolent creature!'

'Yes, but His Grace is impressed by his fishing.'

Calum was reassured by what he heard and decided to return to the boat. He could be baiting some lines instead of watching the ploughing. As he sat on pier fitting mussels onto the hooks, he tried to work out whether either of the men knew of the new house. Elliott, of course, lived on the other side of the island and rarely visited Scoor so it was possible that he was not aware of it, unless one of his shepherds had told him, but there was no hint of it in what he said. The Factor. You never knew with him. His thoughts and knowledge were concealed behind that stern, permanently furrowed brow.

That night he wrote to Catherine,

My dearest Catherine,
Today I attended a ploughing match! I know you will think that a curious form of amusement for a fisherman, but young Hugh was keen to go and, as it happens, I met the Factor. Campbell had organised the affair and all the worthies of the district had been invited. Needless to say, his own ploughmen won second, fourth and fifth prizes. He came to speak to me with Elliott, the tenant of Shiaba, and he mentioned that my wife seemed to have powerful friends. I don't know what he means by that, but I heard him say that the Duke knows of my fishing and approves of it. I think that must be good news.

I don't know if they are aware of the new house. Neither of them talked of it. It will be finished by the summer, all being well.

I was speaking to MacQuarrie about a school for you and he tells me that Campbell does not control all the schools in the Ross. He has sway in the two parochial schools, the Assembly one and the female charity one, but he has less influence in the Society one and the Gaelic school and none in the Free Kirk one. So you do not need to worry so much about his influence. Surely a place will become available in one of them.

The fishing is going well and, if it holds up, I might be able to buy a second boat. The problem is that other men have seen the profit to be made in lobsters and there will soon be more boats than lobsters. There must be twenty or thirty men working at it now and another two score fishing cod and ling. It is becoming hard to find crew.

I hope that your college work is going well and that you will find time to come back for a day or two at some point. The few days we had together the last time you were here were the best days of my life. I will never forget them.

Your loving husband, Calum

34

Catherine continued to help Bella with her aunt during the week, but found that she had to keep the weekends for her college work. As the time spent in class with the children increased, she found the evenings spent with the old lady more taxing. She had barely the energy to talk to Archie and felt guilty about that, frequently falling asleep as he spoke to her. Eventually, she was forced to tell Bella that she could no longer help.

At Christmas she attended the new Free Church in the Gorbals with Archie. It was good to hear the service conducted in her own language and according to the rituals of her own church, with the singing of the psalms in harmony led by a precentor and the Rev Bremner. Archie, like his father, tolerated subjection to the rituals reluctantly, an attitude which puzzled her, as he had spent so little time with Calum latterly. Perhaps scepticism was a necessary part of engineering. Still, she found it irritating but decided not to pursue the issue.

As she sat in the pews, which still smelt of fresh pine, she thought of Calum's new house and the threat posed by Campbell. She had forgotten to thank Charles for his intervention. Assuming that he had spoken to his friend Johnnie Campbell and that Johnnie, as the 'powerful friend' mentioned by the Factor, had spoken to the Duke, she had to thank Charles. Somehow the summer had passed so quickly, with work in the museum and the old lady at night, that the season had turned almost unnoticed into autumn and then winter. The seasons seemed to matter less in the city. In Shiaba they ruled their lives. There was no excuse, though, for the omission.

It was not until the spring term started that she had the opportunity, when Charles appeared at the college. He was very excited about Johnnie's plans for a new castle on Mull, running up the steps to meet her and Phoebe.

'Magnificent!' he said. 'You must see these plans. I've brought a drawing with me. We've demolished old Achnacroish and are replacing it with this sensational new castle overlooking the sea. You must come and stay when it's completed, both of you. I'll arrange it with Johnnie. Let's take a cab to the Tontine so that I can show you these plans. David Bryce, the architect. Designed to look like a French chateau with turrets and tall windows. I've been asked to help with the interior designs. Come.'

He ran out into the street and, waving the plans above his head, hailed a cab. When they were seated in the hotel, he cleared everything off the table, rolled out the drawing and told the waitress to come back in ten minutes.

'There!' he said proudly. 'What do you think? This is to be the central hall with a splendid staircase, and this the library and the billiard room, here the conservatory. Sixteen bedrooms. Don't you think it's wonderful?'

'Extravagant certainly,' said Phoebe. 'His purse must be bottomless.'

'West Indian money, Phoebe. A cornucopia.'

'Slave money, but I suppose it will provide a lot of work in the parish,' Catherine said. 'Much needed. I want to thank you, Charles, for speaking to Johnnie on our behalf. It seems to have had some effect—it seems to have reached the Duke's Factor.'

'I'm glad. To be honest, I'd forgotten all about it, but clearly Johnnie hadn't. Good man, Johnnie. Now, what colour do you think we should have in the library? Nothing too garish, something restful and elegant. What do you think, ladies?'

Catherine looked at the plans and listened to his description with astonishment, comparing the extravagance with the wretchedness and misery which she had seen in the vennels of the city and in the meal queues of the Ross. She was tempted to draw his attention to the difference, but his grin and boyish enthusiasm dissuaded her. Clearly, he was completely oblivious to the distinction, yet he was a kind and generous young man. It was not his fault that he was sheltered from the poverty around him, unaware even of the savage cruelty involved in the creation of Johnnie's wealth.

Phoebe, on the other hand, had no reservation in criticising the extravagance.

'Should be investing in industry, Charles. He may create work in the building, but it ends there. A sterile display of wealth. Put his money into manufacturing and it will multiply, creating work and wealth at every step.'

'You're biased, Phoebe. Just because Torquil's an engineer.'

Catherine listened quietly to their argument as it progressed, thinking of Archie and feeling that her time would be better spent cooking a meal for him at home. She realised that, although Charles and Phoebe had become good friends, there was a chasm between their lives and hers and that their futures lay in a very different direction. Eventually she excused herself, thanked Charles again and rose to leave.

'But you have had no tea. Have I been boring you with my plans?'

'Not at all. They're fascinating, but I must see to Archie. I will see you tomdorrow.'

§

As the Certificate of Merit examinations approached, she spent an increasing amount of time studying in the evenings. Quite often they would sit companionably on opposite sides of the table, she engrossed in her college work, Archie reading books on engineering. Occasionally, on fine evenings, they would abandon their studies to walk along the river or round to the gardens at the cemetery. While they walked, they would discuss their futures, which were clearly diverging. It saddened her to contemplate losing her other child when she returned to the Ross and he was left in the city. She knew that he had no intention of going back to the island; his work in Tradeston was far more satisfying than anything Mull could offer, yet she worried about him being left alone in the city. He constantly reassured her that he would not only manage but might enjoy being on his own, responsible for himself.

Just before the first examination, she received a letter from Calum.

My Dearest Catherine,

I know you will be preparing for your final examinations and I want to wish you every success. I'm certain that you will have done all the work necessary to pass because you have always had the strength to persist with a task, regardless of the circumstances. It is that strength that I have always admired and I'm sure it will lead to success.

I must admit that, when you said that you were going to train as a teacher, I thought it was just a dream and that the notion would soon melt away. I did not doubt your ability, but I thought that it was just a passing fancy to impress Mr Lamont. I failed to see how serious you were and I apologise for not encouraging you from the start. I know that you will be an excellent teacher for you not only have the intelligence but you have a way with children which has often caused me to pause in wonder. Once you qualify—and I'm sure you will—I will do everything I can to help you with your work as a teacher.

The new house is almost finished and Hugh has started on the inside work. It is strange to be under an iron roof, as the rain sounds like thunder and I think it will be colder in the winter. I'm thinking of laying boards across the rafters to deal with those faults. I wish I had planted some potatoes but there has been no time. I will make sure to get healthy seed for next year. There has been no sign of the Factor and Elliott has not visited.

Each morning I wake thinking that this is one more day nearer to your return and that thought keeps me warm for the day even when a sharp east wind cuts through my jacket.

I wish you success with the examination, dearest Catherine, and a swift return to me afterwards.

Your loving husband and most faithful admirer, Calum.

As she walked over bridge on the way to the first exam, she kept going over the shorter catechism and the Bible stories which she thought might arise in the test. Concentrating on such details helped to calm the nerves which were fluttering inside her. She knew that, in the subjects which interested her, such as Geography and History, she would be able to answer most questions but, when it came to Scripture and Management, her memory was weakened by her lack of enthusiasm. Still, she had performed well in her teaching practise, being commended for her kindly discipline. Her future depended on her knowledge of subjects which she found tedious. If she failed, all her months of study and her separation from Calum would have been in vain. Her future then would be as bleak as ever.

35

Calum stood outside the house in the early morning, watching the shepherd on the hill gathering the flock towards Scoor for shearing. In the still air he could hear the ewes and lambs bleating and the shepherd whistling to his dogs. Lambs, which he had seen born as staggering, scrawny creatures, had filled out and were as able as their mothers. By that evening the male lambs would be castrated and the ewes stripped of their heavy fleeces. A flash of sunlight on the iron roof made him look across at the new house. He was proud of it, so different from the others with its chimneys and gables. Yet he remembered that the old houses had cost nothing but the time and labour of the men of Shiaba. Like his own, they had been built by the people out of the land on which they stood.

He looked along the row of houses, most of them empty now, and wondered how long it would take for the thatch to rot and fall in, how many storms would snatch at the roofs before they collapsed, how many generations would be born in Canada before the walls crumbled and collapsed. He imagined sheep sheltering where the cattle slept, rabbit warrens in the corn ridges, wrens nesting above the lintels. It would be silent then. No clattering of thrashing flails or children chasing birds off the crops. No women singing as they made cloth. Silent. He felt sad thinking of Shiaba as it would be after he and Catherine had gone. Even the new house would become a ruin. He shook his head to cast off the gloomy thoughts and headed for Bunessan.

'I want to try a new way of using the long lines,' he said to Hugh. 'A different way. When I sailed to Glasgow a few years ago, I saw the fishermen in Campbeltown laying out one long line on floats and hanging hooked lines down from that single one.'

'Would it not need good floats, better than cork?'

'Glass. I think they had glass. I suppose you get iron buoys at the ends.'

'Sounds like a good idea, but I've already baited the lines for today.'

'I'm going to think about it, all the same. Find out about glass floats and buoys.'

They climbed down into the boat and Hugh hoisted the sail, but there was little wind and they had to row out into the bay before the sail filled at all. Even then, it was slow progress. Still, it was quite pleasant to drift along in the sun until a breeze finally gave them some speed and they headed round the north of Iona towards the deep water in the west. It was nearly midday when they lowered the lines.

'I forgot to tell you that Bridget was looking for you early this morning.' Hugh said.

'Oh? What did she want?'

'I don't think it was important. She didn't seem anxious or upset. She said that Mima was asking to see you.'

'That would make a change. Usually, Mima can't wait to see the back of me. Still, I'll call on the way home.'

He couldn't fathom why the old lady would ask to see him, unless she had had word from Catherine. That worried him. Why would Catherine write to her before him? Perhaps, on the other hand, Mima wanted help with a task beyond the strength of Bridget or her mother. He knew that the old lady would not ask a favour from him unless she was driven to it.

'The line's caught,' said Hugh suddenly. 'Something on the bottom. Can't be kelp. There's no weed here.'

'Is it caught fast? Like on a rock.'

'It is. Not a movement.'

'Good God! We can't lose the line. You hold on and I'll try moving the boat round so that the pull's in a different direction but I'll take in my line first.'

He hauled in his line, unhooking the fish and tossing them into a barrel, and then put out the oars to shift the boat.

'Try again, Hugh. Give it a good tug.'

'It's moving. Something very heavy below. Can you unhook as I haul it up?'

Calum shipped the oars and moved to the bow to clear the line of fish as Hugh, hand over hand, pulled it up. As the obstruction neared the surface, they could make it a long, dark shape with what looked like tresses of weed flowing from the end.

'Christ Jesus, Calum! It's a body! The weight's caught the clothes.'

As it came to the surface, they could see that it was a woman with long, dark hair. They gripped the clothes and hauled it on board, horrified to find that most of the face had been eaten away, exposing the teeth and the skull. There was little left of the fingers and the feet had been cleaned to the bone. A small crab scuttled out of her hair.

'What will you do, Calum? Take her to Iona? That's the nearest. Maybe we should just put her back. Say nothing. There might be a lot of trouble.'

'Can't do that. There'll be grieving relatives somewhere.'

'We'll take her to Iona, then They might know who she is, though she might be off a ship. God knows. Let's do it. Iona.'

They hoisted sail again and turned east.

Arriving at the jetty on Iona, Calum asked one of the fishermen to go for Mr MacVean, the Free Church minister, who came almost immediately.

'We have the remains of a woman on board, Reverend,' Calum explained. 'She was caught on our lines and we brought her up. I don't know what to do.'

The minister stepped on board and looked at the body.

'I think I know who it is,' he said. 'A poor widow from that bog land at Kinloch who was evicted and whose children died of hunger and disease. She just walked out into the loch. A tragedy, one of many, I'm afraid. We'll bring her ashore and I'll get in touch with the minister over there.'

'Do we need to let the constables know?'

'I'll see to all that, Calum. It was good of you to bring her ashore. Many a man would have tossed her back to avoid trouble. You rescued another widow from the same place, I seem to remember. Maybe saved her from the same fate. That was a great kindness when you were near starving yourselves. What became of her?'

'She went to Australia to join her husband.'

'God be praised. I'll take care of this one, if you want to be on your way.'

'Thank you, reverend.'

'God bless you, Calum, and you too, Hugh. This is a good deed you have done.'

They sailed back to Bunessan and unloaded the catch for salting. When they had finished, Calum walked round to Ardtun to see Mima. She was sitting alone, staring at the embers of the fire with her hands on her lap.

'Well, MacGillivray. I asked to see you. You were a long time coming, but then I'm only an old woman of little use to you.'

'What is it you want, Mima?'

'You will go to that dresser there and look in the drawer and in it you will find a small box.'

Calum obediently followed her instructions.

'I have the box, Mima.'

'You may open it.'

In it, he found a gold nugget.

'For God's sake, Mima! What's this?'

'It's from Australia. My brother in Ballarat sent it.'

'It's worth a fortune. All these years you've starved, you've frozen, you've nearly drowned and you have had this. All that time. You could have saved lives with it. I don't understand.'

'You wouldn't. I didn't want John to get his hands on it. You will take this to Oban or wherever and exchange it for coins. You will give half of it to Bridget and Tina and the children. They have been good to me. The other half is for Catherine to help set her up as a teacher and to pay for a decent coffin at my funeral.'

'But I don't know where to go, who to ask.'

'A clever man like you will soon find an answer. Will you do this for me? I am not long for this world and I want to see this settled.'

'You seem very healthy to me, but, yes, I will do it for you.'

'What you see is not always what is fact. Take it and say nothing to anyone.'

He left the house, astonished and incredulous and wondering how long she had possessed the nugget. He could not understand her reason for concealing it and for keeping it while people in the parish were dying of hunger.

When he reached home that evening, he found the Factor sitting on his horse with the Ground Officer by his side, both examining the new house.

'I take it that this edifice is your doing, MacGillivray.'

'It is.'

'It is illegal. I have not given permission for such a building on the Duke's land.'

'My grandfather did not need permission from the Duke to build his house; nor did any of the tenants here.'

'You have been given a summons of removal from the Sheriff.'

'The summons was for the old house. In any case, I have no intention of leaving.'

'I will report the matter to his Grace the Duke and leave it in his hands. You may defy me but it would be unwise to defy him.'

'Perhaps I will not need to defy him. He may see the justice of my case.'

'I doubt it. I'm sure he will fulfil his obligations to the legal tenant of the farm and have it cleared of inhabitants.'

'We will see then.'

Calum turned his back on the men and walked into the old house.

36

Catherine hurried over to the college to see if she had passed the examination. She was more nervous climbing the stairs that morning than she had been when sitting the papers or answering questions orally. She arrived before any other students, so the corridor in which the lists were displayed was empty. Her finger trembling, she read down the list and there it was. Certificate of Merit—Catherine MacGillivray. The text blurred as tears of relief filled her eyes and she stepped away to look out of the window, leaning on the sill.

Phoebe arrived with two other women, all of whom shrieked with joy when they read the results. Phoebe flew over to embrace her.

'I knew you would pass,' she said. 'I'm delighted for you. Congratulations.'

'And you too. You were so sure you'd failed.'

'We must celebrate. Let's go the Tontine for a toast.'

'I can't, Phoebe. I'm catching the steamer to Mull.'

'You'll be back for the presentation next week, surely.'

'I will. I promise. You go with the other girls to celebrate. I want to tell Calum in person.'

'You will come, won't you?'

'Promise.'

Phoebe joined the other women and they hurried away, chattering like starlings. Catherine stood by the window, remembering her arrival in Glasgow, with Mary so near to death and rank with flux, saved by Jacob. Stripped of all hope, she herself had been close to despair, struggling to survive for the sake of the children. So much had happened since then—working for McBride, meeting Eoin, working in the museum and coming to College. Her life had changed utterly, emerging from the dark shadow of starvation and hopelessness to the bright space of aspiration and confidence. She felt that she was in charge of her destiny for the first time. She smiled and left the corridor.

Archie was waiting for her on the quay, her bag in his hand.

'Thanks, Archie. I hope you'll be alright on your own. If anything goes wrong, call on Mr Lamont. If you go round to see Hector, tell Mr Lamont I'll call on him as soon as I come back.'

'I'll be fine, Mother. Don't worry.'

'I'll be back next week.'

The steamer sounded its siren as she hugged him.

'Better go before they let down the gangway,' she said, lifting her bag.

§

It was a long journey to Shiaba, as she had to stay a night in Tobermory and walk all the way from Bunessan to the township, so it was evening before she smelt the peat smoke of home and saw the new house. Stopping to admire the iron roof, the chimneys and the square gables, she realised how much work Calum had put into the building. The thought worried her too, for she knew it would prove to be too far from any school in which she taught. That defect might lead to another painful argument.

Calum was standing with his back against the wall, gazing over the sea, as she rounded the corner. He did not see her at first so she was able to watch him. He had taken to smoking a pipe, holding the clay bowl in his hand with the stem in his teeth. His hair and threads of his thin beard had turned grey, but the skin on his face, though weathered, was still fresh. His chin, still thrust forward, and his long nose still gave him that air of defiance. She wanted to keep that moment, stamp it on her memory, and the love for him that went with it, but he turned and saw her, dropping his pipe, which shattered on the ground. The frown of confusion vanished as he recognised her and took her in his arms.

'Catherine, Catherine, Catherine,' he whispered. 'You should have said. I would have met you off the coach, if I'd known.'

'There was no time to write. I had to come first thing.'

'You've had the results. I can see it in your eyes. You've passed, haven't you?'

'Yes. I've passed.'

'I knew you would. That's wonderful. You're an amazing woman, so clever, so strong, so brave. I'm proud of you, Catherine. Really proud of you.'

'It's been a long, hard journey—as hard for you as for me.'

'But worth every minute. Come into the house. The water's boiled for tea. You must be exhausted after the journey.'

'I'm tired, but not too tired.'

She smiled mischievously and squeezed herself against him.

§

The next morning they walked down to the village, holding hands. In spite of their time together the night before, Calum seemed to be troubled and she guessed that he was concealing something unpleasant. That worried her, given his previous dishonesty.

'What's wrong, Calum?' she said as they reached the turning for Saorphin.

'Nothing. I'm thinking about the boat.'

'It's not that. Last night we promised to be honest with each other, a pledge that we must not break.'

'You're right. I did not want to tell you of the Factor's visit. I didn't want to spoil the evening.'

'What has he done this time?'

'He saw the new house and said it wasn't lawful and that he would report the matter to the Duke. He said that I should have had permission to build it and I told him that my grandfather had built our house without seeking consent. God knows what will happen.'

'Don't worry. The Duke may decide to do nothing. If Campbell had been sure of his ground, he would have had the Sheriff's men down from Tobermory.'

'Perhaps you're right. There's nothing I can do anyway. Will you not come on the boat with us? You would enjoy the sail.'

'No. I want to see Mother about the gold and MacQuarrie about a teaching position.'

'Yes. That's a mystery, isn't it? Maybe she'll tell you why she kept it. I can't understand it. Maybe she's more wandered than I thought.'

'There's nothing wrong with her mind. She's as fly as a bag of monkeys.'

They parted just before the village, Calum heading for the pier, Catherine turning over the bridge towards Ardtun.

'Catherine, love. How are you? Come and give me a hug.'

She was too astonished to reject the invitation. It was such a long time since her mother had shown her any affection.

'You look well, Mother.'

'I'm well looked after. Are you home for good now?'

'Yes. I've to go back for the presentation, but, after that, home.'

'At last. That's good news. You have passed, then?'

'Yes. I'm qualified to teach.'

'You've done well. I always knew you were clever—like your mother.'

She laughed as she said this.

'Did Calum give you the gift from Australia?'

'He did and he told me what you want him to do with it. Why on earth did you keep it safe while you and the folk round you were starving? I don't understand.'

'For one thing, I didn't want John to know of it. You can understand that at least. If people got to hear of it, there would have been mobs round my door, fighting and squabbling over it. Someone might have killed me to lay hands on it. I was frightened of it.'

'No-one here would want to kill you.'

'You never know, do you? Anyway, it can be put to good use now. Bridget and Tina have been kind to me and deserve a reward and I want a good coffin when I go to my grave. The rest will give you a start when you find work as a teacher.'

'You don't need to do that for me, Mother.'

'No, I don't, but I want to, and your Calum has been a great help to me—never looking for thanks or making a fuss—but a help nonetheless.'

'And I thought that you had no time for him.'

'He took you away. I resented that and he took that widow into his house because he felt sorry for her, but I could see the good side of him too.'

'I could take the gold to Glasgow and sell it for you.'

'That would be good. I want to see the matter settled before I go.'

'You're not going yet. You're perfectly healthy.'

'There's never a moment promised, as my father used to say.'

'Very gloomy. Now, I'm going to the village to see MacQuarrie. Is there anything you need?'

'No. I'm fine, dear. Come back and tell me what he says, will you?'

'I will.'

As Catherine walked away from the house, she was puzzled and a little worried by the change in her mother. Having been such a cantankerous and bitter woman, she was transformed into a kindly old soul. Perhaps she was not as healthy as she seemed. Perhaps she felt that she was nearing the Judgment Day and needed to become a better person. Whatever the reason, it was a pleasant change, particularly the change in her attitude towards Calum.

'I thought you would be the best person to speak to about teaching posts in the parish,' she said to MacQuarrie.

'You've done well, Catherine. For a person who rarely saw the inside of a school to become a teacher is truly remarkable, an example to us all, but I'm sorry to say there are no posts here at the moment. During the hunger, many children couldn't go to school and hundreds have left. Some schools had to close their doors. The parish has not recovered yet. A couple of the older teachers should have retired years ago, but cling to their salaries as if they were drowning. I'm afraid you will have to wait.'

'I don't mind waiting, but could you let me know if there's any sign of a post becoming available?'

'I will, of course, Catherine. How are the children? Calum tells me that Archie is to be an engineer.'

'Yes, he's doing well, though it means he's unlikely to come back here.'

'At least he's in a trade with a future. And Mary, has she settled in Jamaica?'

'She seems very happy there.'

'Isn't that a blessing? And Calum is considering another boat. I'm very pleased for him. I've heard that the Duke is keen to encourage the fishing.'

'It's not the Duke I worry about. It's the Factor and the new house, claiming it's not legal.'

'I don't think you should worry about it.'

'Why do you say that?'

'If Campbell was going to force an eviction or demolish the house, he would have done it before now.'

'I hope you're right. I'm going back to Glasgow to collect my certificate and I'll call again when I return.'

'God be with you. Have a safe journey.'

Reckoning that Calum would have set sail, she headed back to Shiaba.

§

The sun was warm when she reached the house and a soft south-west breeze blew in from the sea. She walked across to the new house to look inside. The fresh larch door opened easily on its hinges and the kitchen smelt of pine resin and lime mortar. There was wood ash in the fire grate where the men had tested the chimney and a pile of wood shavings in the corner. She looked up through the rafters to see the iron roof but it was hidden by sarking boards. She remembered how the hens used to roost in the rafters in the old house and the beasts chewed their cuds behind the hessian partition. That space, in this house, was divided off with pine boarding to make a bedroom. She was impressed. The flag flooring would make it easy to keep clean. It was an improvement, but it didn't contain the memories of the old house—the memories of the days when they were young and still childless and the night when they lay together for the first time, memories which she cherished still.

37

Returning to Glasgow, she left the quay and walked straight up to the bridge and over to the Gorbals. As she approached the house, she was glad to see lamplight in the window. Archie was home. When she opened the door, he was sitting at the table, a cigarette in his fingers and a book in his hand.

'Good God, Mother! You startled me.'

'I couldn't tell you when I was coming. Are you studying?'

She moved round to lay her hand on his shoulder.

'I was reading about steam engines. Have you had something to eat? There's some salt herring.'

'That would be perfect. I'm really hungry.'

'You sit down and I'll see to it. I'll make some tea as well.'

He stood and hung the kettle over the fire.

'How's Father? Has he finished the new house?'

'It's finished but we haven't moved in yet and he's fine.'

'Is there teaching work for you?'

'Sadly, not yet. I can wait. Father makes enough from the fishing to see us through.'

Archie laid a plate of salt herring and a mug of tea in front of her. They talked for a while about Mary and his work in Tradeston before she went to bed, exhausted after the journey.

§

The following morning she woke to find Archie stoking the fire, having slept in the other flat. Clearly he had decided that he was too mature to share a bed with his mother. She rose and went over to the window, hoping to see the street dry and the sky no darker than usual. She was relieved to find weak sunlight trying to penetrate the haze. She brushed down her best, green dress, slid into it and looked out her Indian shawl.

'Should you not have a gown and one of those flat hats?'

'A mortar board. I don't possess such a thing. It's not like a graduation. I hope not, anyway.'

'You look very smart.'

'Thank you, kind sir.'

'I'll need to be off. Hope it goes well.'

He kissed her on the cheek and left for work.

After she had eaten, she walked up to the college to find a crowd of students on the steps, most of them wearing gowns. That was discomforting. She searched for Phoebe and found her in the foyer, looking radiant in a crimson skirt and green velvet bodice. She was carrying her teacher's gown over her arm.

'You look wonderful, Phoebe.'

'Thank you. Mama says I look like a trollop. Do you think we should wear gowns? I've brought two in case.'

'That's kind of you. Yes. I suppose we should look like teachers, although I feel more like a tailor's dummy in these clothes. Have you decided where you are going after all this is over?'

'According to Papa, it will likely be India with the 74th.'

'How exciting! What an amazing adventure! You will write to me, won't you?'

'Of course. I have to join Mama and her entourage after the ceremony so I won't be able to see you then. Can we meet before you return to Mull?'

'I'm sailing in the morning.'

'A flying visit. We have to part now then. I will miss you so much, dear Catherine. You have been an inspiration. What you have achieved is an example to every woman. I will not forget you. I will come and find you whenever I return to Scotland. You won't escape my clutches. We will meet again. I promise.'

There were tears in her eyes as she kissed Catherine on both cheeks.

'Thank you for all your help, Phoebe, especially with Archie. He has a future now. I will miss you. You brightened every day in college. It would have been a dull place without you. I hope you find a handsome officer in India and have lots of children.'

'No man, Catherine, will fill the place in my heart reserved for you. I must fly. There's Mama's carriage outside. Au revoir, mon coeur. Keep the gown.'

Catherine watched her hurry down the steps, feeling that her life was changing beneath her, that she was being borne along like a leaf in the wind.

The ceremony was not the same without Phoebe, who sat in a different part of the hall.

Catherine saw her applaud with her hands above her head as she stepped down from the rostrum, having received her Certificate of Merit.

She was just leaving the college with her certificate in her hand when Charles rushed across the street to shake her hand.

'I'm so sorry, Catherine,' he gasped. 'I just couldn't escape in time. I wanted to come to the ceremony and roar my approval when you mounted the platform.'

'I'm glad you didn't. It was embarrassing enough without that.'

'Is there a place for you on Mull—a teaching post, I mean?'

'No. So many children have left. So many schools shut.'

'Something will turn up. I'll speak to Johnnie again. There might be something in his parish. I'm off to London tomorrow but I'll see him when I come back.'

'London? You're not going to live there?'

'No, no. I've won third prize in the design. Is that not amazing?'

'Congratulations. I'm delighted. Well done. You promised me one of your landscapes, remember.'

'I have not forgotten. I will have one framed and sent to you. You must let me have your address on Mull so that I can write to you. I don't want to lose contact with you. You mean a great deal to me.'

'I'll send it to you and I promise to reply to every letter of yours. I'm glad you came today. I wanted to thank you for speaking to Johnnie for us. You've been a good friend.'

'I wish I could have been more than that, Catherine, but it was not to be. Will you at least join me for lunch before you leave?'

'I'm sorry, Charles. I leave in the morning and I want to call on Mr Lamont.'

'Of course, the Classicist. Let me fetch you a cab.'

For a moment she thought about accepting the offer, but then remembered the other task she had undertaken.

'There is something I have to do while I'm in the city and I would welcome your help with it, if you have time.'

'I will make time for you.'

'I have a gold nugget from Australia and want to change it for sovereigns but I have no idea how to proceed. Can you help?'

'Of course I will help. I hope you're not carrying with you. That would be a fearful risk.'

'It's in my purse.'

'Good God! How heavy is it?'

'I don't know. A pound maybe.'

'You don't know! Listen, Mama's jeweller is an honest man. I will take you there and introduce you. If you take it where you are not known, they will fleece you. Come, we'll take a cab.'

They drove into the merchant's part of the city and Charles accompanied her into the hallowed precincts of an expensive jewellery shop. After some time, she came out with a heavy handful of sovereigns in a felt pouch provided by the jeweller.

'You should not carry that with you, Catherine.'

'I'll have to take the risk. There's no other way to take it home.'

'You're a brave lady. Take the cab across the river at least'

It was still waiting in the street.

'Thank you. I will and thank you for your help.'

He kissed her fingers as he handed her into the seat.

'Safe journey, Catherine. We will meet again. I promise you.'

She waved to him as the cab moved away. His boyish grin and untidy fair hair made her smile. She was fond of him—not in a sensual manner but rather in a maternal way. He was not part of her world, though, moving in more influential circles.

When she called on Lamont that afternoon, he opened the door, clearly delighted to see her.

'Congratulations, Catherine. You have now joined the noble profession of pedagogues. I knew you could cope with the work. Do come in. Kathleen is away out with the boys.'

'I won't come in, thank you, Eoin. I'm sailing back to Mull in the morning and I want to spend some time with Archie.'

'Of course. He's doing so well. A clever boy. He made Hector a model steam engine, beautifully crafted.'

'He didn't tell me, but I'm pleased that he did. I called to thank you, Eoin, for all your help and encouragement. Without you, I would still be illiterate, terrified of words. I used to look at them as you would look on scorpions. Without you, I would never have worked in the museum or sat the examination for college. I wish there was a way I could express my gratitude.'

'You've done so already. When I feel overwhelmed by the demands of my pupils or the incompetence of the management, I will think of you. I joined the profession believing that I could bring enlightenment into the ragged hordes in this parish, but I doubt if I achieved any success. One always hopes that one spark might lead to a conflagration, but I fear that is not the pattern. Still, when I'm old and on the edge of senility, I will remember our evenings together and consider that together we lit the spark that fired your thirst for knowledge. Most of all, though I'll recall what I learnt from you.'

'I could never teach you anything.'

'On the contrary. I learnt what resilience and strength of will, in the face of adversity, can accomplish. You're a remarkable woman, Catherine. Keep that in mind always.'

'There are many more remarkable than me. I have seen them, Eoin, women struggling with crippling hunger and disease. I'm one of many who managed to survive.'

'Your modesty merely confirms my description. I will miss you.'

'And I you. I hope each of the boys turn out as fine a man as their father. Now, I must leave before I start to cry. God bless you, Eoin—even if you don't believe in him.'

She turned and walked down the street, conscious of the fact that he was still standing in the doorway watching her. Remembering the intensity with which she had worshipped his intellect and knowledge, she felt slightly embarrassed by it.

§

Determined to see the people who had helped her, she walked back into the town that night to see Mr Fullerton and to speak to Bella.

Unfortunately, Mr Fullerton was not there, but she spoke to Miss Armour, asking her to thank him on her behalf. When she enquired about Bella, Miss Armour told her that she had not appeared at work for the previous two nights. That never happened. Bella didn't miss work, so Catherine decided she had to call on her, in spite of being dressed still for the presentation.

Although it was daylight, it was almost dark in the vennel and it was difficult to see where the gutters ran beside the cobbles. She found the close and climbed through the foul air to Bella's door, which hung open. Inside, she found Bella bent over the bed where her aunt lay on her back with her mouth open. Her breathing was shallow, quick and irregular.

'Not long now,' Bella said, looking up then continuing to talk to her aunt. 'Leaving from Uig now on the way home. A soft wind from the south is filling the sail. Watch the boom as the boatman hoists the sail.'

Catherine knew immediately what Bella was doing, describing to the old lady her journey home as she was dying. She had pulled one of the chairs beside the bed and was holding her aunt's limp hand with one hand and stroking her brow with the other. She began to sing softly: 'Fear a bhata'. Catherine was stunned by the clarity and beauty of Bella's voice, the sorrow and nostalgia of it piercing her heart and filling her eyes with tears. Everything beyond that sound faded into the distance, the world outside, the voices in the vennel, the clatter of carriages, the siren on the river, even the urgent whisper of the old lady's breath—all overwhelmed by the purity and intensity of the singing. It carried Catherine back to her childhood and her mother's crooning by the light of the rush lamp. Long ago. So long ago.

Before the song ended, the breathing had stopped, but Bella finished the song and, on the last note, kissed the old lady's forehead and closed her mouth.

'A good sleep to you, Nan,' she murmured.

Catherine wiped her eyes and took Bella in her arms.

'I'm so glad you're here. I didn't want to be alone when she passed.'

'It was very peaceful.'

'Yes, she seemed content to go.'

'Will you manage everything on your own?'

'I don't know. She has nothing herself. I have saved a little for her funeral.'

'I can help with that, Bella, if you will let me.'

'She wasn't your family. Why should you?'

'She was your aunt, but I did look after her for a short time and you're my friend. Please allow me.'

'You're very kind. It would be good to see her buried properly.'

'I have nothing with me, but I will send Archie tomorrow night. You arrange the funeral. I'm afraid that I have to leave on the steamship in the morning. I came to say goodbye.'

'It's good that you're going back, but I'll miss you. Every night I'll look at the butterflies and expect you to be there. God go with you, Catherine.'

'And with you. I will always remember you and I will never forget the song you sang for Nan's journey home. The song, and you singing it, will be in my heart till my time comes.'

38

The men were cutting hay in the field at Assapol as Catherine walked up the road, a sweet scent which brought back memories of summers in Shiaba. She stopped to watch them, enjoying the rhythm of their action and the hiss of their scythe blades in the grass. The women were working nearer the loch, turning hay, cut the previous day, to dry in the sun. As she walked on, she had to leave the road to avoid the cattle sheltering from the sun under the trees. Flies buzzed on pads of cow dung. A young calf, disturbed by her approach, staggered as it hurried to join its mother.

She was glad to be home, home to stay. Her time in the city had changed her. Although she still felt part of the scene around her, it did not own her. She was conscious of possessing a freedom which she did not have before. It allowed her to enjoy her place in the townland, to appreciate and savour the waves of wind on the meadow hay, the glitter of the sun on the loch, the green rigs of ripening barley, the scent of peat smoke, the lichen on the dry-stone dykes, the white gulls in the blue sky and the people in the fields, her people, speaking her tongue.

When she reached home, Calum was not there. She laid her scroll on the table and dropped her bag and brief case on the chair. It had been a long journey and her feet were sore after walking from Bunessan. Calum had smoored the fire before he left so she lifted some peat from a creel and blew the embers aflame. Fetching water from the burn, she hung the pot over the fire and went outside to wait for the water to boil. Leaning against the wall, she noticed that there was no smoke from the other houses. That was strange. Calum had said nothing about the families leaving.

She walked down the scattered row of houses. In some, where the people had been evicted, the doors were nailed shut. Knowing that these were empty, she passed without stopping. In others, the doors lay open, the houses deserted, the hearthstones cold. She was shocked to find that there was no-one left, that she and Calum were the last people in Shiaba. It seemed to have happened so quickly. More than a hundred people driven out by hunger, despair and oppression, a whole generation swept away in ten years. She stooped under the lintel of the last house and went into the gloom. A blanket was still on the bed and a black pot hung over the cold ashes on the hearthstone. A child's shoe lay on the floor, its sole worn away. A rusting scythe hung on the rafters and a potato spade lay on the floor in the corner. Such an air of sadness pervaded the room that Catherine left before it gripped her.

That evening, when Calum returned, she was loading a creel from the peat stack.

'You never said that they had all left,' she said.

'It was while you were away. I met the widow and her children as I came home. The Sheriff's men had been, she said.'

'Where will they all go?'

'I don't know. The MacLeans, she thought, were for Australia and maybe the MacGillivrays but the others were too old. Neil's over eighty and John Campbell not much younger. God knows, Catherine, where they'll go. The widow's going to Ardtun, though there's far too many there as it is.'

'So, we are the last.'

'We are the last. I never dreamt it would come to this.'

'We can't stay, Calum. I'm sorry. I know that you built the new house for me. I will never forget that, but, if I'm to work, there's not going to be a school here. The woman in the Gaelic school over the hill in Scoor is young. She could be there for years yet. It is a long way to Uisken and Bunessan and even further to Creich. You must see that.'

He looked so dejected that she took his hand in hers.

'I know. I tried to think of a way you could stay here and get to one of the schools—a pony or something—but there was no good answer. I would not want you to walk every day. Still, we can stay just now, can't we? We can get some use out of the new house, surely. I have spent a lot of money and time on it. Stay till a teaching post comes up?'

'I suppose so. No longer, though.'

'No longer. I don't want the Factor to feel that he has won.'

'Good God! Is that still on your mind? What does that matter now?'

'It doesn't really. The thought of his smirk of triumph just smarts., but what matters most is your happiness.'

He put his arm around her shoulder and pulled her against him.

'I have a letter for you. The handwriting is really elegant.'

He reached into his jacket pocket and pulled out an envelope.

'Beautiful writing, as you say.'

Breaking the seal, she opened it.

My Dear Catherine,
Just after you left, I happened to meet Johnnie Campbell and I took the liberty of explaining your predicament. Although his mind is con-

centrated on his castle, which is to be called Duart House, he was most sympathetic.

He said that one or two of the schools in Torosay parish have no teacher at all and advised you to write to the appropriate authority with your curriculum vitae. He would be delighted to have a teacher of your calibre in the parish. He could not recall immediately which schools required teachers, but he told me that there were four parochial ones and an Assembly school. He thinks there is also a Gaelic school. However, all of the school buildings are in a deplorable state of repair.

I know that you would wish to find work in your own parish, but perhaps a post in Torosay would suffice until you find one in the Ross.

I have survived the journey to London and Papa is almost enthusiastic about my award, though grumbling that third prize was not as good as first—as if I hadn't noticed the difference. I promised to send you one of my landscapes and I will see to that shortly. The afternoons in college do seem rather dull now, deprived of the prospect of seeing you and Phoebe. I always looked forward to those meetings and miss the laughter—and the occasional scolding!

Please write to me, Catherine, and let me know how you are faring in your beautiful island.

Yours sincerely, Charles.

She read the letter aloud and waited for a comment, but Calum, waiting for her, said nothing.

'It's not really very helpful,' she said eventually. 'Now I don't know what to do. I could write to the board, as he suggests, just to see if there is a vacancy.'

'Even if there was a post, you would have to live over there. You've only just arrived.'

'I could stay there through the week and come back at weekends.'

'How could you do that? There's no service through the glen. You would have to live there, except for school holidays.'

'I don't want to waste the two year's training.'

'No, of course not, but I've missed you so much, Catherine. I don't want to lose you again.'

'You wouldn't lose me. Not ever. I think I'll write to enquire. That won't do any harm and we won't have to decide till we get a reply.'

'I suppose so.'

'Don't be so glum. A post may turn up here. In the meantime, I could help you with the long lines.'

He brightened immediately.

'Would you? That would be great. They say it's unlucky to take a woman on a boat, but I would risk that just to have you with me.'

'First thing tomorrow, though, I must see Mother. I didn't call on her today.'

§

They walked down the road together the next morning. It was a dismal day so wet that Catherine's head and shoulders were soaked in spite of her thick shawl and, by the time they reached the village, her shoes squelched with every step. Calum seemed to be impervious to the rain, his oilskin coat shedding the worst of it. When they reached the bridge where Catherine had to turn off for Ardtun, Calum was clearly concerned for her.

'See that there's a good fire going and try to dry your shawl. You could catch a chill.'

'I'll be fine. Maybe Mother will have another shawl. Call for me when you've landed.'

'I will. See and get warm.'

He kissed her on the cheek and headed for the pier.

When she reached Mima's house, Tina was standing in the doorway.

'I'm glad you're here, Catherine. I wanted to see you. Come round to the barn where we can talk.'

They went round to the shelter of the barn, where Catherine took off her shawl and flicked some of the rain out of it.

'Mima is not great,' Tina said. 'I'm really worried about her. She's stopped eating. I've tried all kinds of food, but she just says that she's not hungry.'

'When did this start?'

'Just after you left for Glasgow. It's as though she had come to a decision. Can you talk to her?'

'Yes, but you know what she's like. If, as you say, she has decided, nothing on God's earth will shift her. Is Bridget with her just now?'

'No. She's in the village for fresh herring.'

'She's on her own, then, so I'll go in.'

Catherine was shocked by the deterioration in such a short time. Her mother's face seemed to be sliding from her skull and, as she raised her head, her eyes were lifeless and dull.

'Well, Catherine. Did you do what I asked?'

'I did and I have a bag of sovereigns on my belt. Tina tells me you are not eating.'

'When you have lived as long as I have, you don't need food.'

'If you don't eat, you'll starve to death.'

'I'm not afraid of that. We all have to embark on that journey at some point.'

'You could live for years yet.'

'I don't think so. Eating causes me pain. I have a ravenous beast within me, Catherine. As long as I don't feed it, it lies sleeping.'

'I could ask the doctor to call.'

'No. Definitely not. Just leave me alone. You have money to pay for a coffin. That's all I want and money to give to Tina.'

Catherine knelt in front of her mother and took her hands in hers.

'I don't want you to leave, Mother.'

'It is time to go. As the book says "To everything there is a season, and a time to every purpose under heaven. A time to be born and a time to die".'

Mima released one of her hands and touched Catherine's cheek, feeling the shape of her face. Catherine felt the tenderness in her fingers as they moved over her forehead, over her eyes, along her lips.

'I remember when you born. Such a small child, but so precious. They said you looked straight into my eyes and smiled.'

Catherine felt the fingers move through her tears.

'The book goes on, "A time to weep and a time to laugh. A time to mourn and a time to dance." Don't weep, Catherine. I go to a better place where, perhaps, I will be able to see my son.'

'I will sleep here, near you.'

'No. Your place is with Calum. He's a good man for all his weaknesses. See and look after him. Now go about your business and leave me in peace. No fuss, Catherine. Lay my head in Kilvickeon when the time comes, but no fuss. Promise me?'

'I promise. No fuss.'

39

Dear Charles,
Thank you for writing so soon after seeing your friend, Johnnie Campbell, and for making enquiries about a teaching post for me. It was very thoughtful of you. However, I have decided to wait for a position in the parish here. It may be that the waiting is in vain, but I would rather take that risk than leave my husband again, having been away from him for the most of two years. I'm sure you will understand.

There is a Gaelic school near us at Scoor, but the teacher is young and unlikely to move, so we may have to leave Shiaba and move to Bunessan, our nearest village.

I must thank you for all your kindness and friendship while I was at college. You and Phoebe made my stay in Glasgow much more pleasurable than I had anticipated. I particularly enjoyed those visits to the Tontine Hotel.

I hope your studies in college bring you success and that your painting leads to an exhibition. Please let me know if they are to appear in a gallery and I will make every attempt to come down. In the meantime, rest assured that I will never forget your friendship—I have the briefcase to remind me!

Yours sincerely, Catherine.

Calum was delighted when she told him of her decision. Doubts about the wisdom of his visit to the Factor still troubled him and he hoped that Catherine would not wait for a post in vain. It was good to have her on the boat, but he knew that she wanted to teach and that she might blame him, if she were to be denied a position. The pouch of sovereigns meant that they did not need to worry about income, but he worried about having it in the house. He was also concerned about the effect her mother's illness was having on her. Every afternoon after landing, she called at the house and each time she seemed to emerge more distressed as Mima deteriorated. There was little he could do to help, other than offer consolation and hold her when she became upset. One night, however, she started to sing. He had never heard her sing before, other than crooning to the children when they were small or chanting as she worked, but never with that deliberate, spontaneous expression of her feelings in a sound which could tear the heart from the sternest listener. She sang with tears glistening on her face in the lamplight.

'That was the most beautiful thing I've ever heard,' he said when she had finished. 'I didn't know you could sing like that.'

'I had to sing in college—in front of a class. It was mortifying. I hadn't sung since my father died.'

'You must keep on singing. Sing for me, if for no other reason.'

'So no-one else will hear?'

'No, that's not what I mean. It's beautiful. I want to hear you singing as often as you can.'

He noticed that she was more relaxed, that the tension in her face faded as she sang, her hands, so often clenched, opened like starfish.

'You were singing for your mother, I think.'

'I was.'

'Maybe you should do that. Go down and sing for her sometimes. She would like that.'

'Yes. Maybe I will.'

§

When she sailed with him, he watched her with pride. Her deft fingers baited hooks faster than Hugh or himself and tied lobster claws with an expertise that surprised him. She seemed to know intuitively where to place herself when the boat swung round at the end of a reach or in a gale. She took the tiller when he had to go forward if a creel was caught in the weed. She could reef the mainsail as quickly as any of his crew. He liked the way her fair hair blew back from her brow in the wind, fine like silk threads, and her blue eyes blinked in the salt spray. Watching her from the tiller, he adored her silently. Very occasionally she caught him, their eyes met, and she smiled. Those moments were precious.

§

Catherine called with her mother every morning and night after she came ashore, often bringing a string of fish for Tina and the children. Calum waited at the boat, baiting lines or storing the lobsters in the floating crate, and met her at the bridge on the way home.

'Will you ask Hugh to make the coffin?' Catherine asked one evening.

'He has the wood already. I asked him the other day.'

'That's good of you. Thanks. I think we'll be needing it soon. She doesn't leave her bed now.'

'Upsetting for you.'

'Not really. She seems content to leave.'

The next morning, sensing that she might have died in the night, Catherine asked Calum to accompany her to the house. She was not surprised when Tina met her at the door to tell her that Mima had indeed passed away in her sleep.

'You go on to the boat,' she told him. 'We will manage here.'

'I'll send Hugh to make the coffin.'

'Do that.'

The three women, Catherine, Tina and Bridget washed the old lady, laid her out ready for the coffin in clean clothes.

'We'll stay with her tonight, Catherine,' Tina said. 'You go home with Calum.'

'Are you sure? It would be a help.'

'I'm sure.'

It was three days before Hugh and Calum carried the coffin across and lifted the old lady into it. Catherine admired Hugh's fine workmanship, the perfectly polished wood, the mouldings and the iron handles. The minister, the Rev MacGregor, walked round from the village to offer his sympathy and to read some texts from the Scriptures, reminding Catherine briefly of her struggles with the subject in college. The small group stood around the coffin as Hugh fixed down the lid—Catherine, Calum, Tina, Bridget and minister. Catherine looked at her mother's face, now wax white and lifeless, but peaceful and purged of all the pain and stress. She almost looked young again. Outside, Catherine could hear the young children laughing. As she emerged from the house, they scuttled into the barn. MacQuarrie had brought round his horse and cart and, lifting the coffin into it, they set off for Kilvickeon, Bridget remaining with the children.

It was a long walk, with the cart rattling and bumping over the rough track. The Minister rode beside MacQuarrie with one foot on a tram while the four followed on foot. Half way to the graveyard, just after the track for Shiaba, they met The Factor and two of his men. Swinging his horse off the road, he turned it to face the coffin and halted respectfully, removing his hat and sitting with his head bowed. At no point did he raise his head to speak or acknowledge the mourners, but waited until they were well past before moving on. Calum kept his eyes on him as they walked past, trying to guess why Campbell should be in the area. It troubled him to see him there. Had it been in other circumstances, he would have established why.

When they reached Kilvickeon, MacQuarrie helped Calum and Hugh to lift the coffin to the open grave and lay it on the grass. MacGregor opened his well-worn book and read the service, leading them in chanting the 23rd Psalm. Calum noticed that Catherine carefully ensured that her voice did not rise above those of the others. When it came to the time to lower the coffin into the grave, she had to help by taking one of the cords. He was impressed by the dignified way she handled the task. A remarkable woman, he thought.

After the blessing, he and Hugh filled in the grave and laid the green sods neatly on top while Catherine and Tina talked to the minister. When the task was finished, MacQuarrie drove off with the cart and MacGregor, with Hugh and Tina in the back, leaving Calum and Catherine to head for Shiaba.

'What do you suppose Campbell was doing here?' Calum asked.

'God knows. At least he was respectful.'

'He was, but I don't trust the man.'

'I wasn't really thinking of him at the time.'

'No. Of course not. I'm sorry. I should have been thinking of you and the mother you have lost and not him.'

He tried to suppress thoughts of Campbell as they walked, but, as soon as they reached Shiaba, he turned aside to examine the new house in case there had been an intrusion. He had already glanced anxiously at the houses as they came over the crest of the hill above the settlement.

'Where are you going?' she asked.

'Just to check the house.'

'You're still thinking of him, aren't you?'

In spite of the rebuke, he carried on to ensure that Campbell had not boarded over the door or trashed the partitions. Nothing had been touched. He searched the grass for signs of the horses, but there was not a mark. Perhaps Campbell had been in Shiaba on other business.

Relieved that he had not damaged the house or nailed a summons on the door, he left to join Catherine, though still trying to find an explanation for the Factor's visit. There would be a reason and it would not be to bring happiness or good news.

40

Dear Catherine,
As you will gather from the stamp, I have been posted to India to join the 93rd with Papa. However, before I could take up my duties officially, Papa insisted that I would join him in Simla for his leave. As I knew the station to be in sight of the Himalayas, how could I refuse? The heat in the plains can reach over 100.

I sailed up the Ganges and then on horseback to Deyrah where I had my first sight of those magnificent, snow-clad mountains. Although the mountains of Glencoe are truly dramatic, the Himalayas exceed in beauty anything I have seen. Arriving at the Jumna, we found the river in spate and had to cross by elephant, an experience which you would not relish.

Our house in Simla is in a perfect place, looking out, on one side, over a deep, tree-clad valley about 3,000 feet below, lined with rhododendrons and cedar trees and, on the other, to the Himalayas. You would love it here. The colours are amazing. The houses, though, are not completely waterproof. The flat, mud roofs tend to leak brown liquid into the rooms below. I wrote my last letter home under a parasol! The rain also brings on a plague of fleas which drives us to distraction at night.

The whole country is still in disarray after the war. Papa has instructed me to convey no details of the campaigns, but I can tell you that Glasgow's son, Colin Campbell, has excelled his Crimean successes by relieving Lucknow. I believe his mother was from Islay—perhaps he is related to the dreaded Factor! It is rumoured here that Sir Charles Trevelyan—yes, Sir Charles Trevelyan - is angling for the post of Governor General. I wonder if his approach to famine in India would be as ruthless as his policy in Ireland and the Highlands. If he achieves his ambition, I'm sure you will celebrate his departure from British shores, knowing that he can inflict no further hardship on your people.

Yesterday we were entertained by a "durbar" where the Sikh horsemen gave a display of shooting from horseback at a mango on a spear with remarkable accuracy. Each success was greeted with applause by the Sikh chiefs dressed in bejewelled turbans and gold tunics woven with pearls. Their wealth stands in such contrast to the half-dressed servants who clean the latrines.

I hope Archie is still pursuing his career with Torquil. My brother never writes so I don't hear of Archie's progress. I hope also that you have found a teaching post in your parish. Do write and let me know. If you write to Simla, I will arrange for the letter to be forwarded to me.

Your friend always, Phoebe.

She folded the letter, having read it aloud to Calum, and smoothed it out on the table.

'I wouldn't like to live in that country,' he said. 'Not in that heat. Perhaps we could get an elephant to take you to school, but, there again, it would take a lot of feeding. The Factor would be mightily impressed.'

'I'm going to see him.'

'What?'

'I've decided. I am going to see him.'

'Why? I've already spoken to him.'

'I don't need anyone to speak for me. I will speak for myself.'

'You're going to plead for a post?'

'No. I'm going to find out if his disputes with you will affect my application for work. I think he would give me an honest reply. Devious and ruthless he may be in some his dealings but, faced with a straight question, I think he would be frank.'

She could see that he wanted to stop her but was fighting to suppress the urge to interfere. His jaw was clenched and he was avoiding her gaze. He reached for his pipe and scraped out the bowl noisily with his pocket-knife then cut slices of black tobacco off the snake-like roll. All in silence. Finally, lighting the pipe and puffing smoke from the side of his mouth, he replied.

'You're right. It might make all the difference. His dispute is not with you. God knows why he was on the road the other day, but maybe you'll find out when you see him. He's a big man, Catherine. Intimidating.'

'I'm not afraid of him.'

'No. I know. You're not afraid of anyone.'

He reached for her hand and smiled at her.

§

She did not sail with him that day but, leaving him at the pier, walked to Ardfenaig. It was a long walk, but it was a fine day and the larks circled high above her, borne upwards in their singing. The green oats in the Factor's fields were tinted with yellow as they ripened. She stopped to admire his new dry-stone dike, impressed by the size of the granite boulders used in the foundations. As she turned off the main road by the mill, the scent of seaweed mixed with that of the ground meal. She started to rehearse her speech to the Factor and then decided that it was a waste of time, that it was impossible to predict his immediate reaction to her visit or her reaction to him. She was not nervous or afraid, but she was keen to conduct the interview to her advantage, to present herself in a professional manner that he would respect.

When she knocked on the door, it was answered by a maid-servant.

'Is Mr Campbell at home?'

'I'll go and see. Who will I say is calling?'

Her supercilious attitude annoyed Catherine. She knew who she was.

'Mrs MacGillivray from Shiaba.'

'Wait a moment, please.'

The door shut in her face. When the maid returned there was a slight change in her approach.

'Please come in, Mrs MacGillivray. Mr Campbell will see you in the study.'

She was escorted through the hall into the study.

The Factor rose to greet her amiably. She had forgotten how tall and imposing he was.

'Good morning, Mrs MacGillivray. Please sit down. Can I offer you some coffee? You have had a long walk.'

'No thank you, Mr Campbell. I'm used to walking.'

He did not sit down until she was seated.

'I'm glad to see you back in the parish,' he said, crossing his legs and placing his long fingers together as if in prayer.

'I'm pleased to be back. I have spent two years in the city and, during that time, I attended the Free Church Training College for teachers and obtained a Certificate of Merit. I am now a qualified teacher.'

'That is a remarkable achievement indeed, Mrs MacGillivray. Congratulations. The island is in need of fully qualified teachers.'

'I was hoping to obtain a post in this parish.'

'I see. Well, I wish you every success.'

The reply unsettled her and, for a moment, she did not know how to proceed.

'I know that, as Factor for His Grace the Duke, you have considerable influence in the appointment of teachers and I wanted to ensure that you would not oppose my application for a post.'

'Why would I do that?'

She sensed that he was forcing her hand on the issue.

'Because of my husband.'

'You misjudge me, Mrs MacGillivray. I would never allow personal animosity to cloud my judgement when it comes to such appointments. The educational and spiritual needs of the children on His Grace's estates take priority over my personal prejudices. I assess people on their merits.'

'That is most reassuring, Mr Campbell.'

'As it happens, a post may become available soon in Bunessan, but it is a long walk for you from Shiaba every day.'

'As it is, I walk in to help my husband with the fishing.'

'A good house is available in Ardtun, which would be much more convenient to you. Your moving to it would assist me with my administration of the Duke's lands.'

'I will keep that in mind.'

'Please do and please accept my sincere condolences on your mother's passing. I should have offered those sentiments earlier. She was a stalwart lady, managing her lack of sight with dignity and courage.'

'Thank you. I will miss her.'

'I must remind you, however, that the family occupying her house do not hold a lease from His Grace and do not seem to have the means to pay a fair rent.'

'I will see that the rent is paid. My mother never failed to pay.'

'She did not. Even so. The family has no lease. The widow must approach me and I will consider her position.'

'I will ask her to speak to you. Now, if you'll excuse me, I must return to the village. Thank you for seeing me.'

She rose to leave and he levered himself out of his chair.

'You're very welcome. Allow me to provide you with a lift. The trap is ready round the back and I'll order the ploughman to take you back.'

'There's no need, thank you.'

'I insist.'

He rang for the maid and gave instructions. She thanked him at the door and he handed her into the trap in a gentlemanly manner.

Talking to the driver about the crops and the price of stirks on the way to the village, she was also thinking about her conversation with the Factor, wondering if he had been offering a deal—he would see that she was offered a post as long as she moved to Ardtun. She wasn't quite sure, but it seemed to be the case. The ploughman dropped in her in the village while he went to the shop.

She walked over to her mother's house where she found Tina outside, beating the chaff mattress with a stick as clouds of dust rose around her. Stopping to talk, she sneezed and threw down the stick.

'I'm just cleaning the place a little.'

'That's good, thanks. You're welcome to have it for the family, but you'll have to see the Factor about a lease.'

'I can't pay for a lease, Catherine.'

'I know, but don't worry about that. Mother has left some money for you which will see you through the winter. You will still have to speak to the Factor, though. When Calum's new boat arrives, we'll need folk to bait lines and fetch mussels. You and Bridget could do that.'

'That would be wonderful. You're very kind. What's to happen with your mother's things? Not that she had much.'

'Put them in a sack and I'll take them away tomorrow. I'm going back to Shiaba just now, but I'll call in the morning.'

§

When Calum returned that evening, he barely took time to greet her he was so anxious to hear the result of her meeting.

'I got the impression that he would not oppose my application. He was very courteous, congenial even. I was asked into the study and offered coffee.'

'He kept me standing on the doorstep. Even threatened to call the dogs on me.'

'I don't think that he blames me for your defiance. He is offering us a house in Ardtun.'

'That sounds like a bit of blackmail. He gives you work as long as we leave Shiaba. Is that it?'

'I don't know. I really don't know. He is so careful in the way he says things. You can never be sure what he means.'

'He's a snake, Catherine. Slippery and deadly.'

'I don't know. There were moments when he seemed to be genuine, kind even. Maybe he's not all bad.'

'Rotten to the core.'

'No. Definitely not. There's a side of him, I think, touched by Christian principles.'

41

Catherine shook out the gold coins onto the table.

'Good God! I didn't know there was so much,' Calum said.

'It was a shock to me too. I still don't understand why she kept it through the hunger. She hid it from John and that was wise, but she could have used to help herself and other folk.'

'Maybe she didn't know the value of the nugget.'

'She was no fool. Anyway, I'm left with it. I have to pay Hugh and give the minister something for his trouble. Take this and give it to Hugh in the morning. It's better it comes from you. He might refuse it from me.'

'I'm putting him in charge of the boat when the new one arrives. He has recruited men from Kintra already.'

'When is it due?'

'God knows. Any day, I suppose. It's a great shame Archie is not here to take over. I had hoped he would join me in the fishing. He and I together. Foolish really. I do miss them, the children.'

'Yes,' she sighed, 'and I worry about Mary. So far away. She left here as a sick child and now she's a young woman in Jamaica.'

'It was my fault, Catherine, that she nearly died and I'm sorry. To strike work at such a time was selfish and arrogant and, worst of all, it drove you away. I'm sorry.'

She took his hand in hers.

'You were young and so stubborn that I could have cracked your head with the broomstick, but perhaps it has been for the best. The children did not suffer in the long run and I would never have qualified as a teacher had I not left. That reminds me, I have something for you. I was keeping it till we moved, but I'll show you now.'

She found her brief case and laid out her paintings on the table. He gasped as, one after another, the brilliant colours covered the surface, iridescent blues and emerald greens. The wings of butterflies. At first, he said nothing, but stood with his fists clenching and unclenching as he fought to stem the tears swelling in his eyes and sliding down his cheeks.

'These are … ' he whispered, clearly struggling to find words. 'They are … beautiful, brilliant. You did these?'

'Yes. While I worked at the museum.'

He remained silent for some time, looking down at the paintings.

'Why did I not know?' he said eventually. 'How could we have been together all these years and I had no idea that you had such a gift? There are so many things I have missed, so many things about you that I failed to see. Had I been blind like your mother, there would be an excuse. I feel as though I'm seeing you for the first time.'

'I am still the same.'

'No. No. You're not the shy girl who met me on the shore at Uisken and you're not the woman who left here with the children. You have grown, inside, in your heart and in your head, like one of your butterflies coming out of its shell into the sun. I'm proud of you, Catherine, all you have survived, all you've achieved.'

She put her arms around him and held him against her, looking up at the strange sadness in his eyes.

§

As they walked up the hill from Shiaba the next morning, they met James MacLean, the farmer from Scoor, a prosperous gentleman who, clearly, had not suffered from the famine.

'I was on my way to see you, Mrs MacGillivray.'

'We have saved you a walk, then, Mr MacLean.'

'It's concerning the school in Scoor. I'm afraid to say that our teacher has developed a fondness for strong drink and appears in the school more than a little inebriated. A shame in one so young and clever. Perhaps, being from the mainland, she found the isolation more difficult than she expected. Anyway, the Factor mentioned that you had qualified as a teacher and might be available.'

'I would not like to deprive her of a living.'

'She has brought that on herself. She will be asked to leave anyway. The post has to be filled.'

'Is there a salary with it?' asked Calum.

'Unfortunately, the salary does not match that of the parochial school, but there are fees which may amount to eight shillings a year for each child. The salary's paid by the Gaelic Society in Edinburgh.'

'And how many children go school?' asked Catherine.

'About a dozen, but there is another half dozen infants coming on.'

'To be honest, I would prefer the parish school, but I would be happy to help you, as long as it is understood that, if a post became vacant in Bunessan, I would apply for it.'

'Of course. That would be fine with us, though I will have to get approval from Edinburgh. I don't suppose there will be any difficulty with that. Splendid. I will let you know as soon as I hear from the Society. Good day to you both.'

As he walked away, Calum grinned at her.

'It's a start, Mistress MacGillivray.'

They walked on together towards Bunessan.

'We can move to the new house now,' he said after a while.

§

Hugh came to help them move the heavier of their belongings—the bed, the table and the meal kist—leaving them to carry the smaller items themselves. When the old house was empty, they stood side by side and looked around the empty space. As a flood of memories surged over her, Catherine leaned her back against the wall, seeing again the children around the hearthstone, hearing their laughter, remembering their wide eyes in the candlelight as their father told stories of ghouls and water-horses. Their childhood was here in this space, between these bare, stone walls, and she had to leave it, let it go, slip away into the past. Glancing at Calum, she sensed that such memories were touching him too. Moving nearer, she took his hand and led him towards the doorway, but, just as she turned, something glistened on the wall head.

'What's up there?' she asked.

He reached up and lifted down the musket.

'You won't be needing that,' she said. 'Not ever. Not for rabbits, not for birds, not for seals, not for stags. I don't want a gun in the house.'

'It was a gift from a man on Lunga for saving his life.'

'Well, give it back or give it to the shepherd.'

She could see that he wanted to argue, to defy her, but was trying to suppress the urge. She watched his face, the eyes flickering as a host of thoughts flashed through his mind, the jaw muscles twitching, the nostrils of the long nose dilating. She waited to see which side of his nature would prevail.

'You're right,' he said finally. 'I'll give it to the shepherd. To be honest, I was keeping it to threaten the Factor, if he came to burn us out. I would never have shot him.'

'Your temper has got the better of you before. God knows what you would have done. Get rid of it.'

'I will.'

'Campbell will face justice one day.'

'But not in this world, sadly. His kind never do.'

As they walked across to the new house, Calum carrying her quern which she was keen to keep, and Catherine the oil lamps, she stopped near the step.

'We should get a new bed,' she said, 'and a mattress. I've never slept on a mattress, one with horsehair. We spend a third of our lives in bed. We can afford a little comfort.'

She smiled as she saw the astonishment in his face.

'A new house. A new bed,' she continued. 'And you should carry me over the threshold.'

Still with a look of amazement, he put down the quern and prepared to lift her.

'I'm jesting, silly man.'

'I'll carry you, if you like.'

'No, no. You could take one of these lamps—it's cutting into my finger.'

It was good to step up into the house and on to a flag floor. Calum had lit the fire and in the kitchen the kettle was steaming. She watched the peat smoke curling up the chimney and, looking up, found that she could not see rafters. Then she remembered that Hugh had covered them with boards to make a low ceiling.

'It'll be warm here in the winter,' she said, 'cosy even.'

'No beasts to warm the place, though.'

'Or keep you awake with their moaning in the night.'

'You like the place, then?'

'Of course I do. I know you built for me. I hadn't forgotten.'

§

The next day, being one of those crisp clear days with a light breeze from the north, they arrived at the pier to find the new boat tied up against the steps. Hugh and two of the Kintra men were standing, admiring it.

'When did it get here?' Calum asked. 'I wasn't expecting it.'

'Must have been yesterday,' Hugh replied. 'Maybe the boatmen spoke to MacQuarrie.'

'I'll need to ask. Isn't she fine? Have a look at the name on her, Catherine.'

She stepped nearer the edge and, looking down, she saw the name Catherine painted on the bow. She did not look round, feeling her face colouring.

'Did you ask them to do this?'

'Yes.' Calum answered. 'The old boat had no name. This will bring us good fortune.'

'Or even disaster.'

'Climb down and I'll take you for a sail.'

She climbed down and sat on one of the newly varnished thwarts. All the timber—the gunwales, ribs, planks—gleamed in the sun. Even the blocks were varnished. Calum joined her and hoisted the sail, the new halyard running almost silently through the truck. He cast off and, as the sail filled with the breeze, he headed north.

'Where are we going?' she asked.

'Somewhere you will never have been. I want to show you something.'

As they left the bay to turn west, she moved to sit beside him, enjoying the lapping of the sea against the planks, the gentle rocking of the boat as it cut through the waves and the way Calum's eyes lifted skywards to watch the top of the sail. This was better than the city. This, she decided, was what the word happiness meant. The salt spray, the clean wind, sunlight and blue sky.

To the north of Iona there was a small island and Calum carefully steered the boat towards its shore, lowering the sail and rowing the last few yards until it touched the sand.

'Shoes off,' he said, removing his own and stepping into the water.

Obediently, she took off her shoes.

'Come,' he said, holding out his hands to lift her over the side. She felt like a small child in his arms. Leading her through the shallows and up the shore, he smiled as he stopped above the dried weed left by the last storm.

'Close your eyes.'

'What?'

'Close your eyes,' he repeated, smiling.

She shut her eyes and let him lead her along the shore. She enjoyed the feeling of the warm, dry sand around her feet and the shrieks of the terns complaining about the intrusion on their sanctuary. Heaven, she thought, could be like this.

He stopped and told her to open her eyes. At first, the glare of the sun on the white sand blinded her, but, as her eyes adjusted, she stepped back, shocked by the bleached bones of a skeleton at her feet, thinking it was that of a seaman. It was large enough. Then she saw the tail and, protruding from the skull, a long, thin tusk.

'What, in the name of God, is that? It's like a unicorn.'

'It's a narwhal, a kind of whale from the ice floes in the north.'

'How did get here, then?'

'God knows. Maybe off a whaler or maybe it lost its way in a storm.'

'It's extraordinary, a freak of nature. A fish with a horn. Can we take it with us?'

'Take it home?'

'Yes. I could use it in a classroom. Show to children.'

'That's a good idea. I hope it doesn't break as I lift it.'

'Just the skull and the tusk.'

The two separated easily from the spine and he carried them back to the boat. He lifted her in and climbed in himself.

She sat next to him in the stern as they sailed back, thinking about him and his notion of taking her to see his discovery. Few men would have taken pleasure in showing their wives such a strange object, but then she remembered how he had always noticed and been excited by unusual things, how he had brought home a white harebell and the feather of a sea-eagle as gifts to her. She glanced at his weathered face, the beard streaked with silver, the veins on his temples thick with blood, the lips dry and peeling, but the eyes as bright as ever. In charge of his boat. She sensed his feeling of ownership, his pride in the vessel, and she was proud of him, for truly he had succeeded where so many had failed. Her man, her husband and, with all his faults, she adored him. She placed her hand on the tiller on top of his and he turned and smiled.

42

The school was almost ruinous when she managed to open the door. The timber floor, sodden under the leaking roof, had collapsed in places. The wood around the windows was rotten and green moss was growing on the sills. The panelling beneath was streaked with rust from the iron roof. Drawings made by the pupils peeled off the walls, waving like wings in the breeze. In the middle of the room damp ash was piled against the round iron stove, which was cracked down one side. Three tables lay at various angles at one end of the room with rough wooden benches beneath them. It was a depressing sight. Little education could have been effected in such conditions. She wondered if she had made a mistake in accepting the position. It was not how she had imagined the start of her teaching career.

She closed the door and walked up to Scoor to find Captain MacLean.

'He's in the stable,' replied one of the ploughmen when she asked where he was.

She found him fitting a collar over the head of one of the heavy horses.

'I can't teach with the school in that state. I'm going to ask my husband and Hugh Cameron to do the necessary repairs. I don't suppose the parents can afford to pay, but maybe they could help with work.'

'I'm sure they will, Mrs MacGillivray. I was worried that the inspectors would arrive and close the school altogether.'

'They would close it immediately in its present state.'

'I know. We'll do all we can to help.'

'I'll speak to Calum.'

'Thank you. We would be most grateful.'

There was little she could do with the school in such condition, so she walked into Bunessan to see if she could help Calum. As she reached MacQuarrie's, she found him loading a cart with sacks of meal.

'Good morning, Catherine. You've missed Calum, I'm afraid. I saw his sail heading round the point a minute ago.'

'I thought he would have left. Did he have crew with him?'

'I think not. He asked me to take meal to a couple of the families in Kintra, seeing that the men there, men who were to crew for him, were too weak to work.'

'Could the parish not feed them?'

'There are still so many in need it's hard to see to them all. I spend my day carting meal to cottar families. These ones, Calum says, are in a bad way, but are keen to crew for him.'

'Can I come with you? I might see his boat from Kintra.'

'You can. It would be good to have company.'

As they passed the pier she saw Tina and Bridget baiting lines, with the boys throwing stones into the sea.

She told him about her time in Glasgow, about the museum and the college, about Phoebe and Charles and her cousins in Australia.

'So many have left,' he said. 'More than a thousand I would say. A third of the parish, Catherine. So many good people too. It grieves me to think about it. Canada, Australia, Glasgow. Will we ever recover from it?'

'The Duke seems to think we will better off in the end. Sweep away the dross and the remainder will thrive. That's his theory.'

'They were not dross, though. They were good, God-fearing people, laid waste by hunger and disease. A plague sent to try us. The Lord must have a plan, but it tests my faith to see the suffering and pain which are part of it. "The Lord giveth and the Lord taketh away. Blessed be the Name of the Lord," Job said. I fear I have not his faith—nor that of His Grace the Duke.'

'We will see.'

As they drove over to Kintra, she could see the Sound of Iona, but there was no sign of Calum's boat. There was one with a similar sail which she thought might be the old boat with Hugh on board. When they descended to the village, she found that the tide was far out, leaving the shallow shore in front of the houses drying in the wind. MacQuarrie drove past the row of houses to the far end and, as they passed, people emerged from the doorways, clearly suspicious of strangers with a cart. She helped MacQuarrie carry meal to two houses on the hill.

'These are the ones,' he said as they climbed towards them.

No-one came to the door as they approached. She had to stoop under the low lintel as she followed him into the gloom. She was shocked by what she saw. She had seen destitution in many places and witnessed starvation in many families, but she had never seen figures so emaciated and lifeless. The men, struggling to their feet, greeted them, thanking MacQuarrie profusely for the meal. Catherine found it hard to believe that these men would ever be fit for work. Two of the children, naked from the waist down below their shirts, came over to her and stood with their hands out, the palms black with grime. The eyes, though, did not plead, but looked on her with kindness, as though it were she who should be pitied.

'We must carry on,' MacQuarrie said. 'There are others.'

'You said they were in a bad way,' Catherine said as they walked back towards the cart. 'That was far short of the truth. They are weeks short of death.'

'I know. Calum has saved their lives. He has done that for many families after he recovered himself. I don't know to whom or to what he owes his salvation, but he has made the most of his chances since. The Lord has looked after him. You must thank the Lord for his good fortune.'

'I do, particularly when I see these poor souls.'

They carried meal to the other house and drove back towards Bunessan, MacQuarrie stopping at the mill to collect more meal.

'So you're to teach at Scoor?' he said as they moved off.

'Yes. The school is just about derelict.'

'I know. Don't despair of a post in the village.'

'Why? Is there likely to be one? The Factor may oppose my application anyway.'

'On the contrary. He speaks very highly of you.'

She turned to stare at him, astonished.

'Oh yes,' he continued. 'He was most impressed.'

'Good God!'

'Good God indeed.'

They arrived in the village and, as she climbed down off the cart, he repeated his encouragement.

'I meant what I said. Don't despair.'

§

When Calum came home that night, she told him what MacQuarrie had said about the Factor.

'What that man says and what he does are two different things. He's a great Christian in the kirk on Sunday and a ruthless tyrant through the week. I wouldn't trust him.'

'I've no need to trust him. MacQuarrie seems to believe him and, if he's right, I may have a post in a parish school yet.'

'Campbell may not be the only problem. They seem to favour men as schoolmasters. All the bigger schools on the island have men in charge.'

'We'll have to change that then, won't we?'

'You're beginning to sound like me. Anyway, tell me about the school in Scoor. You said you had visited it.'

She described the state of the building, confessing that she had told Captain MacLean that he and Hugh would help to repair it.

'It will mean more time off the fishing, but I'll do what we can. I've no crew yet for the new boat so I can work on the school, but Hugh's needed on the old one. He might be able to come when the weather's bad. We'll need tar for the roof and timber for the floor. I'll order that.'

She was surprised by his enthusiasm, having thought that she would have to persuade him to help, that he would resent any hours spent away from his boat.

§

It was the end of October, the season when the children would normally have been lifting potatoes, before the school was fit for use. The day before it opened to the children, Calum lit the stove in the morning so that the fabric of the building could absorb a little heat. The following morning, he went down early and lit it again, leaving some peats beside it. When the children arrived, it was still cold, just warmer than the winter outside.

Catherine had bought a proper school register as there didn't appear to be one and she started by entering the names of the eight children who attended that day. She arranged the eight around two tables, four at each. Relieved to find that they were not as wasted by destitution as those at Kintra, she noticed, nevertheless, that the younger ones had no shoes. They were very different from the pupils she had taught in Glasgow, lacking their vitality, resistance and humour. These were shy, submissive and reticent. In spite of that, she was nervous, her fingers trembling as she completed the roll.

She gave each a pencil and paper and asked them to spread one hand on the paper and, using the pencil, trace the outline of their hand onto the paper. Once they had finished, she asked them to write their names above the drawing. She went round the class, surprised to find that all of them—even the youngest—succeeded. At least the teacher had accomplished that. If an inspector called, he would not meet a class of illiterates in her care. She began to feel more confident as she collected the sheets and read them the story of the Good Samaritan.

Having discovered a few Gaelic bibles in a cupboard, wrinkled with damp and badly scuffed, she handed them to the older pupils and asked them to read from the Psalms, again surprised by their prowess. All of them had a sound knowledge of the Scriptures. She would have liked to teach in English, remembering the struggle of the Barra refugees in Glasgow to make themselves understood, but had a duty to use Gaelic, the school being funded by the Edinburgh Society.

It was not that she could ever abandon her native language, but, having lived in the city and moved among influential people there, she knew that fluency in English was essential for survival and progress in the world beyond the island. She was glad that her mother had taught her English, though she found that the meaning of Gaelic words could not always be conveyed in English. Still, she was pleased she had passed on her English to Archie and Mary, but she was glad that they had kept their native tongue and knew Gaelic poems and songs. Calum's stories had always been rooted in his language and culture. If she gained a place in the parochial school, she would see that her students never lost their Gaelic roots, even if some of the gentry disapproved of the 'barbaric' tongue.

Taking the drawings of the children home at night, she opened her paints and coloured them with bright patterns, each one unique. They would add some colour to the drab classroom. Thinking about the bare walls, she decided to pin some of her own paintings on the panelling. There had been some illustrations from scripture behind her desk, but they had fallen some time before she had arrived and the mice had eaten through the paper. An Inspector, no doubt, would condemn the absence of scriptural pictures on the wall, but she felt that the Society was lucky to have a teacher there at all and that gave her some freedom to choose her own subjects and way of teaching.

'Is the roof watertight?' Calum asked.

'I think so. It hasn't been tested, though.'

'Tell me, if it leaks.'

'I will. The floor is perfect.'

'Good. I'm going to try the Kintra men tomorrow. Hugh says they have a bit more strength. I can take the boat right in on the high springs. Is there no word from Mary yet?'

'No. I expect she's too busy with the children.'

He was sitting in a round-backed armchair in front of the fire, his pipe in his mouth and his socks drying on a string below the mantle-shelf. His bare feet stretched towards the fire and his eyes glistened in the lamplight.

'Did you see the shepherd about the gun?' she asked without looking up.

'No. Not yet. I will. I will.'

'Tomorrow.'

43

Ben Armine Estate
Portland
Jamaica.

Dear Mother,

Please do not show this letter to Father. I know how angry he can be when he sees injustice. I would not trouble you with this matter, but I need your advice.

A young nephew of Mrs Buchanan has come to live here. I think he will be much younger than I am, but he sees himself as an adult. The problem is that he comes to my room and walks in without knocking. There is no lock on the door. At first, he seemed very friendly and interested in my family and the Ross, but recently he has become more forward and animated, attempting to kiss me and pressing himself against me. I have done everything I can to dissuade him politely but my protestations have no effect.

I could tell the mistress but, knowing how these matters usually go with staff, she would blame me or make little of his behaviour. She is very kind to me, but I'm sure such a complaint from me would change her attitude. What should I do? What would you do in the circumstance?

Until his arrival, I was happy here. The weather is wonderful compared to that of Scotland and it is possible to bathe in the sea. The potatoes are healthy and sweet to eat. How is the crop there? Has it failed again? We sometimes have salt herring and I noticed a barrel on the quay branded with the word "Wick". It made me quite homesick and reminded me of the girls who used to go to the East Coast for the herring.

Father might like to know that land is very cheap here. I heard Mr Buchanan say that it could be had for five cents an acre. Since the slaves were freed, many of the big plantations are lying idle and some are derelict. Would Father not consider buying a farm here? Could you persuade him? And there is plenty of work for teachers!

I have heard nothing from Archie. Could you ask him to write? I look forward to hearing from you and for some sound advice.

Your loving daughter, Mary.

Contrary to Mary's advice, Catherine showed the letter to Calum. He did not, as Mary hinted, rise in a rage from his chair, but sighed deeply and handed it back to her.

'She should never have gone to that place,' he said.

'What can we do? We can't write to her mistress. That could make the situation worse.'

'There's little we can do at this distance. I know no-one in Jamaica.'

'There must be a minister near her, a Free Kirk minister.'

'No sensible minister would go to such a dangerous place.'

'There must be. I will write to Edinburgh, to headquarters, and ask.'

'Do you think that they will pay any heed? A distressed woman in a distant parish. Likely, they won't have heard of Kilvickeon.'

'Of course they will. Or I could persuade MacVean to write for us.'

'More delay. Write yourself. It's a good idea.'

§

The following morning, she and Calum parted company on the Scoor road, she turning towards the school and he for Bunessan. A cold morning, with flurries of snow from the north-west and skins of ice on the puddles. She watched him walk away, his coat collar turned up and his hands deep in his pockets. He had taken to wearing a seaman's cap with a peak which, he said, was what fishermen were supposed to wear. She remembered that he was carrying the letter to the Free Kirk and she hoped that he would remember to leave it with the postmaster. She was worried about Mary in her predicament, so far away and helpless, and prayed that nothing untoward would happen in the meantime, that intervention would not come too late. She imagined Mary fighting off the boy as he tried to force himself on her and shivered.

She arrived in the school before the children and pinned up two of her butterflies on the wall. Her hands were so cold that her fingers could barely hold the pins. Using the old scriptural posters and some kindling that Calum had cut, she lit the fire, watching the face of John the Baptist shrivel and burn in the grate. It would be noon before the classroom had any heat. When the children arrived, there were two more than the day before. That was promising, yet she wondered if she could ask their parents for fees as she looked at their bare legs, blue with cold, and their shoes without socks. It occurred to her that she had not discussed fees with any of the parents. She would have to see to that.

'Margaret and Archibald MacFadyen, Miss,' the oldest boy in the class announced to introduce the new children. He was a tall boy, more confident than the others, with stout shoes, socks, thick jersey and good trousers—the ploughman's boy, she thought.

'Thank you, Murdo. Can you make space for them at your table?'

She entered the names on the roll and then handed out their drawings which she had coloured. They could not hide their delight and enthusiasm, examining each other's and passing them round. She watched their excitement and exchanges and smiled, pleased with their reaction.

'Did you do these, Miss?' said Murdo.

'You drew them, Murdo. I merely coloured them.'

'They're wonderful. Can we keep them?'

'Yes. Of course. They're yours. Perhaps you could show the new arrivals how to do them. Then we must have prayers to start the day and, after that, a story and a song.'

After they said the Lord's Prayer she told them a story.

'There was a young man, boastful and proud, who lived near Aros. He boasted that there was not a horse in the kingdom that he could not tame and ride. To prove how able he was, he saddled a horse which his neighbour could not handle and rode it by Loch Frisa. Beside the loch, the horse reared and dragged him into the water. Now, some say that a water horse rose out of the loch and devoured him. So, which story do you believe? Who believes in water horses?'

All of the younger children raised their hands, their eyes dark with imaginings. Murdo and his friend shook their heads and kept their hands below the table.

'As we get older, we get wiser. To continue with the story. The man's true love, heart-broken, wrote a song for him and a priest from Lochaber made it into a hymn for Christmas. It has a beautiful tune called The Man of Aros. We will learn the hymn for Christmas and ask your parents to come to the school to hear us.'

She sang the first verse of Taladh ar Slanaigheir and taught them the tune. At first, they were slow to join in, but gradually they overcame their inhibitions and sang along with her, some of them having fine soprano voices.

The rest of the morning, as the stove began to heat the room, she tested the four older ones for reading, surprised to find that they read well. When she asked them questions about the text—the feeding of the five thousand—she was impressed by their comprehension. The previous teacher, for all her flaws, appeared to have been more successful than she expected, in spite of working in the midst of decay.

She spent some time on the Gaelic alphabet with the young ones, but resolved to obtain a proper chalk board as quickly as possible and some exercise books. She remembered the classrooms in the school attached to the college, with their polished desks, blackboards, globes of the earth, pointers and high desks for the teacher. She wondered what Phoebe would make of the premises at Scoor. No shining kitchen with rows of utensils, mixing bowls, running water and jars of fruit. Her classes of cooking and kitchen hygiene would be of little help. Yet Phoebe, resilient and determined, would probably make the best of it. That's what she would have to do.

At the end of the day, as he was leaving, Murdo halted at the door.

'Is your husband a fisherman, Miss?'

'He is.'

'Would he take me out in his boat one day?'

'I'm sure he would, if your father allows it.'

'He wants me to be a ploughman like him. I want to be a sailor and go to sea.'

'You'd be safer on dry land. You could be drowned at sea. Too many folk are. Ask your father to tell you of the Katherine of Iona. Still, I will speak to my husband and you will ask your father.'

As she walked over the hill towards Shiaba, she saw the ploughman loading turnips into a cart in the Crossan above Scoor house. Progress, she thought, new crops, new ways. There was even new wire fencing around one of the fields. From the top of the hill, she noticed a plume of smoke rising from their chimney, tall and straight like a lance it was almost stationery in the cold air. It meant that Calum was home before her, a thought which pleased her and prompted a smile. It was good to come home to a fire and a welcome on a winter evening.

'You're home early,' she said, stepping into the kitchen, where the blazing fire lit the room in a warm glow.

'The Kintra men tire easily. They tried to hide it, but I could see they were weary, so I left the creels for another day. I brought home a lithe for us.'

'Is it gutted?'

'Gutted and in the pot. I met MacVean on his way to Iona and spoke to him of our troubles in Jamaica. He thinks there is a Free Kirk man in Jamaica, a place called Falmouth. He offered to write to Edinburgh for us and I agreed.'

'Good. He's bound to get a reply. The ploughman's son, Murdo, is asking if he could come in the boat with you.'

'He's far too young.'

'I think he means for a trip only.'

'Oh. That's different. He'll have to wear a cork jacket. I got four for the Kintra men.'

'But none for yourself, of course. Calum the indestructible.'

'They're such awkward things. It's like wearing a suit of armour.'

'It might save your life one day.'

'I can walk on water.'

'Very funny. I don't want to be left a widow.'

He turned away and lifted the lamp from the corner, as she laid her brief case on the table. The glow from the fire brightened as he lit the lamp. He moved closer to her and placed his hand on her shoulder.

'You will not be left a widow—not yet anyway.'

'You can't know that.'

The following morning, she rose before dark, slipped quietly out of the bedroom and dressed in the kitchen, stoking the fire and lighting the lamp before making some porridge. Calum was still asleep in the bedroom. She had decided to call on Captain MacLean about school fees before the children arrived.

She knocked on his door just as a grey day dawned.

'Good Heavens, you're early Mrs MacGillivray,' he said, his white hair like a briar bush and eyes blinking.

'I'm sorry. I wanted to speak to you before the pupils came to school. It's about school fees.'

'Ah yes. Miss Archibald was continually at our doors for the fees. I'm afraid they come to little more than eight shillings in a year—two shillings a term roughly—and they are not always forthcoming. Some are more diligent than others.'

'Perhaps those who can't pay can find another way of contributing.'

'I'm sure they will.'

'I don't want it to appear that I'm pressing them for payment by calling on every house so could you let them know that I hope the fees can be paid by Christmas. I'm keen to buy more books.'

'Of course. I'll go round the houses myself.'

'Thank you. That would be most helpful. Please don't harass them, though.'

'No indeed.'

She bid him good day and walked to the school.

44

The new Gaelic bibles arrived in the school at Martinmas and, by the end of November, Catherine had a blackboard, coloured chalks, pencils and even exercise books. Attendance, however, fluctuated, often depending on work on the farm, such as thrashing or lifting turnips. In spite of that, she saw the reading and spelling improving and the singing of Taladh ar Slanuighear was in time and in harmony. The whole hymn was too long so she helped them to learn verses which she had selected. She decided to organise a service, inviting not only the parents but also Rev MacVean and Mr MacQuarrie.

When the day arrived, she made sure that the classroom was warm and clean. The children had drawn pictures of events from the scriptures and these were coloured and pinned on the wall along with the hands painted on their first day. The children, their faces and knees shining, their feet boasting socks and shoes, lined up in front of the blackboard as a few of the parents shuffled in, trying not to look at each other. Catherine was pleased to see MacQuarrie and Tina follow them. The minister, looking quite stern beneath his bald head edged with dark locks and whiskers, started with a prayer, but was transformed into a smiling, amiable minister immediately after the word "Amen". Catherine introduced herself and each of the children and then led them in their chosen hymn, noticing that some of the mothers were visibly moved by the music. Recitations in Gaelic followed and readings from the psalms.

The minister finished the proceedings by congratulating the children and their teacher and by blessing the company. The parents, much more relaxed, filed out, thanking her for all her work. MacQuarrie, waiting until they had left, came to stand in front of her.

'I am lost for words, Catherine. You have done wonders here. You left this parish under terrible circumstances and have returned as a gifted teacher. I'm overcome with admiration. The Lord works in mysterious ways indeed. God bless you.'

She was moved by his sincerity and embarrassed by the compliments.

'Thank you, Mr MacQuarrie,' was all she could say.

'I agree with every word of that,' said the minister. 'I'm most impressed.'

They left the classroom together, nodding like sandpipers.

She had not noticed that Tina had waited behind until the men left.

'Tina,' she said, walking across to take her hands. 'I'm so glad you could come. You should have brought the children.'

'I did not want to see a riot, but now I wish they could have been here. It was wonderful, Catherine.'

'They have worked hard, the children.'

'And you too.'

Having been so apprehensive when she started in the school, she was relieved to find that she could manage, that she could win the respect of the children and inspire the kind of enthusiasm for learning that she had found with Eoin. She thought of him and decided that he would approve of her efforts—even if the language was Gaelic rather than Latin.

§

One morning in the new year, Captain MacLean was waiting for her at the school. Surprised to see him so early in the morning, she stopped suddenly as she came round the corner and saw him. He seemed strangely nervous and ill-at-ease.

'I'm sorry if I startled you, Mrs MacGillivray.'

'I was not expecting anyone so early.'

'I wanted to speak to you before the children arrived.'

'Come inside,' she said, opening the door.

'A few of the parents—a very few I might add—are complaining about the lessons.'

'Really?'

'They say that there is too much music and art and geography—what they describe as frivolous subjects—and too little concentration on scripture and morality. I must emphasise that these are not my opinions, but I thought I should warn you in case they reach the inspectors.'

'That's good of you. I'm afraid I have been trained as a teacher and not a minister and, as such, I have a duty to prepare children for their place in the world and not just for the Kirk. This is a school, not a seminary. I have no intention of changing the curriculum.'

'I understand and agree with you, but I would advise you to keep their complaints in mind.'

'I will indeed. Thank you for the warning.'

§

That evening, when she told Calum about the complaint, he wanted her to resign.

'You gave their children the best possible education and, to thank you for it, they complain. They don't deserve a good teacher. You should resign.'

'No. Think of the children. It's not their fault. I'll carry on and wait till the Inspector comes. See what happens then. They don't visit very often. I suppose the parents who are complaining may remove their children, but I suspect they won't. In the meantime, we will wait and see. My duty lies with the children.'

'I still think you should resign. The children can walk to Bunessan.'

'Punish the children because of the parents?'

'They are narrow-minded people. Whatever you think best. There's a letter on the table from Jamaica.'

'From Mary?'

'It's her writing, I think.'

Ben Armine Estate
Portland
Jamaica

Dear Mother and Father,

Very many thanks for your help. I had a visit from the Reverend Robert Thorburn who rode all the way from Falmouth at your request. He is a Scot from Bowden, gruff but kind, and very helpful. He spoke with both Mrs Buchanan and her nephew who has never been a trouble to me since. I am relieved to find that Mrs Buchanan's kindness to me has not been affected so he must have handled the affair with great skill. Anyway, the situation here is much improved and I must thank you for all your help in rescuing me from the crisis.

I wish that the Reverend lived nearer at hand so that I could attend his church, but Falmouth is in the far north-west of the island.

The other day I was hanging out washing when a stranger came to the gate. It was Jacob! He had come all the way to see that I was happy here. It was so good to see someone who knew you—it seemed to bring you closer. He stayed most of the day and has struck up a friendship with cook. I think I'll be seeing more of him!

Although this is a wonderful place, with all kinds of fascinating things to see, I miss Shiaba and the smell of the peat fires. Most of all, I miss you both and my wee brother. Please write soon.

Your loving daughter, Mary.

'That's such a relief. I was worried that the minister might cause more trouble for her.'

'He seems to have handled it well. I was tempted to go out myself.'

'And cause even more trouble. At least you had the sense to stay at home. God knows what would have happened, had you interfered. Have you given the gun to the shepherd yet?'

'No. I will do it tomorrow.'

'You must. I don't want a gun in the house.'

44

The sheep started to come down around their doors during the day, almost as if the shepherd herded them in the direction of Shiaba. Their presence annoyed Calum, particularly at lambing time when lambs lay on his doorstep in the sun. Still, it gave him an opportunity to speak to the shepherd about the gun.

The man came down one morning to lamb an ewe with a hung lamb near the house, so Calum went round to make the offer. The shepherd already had the ewe on the ground with the swollen head of the lamb hanging from her back end.

'I have a gun in the house which I never use. It's in good order, well oiled and polished. Would you like to take it?'

'Are you selling it?' he answered over his shoulder, kneeling as he tried to ease down a leg of the stuck lamb.

'No. You can have it.'

'I have no use for such a thing. There are no foxes here. The man that I work for might take it, though. He shoots deer.'

The ewe, lying in front of him, groaned as he pulled the lamb from her.

'I'll tell him,' he continued.

'Can I give you a hand?'

'No. She'll be fine. You could keep an eye on the lamb for me. I'll see that it gets a drink, but it'll take a while to recover. A big tupp lamb too.'

'I'll be going to lift creels shortly, but I'll watch the lamb.'

'Thanks. I'll need to see round the others.'

Calum returned to the house to fetch his bread and cheese and left for Bunessan soon afterwards, pleased with himself for asking about the gun. Catherine would be delighted.

The Kintra men were waiting in the boat when he reached the pier.

'You haven't walked from Kintra, have you?' Calum asked.

'No. Hugh lets us sleep in the shed behind his house.' said Neil, the older one.

'Have you eaten?'

'He made us porridge.'

'Is he away out?'

'Yes. The boat left about an hour ago. Said to tell you he was taking lines west of Iona.'

'We'll lift the creels off Erraid. Are you ready?'

'We are. Do you think we could call at Kintra? I've a bag of meal for the family.'

'Have you enough?'

'For now. Angus has some too.'

'Right. We'll call at Kintra.'

The Kintra men carried their bags of meal into the boat and Calum lifted down a basket of saithe for bait. A squall caught the sail as they left the bay and heeled the boat over suddenly, the men moving quickly to the windward gunwale to steady it.

'Squalls all day, I think,' said Neil. 'See the black sky over Ulva.'

'At least there are breaks in between.'

When they reached Kintra, the spring tide allowed them to beach near the houses. The two men carried their bags up to the houses, while Calum took out his pipe, cleaned it out and filled, but then realised he had nothing to light it with, so sat there with the pipe dangling from his teeth, waiting impatiently.

He did not have to wait long as they hurried back.

'The Inspector has been at Creich school,' Neil said, 'complaining about the poor attendance. I don't think these people know how hard it is to get children to school when they are starving. They live in a different world from us.'

They pushed the boat out and Calum lifted the oars to turn it into the wind.

'That's a Society school, isn't it?'

'It is. He is a good teacher who will have nothing to fear from the inspector.'

'Does he inspect all the schools in the parish?'

'I don't know. Maybe just Creich and Ardchiavaig. I don't know.'

Calum frowned, worried that Catherine might receive a sudden inspection.

They turned south and headed for the back of Erraid, the wind behind them and the sail almost at right angles to the boat. They raced through the Sound of Iona, the bow slicing through the swell. Heaving to near the floats, Calum thought it better to lower the sail so he was able to help with the creels. As Neil hauled them up, Angus took out any lobsters or crabs and Calum tied the claws and baited the creels. There were too many empty ones.

'Not good, boys,' Calum said. 'We'll need to move them.'

They laid the creels further round the island and headed home. Calum put the men ashore at Kentra so that they could see their families.

'I'll pick you up tomorrow.'

He sailed back to Bunessan himself just as Hugh was arriving with the other boat.

'How was it out there?' he asked Hugh.

'Great fishing. Scores of boats all over the place, though. There won't be a fish in the sea, if this goes on. Where's your crew?'

'I left them off at Kentra. Was good of you to let them have the shed.'

Calum helped them to land the fish and then had to store his catch in the floating crate, keeping the big lobster as a gift for MacQuarrie.

§

Several days later Mr Elliott rode in to Shiaba in the late afternoon.

'Calum MacGillivray?'

'I am. You know that.'

A rude man, Calum thought, without the manners to raise his hat to Catherine, who was standing in the doorway behind him.

'I believe you have a gun for sale.'

Calum had been happy to give it away, but decided that this man could pay.

'Yes. It's a fine weapon, shoots as straight as an arrow.'

'Can I see it?'

Calum went into the house, brought out the musket and handed it to him.

'It is a handsome piece,' said Elliott with some surprise. 'What's your price?'

'Ten guineas,' he replied, having no idea what it was worth.

'That's a lot, but I'll give you that because there's another matter I want to discuss with you.'

'What might that be?'

'I need your house for my shepherd here. I will pay you handsomely for it. I know that you have just moved in, but the Duke's factor claims that you had no right to build it there in the first place. He tells me that he is prepared to offer you a bigger house in Ardtun—near your fishing. It would be more convenient for both of you, if your good lady is given a place in the village school.'

'I have no intention of leaving Shiaba. We are managing perfectly well.'

'Think about it carefully, MacGillivray. You may regret refusing the offer, particularly if you're served with a warrant and thereby lose all hope of compensation.'

'I'll stay.'

'As you wish. Here is your ten guineas. Keep my offer in mind. Good evening to you. Mistress.'

On this occasion he raised his hat to Catherine.

'I'm not leaving,' Calum said as they returned to the kitchen.

'Not at the moment, but, as he said, if I was to be given a post in Bunessan, it would make sense for both of us. That's the truth of it.'

He did not reply, but stormed out of the kitchen, brushing past her as he left.

45

Lucknow
India
Dear Catherine.
Our regiment was posted here because there was fear of unrest, one irresponsible newspaper predicting bloodshed. The cause of the panic? Your 'bete noir', Sir Charles Trevelyan! He was no sooner here than he provoked outrage by writing to the press attacking the Madras Government over income tax. As Governor, it is considered to be a gross violation of etiquette to criticise one's Government. It is said that he is being summoned home in disgrace. His poor wife, having just arrived, has barely had time to unpack.

Mind you, I admire the man's courage and unshakeable belief in his own convictions. I'm sure that you would approve of his sympathy for the native people here and his respect for their religions. He has worked for the education of the Indian elite in the English language and for the expansion of education generally in the country. He has even invited Indians to the durbars and balls in Government House. Yet I'm sure he will be remembered at home for his callous treatment of the Irish and your Highlanders. I can't forget your descriptions of the hunger and disease which he seemed to ignore.

I'm delighted to hear that you have found a post, even if it is not in a parochial school. The college did not really prepare me for teaching soldiers. They are rough and inclined to blaspheme when frustrated but very keen to learn. In India they seem to have developed a language of their own with words stolen from the natives—including swear words. Some of the men speak Gaelic and have services in their native tongue. I love to hear them chanting the psalms in harmony. The sound reminds me of home.

There are times when I feel unbearably homesick and miss the walks we had on Glasgow Green. I envy Lady Trevelyan who will be sailing for home shortly. Do you ever hear from Charles? He never writes, but I'm sure he will be busy with his designs for Duart House.

Please write again soon. I enjoy your letters and hearing about your beautiful island.
Your exiled friend, Phoebe.

Catherine folded the letter, intending to reply with her good news. An unexpected vacancy had arisen in the parish school in Bunessan, and she was about to apply for the position. She had been worried about the inspector's visit, dreading his contact with the disenchanted parents, but he had been delighted with her work in the school. She was not sure whether he had spoken to the parents. If he had, he had dismissed their complaints, so it did not matter. Now she had to concentrate on the application. She was glad that she had taken the post in Scoor. Apart from giving her confidence, it would add experience to her curriculum vitae.

Calum had heard about the vacancy from MacQuarrie and had hurried home to tell her, surprisingly enthusiastic. He had not mentioned leaving Shiaba, but she knew that, behind his encouragement, lay the prospect of moving and that he would find leaving difficult. She felt sorry for him, knowing that tearing himself away from the place where he had been born and lived all his life would be painful. He would do it for her this time. She knew that. Of course, her application might fail and she would have to remain in the Gaelic school. In which case, there would be no need for a flit.

Calum had not arrived home, so she stoked the fire, placed the kettle over the peats and sat down to compose a letter. She had to plan it carefully, deciding whether to make it a formal introduction or to express herself freely and hope that the Board would appreciate such an approach. She was quite sure that other applicants, being almost entirely men, would choose to be stiff and formal, expressing themselves in scriptural or classical terms designed to impress the Board. She could do that now. She felt she had sufficiently sound command of English to compose such a letter. Yet, she felt that a personal approach, expressing herself as a person, might carry more weight. She decided to risk that and composed a draft in her mind.

Dear Sirs, I understand that a vacancy has arisen for a teacher in the Parish school. I would like to apply for the position.

I know what it is like to be illiterate, having grown up without schooling, when words have no meaning, when they sit on the page as dead and as silent as corpses. No child should have to grow up with that disability. At the age of thirty, having had two children, I had the opportunity to learn to read and write and remember the delight of reading for the first time. It was like discovering a whole new world, where each word was a picture or a sensation. Having learnt, I was determined to teach others so that they should not suffer from the deficiencies as I did.

I gained a scholarship to the Free Church College to train as a teacher and obtained a Certificate of Merit. As part of that course, I was required to teach classes of all ages in the Model School attached to the college, this gaining experience. Since returning to the parish, I have been teaching in the Gaelic School at Scoor for more than a year and Her Majesty's Inspector has expressed his approval of my methods there.

If I were to be appointed to the position in the parish school, I can assure you that I would approach the responsibility with the same diligence, imagination and expertise that I have applied in Scoor.

Calum returned, grinning and carrying a salmon.

'Where did you get that?' she asked.

'I saw it leap in the estuary to get rid of the sea lice, followed it up the burn and caught it by the tail under a bank. Fresh-run grilse.'

'Did no-one see you?'

'Don't worry. No-one saw me. We'll have to half it to fit in the pot.'

He laid it on the table to cut it in half. The silver scales glittered in the evening sun. She admired the slim, elegant shape until the knife cut through the skin and an ooze of blood marked the table.

'We'll have some of it tonight,' he said, fitting it into a pot with water and laying it over the fire. He sat in his armchair, waiting for it to cook.

'I want you to read this and tell me what you think.'

She handed him the application, which he read several times before commenting.

'There's very little here about teaching scripture or the catechisms. I'm sure you should tell them that you are a devout Musselman or Mussel-lady and that you pray to Mecca morning and night. They will want to hear how godly you are and that you'll teach the shorter catechism four times a day.'

'They're not all like that surely?'

'I don't know. They will be from the Presbytery. I don't know any of them.'

'Maybe I'll change it a little. You're right about the scripture.'

She showed him Phoebe's letter.

'Trevelyan seems to annoy people wherever he goes. I'm not sorry for him. They say that more than a million people died in Ireland because of him and he brought great suffering here when he stopped the relief. A cruel, heartless creature. I'm glad he's in disgrace.'

§

After they had eaten, they walked eastward along the track above the shore. The sun was setting behind them, casting an amber glow on the snow on the distant Beinn Cruachan. On the steep slope beneath them, a herd of wild goats grazed on the heather, a pungent smell rising to announce their presence. Catherine grimaced and put her hand across her nose.

Down on the shore, a cormorant was drying its wings like a small, black angel. As they walked, the matter of leaving walked beside them, silent, invisible but powerfully potent. They talked about the children—Archie's future and Mary's vulnerable position in Jamaica—but never Shiaba. It was as if they were both afraid to step into that path, as if they knew it would spoil the evening.

46

When Catherine was to be interviewed for the position, Calum walked with her to the school in the evening, asking her test questions from scripture. As she reached the steps, he took her hands in his and kissed her.

'God go with you, Catherine MacGillivray, though I'm sure you'll manage proceedings perfectly well on your own.'

'You know that I detest this sort of affair, all the attention focussed on me.'

'You've nothing to be afraid of. You're as able as any of them.'

They were interrupted by the door opening and the monk-like figure of Rev MacVean appearing.

'Come away in, Catherine. I saw you approach through the window. Good evening, Calum. Will you be waiting for her?'

'I will indeed.'

As she stepped into the school, she raised her hand to him and smiled. He walked down to the tide-edge and sat on a grassy bank to light his pipe. Gazing out over the bay, he reflected on how far she had come since they met on the shore at Uisken. Such a shy, self-effacing girl had nevertheless found the strength and will to leave him when starvation threatened her children. He regretted his stubborn refusal to work at that time. Looking back on it, it was embarrassing, his pride, his foolish opposition which threatened their children. He should have put his family first. She had been right to leave and he had betrayed her. He shook his head in disbelief as he remembered Peggy. How could he have done that to Catherine, his lust for the woman sweeping aside any thought of the pain inflicted on her? Dreadful. And yet her love for him had survived it, proving to be stronger than all his flaws. That was what he found astonishing, her capacity to forgive, her constancy.

He realised for the first time how hard it must have been for her to leave him, torn between her love for him and her love for her children. How she must have suffered in having to make that choice.

Yet had she not made that sacrifice, she would never have become a teacher. He thought of the children, how they had survived and were doing well, making their own way in life, and that was due to her. Their resilience, their good nature and honesty were due to her influence. He had not appreciated that.

He heard voices behind him, rose from the bank and knocked out his pipe. Looking up at the school, he saw Catherine saying good night to Rev MacVean and he walked across to meet her.

'Well?' he said as he reached her. 'How was it?'

'They were very kind to me and seemed to like my answers. They have decided to appoint two teachers and I am to be in charge of the infants' class.'

He flung his arms around her and squeezed her body against his.

'What a remarkable wife I have! Well done.'

'And there's talk of a new school, a new building. I don't know what to do about the school in Scoor. I feel I'm betraying them. They have worked so hard.'

'They'll manage. Just have to rise earlier and walk further.'

'Yes, but the classes will be in English, not Gaelic.'

'That's the future, I'm afraid. "The old ways are gone," you said once. Maybe it's true.'

'I will keep them alive somehow.'

'We'd best get home now. There's a fearful storm brewing. Look at that sky, the black clouds bulging with anger and that soft wind breathing a warning. I don't like the look of it at all.'

§

During the night the wind roared around the house, carrying the thunder of swell on the Torran rocks. Calum, worried about the boats, slipped out of bed and went to the front door. The minute he raised the latch, the door flew open, crashing against the wall. Staggering against the gale, he went outside. It was not completely dark and he could see the thatch peeling off the old houses. The wind was warm and so fierce that he could not stand upright. He would have to go down to the pier. Turning back into the house, he got dressed and put on his oilskin coat. The whole house seemed to be vibrating in the storm.

'I'm going to check the boats,' he said to Catherine. 'You stay where you are. You're as well in bed as anywhere else.'

As he left, he had to use all his strength to close the door and had to crawl against the wind at the top of the hill. The gale was coming in violent gusts, whipping the grass against his face, and bellowing like a bull. Three times he was blown off his feet into the heather. It too him twice as long as usual to reach the pier, where he found Hugh and the Kentra men huddled together in the shelter of the hut. A tangle of long lines was blown into the sea. He checked the boats and was relieved to find that they were safe. He joined the others at hut.

'There's a skiff ashore on the rocks out there. Look, you can see the sail. On the rocks just outside the bay there,' Hugh yelled.

He was pointing to the north and, as Calum looked in that direction, he saw the long shreds of the sail fluttering in the gale and the broken mast swaying dangerously.

'Are the men aboard, Hugh?'

'God knows but if there are, they'll surely be drowned. I'm sure I saw folk in the bow.'

'We'll need to go out.'

'What? That would be madness.'

'No matter. You don't need to come. Stay here so that someone knows I have gone.'

'I'll come with you,' shouted Neil, fitting on a cork lifejacket.

'And me,' called Angus.

'You don't need to come, either of you.'

'You'll never manage on your own.'

'Right. We'll use the oars and maybe the jib.'

The three men climbed down into the nearest boat and clambered over the rest until they reached their own. Calum cast off and they fitted the oars and started to row, heavy slow work. Although the worst of the swell was outside the bay, the sea was lashed into short, dangerously uneven waves as they fought to keep the boat heading for the rocks, where the massive swell was breaking white over the stricken vessel. Hoisting the jib helped a little.

Calum held the tiller and the jib sheet while the other two strained on the oars. Slowly, bit by bit, the distance between them and the wreck narrowed and they could see figures clinging to the mast. When they reached the open sea, the full force of the hurricane hit the boat. It rolled precariously in the swell broadside on, its gunwales dipping into tide. Water poured in, weighing down the lee side. The boat became sluggish and hard to steer. Suddenly an immense roller towered above them. Calum stared into its dark, malevolent depths as the boat heeled over. The Kentra men were thrown off the thwart to land on the lee gunwale, the oars left swinging. He saw the terror in their faces as the sea swamped the boat.

47

The hurricane was still roaring round the house when Catherine arose at daylight. Looking out of the window in the kitchen, she could see the slate-grey sea and the white crests racing towards the shore below Shiaba. She stoked the fire, noticing that she was using the last of the peats in the basket, and hung the kettle over the heat. She sat at the table, worrying about Calum. He said that he was going to check the boats and should be back. Perhaps one of them had been damaged by the storm and he had stayed to help Hugh with repairs. She decided not to open the school. The parents would probably keep their children at home anyway.

As the kettle boiled, she carried the teapot over to the fire and swilled it round with hot water, emptied that out and then put three spoonfuls of tea from the caddy into the teapot.

She liked the scent of the dry, black leaves. Phoebe had told her how they were harvested by the Indian women on the plantations. Sitting at the table with her hands wrapped around the mug, she wondered what could be keeping Calum. Maybe he had called at Mima's house to speak to Tina, tell her the news of her new position. Maybe he was speaking to MacQuarrie about sales of fish. The one possibility, hovering on the edge of her mind but quickly suppressed, was that he had put to sea. He wouldn't do that surely. Not in a hurricane.

She passed the time by making some porridge in case he came back soaked to the skin and shivering. She stirred it slowly, wondering if Mary had porridge for breakfast in Jamaica. Maybe they had some other grain like oats or maybe they just ate fruit or fish. She forced her imagination to build a picture of the place in Jamaica with palm trees, white sands like Iona and azure sea. She remembered the description in the last letter of waterfalls with rainbows in the spray and imagined Mary walking among the strange plants in a green cathedral of trees. She imagined the negro servant, laughing, with her ivory teeth flashing She built pictures of the minister confronting the lascivious nephew. Pictures to keep her mind occupied.

As the morning wore on, she became increasingly anxious, looking out paper and pencil to draw, draw anything—swirling designs, caricatures of people, houses, cattle—anything to keep her fingers busy. She drew Shiaba as it was before the hunger, with stooks of corn in the rigs behind the house, with cows and calves coming back from the hill grazings, with peat stacks at the gables, with ling drying on a line, butter churns by the doors. Anything but the sea and ships.

In the afternoon, the storm began to ease. She looked out of the window to see if the swell at sea had calmed, but, as she did so, Hugh passed the window. When he knocked, she did not answer at first but stood still, leaning on the table, afraid to move, afraid to open the door. He knocked again and she called him in. He removed his cap and stopped in the kitchen doorway, wringing the cap in hands. Neither of them spoke at first. Catherine stared at knots in the pine table, thinking one looked like an eye. He's gone, she said to herself, Calum's gone and, as she said it, the words swelled into a monstrous pain within in her, a pain as fierce as childbirth, uncontainable, unbearable, bursting out in a single sob that shook her whole body. She did not break down and weep but tears slipped silently down her cheeks.

'What happened?' she said eventually.

'There was a skiff on the rocks out from the bay. Three men on it. He took the boat out to help. The swell was too much for it. It was swamped.'

'He was on his own?'

'No. The Kentra men were with him.'

'All drowned?'

'No. The men had cork jackets. They reached the shore at Ardtun.'

'He wouldn't wear a jacket.'

Hugh didn't reply.

'Where is he?'

'They have not found him yet. The whole village and people of Ardtun are out looking.'

'He might be alive still.'

'No, Catherine. The men saw him sink but couldn't reach him. They are distraught and badly hurt.'

'And the men on the skiff?'

'The sea has them too.'

'I will come with you. We'll join the search. I must find him. However long it takes, I must find him. Come.'

She lifted her shawl, wiped her eyes with the hem, and left the house. When they reached Ardtun, she was astonished and touched by the hundreds of people searching the shore.

§

For three days and well into the dusk they searched the coastline, Catherine's shins torn by briars and long heather as she tried to cover every inlet and rock. One of her knees was bleeding where she had fallen. As darkness made the search impossible, people of the parish, people she barely knew, gave her a bed for the night, while Hugh returned to Bunessan to join her again the next morning. They searched below Knockan and Luib, round Ardchrishnish to Ormsaig without success, Catherine becoming more desperate and obsessed with each day.

On the fourth day, standing on the point beyond Ormsaig, Hugh saw a small skiff sailing across from the cliffs of Burg towards Bunessan. He guessed instantly its purpose.

'We should go back to Bunessan now,' he said.

'No. We have the whole afternoon.'

'We need search no further, Catherine. He is in the boat there.'

'What?' she said, following his gaze.

'It's heading for Bunessan. He'll be on it.'

'How do you know that?'

'I'm sure of it. Come. We'll go back by the road.'

There was something about his certainty that made her follow him.

The skiff was already at the pier when they reached the village. Out on Ardtun the search parties were returning to their homes. A group of fishermen were helping to unload a bundle from the skiff. They laid it on the ground and stood over it with their heads bowed. As they approached the pier, she started to run. She saw one of the fishermen take off his coat and lay it over the bundle. She could hear Hugh running behind her. It was Calum. Her Calum. She sprinted down the pier and dropped beside him, tossing aside the coat. His face, white and cold as marble, was still wet. Seaweed was tangled in his hair. She kissed his forehead, tasting the salt, and lifted his head into her arms, but he was not there. There was nothing there. No matter how much she rocked him in her arms or called him back, he would not come. The finality of his leaving broke over her, a wave drowning her in grief, and she howled.

The fishermen stood quietly around her, folding her in their sorrow, sharing her grief. They had lost one of their own. They waited patiently, not moving, while she wept. As the tide of weeping slowly ebbed from her, she felt Hugh's hand on her shoulder.

'We will take him to Mima's.'

'No. Shiaba. He must go back to Shiaba.'

'Of course.'

One of the fishermen knelt beside her.

'We will take him. Let us carry him.'

He slid his arm beneath the body and others helped to lift him onto a board. As she felt him slipping out of her arms, another wave of grief swirled around her, and she held on to his sleeve as they hoisted him up to their shoulders. Taking turns the fishermen carried him the whole way to Shiaba, as she walked beside them, never letting go of his sleeve.

Tina and Bridget followed them and helped her to lay him out on his bed. She thanked the fishermen and, as Hugh left with them, he told her that he would be making a coffin.

'I will wash him myself,' she said to Tina, 'and change his clothes. I don't want the salt of the sea on him.'

'I can help, if you like.'

'No. I must do it myself, thank you. And I must write to the children tonight and send word to the minister.'

Tina and Bridget stayed with her that night.

§

The next afternoon, MacQuarrie drove in with Hugh on the cart with him. In the back was a new coffin. The three women were sitting at the table when, the men came in.

'I'm truly sorry, Catherine,' MacQuarrie said. 'It was just like him to go the rescue of others. He was a fine man. It has been a privilege to know him.'

'You have been a good friend. I won't forget your kindness.'

'He's in the bedroom?'

'He is.'

'You stay there and we'll see to him.'

She allowed them all to lay him in the coffin and carry it through to the kitchen table. The new wood smelt of resin and sawdust. She didn't look on his face. She had covered his mouth with a piece of her dress to hide the lips marked by gulls.

'If we can get the minister, we'll bury him tomorrow,' said MacQuarrie. 'Will that be too soon?'

'That will be fine.'

'We'll go then. God be with you, Catherine.'

'Thank you, both of you, for all your help.'

§

That night Tina tried to persuade Catherine to have some sleep in the bed, but she didn't want to leave the kitchen. It was a long night for the three women.

When Hugh arrived the next day to fix the lid on the coffin, she felt as though all her feelings had drained out of her. She felt empty, dazed, stunned—as though she was not there.

She watched him finish and the fishermen come in to carry out the coffin. She covered her head in her best scarf and, with and Tina and Bridget on either side, followed the men to Kilvickeon.

At the top of the hill overlooking the graveyard she stopped. Hundreds of people from all parts of the parish had gathered at the ancient church. She was astonished.

'All these people,' she said to Tina.

'He touched many, Catherine, with small acts of kindness. All through the hunger, a bag of meal here, a string of fish there. No-one will ever know how many he helped.'

Catherine shook her head in disbelief and walked on.

Rev MacVean met her at the gate.

'I'm sorry for your loss, Catherine, in such tragic circumstances. A great loss to the parish too as you can see by the size of this congregation. He gave his life in a brave attempt to save others. We are not blessed with many like him.'

He led the way to the grave, where the fishermen laid the coffin on the ground. The minister held the service in the open, there being so many people.

After an opening prayer, he read from Isaiah 43.

When thou passest through the water, I will be with thee; and through the rivers, they shall not overflow thee; when thou walkest through the fire, thou shalt not be burned; neither shall the flame kindle upon thee.

Then they sang Psalm 46.

God is our refuge and our strength, a very present help in trouble. Therefore will not we fear, though the earth be removed, and though the mountains be carried into the midst of the sea; though the waters *thereof roar and be troubled, though the mountains shake with the swelling thereof.*

The voices in harmony seemed to rise into the air above the graveyard, forming a mantle of sound over the ancient, crumbling church, and the congregation. Catherine did not sing, but listened to the sound, remembering Bella singing to her aunt.

When the minister gave a eulogy, she hardly heard the words, but was conscious of Tina nodding her agreement occasionally. She watched Hugh, MacQuarrie, Donald MacLean and two fishermen lower the coffin into the grave, surprised that she did not feel sorrow or distress. After the blessing, she took her place at the gate to thank every person for attending the funeral. It was a task which she would have preferred to avoid, but felt that Calum would have wanted her to show his gratitude.

48

Tina had offered to stay with her the night after the funeral, but she wanted to be alone in the house that Calum had built for her. Returning to it, she felt at first that he was still there, that he would walk in the door at any minute with a grin and a string of saithe. Yet moments of grief, of realisation, swept over her, engulfing her in a sea of longing, leaving her weak and empty. She read aloud to him in Gaelic in the evenings, pages from the Song of Solomon or the Rights of Man—things she thought he would like. She talked to him through the day but there were dark times when logic told her that he had gone, never, never to be seen again. She started to attend church, thinking there would be solace there, that the faith of the people in resurrection would be passed to her, but she could not share their unshakeable belief.

She knew that she should return to work but a lethargy, sweet with memories, settled over her. She wanted to be alone, wrapped in her grief, clinging to the pain because it kept her close to him. Even the effort of carrying in peat or making tea was an interruption. She had no idea what she had eaten or when she slept. The passing of time was marked lighting the lamp or turning it off. It was a sharp knock on the door which brought her to the surface.

'Good day to you, Catherine. I came to see that you were managing alright, if there's anything you need.'

She passed her fingers through her hair, brushing it off her face, realising that she had been sleeping in her clothes. Mr MacLean looked her straight in the eye, clearly to avoid seeing her bare feet and her crumpled clothes.

'I'm fine, thank you, Mr MacLean. It's good of you to call. Can you tell the parents that I'll return to school tomorrow.'

'Don't feel you have to hurry back, Catherine. Take as long as you want.'

'Thank you but I'll need to get back, see to the children.'

'Whatever is best for you. I'll light the fire for you in the morning.'

She had to leave in an orderly manner, give them time to find a replacement or make arrangements to enrol the children elsewhere. She had to see the children and talk to them about leaving. Her sense of responsibility resurfaced, driving away the inertia.

She was touched when all the children turned up on her first day back after the funeral and impressed when they studiously avoided any mention of her bereavement. The oldest girl, Seonaid, handed her a bunch of daffodils, saying that they were from the whole class. That was the only sign of sympathy. She followed her usual curriculum, but told them the tale of Fingal and the Irish giant to lighten proceedings at the end of the day.

As they were leaving, Murdo turned to her and said, 'Sorry for your loss, Miss. It was good of your husband to take me in the boat.'

'Thank you, Murdo. I will miss him.'

Returning to an empty house was an unpleasant experience. It was cold and lifeless. She would not have cooked for herself, but Hugh brought her fish every few days, always asking later if she had enjoyed it, and the children brought eggs to the school. It was bleak, sitting alone at the table while she ate. She could hear herself chewing and swallowing.

She was picking fine herring bones out of her teeth one evening when Archie arrived. He had grown and filled out to be a sturdy and handsome young man. She rushed to the door to greet him. He threw his arms around her and she could feel his strength and smell coal smoke off his clothes. They were locked together for some time, silently sharing their sorrow and taking comfort from the sensation of touching each other again.

'Och, Mother. How are you?' he said, drawing back to look at her.

'I'm well.'

'You're not. I can tell. You look like you did when we went to Glasgow. Let's go inside.'

He dropped his bag on the table and turned to look at her. His expression told her that the pain and distress of the whole affair were showing in her face.

'I received your letter only two days ago and came as fast as I could. I'm sorry. I would never have missed the funeral. You know that.'

'I do and don't worry. I'm glad you're here. That's what matters.'

'What happened? Your letter didn't tell me.'

She sat down and told him everything she knew.

'So the others had cork jackets and he refused to wear one,' he said. 'Is that not just like him? '

'I tried to persuade him.'

'I'm sure you did. He never listened.'

'He was a good man, Archie. He was trying to save lives.'

'I know. I know. I should not have spoken that way. I'm sorry.'

'Can you stay a while? I have nothing in the house but bread and cheese and some eggs.'

'I can't stay for long. We have a big order for Grenada to finish. What food you have is fine. I can walk to Bunessan tomorrow and get more.'

'I'm so glad you're here. The house is a strange place to me.'

'This is the one he built for you? It's a big improvement on the old one. I would miss the hens in the rafters, though.'

She smiled for the first time in days.

'Will you stay here?' he asked.

'I don't know. Because he built it for me, I feel that I should stay. Yet it is a long way from the school. It would be sensible to move.'

'Why a long way from the school? Scoor is just over the hill.'

'Of course. You won't know. I have a post in the parish school.'

'That's wonderful. That's what you wanted. No more fees and better pay.'

'Yes, but it's a long walk from Shiaba in all weathers. You know, your father said he would never leave Shiaba. The only way he would ever leave would be on a coffin. That's what he said. I had no idea then that it might be true.'

'You must do what is best for you.'

'I need time to think about it.'

'When God made time, he made plenty of it.'

She smiled again. It was good to have Archie home. He was always able to make her laugh.

'Can the new boat be salvaged?' he asked.

'I have no idea. Ask Hugh. He'll know.'

'I'll go down and see him in the morning. Have you heard from Mary?'

'Not yet. I gave her strict instructions not to come.'

'I never hear from her. No, that's not true. I had two letters from her.'

'She might write, if you wrote to her now and then.'

'I'm not good at the letter writing.'

'You can write perfectly well. Sit and I'll make some tea.'

§

Archie slept in the bedroom that night, Catherine insisting that they made a place for her in the kitchen.

In the morning they walked together towards Bunessan, parting on the Scoor road as she turned for the school.

'I have to tell them I'm leaving. I'm not looking forward to the task.'

'They will follow you to Bunessan. I'm sure of it. If was me, I would use the chance not to go at all.'

'Away with you!'

When she reached the school, the children were already lined up at the door. Murdo handed her a bundle of kindling for the stove and Seonaid gave her a basket of eggs. She opened the door and they filed in, Murdo heading straight for the stove to light the fire. When they had settled on their benches, she led them in a prayer and then stood silently in front of them, waiting for their full attention. When all the eyes were focused on her, she spoke.

'You may have heard that I am going to teach in the parish school and that I will have to leave you. I want you to know that I have loved every minute in this school and that I will always remember my time with you. I could not have wished for better pupils. You have worked hard and behaved perfectly. I hope that you will be just as good when the next teacher comes but, if a new teacher can't be found, I hope you will follow me to Bunessan. I know it is a long walk, especially for the wee ones, but nothing would please me more than to see your faces in my new school. I will be leaving in two weeks' time. Now, on a happier note, I'm going to read you a poem about Iona by a famous Glenorchy bard called Donncha-ban nan-Oran.

As the children left in the afternoon, Murdo spoke to her from the door.

'I will come to Bunessan, Miss, and Seonaid says she's coming too.'

'That would be good, Murdo, but you'll need to ask your parents.'

§

'Did you see Hugh?' she asked when Archie returned that evening.

'I did. He was away searching for the creels after the storm. Tina and Bridget were there so I helped them gather mussels on the ebb tide. She's a pretty girl, Bridget.'

'Maybe she could coax you to come back.'

'Or maybe I could coax her to join me in Glasgow. She wouldn't have to break her fingernails fetching mussels. She'd have a better life with me.'

'Don't you be seducing her with tales like that. What would Tina do without her?'

'She has other children. I've no intention of seducing her daughter. Don't worry.'

Catherine was not altogether convinced. He was clearly attracted to her.

'What did Hugh say about the new boat. Can it be retrieved?'

'He thinks not. He wondered if the derrick on the steamboat might lift it but reckoned it would be too heavy.'

'So it's lost.'

She thought of the shining new boat lying on the seabed, slowly decaying as weed grew over the rigging and sand built up over the gunwales. She remembered their sail to the island off Iona, his pleasure as he showed her the narwhal, the happiness of that day. The blinding sun on the white sand, the turquoise sea, the warmth of the sand on her feet. His eyes as he looked up at the sail, his hand in hers. How she had wished it would never end, that they could sail forever in that sunlight. As she remembered, another wave of grief washed over her, she could feel it rising from somewhere deep inside, unstoppable, and she wept.

Archie came over and put his arm around her.

'It's alright, Mother. He's still here. He'll never leave. He said that.'

She felt his shoulders shaking like hers and heard the crack in his voice.

§

They walked down the road together as before and parted in the same way. When she reached the school, Mr MacLean was waiting for her.

'I came to tell you that the parents are begging you to stay, particularly the ones who complained. They're sorry they complained and hope that it has had nothing to do with your decision to leave.'

'I made it clear at the beginning that I would apply for a position in Bunessan should one arise, but their narrow-minded attitude did not encourage me to stay.'

'In spite of those views all the parents—all of them—say that their children will walk to whatever school you are in.'

'Good heavens. I hope I can live up to their expectations.'

'I'm sure you will. Personally, I'm very sorry to see you leave. I'm perfectly sure that we will not find a replacement. May I wish you every success in your new position.'

'Thank you, Mr MacLean. I will miss the school.'

He marched stiffly away as the children approached.

§

That evening Archie returned from the village with Bridget. Catherine saw them coming down the hill, hand in hand. At first, she was irritated, feeling that he was taking advantage of her friendship with Tina, but then remembered that Bridget was a clever girl, well able to look after herself and make her own decisions. When they saw her, they unclasped their hands, looking embarrassed.

'It's good to see you, Bridget,' she said. 'How's your mother?'

'She's fine, thank you. I'm sorry I have not been out to see you. I should have come earlier.'

'Don't worry about me. I have an engineer for company. Come inside. There's another shower coming.'

In the kitchen, Bridget and Archie chose to sit on opposite sides of the table.

'Calum saved our lives,' Bridget said. 'I don't know if Tina told you.'

'She did. She also told me that you nursed him through his sickness and I've never thanked you for that.'

'It was the least I could do. He was very poorly, wild with fever. He kept calling for you.'

'And I wasn't here. I can't forgive myself for that.'

'Will you stay here?'

Catherine looked at her, noticing how she had changed from a little girl into a beautiful young woman, far more mature than her years. Her dark eyes met hers as an equal, fearless but kind. It flashed through her mind that she would be a good partner for her son.

'I don't know, Bridget. I feel he is here sometimes, in the house, and I couldn't leave feeling that. At other times, it is just a house, a place to lay my head at night.'

'It would be sensible to move,' Archie said. 'These are only shadows, ghosts. He would want you to do what is best for you.'

She saw Bridget glance at him with admiration.

49

When Catherine joined the village school, she found the senior teacher distinctly unwelcoming. He made it quite clear that, in his opinion, women should be confined to the household, that teaching was a profession for men. However, she discovered within a week that he had never been trained and that her knowledge of geography, history and the Classics was superior to his, so she decided that his resentment had its origins in a sense of inferiority, that he saw her as a threat. After some thought, she planned to convince him that she had no intention of supplanting him.

He was a tall, gaunt figure, held together by chalk and his tattered gown. His knowledge of the scriptures was prodigious and his commitment to imparting it to his pupils unrelenting. He viewed her attention to art and music as frivolous, if not sinful. Yet she liked the man. In spite of his occasional resort to the cane, he had the best interests of the pupils at heart. Stern and strict, but kindly. Murdo, who had followed her to the school, was a constant thorn in his flesh, testing his patience with awkward but incisive questions. He complained about him frequently after school, implying that the child had been badly taught. She suspected that he resented the inclusion of the Scoor children and their loyalty to her, most of them having followed her to Bunessan.

The day that Archie left for Glasgow, she brought all her paintings to the school and pinned them to the wall, adding a blaze of colour to her part of the room. Although Mr Matheson frowned at the display, he did not complain. When Archie had seen them laid out on the table the night before, he had warned her that Matheson might object. They had spent his last evening reminiscing about Sine and Duncan, Marion and Sarah, and wondering what had become of them in Australia. It was strange how they never wrote. Archie confessed that he rarely saw Lamont or Hector, being too tired to call most evenings and Hector was studying for university. He had walked to the village with her that morning and it had been hard parting with him, but she was glad that it was outside the school and not in the house. Remaining alone in the kitchen as he left would have brought back all the grief of parting.

After school that afternoon, she was just leaving when she met the Factor outside the postmaster's house. Raising his hat and holding it like a shield in front of him, he spoke respectfully to her.

'I'm truly sorry for your loss, Mrs MacGillivray. As you know, your husband and I did not always agree, but I respected him. He was a good man, forthright and hard-working. I have learned only recently of his generosity to those in need. I'm sure you will miss him.'

She looked up at his doleful face, surprised to find a hint of sincerity sheltering under the heavy brows,

'Thank you for your kind words, Mr Campbell. I wish he had not perished in the manner that he did. I can't think of a more dreadful way to go.'

'Indeed. I'm glad to see you have a post in the school here. I'm sure the pupils will benefit from your expertise. It is a long walk from Shiaba and that must make demands on your time and on your strength. I have a house in Ardtun which would suit you, if you could see your way to leave Shiaba.'

'You know what my husband felt about that.'

'I know that Mr Elliott offered to pay him handsomely for the new house, which, as you know, was built without the Duke's permission.'

'I will think about it, Mr Campbell. I'm still trying to adjust to being on my own.'

'Of course. My apologies. I should not have raised the matter so soon. There is no hurry. Good day to you.'

He walked past to where his horse was tethered.

As Catherine passed the postmaster's house, she met Tina.

'How can you be civil to that man? I saw you talking to him.'

'He approached me. I did not approach him. Because I'm civil to him does not mean I don't dislike him after all the suffering he has inflicted on us.'

'He's a monster.'

'He'll face the same judgement as the rest of us.'

'It's the harm he does in the meantime that frightens me. Are you coming over? We can make you some tea.'

'Yes. That would be very welcome.'

They set off for Ardtun, Tina carrying Catherine's bag.

'Bridget is talking of going to Glasgow,' Tina said.

'What? Is that Archie's mischief? If it is, I'm really sorry, Tina.'

'He's told her that she can easily find well-paid work down there. I'm afraid that he has fallen for her.'

'I'll speak to her. Put the nonsense out of her head.'

'No, no. Don't do that. She'll think I've been whining to you. The notion may pass yet. I don't want her to think that I'm going behind her back. I don't want to make an enemy of her, but she's very young and impressionable.'

'I can write to Archie.'

'No. He would tell her. Leave it be. Let's wait and see. Mind you, I would be delighted if she married Archie but not yet. He's a handsome boy and in steady work. They're always in such a hurry, the young ones.'

'I'm sure we were not any more patient ourselves.'

The two women laughed and walked on arm-in-arm.

When she reached Shiaba that evening, she carried a chair outside to sit and enjoy the peace. The sea below was so calm that the eider ducks left trails behind them and the cooing of the drakes echoed right around the coast. A few small clouds, like lambs' tails, hung in the sky high above the hills. She wondered what Calum would think of his son. Proud, probably, of his skills in engineering, but sad that he couldn't take over the boat. He would approve of a liaison with Bridget. She knew that he was very fond of her. She would leave the Ross one day. Catherine sensed her restlessness. They were all leaving, One after another. She would be left. She saw herself in years to come, an old widow sitting outside a cottage with only cats and memories for company. The vision did not make her sad or anxious. That's how it would be.

§

She settled into the village school, enjoying her time with the infants where there was less pressure to conform to Matheson's strict curriculum. Often, on her way home, she called in to see Tina. A few weeks into the autumn term, as she approached the cottage, she saw a stranger talking to Bridget at the door. At first, she thought about turning back, but then curiosity nudged her forward. The stranger was a tall young lady, deeply tanned, and well dressed with a bonnet and brilliantly coloured shawl. Beside her there lay a travelling bag, suggesting that she had just arrived. Catherine did not recognise the voice, deep and ringing with a foreign accent. She thought it might be Phoebe, but, as the lady turned, she was so shocked she dropped her briefcase.

'Mary! What are you doing here?'

'That's hardly a welcome, Mother,' she said, as she came forward to embrace her.

As she clutched her daughter, she noticed that she smelt different, her clothes perfumed with foreign soaps and oils.

'I don't understand. How did you come to be here? Have you been dismissed?'

'Are you not pleased to see me?'

''Och, Mary! You know I am. I'm overcome, that's all.'

'When I told Mrs Buchanan about father's passing, she insisted on paying for me to come home. She knew it would be too late for the funeral, but she said I should come anyway to see that you were well. I told her that you had instructed me to stay in Jamaica, but she said that there were times to disobey one's parents. She paid the fare on the condition that I returned. She has come to rely on me for company. So I'm here.'

'It's wonderful. Just wonderful. I'm so pleased. But I have no food in the house.'

'It's not a problem. I knew that you would not be prepared, so I have arranged a meal for us both in the inn. Tonight we will pretend to be ladies of the manor, the wives of nabobs visiting from the Colonies.'

'Have you seen Archie?' asked Bridget.

'No. I'll see him on the way back. Has he not been here?'

'Yes. Just for a few days. 'He had to go back for a big contract of some kind,' added Catherine, picking up her briefcase.

'He never writes,' said Mary. 'I did write at the beginning, but he didn't reply. Too busy being an engineer. Anyway, let's go over to the inn. Will you join us, Bridget?'

'No, no. You should have time with your mother. You haven't seen her for years.

'I'll see you before I leave. Come, Mother.'

Mary stooped to lift her travelling bag and they set off for the inn.

§

As they sat opposite one another at a table, Catherine noticed how much Mary's features had changed, the smooth skin of her childhood replaced by a rougher, more weathered adult surface. An image of a snake sloughing its skin passed through her mind. It was not only her appearance which was different. There was an assurance, a maturity in her behaviour, a sophistication almost. She dealt with the innkeeper and ordered the meal.

'You are still living in Shiaba, then?' Mary asked.

'For the moment, yes.'

'It's far too far from the school, Mother. On wet days you must sit in your sodden clothes all day. Why don't you move into seanamhair's house?'

'Tina and Bridget are there. The Factor has offered a house in Ardtun.'

'There you are, then Why not move?'

'I feel I would be betraying your father. He built the new house for me. You have not seen it yet. It's much better than the old one, with chimneys and a separate bedroom.'

'Father would want you to be comfortable. You're being silly.'

Catherine did not hide her surprise at the remark.

'It's true, Mother. You can't stay away out there for the sake of a ghost. I worry about you being there on your own.'

'I will think about it. I told the Factor I would. Tell me about your life. That's much more interesting.'

Mary laughed.

'You're changing the subject.'

'I am.'

'Very well. I'm very happy there. That's not to say I don't miss you and Archie. I think about you every day, but I enjoy living with the Buchanans. I spend the day with the children, helping them with their lessons, and, in the evenings, when Mr Buchanan is not there—which is very often—I sit with the mistress in her drawing room. We read novels and talk about them. She teaches me French and how to play the piano, how to play cards and make tapestry.'

'Becoming a lady.'

'Hardly. I help with the milking, clean the stables and churn butter.'

'Is there a beau on the horizon.'

'No. I've had enough trouble with that. Thank you for asking the minister to intervene. Whatever he said had the desired effect without causing any trouble for me. Jacob, by the way, came all the way from their estate to see me. He brought me your stone from Iona which I have made into a pendant and wear it wherever I go. See.'

She pulled it out from the neck of her frock.

'I should have thought of him when you were being pestered, but perhaps the minister was the best solution. I feel very guilty about not writing to Jacob. When I met him in Glasgow I promised I would write. I shall have to remedy that.'

They ate a steak pie with turnip, followed by an apple pie and custard. Catherine found it difficult to finish, having lived on so little for many months.

'You'll stay with me tonight, won't you?' she asked.

'Of course. I want to see the new house and I would like to visit Kilvickeon.'

Mary summoned the innkeeper, thanked him for an excellent meal and paid him for it.

Her assurance made Catherine feel like an old woman, a frail specimen of humanity who needed kindly attention. She knew that Mary did not think she was helpless so she was quite happy to let her mother her.

'Was it the island out there?' Mary asked as they left the inn, pointing out to sea.

'Yes. The skiff had been driven on to the rocks. There were men drowning out there. That's why he went. You should be proud of him.'

'I am. I should have been here.'

'He would have gone, no matter who tried to stop him.'

'Stubborn.'

'And brave.'

They set off for Shiaba, leaving the sea behind them.

50

When, after a few days, Mary had to leave, she decided to spend her last night in the inn so that she did not have to walk all the way to the village in the morning. Catherine would have preferred her to spend the evening in Shiaba with her, but knew that her daughter's mind was set and, like Calum's, would be unlikely to change. Mary walked with her after school to the road-end above the village and they parted there. Neither of them wept or dared to show sorrow— two strong women with too much respect for each other to expose their frailty and thereby cause the other to crack.

'Promise me to move to Ardtun,' Mary said.

'I won't promise but I'll go and see the house.'

'You're every bit as stubborn as he was.'

'You will write, won't you? I need to know you're safe and happy.'

'I promise.'

'And one day, you'll come back for good.'

'When you are old and can no longer tell a loaf from a pair of stockings, I will come back but not forever. Never for good. Never to live in the Ross.'

'A pity. The Ross could do with women like you. Still, I can understand.'

'I'll be back before then. Don't worry.'

They embraced and Mary walked away without looking back. Catherine felt the surge of grief, which she had managed to suppress, rising to engulf her so she turned away and hurried up the road, walking as fast as she could to stem the flood. She felt she was losing everyone she loved, one after another.

There were so many things she should have said, so many memories she should have shared. Mary, her first-born child, her flesh until the cord was cut. She could have told her of the gasp of relief when she heard her first cry, when she saw her breathe. How the love that she felt for her at that moment was like pain, swelling like a leviathan inside her. How her small, slippery body against her own brought a form of ecstasy that she didn't think possible. How her tiny fist gripping her finger was so wonderful that she wept with joy. She could have told her how she wrapped her tenderly in a blanket and how the cow sniffed the bundle as it passed. She had laid her beside a sheaf in the sun as her father scythed the barley. A child who never cried. Happiness seemed to be hers then, a gift bestowed on her. As eager for the world around her as she was for milk, amazed, like her father, by the smallest plant or the movement of the skies, to touch, to hear, to smell, to see the wonder of it all. Her child. To have her torn from her by hunger and disease would have been death indeed. She should have told her what it did to her to make that choice, the pain, the grief, the terror. Yet it was not her own sorrow that she wanted to hand her as she left but a token of her love. Something, anything that could convey the love that blazed in her heart for her only daughter but no material gift, however perfect, would have been good enough so she stopped and sang, sang in full voice, as she had heard Bella sing for her aunt, sang as the tears slid down her cheeks.

No-one else was on the road, but a man cutting peats on the moss heard the sound, laid down his spade and for no reason, found himself weeping.

§

On Saturday she walked round to Ardtun to see the house, collecting Tina on the way.

It was not unlike the new house at Shiaba, having chimneys, gables and separate rooms. Set in a hollow, it was sheltered from the prevailing south-west wind. The stackyard, enclosed in a dry-stone dike, was empty and had not seen corn for some years. Behind it, the potato beds and cornland had been abandoned, growing only dockens and weeds.

'I could keep a cow,' she said to Tina.

'As if you hadn't enough to do.'

'I would like to do that.'

'Time enough for things like that. Let's look inside.'

The kitchen, cold and smelling of damp, was as the people had left it, as if they had just risen from the table and walked out. There were four bowls on the table, encrusted with the remains of porridge, and an oil lamp with a cracked and blackened glass. A chaff cushion on one of the chairs still bore the imprint of the last person to be there and a pair of socks hung from a string above the fireplace. The walls were lined with old newspapers, which, in one corner, were peeling off and a piece of sacking, used as a curtain, hung from a nail in the window.

'They must have left in a hurry,' said Tina.

'Evicted, perhaps, or away to Canada. MacInnes, I think.'

'Could be a nice room, with a fire going and whitewash.'

'Yes. A fire would make a difference. I don't suppose there will be peats left, though.'

'You could have your mother's house. It is yours by rights, Catherine. We can find somewhere else.'

'No. It is yours. I want you to stay. Yours as long as you wish. My mother wanted you to have it.'

'That's kind of you. I'll be alone with the younger children shortly. Bridget is set on going to Glasgow.'

'I'm sorry. That's Archie's fault. I feel bad about that.'

'No need. She would have left anyway. You could see the restlessness in her. It was worse after Calum's passing. She was very close to him.'

'I know. Poor child. I saw how distressed she was.'

'I would be glad if you moved here. We would be neighbours almost.'

'Perhaps I will. Yes, I think I will.'

She left the room, followed by Tina, and stood outside the door, gazing out over the sea to the cliffs of Burg. That's where he was washed ashore, she remembered, on the rocks beneath those cliffs. She wondered who had found him. It must have been a shock to them to see a body on the rocks.

'You think too much,' Tina interrupted, 'I know what you're thinking. Come back with me and have some broth.'

Catherine was comforted. It was good to have a friend like Tina.

§

She left Shiaba, riding on a cart hired from MacQuarrie and sitting beside Hugh.

Behind her were all their belongings from the new house. As the cart swayed and rattled up the hill, she gripped the board beneath her tightly and did not look back.

§

In the early spring, she bought bulbs to plant around the new house and stole cuttings from veronica hedge on Iona. Hugh and the Kentra men built a wall around the house so that it would have a garden with flowers and vegetables. They were working there one morning while a gale whipped the hems of their coats and clawed at their sou' westers, when Mr Elliott rode down from the main road.

'Is Mrs MacGillivray in?' he shouted, holding on to his hat.

'She's inside,' answered Hugh, dropping the stone in his hands. 'I'll fetch her.'

He went into the kitchen where she was kneading dough on the table.

'That man Elliott is here, Catherine.'

'You'd better ask him in.'

'Are you sure? He's a snake. You'll need to be careful.'

'He's just a man like any other. Tell him to come in.'

Hugh left and shortly afterwards Elliott stepped in, removing his hat and apologising as his cape dripped over the floor.

'I spoke to your husband when he was alive about the house at Shiaba, the new one he built there. I would like to put a shepherd into it. The Factor is not opposed to that but insists that I pay you compensation,' he said.

'That's unusually generous of him.'

'In fact I had already offered to pay your husband. What do you think would be a fair price?'

'I have no idea. The man to ask is out there. Hugh Cameron helped to build it and did all the carpentry. Go and ask him.'

'You will trust him to fix the price with me?'

'I would trust Hugh with my life.'

Elliott replaced his hat and strutted out of the kitchen, leaving Catherine smiling over her dough.

Hugh came in a few minutes later, clearly pleased with himself.

'I managed to get hm to £200. Is that enough, do you think?'

'You know better than I do. He would not have it with him of course.'

'No. I expect we will have to draw it out of him like an anchor out of clay.'

'We will, though. Every penny.'

'I'll go and get on.'

She had already decided that the money would go to him anyway.

At the spring sale, she sent Hugh to buy her a cow in calf, which she grazed in the field at the back. He built her an iron shed to act as a byre and, when the cow calved, she rose early every morning before school for the milking. She liked the sensation of her brow against the warm flank of the cow, the sweet smell of her hide, the sound of her chewing her cud contentedly. Every morning and night as she had done that in Shiaba. It became a routine.

In the early summer, the garden was ablaze with a mass of blooms, the hill behind being already golden with whin flowers. She ordered clematis to grow on the western gable and hydrangea on the east. Sending the cow and calf with those of the township to the high grazing for the summer, she made hay, teaching herself to use a scythe. During the school holidays, she white-washed the house so that the walls hurt her eyes in the sunlight. Having no classes on a Sunday at that time she walked out to Kilvickeon, often plucking posies of wild flowers to lay on his grave.

On one occasion, she walked out to Shiaba. The shepherd had not moved in, so the place was deserted. Sheep were grazing among the houses, their lambs lying in the sun against the walls. She walked past the new house and along the row, the ewes moving away as she approached, muttering to their lambs. Apart from their quiet complaints, silence hung heavily over the abandoned houses. There were no voices, no hissing of scythes, or laughter of children. Shiaba was dead. An air of melancholy pervaded the walls, as if the people departing had left their sorrow in the stones. As the memories flooded back, she felt the pain returning, the physical upheaval of grief. She turned quickly and walked away before it could overwhelm her.

The autumn of 1862 proved to be one of the worst for generations. Gales and heavy rain, week after week, flattened the corn crop, wasting half and sometimes two-thirds of the harvest. The spectre of hardship and famine once again stalked the doors of the poor.

John Campbell wrote to the Duke in December.

> *I fear this is to be a very serious year, given the effects of a short crop last year and worse this year ... I will employ no-one save from necessity. Their daily applications for work saying they are starving are legion. I have kept them off with the exception of about 22. These are employed principally in making roads or a few on their crofts draining.*

Some families, weary of the struggle to survive, left the Ross at the end of the winter. Another eight houses were to be deserted as the families—thirty-three souls—boarded the emigrant ships.

School rolls fell again and empty desks indicated the households which were suffering. Catherine wondered if it would ever end, if a day would come when the people of the Ross would have the resilience and resources to withstand harvest failure. When she saw the gaunt faces of the cottar children, she was not hopeful. At such times, she was glad that Mary and Archie led different lives.

§

Six years later, in the spring of 1868, John Campbell again had to write to the Duke,

'I enclose a list of 54 destitute persons who have nothing whatever to depend upon and will require to get employment for some little time. They are all cottars. I think the crofters will be able to support themselves for the present, at least I will employ the people as much as possible on works for which the tenants will pay interest on the outlay.'

However, the year ended on a more optimistic note. In August he wrote:

The people are not at all ill off at present. They get work here and there among the larger farmers, haymaking, shearing etc.

In that year there were rumours of a new school in Bunessan, a building suitable for the education of all the children. The expectations of the wealthier tenants rose with their incomes.

In the evenings, Catherine read or wrote letters to Phoebe and Mary. As the years passed, Phoebe's letters became less frequent, eventually arriving only at Christmas and finally ceasing altogether. She was not troubled greatly by the loss, but it was sad to find friends fading into memory. She was comforted by the regular letter from Jamaica and her friendship with Tina and Hugh. Charles had not forgotten his promise to send a painting and one of his oils, a bright painting of a French canal, hung on her wall.

Murdo finished school and left the Ross to join Archie as an apprentice engineer. Seonaidh ,her pupil from Scoor, left to train as a nurse. She was sad to see them go, but was pleased that she had seen them grow into confident and considerate people. She maintained her correspondence with Phoebe, always looking forward to her letters until they ceased without any explanation. She thought she might have been killed in her forays into the northern passes or died of fever but could not discover why her letters had come to an end. She still exchanged letters with Mary, hearing of Jacob's courtship and marriage with the cook.

51

The new school opened in October 1869, when Catherine was fifty-two. Mr Matheson had been replaced by William Telford as head teacher, a change which she regretted as she had become accustomed to Matheson's idiosyncrasies. The opening was a grand affair with a fete and influential guests—the Factor and his wife, Rev MacVean and his family, Dr Black and Mr MacQuarrie. and a flurry of Campbells from other parts of the Duke's lands. Catherine was more than a little apprehensive, having tutored the children in the psalms and hymns which they were to sing before the guests. By the time everyone had arrived, Catherine reckoned that there was more than a hundred and fifty in the crowd. She was not looking forward to conducting her pupils in front of them.

As they circulated around the room, admiring the profusion of flowers and the children's paintings which she had displayed on the wall, she found herself beside the Factor's wife.

'The butterflies,' she said, 'they are yours?'

'Yes. Mr Telford insisted. He said they would add colour to the room, but that was before the flowers arrived.'

'They're absolutely beautiful. From all over the world too. How did you find them?'

'In the museum in Glasgow. They're just copies of specimens there.'

'You have a great talent. I'm sure the children will benefit from it.'

She swept on to talk to Miss Campbell of Garmony.

The Factor, naturally, opened proceedings after MacVean had led the people in prayer.

'It gives me great pleasure,' he announced, 'to be present on such an auspicious occasion. I do regret that education has, until now, not been properly appreciated by the people of the Ross.'

He paused to allow dissenting murmurings to subside.

'I hope their ideas on this subject will now undergo a change. It is my wish that the rising generation will obtain the benefits that a liberal education is calculated to confer. It was with this in view that the erection of this school was undertaken. His Grace the Duke of Argyll expects that people will appreciate such privileges and is anxious that every child on his property will be properly educated. With this in mind, I declare the school open and will hand the keys to Mr Telford, our worthy head teacher.'

Other speakers followed, with Catherine conducting the children as they sang Gaelic songs between each one. She was relieved when Mr Telford rose to propose a vote of thanks to the Factor and his wife for the interest they had shown over the years in the education of the children in the parish. She handed her pupils over to their parents and escaped to take a walk round the back of the school from where she could see Ardtun and the cliffs of Burg. She was not alone for long, as Tina came over to join her.

'Is everything arranged?' Catherine asked her.

'Yes, I think so. Bridget says she has everything in hand.'

'We should have a meal in the inn after the wedding.'

'I can't afford that.'

'I can, though, and the happy couple can stay in my house. You will have to put up with me for a night or two. Have you spoken to the minister about the banns?'

'I have. He's going to call them next Sunday.'

'Good. Soon we will be related.'

'Yes. Who would have guessed? All those years ago. Archie and Bridget. I'm delighted, Catherine. She could not have found a better man.'

'And he could not have found a more beautiful wife and not just beautiful but intelligent, kind, competent and courageous.'

'Hope she can live up to that accolade!'

§

Catherine was proud of her son as he stood in front of the congregation that day. Dressed in a tweed suit and adorned with side whiskers, he looked like a gentleman. Calum would have been amused by the transformation and teased him about the whiskers. She was sad that he was not there beside her and she remembered the sunlight, the glittering sea and his grin as they sailed the new boat north of Iona. An image of the boat on the seabed, gradually sinking into the mud, tried to invade her mind, but she swept it away and thought of the narwhal. She would have to carry the tusk up to the new school.

Archie smiled at her as he passed with his new bride on his arm. Bridget's happiness was obvious in the way she glanced at him. Catherine thought of them leaving. They would return to the city and make a life there, very different from hers, very different from that of their people. They would have a flat like that of McBride's and children like Lamont's, children who would attend university and become professionals. She wondered what those children, her grandchildren, would make of her early life in Shiaba or the years of hunger and destitution.

She was sorry that Mary could not be there, and she wondered if she would ever return to the island. She missed her, her friendship and her thoughtful support. What a strong woman she had become from that emaciated creature, wasted with flux and hunger, on the ship to Glasgow. It would be such a comfort to have her beside her when she could no longer carry peat to the fire or milk the cow, when she couldn't see to thread needles or hear the church bell on the Sabbath. She would want her then, but Mary had her own life in Jamaica and she would never ask her to come back. She might even have a lover there.

§

Two years later, as scythes were being sharpened for the harvest and the children had reluctantly returned to school, Tina rushed into the classroom, heedless of Mr Telford and the pupils.

'Campbell's dead!' she shouted breathlessly. 'The Factor Mor is no more!'

'Get out of here, woman!' Telford roared. 'You can't come in here like that!'

Catherine instructed her children to return to their work and left the room to join Tina outside.

'Is this true?' she asked.

'It is. The postmaster told me and I just had to tell you.'

'How did it happen? '

'His heart failed, they say, though I didn't know he had one.'

'I have to go back in, Tina. I'll call down after school.'

'You don't seem overjoyed. I thought you would be celebrating.'

'He was just a man like any other and his wife will be distressed.'

She left Tina standing there and returned to the classroom, meeting Mr Telford at the door.

'You must tell your friend that must never happen again, Mrs MacGillivray.'

'I doubt if he will die twice, Mr Telford.'

§

After school, she called on Tina.

'There's some terrible rumours circulating, Catherine. They say that he was eaten alive by maggots in his bed, with them crawling out of his mouth and ears and his manservant using a shovel to sweep them into the fire.'

'I hope you don't believe that one.'

'Another says that all his beasts broke their chains and that his dogs in Ardfenaig could be heard howling here in Ardtun'

'Did you hear them?'

'No.'

'Well, there you are, then.'

'Calum would be celebrating.'

'He would. He had no time for the man.'

'Will you go to the funeral?"

'I don't know. They'll take him back to Islay likely. He won't be buried here.'

'We wouldn't want him.'

'I feel for his wife. Now, I must go and milk the cow.'

§

She did go to Ardfenaig gates to watch John Campbell's cortege, joining the hundreds of people lining the roadway. The crowd was drawn from all ranks in the Ross, from the poorest cottar to the wealthier farmers. Hugh moved to stand beside her.

'Calum should have seen this,' he said.

'Yes. He should. I didn't think you would come.'

'I came to make sure he was dead. Most of the folk are here for the same reason.'

'I heard some of the crofters asking if they could accompany the coffin to Islay.'

'They would make sure that their request was heard and noted. There are to be bonfires tonight all over the Ross and a telegram has been sent to the folk in Owen Sound in Canada. There will be bonfires there too.'

As the bier passed them, Hugh removed his hat, as did all the men on the roadside. They would still respect the dead, in spite of his flaws. The coffin was laid in a carriage drawn by two horses, dressed with black plumes and followed by a long column of mourners.

'He goes to be judged by someone more powerful than himself,' Hugh said.

'As do all of us.'

§

She walked out to Shiaba that evening as the sun set. She did not go down to the houses but sat on the grass overlooking the township. It had been such a sweltering day that nothing moved; the whole earth, stunned by the heat, lay still and silent, recovering from the blaze. In the haze on the horizon there was no distinction between sea and sky. She closed her eyes and pretended that Calum was sitting beside her. She remembered the first time she saw Shiaba as he brought her back from the wedding and the hesitant touch of his hand as he touched hers. She reached out, still with her eyes closed, longing to feel him there.

'Please,' she whispered, 'just a touch. Just one moment. Just a breath to know you are still there. Somewhere. A sign. A whisper to hear you again. I miss you so much.'

Tears glistened in the lashes of her closed eyes as she clutched the grass to squeeze the hand that was not there.

She swung between moments of certainty when she was sure that they would meet again and moments of despair when she felt that it would not happen, that it was all a fantasy, the afterlife, the resurrection, that what lay beyond was infinite darkness and the loneliness which sliced open her heart at that moment.

Opening her eyes, she looked down on Shiaba, the empty houses, the fallen roofs, the windows staring blindly out to sea, and, for a moment, he was there, swinging a scythe in the corn, and she behind him, gathering the sheaves.

'Wait for me, mo chroidhe,' she said. 'Wait for me.'